The Older Woman

Anna Leigh Brooks

Clink
Street

London | New York

Published by Clink Street Publishing 2021

Copyright © 2021

First edition.

ISBN:

978-1-913568-75-7 - paperback
978-1-913568-76-4 - ebook

Prologue

It was a long drive, but Jessica Willets enjoyed every minute of it, every mile was a mile closer to her new life. Sure, she would miss her old house and her old friends, but hopefully she would make some new ones.

The village is only one hour away from her parent's house too, which means she will be able to visit as often as she feels like, but they won't need to be in her pockets. She smiled inwardly at the thought of her dad popping round for a coffee and a chat, then a mild shudder went through her when she thought of her mother in the same situation. Not that they argue or anything, in fact they have enjoyed many nice times together.

Anyway, she brought her thoughts back to the village, with a population of around two thousand people, mostly ex-military, located at the edge of an army barracks. That could be interesting, all those young soldiers on marching drill to gaze at hopefully from her office window – when she finds a job that is. With her education and background that shouldn't be too hard, she has a few interviews lined up at the nearest town, so fingers crossed she'll be on the payroll somewhere in no time at all.

There's also a local pub, she's heard, right on the base itself, so when she's made some friends there'll be somewhere local to go and with a bit of luck some of the local squaddies will go there too. She let herself daydream a little. *Mmm, young, fit soldiers will be a welcome fantasy after such a sexless marriage.* She felt warm between the legs just thinking about it. *Enough of that Jessica, whatever would people think.* There are certainly some who would not approve, "only after one thing, they are," her mother's voice popped into her head and spoiled the moment.

'You have arrived at your destination,' the satnav stated in a mock-posh digital accent and she pulled on to the driveway. She dug around in her bag for the shiny new key from the Estate Agents' and got out of the car, unlocked the front door and stepped inside, dumping her bag on the hall table.

Dropping her keys on the kitchen worktop, she stepped back to look around. It was hers, finally hers. Her own house, with her own mortgage payments to keep up unfortunately, but she didn't care about that. Her marriage was over and she was glad to be free.

CHAPTER 1

Lad's Night Out

A splash of my best cologne, and I was ready to head out into town with the lads. Tonight was going to be a good night, I could feel it in my loins. Feeling certain I'd be getting laid tonight, I'd commented as much to the lads earlier in our WhatsApp group. After all "everyone loves a squaddie" I'd said.

I took one last glance in the mirror to check that my T-shirt wasn't creased and my jeans hadn't somehow got dirty, even though I'd very carefully washed and ironed it all, especially for tonight.

It's been a little over a year now, since I joined the British Army, and I'm enjoying being stationed at the new base. Like most of my generation, I work hard and party harder. I know for a fact that's one of the first things my buddies would say about me if they were asked.

So far I've found the locals to be very friendly and although there have been a few encounters with the odd girl here and there, I'm really looking out for someone a bit different. Someone more adventurous. Someone who's going to tease me and above all, someone I can live out all my fantasies with. Put very simply, I know I'm lusting for an older woman.

Recently turned nineteen, I understand from slightly unfortunate experience that many women in their forties laugh at me when I flirt with them, but I'm still determined. After all, I am a squaddie; therefore failure is not in my nature.

'Right then, who's up for shots?' I shout to my mates as we walk into The Bowl. Unanimously we chose our local, the only pub on camp as it was cheap, therefore saving ourselves for splashing out when we reach the nearby town a bit later. *Hell, it's busy in 'ere tonight*, I think to myself but I manage to get to the bar to order four shots and four pints. Scrambling back to the lads through the heaving crowd, I notice someone new standing with a couple of more familiar faces, just a few feet from the bar.

I'm pretty sure I've not seen her before, either in here or in the village – I'd definitely remember her if I had. By my judgment, she is an older woman in her late thirties at the most. She has gorgeous, long, blond hair and from where I'm standing she seems quite tall and she's got a really lovely smile. I take another look at the smile and notice her lips and the pink lipstick she is wearing.

I've done my shot and started on my pint, but all the time my mind is wandering. I keep glancing her way, to get another look at that smile, at those lips with that pink lipstick. It's all I can do not to think about her and how she would take my hard cock into her mouth. How it would feel to have those lips wrapped around my length. I realise my cock is beginning to twitch every time I even glance her way. Yet I just can't seem to stop looking at her lips as she's taking her glass to her mouth, thinking and fantasising that it's my erect cock she is placing in her mouth, sliding her lips up and down over the full length of it.

My pint is finished now and it's time to leave, but somehow I manage to persuade the lads to stay for one more. I even get the round in again as I don't want to leave yet. I need to find out who this older woman is. This older woman who is totally unaware of how much she's teasing me.

'Taxi for Jamie,' someone shouts.

'Come on lads, it's time to get out and get smashed. Who's up for some pussy as well?' I say, realising a little too late that it was loud enough for the whole pub to hear. I can't help glancing over to look at her as I say it, taking in every detail about her. Watching her lips move as she's talking and smiling and lost in my thoughts I see her turn to look around the pub, to see who is the gobby guy in the room and she looks straight at me. My heart stops, my mouth goes dry, my palms are sweaty and my cock is throbbing. It's so hard already and all she's done is look and smile at me with that smile I've been watching for the past hour while thinking about her lips and what they will look like around my six inch cock.

The taxi journey was short as the base is only three miles from the town centre. Even so, I don't want to get out when we get there. I feel like telling the driver to turn the taxi around and go straight back to camp. I force myself to get out of the taxi and be the loud, lairy lad that all my mates have come to expect when we're all together.

Since leaving The Bowl my thoughts continue to wander towards blond hair and pink lips….and the time passes in a bit of a haze of distraction all the way through the next two pubs on our pub crawl.

'What's up J?' one of the crowd asks me.

I shrug my shoulders and take a drink of my pint, not wanting to let on even to myself that I'm not really interested in being out now with them. I want to go back to The Bowl. I need to see if this woman is still there and most of all, find out who she is and why she is here. Is she visiting? Has she moved into the village? My head spins with a thousand questions all on the same subject newly resident in my mind - the older woman.

There are often times in life when instinct or intuition, whatever you want to call it, will occur. It's now almost 2200hrs and we've been out since 1930hrs. There are loads of conversations going on now all around me, as a lot more people have joined the group without me really noticing.

'And you must be Jamie,' someone says.

My brain is running at a million miles an hour trying to place the voice as I've definitely not heard it before. It's sweet and soft, most definitely a more mature woman's voice but it doesn't sound old. Turning around to check it out, I can see some familiar faces. A couple of them are from the village, I've often chatted to them either in The Bowl on camp or at the Sports and Social Club in the village.

Focusing in I notice something familiar, which I hadn't noticed earlier when our group was growing. While my mind was elsewhere, back at The Bowl mainly, I hadn't paid any attention to who was joining us, but as I'm looking for the voice I see the blond hair.

CHAPTER 2

Testosterone

He is even more beautiful up close. That smile, with perfect white teeth and those sparkly blue eyes. His hair is slightly longer on top even though it's brushed to one side. I imagine running my fingers through it, gripping it between them and feeling how soft it is. I notice the natural blond flecks going through it, although it's actually more of a dark blond that I can see will go lighter in the sun.

I watch him for a brief moment, before he turns around and I take in his physique. His back and shoulders are very muscular, with his T-Shirt fitting in all the right places, emphasising his muscle tone. His bum is a perfect peach, in dark blue jeans, not too tight but a comfortable fit against his bum and thighs. As I move my gaze down I can see his legs are the perfect length for wrapping around me. I'm not a fan of tall men - even though I myself am five feet six inches, I like a man who is around five feet seven to five-nine inches tall.

He turns a little more and I notice his chest and biceps, the sleeve of his T-shirt hugging the well-defined muscles tightly. I can't help but look down at his crotch and see the shape of his balls cradled by his jeans, also showing the bulge of his resting cock.

I look straight at him to see his expression. I want to see that smile, imagining what he would look like glancing up from in between my thighs, covered in my juices, knowing he's just been licking out my pussy and tasted my cum. He'll say it's as sweet as I know it is and I'll lick it from his gorgeous lips, his tongue and his fingers, one by one.

I lean forward to say, 'Hi,' into his ear knowing my blouse is slightly baggy. I know it will fall forward revealing my perfect shaped boobs sitting nicely in my cream lace balconette bra, with my nipples currently erect at the sight of him. I take in the smell of his cologne, he smells amazing.

I look down at the hand holding his pint. His fingers are slim with chunky knuckles and I think of them deep inside my pussy, my juices swishing over them, feeling his knuckles sliding in and out. The thought of this alone is turning me on, this man is making me so horny. I want to tease him and fuck him, I want him lusting after me. I want to live out all my fantasies with him.

At thirty-six I'm probably twice his age, but he looks so damn sexy. I never thought moving to a new town after my marriage breakdown could be so exciting. I've started a new job, and I'm already making new friends and meeting new and adventurous people.

I'm a city girl at heart, I know I am, but this village life is good. It's exciting. I'm definitely going to like it here, after all there is an army base full of virile young men, full of testosterone, basically attached to the village. Yes, I can see I am going to like it here.

***

Jamie

'Hi, I'm Jessica but my friends call me Jess.'

She's leaned in closer, right by my ear and I can smell her perfume. I've no idea what it is but it smells amazing on her. I can't talk. My mouth is dry, my heart is pounding, my hands are sweating and I can feel the blood running to my head. Jessica, Jess for short. Her confidence, her smile - what has this woman done to me?

She's leaning forward introducing herself and I can't help looking down. Her blouse is falling forward revealing a glimpse of her breasts. They're perfectly shaped, nestling nicely in her bra, and from my self-confessed expert judgment I would guess she must be a C cup. I imagine my hands cupping them, my cock in between them, squirting my cum all over them. Mmm, that's what I want do. Right here, right now. Squirt my cum all over her tits.

I've got to find my voice, after all I'm the loud one. The one who is always up for a laugh, the one who is always first in the pub or club, confident and cocky, that's me. That's who I am, Private Jamie Michael O'Halloran.

'Hi Jess,' I say with a smile.

My cock is already twitching at the sight of her. She is slightly taller than me and has to lean forward to hear me. I don't mind of course, as I get to see her tits. I look down and see she is wearing tight fitting jeans and black high heeled shoes. So that's why she is taller than me, I realise thankfully.

But that's fine, I picture her in her high heels, with black stockings and suspenders, teasing me as she walks provocatively towards me. In my vision I'm lying on her bed, my cock erect, my balls throbbing. I want her to sit on my face, with her smooth fanny on my mouth, her wet pussy juices flowing down my throat.

A voice interjects my thoughts, it's someone in our group next to me, telling me that Jess has recently moved into the village. That she's started a new job and relocated here after separating from her husband.

'A fresh start, Jamie lad. We all need one of them at some point in our lives, don't we?' he says.

'Erm, yeah, definitely,' I answer. The only part of the conversation that's in my head, out of all that was said is the word *separated*.

Jess and I manage to snatch a few words together over the din of the still crowded pub, though I have to concentrate hard to pay attention to everything she says to me. My mind continues to wander through the unadulterated thoughts that are controlling my mind, ever since I first laid eyes on her just a few hours ago.

'Time to get a taxi,' someone suggests.

'You up for a kebab J?' comes another voice.

'Yeah, why not?' I say, and we say our goodbyes to the rest of the group including Jess. I don't want this to be the end of our first meeting, but it's not all bad. I told her earlier that I'm going away on Monday for three weeks training and then she added me on Facebook, so I guess all's not lost.

CHAPTER 3

Salt of the Earth

I'm lounging on my bed after what seemed like the hardest day of my Army career so far. Every muscle is aching and my joints feel like they belong to an old man even though I'm actually really physically fit, probably fitter than any of the lads here now. But today has really taken it out of me, both mentally and physically.

My gear is cleaned and ready for tomorrow, uniform pressed and hanging up ready, and a couple of the lads are trying to talk to the *Missus* - their girl back home. They're knackered too, can't even be arsed to get off their beds and go out of the room for some privacy.

'Nah babe I can't, I'm exhausted and I have to be up at 0300hrs but I promise when I'm back I'm all yours. You can do whatever you want, I'll even take you shopping!' says Jake, or Nobby as he's known amongst the lads, talking to his girlfriend.

'Yeah I promise baby, love you, I need to go now, bye,' he finishes his call. 'Jamie mate, this three weeks had better be fucking worth it. A day fucking clothes shopping this is costing me!' he says, pissed off with himself that he offered to do it, I can tell from his tone. 'But hey, it's good to keep the little lady happy,' he says with a shrug of the shoulders.

'Yeah mate, you might wanna see if yer can get a year's advance on your wages. Yer gonna need it Nobs!' I say, laughing at him and his sulky face, lying on his bed.

I lay on my bed, not thinking about anything other than sleep as I need to get my head down. I sigh, it's been a hard four days and we still have seventeen more to go. I haven't had much time to think about Jess. Been too busy with everything else, but I know there'll be plenty of opportunity for that when I get back to camp. My phone is on charge on the bedside table and I hear it vibrate, probably a message from my mum, bless her, so I leave it as I can't be arsed to pick it up.

My mum, what an amazing woman she is. She single handedly raised me, my two brothers and my two sisters. Kept us all in line, even during our teenage years. She only worked part time in an office, so money was often a little tight but we never went without a meal or without birthday or Christmas presents.

My dad, God rest his soul, I'm sure, was a good man, albeit a strict Irishman. He grew up in Dublin, that's all I ever knew about him. Sadly he was killed when I was three years old, my mum pregnant with our Sean. She named him Sean because that was my dad's name.

Growing up was fun. I guess we were like any other single parent family. The girls, my two sisters Breda (named after my dad's mum I found out some years later) and Rosie, would cook and clean up after us boys, which I can imagine was a nightmare. Our Joseph (Joe for short) would tell them "it's what women do," but I would always tell him to "shut up, don't be rude, you should help, Mam has a lot to do". Our Joe was and still is a kind soul, he would always say "Mam, when I get me apprenticeship I'm gonna take you out for a slap up meal, like you deserve," and he did as well, he made the girls pick something nice for our mum to wear and he took her out for a lovely meal. We laugh about it now, but it was a big deal for us. Our mum never got to go out, raising five kids all on her own. Four kids under ten years old with another on the way when dad was killed.

There's only Sean left at home now, but we all still look after our mum. She texted me before I came away to say Rosie and Jed (her fella) had got engaged, Joe bought Mum a new washing machine and when will I be coming home.

I knew Rosie and Jed were getting engaged. Jed texted me as he had already spoken to Joe about it. Joe being the 'head of the family' in our dad's absence. He also spoke to Breda, asked her if she would help him pick out a ring. From what he tells me our Breda cried in every shop they went into and told the sales woman the story of our dad and how Jed has come to us for permission. It wasn't all just sentimental claptrap either, the last shop assistant was so impressed by Jed that they knocked a hundred quid off the ring. Result! He's a good lad is Jed. Salt of the earth, and I'm sure he'll look after Rosie.

My phone is buzzing again, reminding me I have a message. I've been waiting for the other messages to follow, as mum always sends me two or three text messages, one after the other. I swear she saves it all up and then bombards me with everything she's been wanting to tell me. I muster up the energy to lean over my bed and pick my phone up. I can't see any text messages from mum but I've definitely got a message because it's still buzzing. The Facebook messenger icon is showing at the top of the screen, so I open it. In black bold writing is the name Jessica Willets. My heart misses a beat, my stomach is amass with butterflies and I'm shaking with excitement as I open up her message.

Jess: [Hey, how's training?]

What do I write back? *Yeah it's good but when I get back I want to fuck your brains out.* I chuckle at myself, of course I can't write that. I'll keep it simple, I'm in no mood to get into lengthy text messaging and besides if I'm honest, I don't want the distraction she brings, not here anyway.

Me: [Hi Jess, yeah good thanks. Have you settled into your new job?]

I know, I didn't want to get into conversation but it would have been rude for me not to ask her about her new job, besides I ought to show a bit of interest, especially while I'm away.

Lying on my bed looking at Messenger, waiting for her to reply I decide that when I get back I'm going to tell her, well actually ask her, if she fancies being 'friends with benefits'. There's no point in asking her out, she is nearly twice my age and also, she's just recently come out of a marriage. So I think friends who want to fuck each other is a good combination. It's taking forever for her to reply and I'm too tired to worry about a response, so I put my phone back on charge, but not for long as I hear that unmistakable new message sound.

Jess: [I've settled in really well, thanks for asking. When are you back?]

I mean it, this time I really haven't got the energy, but I so want to see her and smell her again. I want to see her lips with her pink lipstick on, her perfect shaped tits sitting perfectly in her bra, I want to feel her smooth pussy, the juices running down my fingers, the warmth of her wetness. There's so much I want to do with her, I want to see what it's like and what it feels like to fuck her in the arse.

Me: [I'm due back Sat 31st, Halloween]

Jess: [Not long then now, see you when your back Jamie? x]

CHAPTER 4

Halloween Party

I've decided I'm not going out for Halloween. I'm too tired from a really busy week in work made worse by my late nights, unable to sleep from the thoughts of Jamie and what I would do to him, or more likely what I want him to do to me!

I've been thinking about all the things I'd like to try. My marriage was good on the outside but dead on the inside, especially in the bedroom. He was always busy with work and didn't really care much for sex, he just wasn't interested. He only wanted to make money. He'd say that with more money comes a better lifestyle, bigger house, bigger cars and better holidays. But *definitely* no children. He even made sure of it, by having a vasectomy for his thirtieth birthday, a present to himself. Yet to have a child was something I had always yearned for, as much as I did for sex.

But that's all in the past. I have my new job which is fun, a new house which I'm slowly doing up - putting my mark on it, as they say - and I've even bought some toys. Toys of the sexual kind, again something I often thought about but never had the courage to go out and buy any or order from a website.

I felt really embarrassed when I walked into the private shop. I drive past it every day on my way to work, it's set back off the dual carriageway surrounded by big hedges. It really is private and I was sure I wouldn't be seen going in, but that wasn't the cause of my embarrassment . I was desperate. Desperate for someone to take me and explore my body, taste my juices, lick my pussy out. I've never experienced that, although I did see a lot of it on the porn sites I watched.

What was I missing out on?

The young girl behind the counter was so sweet, no more than twenty-five, she could see I was nervous but she really put me at ease. I told her that I was recently separated and new to the area, I don't do online dating as I'm not sure if it's safe yet but I really miss my sex life. I made it sound so exciting, like I had an amazing sex life when I was married, but of course that was just a dream. She showed me a couple of vibrators that she highly recommended and some dildos. I never realised there was so much choice.

I've put some pumpkins on my doorstep, a few little decorations for Halloween and bought a load of sweets to give to the kiddies when they come knocking. I've had a hot bath and touched up my make-up. Anyone would think I have a 'hot date' but it's just a quiet drink with a male work colleague after the trick or treaters have been.

I've arranged to meet him at a pub in the next village, that way no one sees us in this village, I don't want anyone jumping to conclusions. After all he is a work colleague and nothing more, he doesn't turn me on in the slightest. I definitely won't make that mistake again!

I hear my phone go as I pull onto my drive. I check the clock and it's just after 11.30pm. Who would be messaging me at this time of night? The house is quiet but as always the radio is left on for when I come home, and even over this I can hear my phone vibrating every so often reminding me I have a message. I'll check it in a minute, but first I need a wee as all that pop seems to have gone right through me, no alcohol of course - the down side to driving!

I hope it's nothing bad. My mum lives sixty miles away though I could be there in an hour if it's her but then if it was my mum surely my dad would call me?

My poor mum, she was more devastated when my marriage ended than I was. She'd say to me "Oh Jessica, can you not just give it another go? Are you sure you want to sell your home, it's just so beautiful." These were her 'go to' phrases that I heard more often than not. But it was only a house. Albeit a beautiful house that we bought nearly four years ago when Anthony got his promotion to 'Director of Sales' with a nice big pay rise and bonuses.

The house deserved to be loved, as did I. It was the right thing to do - to sell it, to a family who will love it and have kids growing up in it. After all that is what I dreamed of and longed for, my very own little family.

Oh well, no point dwelling on the past, that's not going to help move on with the future especially now, being sixty miles away, living in my modest little two bedroomed ex MOD house. It's a far cry from the detached four bedroom Georgian style house with a price tag for offers over £750,000. I know one thing, with my settlement I'll be able to pay my mortgage off and have some left over for the little luxuries in life. Who knows I may even get the chance to have my own family…

Ok, let's check what this message is all about.

Jamie: [Hey Jess, where are you? I was looking forward to seeing you in The Bowl for the Halloween party]

I look at the name at the top of Messenger, Jamie. It's just coming up to 11.45pm but my adrenaline just kicked in. Is he really looking for me? My juices start flowing and I'm getting wet already. My nipples are erect at the thought of his handsome face above his perfectly toned muscular body and his peachy bum along with his balls and erect cock. I've imagined what it looks like so often over the past three weeks, I've as good as tasted his cum, felt his knuckles inside my pussy and felt my juices running all over them. Every time I get my new vibrator out I imagine it's him. My big blue vibrator deep inside me and my cum all over it. I always lick it off while fantasizing that I'm licking it off his thick, erect cock.

***

Jamie

Jess: [Hi, sorry, I've been out for a drink with some work colleagues, I forgot it had been arranged otherwise I would've. I could do with a beer tbh, I had to drive but hey, you're back, it's lovely to hear from you? xx]

Two kisses, my heart is pumping, I'm so pissed right now, back from training straight to The Bowl. Three weeks without a beer and I'm bladdered. But my cock is erect, I'm home alone, the house is empty and my house buddies are away for another month.

Me: [That's ok, I'm a little pissed but have some beers in if you fancy one? Pop round!]

Me: [Xx]

Have I got beers in? Because I don't even have a pint of milk in, I dropped my Bergan off, got changed and went straight out. What if she says "Yes" how do I explain to her that "I don't have anything in, I just needed to see you, to kiss you, to smell you and most of all I need to fuck you"!

Jess: [Yeah that will be nice, I have a bottle of wine I was about to open, I'll bring it with me or you can come to mine if it's easier? Xx]

Me: [I'll come to you, send me your address xx]

CHAPTER 5

Intuition

She must have known I don't have any beers in. They say women have this knack, my mum calls it intuition. They know when something isn't right or *he's lying, he doesn't have any beers,* in this particular case. That it's just a ploy to get you to go to his house. Perhaps she knew that my house, that I share with two other squaddies, has been empty for the past three weeks and I wouldn't have bothered picking anything up on my way home as all I wanted to do was drop my kit off, get changed and get out.

My house is pretty basic as it goes but I have everything I need in my bedroom including condoms and lube. You never know when you're going to pull a bird that wants a good arse fucking, so it's better to be prepared, I say.

So, about this intuition thing. I'm sure she knows that there isn't anything in, that's why she wants me to go to hers. Perhaps she wants me to fuck her after all, *one can only hope, hey Jamie lad*?

My cock is throbbing at the mere thought of her. I need a blow job, I need to fuck her, cum deep inside her and all over her. All over her perfect shaped tits, which I have kissed and caressed in my thoughts hundreds, no, more like thousands of times by now.

Thank God she only lives three streets away or I'd be in trouble as I try not to stagger on my way there. I try not to seem too pissed, after all I was only out for seven hours – *only?*

23

I was out at 1600hrs and back home by 2330hrs. I actually should've gone into town with everyone else. That was the original plan. I continue my slightly more controlled stagger and try to compose myself in every way. I don't want her to see my erect cock or see that I want to fuck her so bad. I almost feel desperate - not just for a shag, I can get that anywhere but desperate for her, I know I am.

***

Jess

I need a drink before he gets here, my adrenaline is pumping and my hands are shaking. I'll pour a glass, so when he knocks at the door I will already be drinking. That way it will keep me calmer than answering the door without one, I convince myself.

Wandering over to the window to look out into the pitch black, the street lights give some welcome illumination. A figure is walking up the path and my heart misses a beat, my hands are still shaking and my stomach is full of butterflies. I open the door and he stands there a little wobbly but trying his best not to sway.

I chuckle - definitely more of a nervous laugh than anything else - and invite him in. He leans forward and gives me a kiss on the lips. Not a lingering kiss, just a quick kiss.

'Hi,' he says, with a cheeky grin.

I can see he is nervous. This is the first time I've seen this side of him, this usually cocky, loud mouth, confident soldier. He is vulnerable, I see it now. He is just a boy, a very drunken one admittedly. I can see in his eyes what it's taken for him to pluck up the confidence to message me. But I'm glad, really glad and so happy he did. I will have some fun with this soldier, I know I will!

***

24

Jamie

Oh no, she's standing in the window watching my (hopefully not too drunken) approach, her long blond hair loosely hanging down her front. It's covering her tits but I can still make out her lace bra through her tight fitting top which shows the full shape of them. They are perfect, waiting for my hands to cup them and my mouth to suck on them. I try to hang back for a second, I need to focus more but as I'm taking in her beauty through the window, I know full well what I want to do with her. My cock is throbbing and hard again - this uncontrollable piece of meat will get me into trouble one of these days!

She answers the door before I can knock and she is already holding a glass of wine. Ha! She must need some Dutch courage. Not bad going really, if it's only one glass of wine - it's taken me seven hours and countless shots and beers to get here. I'll give her a quick peck on the lips, I decide. I know I'm being cheeky but it will help calm my nerves, also it means I get a quick taste of her.

She chuckles when I kiss her. It's the cutest thing I've ever heard, really girly, but I know she is all woman and that's what I want, not a girl. I want to experience all my desires that only a mature woman can fulfil, especially one who's been married. I bet she's done everything. I bet she'll be open to everything - indoor, outdoor, anal sex - yes I definitely want to fuck her arse. I want to fuck her pussy and her arse with one of her vibrators at the same time. I wonder how many vibes she has….

'Hey, come in, glad you could make it!' she says as she motions for me to follow her into the house.

'Hellooo,' I slur a little, trying very hard not to.

'Do you want a glass of wine?' she asks.

'Yeah please,' I say, not that I need any more to drink but I'm thinking that it will help my nerves. I'm not sure what this case of nerves is all about, I've only ever once been nervous and that was on my final interview for the army.

Following her into the kitchen I watch her bum in her black tight fitting Jeans which emphasise its perfect shape. I can just imagine my cock sliding in and out of that arse, those butt cheeks raw from being slapped by my hands, her perfectly shaped tits bouncing while I'm fucking her doggy style.

I'm going to take her here and now.....No I'm not.

What am I thinking? *No, no, I'm going to wait, how do I even know she wants me?*

***

Jess

I really hope he is watching my bum move to the motion of my walk. I wonder if he is thinking about fucking my bum, and my pussy, in fact every orifice on my body. I want to know what it's like to be truly 'fucked'. The feeling of sheer exhaustion from hours of foreplay and fucking. Will he want to use my vibrator? I hope so, but I don't want to make him feel inadequate because I've suggested it. *I wonder if he's ever used a wine bottle before,* I think as I pour him a glass.

I bet it's amazing, especially if there's still wine left in the bottle. Oh yes, he can share that with me, it's like 'cum swapping' only 'wine-cum swapping' instead. Did I just invent a new word??? Well whatever you call it, I want to try it!

***

Jamie

'Here you go,' she says handing me a glass of wine.

'Thanks. Hope you don't mind me being piss... er, drunk. I went out really early - it's the first time,' I hiccup mid-sentence, 'first time out since the last time.'

Oh god! What was I thinking? I can't even speak properly. I bet I'm slurring too, she's going to think I'm a drunken twat.

'Can I tell yer something, Jess?' I ask.

'Sure. Do you want to sit in the living room?' she says and leads the way.

'Yeah, please,' I answer, thankful for the suggestion.

I swear my legs were about to give way. She must have sensed it, that's why she's asking. *Jamie lad, get yer shit together. Yer gonna blow this if you ain't careful.* I need to tell her that I fancy her, I really want to fuck her and that I've never really had a girlfriend so I don't know how to do this. I just fuck them and leave them. I want to say to her, *I don't have time for girls in my life but you, you're different, you're a woman, you can show me the way, show me how it's done.*

I've only got eight months left until my next posting. When I joined this regiment straight from training they were already sixteen months into the three year posting. The next posting I've been told will only be for two years as we may well be going to Cyprus. I am really excited about it, although it's still too early to even think that far ahead. For now all I can think about is Jess and what I want to do with her.

'So how was training?' she asks.

'It was good, intense. Non-stop actually, but,' I hiccup again mid-sentence, 'Oh God, sorry, I'm so sorry Jess. You must think I'm an idiot.'

Why is she laughing? Is she genuinely finding this funny or is she just being polite?

'It's fine. You said you were "pissed" so stop apologising. Honestly if I hadn't had made the arrangements with my work colleagues, I'd have been out early like you. So you definitely wouldn't be the only one who's "pissed". Anyway, relax. I invited you round because I thought we could get to know each other better.'

***

Jess

Would it be wrong of me to take advantage of him when he's really drunk like this? I get the feeling he is interested, he must be to come over and he did peck me on the lips. Should I tell him I want him to fuck me and show me what I've missed out on over the last ten years?

27

When my Decree Nisi is through, according to my solicitor and hoping the soon to be ex-husband doesn't object to the sixty-forty pay off in my favour that's been put forward, it will be eleven years to the month since our wedding.

I should've realised even before we got married that our sex life wasn't going to improve. It had been more than a year before we wed that we last had any sex. Anthony had promised me it would get better, that he'd sort it out, his lack of libido that is. It just didn't seem right - a healthy twenty-seven year old man with no sex drive, well none towards me anyway.

I still feel anger towards Anthony, he denied me so much of what is a perfectly normal human thing, *sex*, but little did I realise that it really wasn't anything to do with me, his lack of libido or his ambition to succeed within the company. He'd been living a lie his whole life, but he couldn't let anyone know, it would have stopped his progression to 'the top' as he called it. The day I found out that my husband of ten years was gay was a huge relief, it was like I'd won the lottery. I finally realised after all this time that it wasn't anything to do with me, I wasn't unattractive as I had been convinced I was for the last five years.

I do believe him when he tells me he always loved me and always will, no matter what. We did have some good times and some good holidays and we got on well.

We agreed to divorce with the understanding that he would not object to anything, on the condition that I would never tell anyone about his secret life.

Which I wouldn't. For the simple reason, I'd be too embarrassed.

***

Jamie

'I wish yer was out,' I say, laughing to myself at how drunk I am, 'Hic! I wouldn't be the only one pissed.' I try to clear my head and begin again. 'Can I tell yer something?'

I need to tell her how I feel and what I want to do to her, that I want to live out my fantasies with her before my next posting.

'Yes, but let me get another drink,' she answers, still completely sober, especially compared to me of course.

'Bring the bottle in with yer,' I say.

'Do you need a top up?' she asks.

'Nah, I'm fine,' I answer as I can't drink anymore, I'm not a wine drinker. I wouldn't mind using that bottle on her though, fucking her with it and licking her pussy after, tasting the wine and her cum at the same time. I can feel my cock getting hard at the closeness of her. I feel like I'm going to burst, close to exploding all over my boxers anytime soon.

'I'm really shocked but chuffed, you asked me to come round,' I say, trying to steer the conversation towards my intended confession.

'Why?' Jess says, grinning at me.

Spurred on by the grin I continue, 'Well, I need to be brutal 'ere, and you can tell me to fuck off when I've told you, but the thing is, I've fantasised about you since that night we met in town. I know I'm way out of order and you're probably thinking of smashing that bottle over me 'ead but I just needed to tell yer.'

Oh God, Jamie O'Halloran you absolute shit for brains wank stain, why did yer say it, why? If she doesn't kick my ass out the door now...wait, what? ....she's smiling!

'How long has it taken you work up the courage to tell me?' she asks me gently.

'Fuck knows, about seven hours, countless shots and pints, plus three weeks of intense training. Possibly not in that order though!' I'm laughing as I say it, and she looks chuffed, she has a big grin on her face, does she feel the same? *Ask her, you idiot!*

'How do you feel? I know we don't know each other and you are new in the village but it doesn't have to be anything serious. We can be friends, but closer,' there, it's out there and I hope she feels the same.

'Well, I do like you otherwise I wouldn't have invited you round, well not at this time of the night. Do you want to kiss?'

Woah, she's just asked me if I want to kiss. Well, *Hello?* Of course I do, but I don't know where to start, if only she knew the right old tizzy she has got me into. Taking her glass from her hand and putting it down with mine, I'm so nervous but I move forward and cup her face in my hands and kiss her.

Her hands move to my forearms, squeezing them as she moves them up to my shoulders and then splits them off, one hand on the back of my head and the other under my arm reaching around my back. She pulls me towards her as my tongue searches for hers. Her mouth and her kisses are soft and warm, exactly how I imagine her pussy to be.

I guide her to lay down so I can lay on top, her legs wrapped around mine and she can feel my erection pressing against her, feel my longing for her.

CHAPTER 6

Animal Instinct

Her breath is on my face as I kiss her neck and caress her tits through her T-shirt, feeling her erect nipples through her bra. My animal instinct is to just rip it off and fuck her here and now, just get straight into it. My adrenaline is pumping, I'm really fucking nervous, but I know I need to take my time, pleasure her as much if not more than myself. I can't let her think that I'm just a lad, out for the fuck.

I can't wait any longer I have to feel the touch of her skin, her erect nipples laid bare. Sitting up, I pull her up towards me and take off her T-shirt, wow! Her tits are just so perfect in that bra, I savour the moment, this isn't just any old fuck, this is special. Kissing her tits, I deftly undo her bra and take it off, lay her back down and slide off the settee. Standing above her now, I can see how totally perfect she is.

We both must have had the same thought, to move to the floor and she joins me and lays down. I kiss her lips, and feel again for her tongue, my hands once again caressing her beautiful, now exposed tits, playing with her nipples, erect and aroused, she's really turned on already, she's definitely horny.

I'm horny. Moving slowly down her body, kissing gently over her perfect skin, I get to her jeans. Her stomach is so flat and there's not a mark to be seen. I undo her button and slide down the zip, a little moan escapes her lips, she knows what's coming - she wants me as much as I want her.

I pull down her jeans, kissing her lower belly along the top of her thong. I run my tongue upwards along the side of it, over the smooth, sexy skin leading toward the hip bones and I can see she is clean shaven down there. Taking her jeans off I begin kissing her calf and move slowly up her left leg, my other hand stroking her right leg as I make my way up. I reach her inner thigh and spread her legs apart, seeing that her thong has shifted slightly into her smooth lips, revealing them on one side. Licking gently along this side, I pull her thong up a little tighter between them and she gives out another moan, I can taste her juices already faintly on my tongue.

I tenderly nibble and suck on her exposed and smooth lip, while my finger rubs her clitoris through her thong, and her moaning becomes more frequent. I move her thong over to one side and look at her pussy in all its glory, making my cock so erect it's going to burst through my jeans any minute. He'll have to wait though, she's not ready for him just yet. I move my fingers around the lips of her pussy, feeling how wet she is. Slowly I insert one finger, it feels so soft and warm, then another, she feels a little tight with both fingers inside. Sliding them in and out makes her juices run and soak her lips and her thong. Her whole fanny is so wet. She smells so good I have to taste her, licking and sucking on her clitoris once more. She's groaning with pleasure, my fingers are deep inside her pussy and I can feel her body shaking. I can't stop now, my fingers moving faster and deeper, she's going to climax I can feel it, but I don't want her to just yet, I'm saving that for him, my hard erect cock. I slow right down and take my fingers out moving my head down to gently tease and lick her pussy, tasting her juices, and giving her time to calm down.

With her juices all over my lips and chin I move up to kiss her and let her lick her juices from my face. She knows how good she tastes, I bet she's tasted herself a thousand times before now.

She wriggles out from under me and kneels up, reaching over to the sofa, and pulls a big blue vibrator and lube from underneath one of the cushions and hands it to me.

'You can use this if you like, Jamie,' she says softly, between ragged breaths.

Though a little surprised, I don't need asking twice, I've been thinking about moments like this for weeks now. I lay her back down and gently slide it into her soaking wet pussy, and turn the vibrations on low. She moans with pleasure and her eyes widen, watching me enjoy every second of every stroke as I push and pull, slowly in and out.

My turn to give the surprises now as I reach for the almost empty wine bottle and swap the vibrator for the bottle neck. Her moans become louder and I feel my cock pressing hard inside my jeans, waiting to be unleashed. I lick her juices from the vibrator, and add a little lube making sure it's fully wet, and gently slide the tip just inside her arse, still vibrating on low. I ask her if she's ok with this and she simply moans with even greater pleasure, so I'm guessing that's a definite confirmation for me to continue. Her moans reach a fever pitch and she's cumming, squirting her juices all over the bottle, and my hands.

My cock is throbbing and my balls feel heavy, waiting to explode deep inside her wet pussy. As I kiss her again, I put my fingers in my mouth, so we both lick her cum from my hand. She reaches up to take control of my hand, to taste more of her own cum and I move her hand down to my cock, to show her how hard it is, to make her think about how much she wants me to fuck her. *Deep and hard just how you like it*, I imagine. Older women love rough sex, this is what I need.

Her hand rubs my crotch, she can feel how hard I am. I help her undo my button and she pulls down the zip, my cock is already springing out of my boxers. Her fingers lightly stroke up the shaft, touching the already wet tip with her thumb and fore finger and I feel the softness of her whole hand as she wraps it around the full length of hard throbbing cock.

I can't wait any longer I have to be inside her soft wet pussy, deep inside her to feel what it's like, to explore where my tongue and fingers have already ventured.

Kicking off my jeans, she pushes my boxers down as far as she can and I slide them off with my feet, my adrenaline pumping at maximum levels. I know any second I'm going to insert my long hard cock into her soft, wet and warm pussy. I wonder should I leave her thong on and just move it to the side?

As I sit up on my knees pulling her closer to me, I move her thong to the side holding it with my thumb as I place the tip of my cock just inside her wet pussy. Damn! It feels so good already. I slide in a little deeper, pulling her closer and holding her on both sides just above her hips. She lets out a little moan as I slide right in - my thick cock is a perfect fit for her pussy. As I thrust in deeper I hear her groan, she wants more, she wants it deeper, harder.

'Don't stop!' She gasps. My cock is throbbing, thrusting faster and deeper. My breathing is heavy as I fuck her as hard and as fast as I can, just like she wants it. I can feel I'm reaching my climax, she groans loud and deep and I know she has orgasmed again and I explode deep inside her, feeling my spunk mixing with her cum. I hold her thighs tight as my body starts to shudder, it's never done that before but I like it, I like the feeling, I know now for sure, this is what I've been waiting for.

CHAPTER 7

Raindrops

Hearing the sound of raindrops on the bedroom windows, looking at him lying on his side with his back to me, I'm listening to him breathe as he sleeps. Just the simple sound of his breath, in and out, is as beautiful as he is. His left hand rests on his right shoulder, twitching while he dreams. I can still smell my cum on his fingers, I'm so tempted just to lick them again, take them one by one into my mouth and suck on them.

It's the first day in November, what a difference a year makes. This time last year I was lying on a beach in the Maldives enjoying our regular winter break. Fast forward one year and here I am in bed with a man practically half my age, after having the best night's sex I've had in the last fifteen years.

The rain seems to be getting heavier, there's definitely something romantic about the sound of raindrops hitting the windows. It's funny but I never understood when people said that before, but now I get it.

8.00am, and I think I've had about three hours sleep, I should probably try to go back to sleep, but I don't want to. I want to think about everything we did, how many orgasms I had, how much I wanted more and more and how good his cum soaked cock tasted. All those fantasies I've had over the past three weeks, but nothing comes close to how it really feels.

Orgasm after orgasm, I've waited fifteen years for this feeling, fifteen long years! His fingers deep inside my wet pussy, squelching with my cum on them, I remember his hair brushing my thighs as he licked my clitoris and tasted my cum. I honestly think I could explode again in only a minute. I'm so glad I was sober so I can savour every memory and replay them in my mind, over and over.

Looking down to the floor I see my vibrator and the empty wine bottle, we brought those up with us after we'd finished in the living room. I didn't realise how much stamina a nineteen year old has or me too for that matter.

Yes, the wine bottle and my vibrator, both just lying there covered in my juices, dried now of course but my juices none the less, I remind myself to wash my vibrator ready for using again as soon as possible, it felt so good in my bum, with his cock in my pussy and the vibration turned on low .

I didn't know it was possible to enjoy something so much the first time, I've never experienced *double penetration* before, not even had anal before let alone this, but wow, this is something on another level. I'm getting warm and wet again just thinking about it, reliving that tightness of the vibrator going into my bum and the smell of the lube to help it penetrate me without hurting. Listening to him telling me how much I would enjoy it, how much we would both enjoy it. "You're amazing" he said, "fucking hell, you are what dreams are made of. You'll tell me won't you, if I'm hurting you? I don't want to hurt you baby" I remember him saying.

We continued upstairs shortly after the first time, another passionate frenzy of licking and playing and teasing until I told him to "Fuck me Jamie, fuck me again". I replay it now, in my mind.

He slides his cock into my pussy, it's so thick, it fits me perfectly even though I'm drenched, still drenched from cum and wine, I'm sure I can smell the wine, slowly he slides in and out, my vibrator on low as he holds it in my arse with one hand. I can feel him getting faster, his cock penetrating deep inside my wet pussy, my cum soaking his balls. He throws my vibe on the floor and grabs my outer thighs, he's holding me tight thrusting his cock deep, fast and hard. Moaning loudly, groaning with pure pleasure, I want to scream, he's groaning with each thrust and telling me how much he's wanted to do this since he first saw me.

I bring my pillows down in between my arms and rest my boobs on them, as they bounce to the motion of my body, my pussy being penetrated by his hard thick cock, finally experiencing the fantasies I've had for so long. He asks if I want him to cum inside me. I don't want him to stop, I can feel he's so deep, I tell him "yes" I need to feel him explode deep inside my wet pussy.

He holds my outer thighs and gives one last thrust, I feel his hard cock pulsating, feel him shudder after the climax, filling me with his cum. Our bodies covered in sweat, dripping onto my back from him, and as he pulls out I feel 'our' cum running out of my pussy as I collapse onto my pillows.

CHAPTER 8

The Taste of Wine

I can't remember the last time I actually woke up in bed with a woman after the night before, but one things for sure I do hope in the next eight months I wake up next to Jess more often because that means I've had a great night of sex. There's no denying it, she really was everything I imagined and more.

Morning glory, he never fails, but this time it's different , I don't have to wank myself off, Jess is lying next to me and I can smell her juices already - this woman who is beautiful and classy on the outside was an animal waiting to be unleashed and Jamie Lad you certainly unleashed the animal.

Turning over I'm greeted with a beautiful smile, her lips a perfect shade of pink even without lipstick on. Every time I look at those lips I can't help thinking of them wrapped around my hard cock, watching her lick all her juices off, seeing her take it in her mouth, right down my shaft. Damn that feels good, sexy as fuck, it always gets me so fucking horny watching a woman take the whole length of my cock in her mouth, even better if she does it without gagging.

'Good morning beautiful,' I say as I go in for a kiss, tenderly caressing her right tit at the same time, I can feel my hard cock throbbing already but I don't want to rush it this morning. I definitely want to take my time, in fact I want to get another bottle of wine, I want to taste it again, I was so pissed last night I can't remember what it tasted like, did it taste like wine or did it taste like cum?

Her fingers are so gentle , she lightly strokes my face down my neck and up to my right ear and back to my face. I've never felt such tenderness, yet her touch is so sexual and she doesn't even realise.

The feel of her soft touch as I'm kissing her, tasting her, feeling her tongue, makes me think about my orgasm, I've not experienced that kind of orgasm before, my whole body shook uncontrollably, I wonder if it's because I went bare back, it's been a long time since I had sex bare back, perhaps I just forgot that feeling, the emotion of it all.

I slide my erect cock into her wet pussy whilst I'm kissing her, moving to the motion of the kisses. I don't recall ever making love before it's always been just sex. My body moves with the motion of the kissing, my hips circling slowly, her tits pressed against my chest. My arms either side of her head and I feel her hands gently on my back, a little scratch here and there but nothing heavy. I'm suddenly full of emotions, the feeling of love and being whole. I've never felt like this before, I always thought that emotions were a sign of weakness, but in the middle of making love to Jess and listening to her muffled moans and groans I realise how powerful it is.

As I rise up on my knees and pull her towards me, still sliding my cock into her wet pussy, not thrusting too deep as I don't want to cum just yet, I look down and see the wine bottle and vibrator. Hmm yes, I remember now, I was fucking her doggy style and inserted her vibe into her arse, the feeling of the vibration next to my cock was amazing. I swear at one point my cock was touching the vibrator. Reliving that feeling and reaching my climax, I thrust my hard cock in deep and explode inside her, my whole body shaking as I orgasm. I'm paralysed for a few seconds and then collapse next to her, breathing heavily whilst trying to catch my breath.

It's a good job I've got the week off, lying here in Jess's bed I see it's almost lunchtime and wonder if she fancies ordering some food in, I'm starving. I'm going home tomorrow, to see my mum and the family. Sean has his final interview soon for the army, he has decided to follow in my footsteps, and I want to help him prepare, not that he needs my help, he's a good kid and a smart one, although he's opted for the REME (Corps of The Royal Electrical and Mechanical Engineers).

I'm going to take my kit home and the rest of my washing. I don't need my mum to do it for me but it gives her a sense of pride whenever I bring it. She'll hang it out on the line and stand there for hours just looking at it. She even takes photos and shows her best friend in work, telling everyone how proud I've made her. The last time I went home, I told her "Dad would be so proud of how you've raised us". I didn't mean to upset her, in fact I hate to see her cry. So I'm careful now of what I say about my Dad. But I know he'd be stoked.

Right, that's food ordered, I'm going to go and grab that bottle of wine in the fridge - may as well make the most of it, after all I've not really drank wine before last night, I always thought it was an older persons drink but surprisingly I really liked the taste of it, either that or I was just too pissed to care.

I hope Jess didn't have any plans today. It's going to be an afternoon of food, wine and sex.

CHAPTER 9

Knock One Out

The two and a half hour journey home wasn't too bad, a few sets of roadworks on the way but nothing serious. I would have made it in two hours, but as much as tried not to, I couldn't help thinking about Jess and the sex we'd had over the last twenty-four hours. It's really uncomfortable driving with a stiffy, and as the junction before mine has a pit stop, all quiet, secluded and set back from the main road, I pulled in (thank God it was deserted) and 'knocked one out' into a bush. I couldn't risk doing it in the car as chances are that mum will have me taxi her around this week.

I notice a new housing estate being built as I turn off the motorway and stop to take a look as I've recently been thinking about 'getting on the property ladder' as they say. I don't need anything too big, just something nice and tidy, something mum can probably live in. Taking the contact details from the sale boards I decide to speak to Joe about it at some point this week.

Joe's not long had another baby, his second, well not Joe of course but his partner Jacqui. They had another girl and called her Annabel. I think there's a tribute to our mum in there, her true name is Anna but everyone calls her Anne.

Jacqui is a lovely girl, very kind and caring and works at the local hospital. She was a student nurse in A&E when she met Joe. He'd not long started work for a local builder after finishing his apprenticeship when he sliced his hand open. According to my mum he nearly lost his thumb but according to Joe it was only a scratch. Anyway he left A&E with a few stitches and Jacqui's phone number, and they've been together ever since.

Joe and Jacqui bought a house when Jacqui was pregnant with their first, Sofia. Seems like Joe kind of led the way, because Breda and her fella Steve, bought one a year later and Rosie and Jed have just moved into their own house. So I think, even though I'm only nineteen, it would be a good idea to look at buying something soon, after all Jess has just bought one and she's on her own. I mean, how difficult can it be?

Pulling into the street where I grew up feels weird these days. I've been gone just over a year now and the lads I use to knock about with before joining up are still hanging around the street, still wearing trackies with their hand tucked inside the waist band or lower, scratching themselves.

I hear a familiar voice shout, 'All right Jamie, come to see yer mum? How long yer back for? We should grab few beers soon.'

It's Ash (Ashton) my best mate from secondary school, he was once a top lad but since I've been gone I hear that he's gotten in with the wrong lot. I shout a greeting back and tell him I'll message him later, as my mum's waiting for me.

I pull up outside and look at the old house that's been our family home since Joe was born and our dad was alive. A typical mid terrace, three bed council house. No front garden but a small yard in the back.

Mum gave up the big bedroom for me and my two brothers, I was on top bunk and Joe on bottom, Sean slept in the single bed but once he was old enough he went on top, me on the bottom and Joe in the single. Looking back we didn't have any privacy growing up, I guess that's why it's easy for me to share a dorm with all the lads, the ones that struggle are the ones who had a room of their own back home. My sisters had the back bedroom, it was smaller but a good size for two single beds and our mum slept in the box room. But now we've nearly all left home she's moved into the front bedroom, the big one.

For her birthday this year we all chipped in a hundred and fifty quid (except Sean because he's only a young'un still) and bought her a new bed, a new carpet and had it decorated. Joe got the chippie to build some nice wardrobes for her too. Breda managed to convince our mum to go away with her for the weekend, by making up some excuse that Steve had to cancel last minute so would she go in his place. I can only imagine what was going through our mum's head when she saw two single beds in the hotel room. But it did all become clear when Breda bought her back on the Monday. I wasn't there but from what Rosie tells me, Mum cried her eyes out. I'm glad I wasn't there, I don't even like seeing her cry tears of happiness.

She must have been watching for me, because as soon as I turn the engine off she's flying out the front door calling for Sean to come and help. Thank God I stopped a couple of streets back, pulling in by the offie to text Jess and tell her I'd arrived safely. What is it with women needing to know you've 'arrived safe' anyway? I've told her I'm in the box room this week and will text as and when I can. With a bit of luck, we might be able to get some 'sexting' in…

I carry the kit bag and Sean grabs the bag of dirty washing, he's looking really strong. He's definitely listened to me, which is nice to see. I've brought all my training kit, so we can go for runs every morning. Ten mile runs will be a breeze for me but I need to make sure he has the speed and stamina, I'll pack my rucksack with weights for him and take him on timed runs. It'll help him prepare for what he'll be doing during his fifteen weeks training.

Mum takes me straight upstairs to show me her new bedroom. Joe and his mate have done a really good job. I tell her it's only what she deserves and give her a big kiss on her cheek. I pop my stuff in the box room and lay on the bed for a bit and my mum goes back down to make us a nice cuppa.

Checking my phone for messages I can see a couple from Jess.

Jess: [Glad to hear you arrived safely xx]

Jess: [Enjoy your time with your mum & family, hopefully we can catch up at some point if not see you when you're back? Xx]

See you when you're back? Is that her asking me or is she just checking I want to see her? Erm… of course she'll see me when I'm back! Well I hope she does, I'd like a repeat of the weekend. I decide to send a simple reply.

Me: [Will do, catch ya soon xx]

CHAPTER 10

No Time Like the Present

I didn't realise sitting around doing nothing is so tiring! I don't know how the lads stand around on street corners all day. Firstly, it's boring and secondly, what can they possibly have to talk about? I reckon that's why they chat so much shit. Sean and I discussed exactly that this morning on our run.

I've got some free time right now, as my mum's at work and Sean's gone swimming with his mates. I know Jess is working so I'll drop her a little message for when she's on lunch, a little teaser, that'll get her juices flowing, the thought alone gives me a hard on. I'll even have a wank and send her a 'dick pic' let her know he's missing her.

The truth is, I am too. I'm missing those perfect shaped tits, her smooth pussy and the sweet taste of her juices.

I rub my cock and think about her tight arse and what it looked like with her vibrator in it. That thought on its own is enough to make me cum, but I can't yet, I need to text her and send her a pic.

Me: [Hey sexy, what you doing?]

Me: [Xx]

I send her a pic of my erect cock with the caption 'someone is horny for you'

Returning to stroking my cock, my phone goes, it's a message back from Jess. I'm a little surprised because she told me she doesn't have her phone on in work.

Jess: [Hey, just on my break, what you up to? Xx]

Jess: [Hmm, you know the sight of your hard cock makes me horny too! Xx]

Oh, she's on a break. I wonder if I can make her cum before it finishes? I laugh as I'm typing.

Me: [I'm home alone, thought I'd have a wank thinking of your wet pussy xx]

I imagine I can even smell her juices and she's one hundred miles away.

Jess: [Lol, no time like the present! Break over, text you later. Mwuah xx]

Ha, she chickened out on me. She won't be able to do that when she's home tonight. I carry on stroking my cock, my balls are full as I've not been able to knock one out since I got here. I know it won't take long, two days without a wank and I'm ready to explode.

A quick shower after, my balls feel so much lighter, I really need to knock one out in the shower if I can't do it in bed, the only problem is it takes me ages, it's not like I can start off in the bedroom then nip across the landing with a hard on, not when my mum's in the next room. In her mind I'm still her little boy!

CHAPTER 11

Registration

I've been in the village for nearly three months now and I still haven't registered with a local doctor. My main objective this week is to find a decent doctor's surgery. They'll need to apply for my medical records to be sent on and I hear that can take up to six months, though how true that is I don't know.

One of my colleagues at work has suggested a nice little practice in the next village, she's registered there and they're "very professional", her exact wording, God knows what she means by that, every doctor I've met over the years has been very professional. Lord knows, I've seen enough of them.

When I was eighteen I was diagnosed with amenorrhea, basically I don't have periods, that's not such a bad thing in itself but the downside is that when I want to have my own little family I may have to go for IVF. Which when you think about it, it isn't so bad, the biggest difficulty is finding a suitor.

I'm on lates this week, so I decided to pop along and get the ball rolling. The receptionist is very polite, which makes a change, especially as doctors receptionists aren't generally known for their politeness in my opinion. Anthony always used to say "you know Jess, it takes seven years of study and training to become a doctor, yet it only takes five minutes to become a bloody receptionist". That always made me laugh, but I honestly think there's a lot of truth in it. Anyway, this receptionist seems really nice, and I book an appointment for Friday morning at 9.00am to see my new doctor, apparently you have to have a medical now before any practice will accept you as a patient.

I've felt really happy this week, and I must have looked it because on more than one occasion someone has commented on it at work. I've just laughed and said "I'm always happy" I'm sure if they did what I did at the weekend they would be happy too!

Just the thought of him gets me wet, even after all the fucking we did over the weekend I still had to get my vibrator out Monday morning. My pussy was a bit sore, I'm not going to lie, in fact my bum is also tender and I can't sit down without inwardly wincing. But its pleasurable pain, and I can't wait for Jamie to get back. I'll be waiting for him at the door in black stockings, suspenders, black lace bra and thong, and even though we've not arranged any further 'sex dates' I'm going to let him know I'm waiting for him by sending him a photo on Sunday morning as he's about to leave his mum's.

We've not communicated much since he's been gone, I know he's busy with his family - catching up seeing his newborn niece, helping his brother get fit and prepare him for his final interview. He actually told me quite a lot about his family, in fact, he talked a lot about them, losing his dad at the tender age of three, how hard his mum worked and how well she's done to raise five kids. It was lovely listening to him. I didn't say anything about my childhood, in retrospect it was the polar opposite and I'm so relieved he didn't even ask about my marriage.

Arriving at work for ten o'clock is a real struggle for parking, I really wished they'd bring a car share scheme in, in fact I'm going to suggest it. I just want to get in, get done and get home. I'm so horny, I'm sure I can even smell my own juices, which isn't good - not when you have an eight hour shift at work ahead of you.

CHAPTER 12

The Unexpected

I thought I'd turn my phone on during this break, I'm waiting for an email from my solicitor regarding the divorce and the settlement figure that's been put forward to Anthony. Oh well, there's a surprise, more disappointment on the divorce front, no bloody email. After speaking with her on Friday, she assured me it would be received by Tuesday and she'd email me by Wednesday lunch time. I'm not spending my lunch time chasing her up, when it can wait, as long as I remember to email her this evening. Perhaps I should consider calling Anthony, hmm perhaps not, he's the last person I want to speak to this week -he'll definitely burst my bubble.

I may not have received an email but I do however, have a text message from Jamie. Totally unexpected, especially considering it's only just after 1.00pm and he knows I usually have my phone off during work. It was lovely to receive it, but wrong timing, I only get a fifteen minute break so I really don't have time to get caught up in explicit texting.

I'll surprise him tonight when I get home, he definitely won't expect it, but hopefully he'll be excited to get it. For now, back to work.

Why is it when you want the day to fly by it drags? Every minute feels like an hour. All I can think about is texting Jamie. I'd never heard the word 'sexting' until he mentioned it in a text, thank God for Google!

Trying not to get distracted with thoughts of what sexting is all about and how it makes me feel, I try to concentrate on work otherwise I'll make mistakes. Imagine if I send an email to Paul in property that says something like "Hey Paul, thanks for your email, I'll arrange for the client to come and suck your big hard cock at her earliest convenience" hmm, that wouldn't go down well. Well it might for Paul but not for me, I think it would be "you can pick up your P45 on your way out, Jessica".

Stopping off at the food store in the village to pick up some milk and a fresh loaf, I realise I need some inspiration for dinner tonight, I can't have tea and toast again. I need to start cooking and start eating properly, it's so easy to be lazy when it's only yourself to cook for.

I've learned some things from living on my own, like if I can't be bothered to cook or don't want to, I don't have to. I just think f*uck it, I'll have tea and toast tonight,* or if I don't want to get dressed today *fuck it, I'll have a PJ day*. I don't want to ... *fuck it, I can't be arsed ... fuck it. Fuck it, fuck it, fuck it*. I have no one else I have to worry about or to try and please. This is definitely an easier way of living and I can honestly say I'm enjoying my new found freedom or 'singleton lifestyle' as my mum calls it.

The shop wasn't very busy, I picked up some milk and bread and Fred walked in as I was walking out. He invited me for dinner on Saturday with him and his wife Hazel, I'll look forward to that - Hazel is a mean cook, traditional tasty food. Fred and Hazel have lived in the village for nearly twenty years, since Fred left the army. They have both become really good friends of mine and I'm very lucky to have found them.

I take a quick shower after my cup of tea and scrambled eggs on toast, honestly I've eaten more bread in the last few months than I've eaten in my whole life I think!

Looking out of my window, the street light illuminates the front garden, and it makes me think of Jamie walking up the path and how he made me feel that night and what it's like to actually have an orgasm with a man. How much fun there is to be had with a bottle of wine, empty or not. It surprised me how gentle he was, not that I'm the most experienced but I was expecting him to be rough. Talking of Jamie, I wonder if he's up for some texting…

Me: [Hey, sorry about today, I'm on late shift this week (10-6pm). If you're free we can chat now? Xx]

Hmm, it's not delivering he must be out with his family. That's a shame, I'd really like to see what this sexting is all about!

Jamie: [Hi, It's ok I just had some free time on my own, are you ok? Xx]

Damn, I really wish I'd had time to text back earlier, when he was free.

Me: [Yeah, I'm good, feeling horny xx]

Me: [Sorry, you're probably with your family? Xx]

Jamie: [Ooh, how horny? Show me xx]

Jamie: [Nah, it's cool, I've come up to my room, said I'm tired, could do with an early night. Fancy joining me?]

Join him? How can I do that, is that a metaphor? I know one thing, I need to catch up quick on all this dating, sexting and general texting I'm so out of touch.

Me: [I'd love to join you. Show you, how?]

Me: [I'm sorry, I'm a little rusty, we didn't really have sexting before I got married xx]

Jamie: [Lol it's fine, send me a photo of your wet pussy, my cock is hard & ready for it]

A photo, shit! Do people really send photos? Well he'd better send one back!

I somehow manage to take a photo, all awkward angles and struggling to press the button.

Me: [Here you go, as you can see all wet & horny for you]

Jamie: [Mmm you are, my cock is throbbing]

Jamie: [Get your big blue vibrator out baby xx]

Me: [I have it, I can smell my juices already, flowing for you]

Jamie: [Mmm imagine my fingers deep inside your lovely wet pussy, my tongue licking your clitoris, tasting your sweet juices]

Me: [Oh yes, my juices running down your fingers xx]

Jamie: [Turn your vibe on baby, I want you to put it in your pussy and imagine it's my thick hard cock]

Jamie: [Do that for me baby]

Jamie: [Tell me how it feels sexy xx]

Me: [It's deep inside me, it feels so good, just like your hard cock feels when you're thrusting it deep x]

I'm really enjoying this now, it's much easier than I imagined it would be.

Me: [My juices taste so good, I'm rubbing them on my nipples for you to suck off xx]

Jamie: [Mmm yes, I'll suck your nipples tasting your juices]

Jamie: [My cock is hard for you]

Jamie: [Open your mouth baby, suck my cock, tasting your juices, do they taste good? Xx]

Me: [Yes darling, your hard cock with my juices on tastes good, your cock is throbbing as I slide my tongue up and down it xx]

Damn, I'm getting good at this. This is really erotic, I can't believe how horny it's making me. Oh, I really hope he doesn't mind me calling him darling, I was a little hesitant to write it but it just felt right

Jamie: [Good girl, now turn your vibe up]

Jamie: [I want to know how much it makes you cum]

Jamie: [I want you to cum for me baby, will you cum for me?]

Jamie: [Tell me how good it feels? Xx]

Me: [I'm cumming darling, cumming all over my vibrator thinking it's you, your thick hard cock, oh how I wish it was. It feels so good xx]

Jamie: [It will be my sexy, at the weekend, I will be deep inside you cumming deep inside your pussy]

Jamie: [I'm so hard, I'm going to cum soon x]

At the weekend, so he *does* want to see me when he's back.

Me: [Think of me when you cum, how much you want me]

Jamie: [I was thinking of you when I came.]

Jamie: [I want you so bad Jess, I think you know that?]

Me: [Yes, I know you do]

Jamie: [Good, now that's out the way, I need to sort myself out. Gonna jump in shower. I'll text you in a bit xx]

Me: [Ok, me too. Xx]

My third shower today, *I really need to get a good body moisturiser at this rate,* I laugh at myself. Oh, how this boy has turned my world upside down, I know he's only got a limited time left until his next posting, so I'm going to make the most of these next eight months.

I think I'll pop to that private shop tomorrow night on my way home from work. It would be nice to see what else they have. I was so nervous last time I didn't really pay much attention to anything else. I do remember something about a 'butt plug' though. I want to see what that is exactly…

Jamie: [Hey sexy xx]

Me: [Hey, is that better? xx]

Jamie: [Yes, at least I won't have to sleep with a hard-on and wake up with sticky sheets]

Jamie: [Ooh, probably too much info there! Sorry lol xx]

Me: [Lol, yes very, lol xx]

Me: [I'm shattered now, going to get some sleep. Xx]

Jamie: [Me too, night gorgeous, sweet dreams xx]

Me: [Sweet dreams darling xx]

CHAPTER 13

Celebration

'Jamie, Son, could you get me 'andbag off me bed?' my mum's asking me, all in a fluster because it's our Rosie and Jed's engagement party tonight, they booked it quickly because they knew I was coming home this week. I told them not to worry about me, do it for when *they* want it, but Rosie insisted she wanted her 'little soldier brother' there. I think she might be proud of me.

That's the problem with what I do, being a soldier in the army is the best job in the world but you can't make plans as such, you can't go in to the Serge on Monday morning and say "Hey Serge, me sister's getting engaged on Saturday whenever, I need to book that weekend off" I can just imagine his face and the response I'd get, in fact I think I'd be cleaning toilets with a toothbrush for a very long time. No, if you join up you can almost guarantee that any family get together, a mate's birthday or wedding, you'll be missing them, well ninety percent of them anyway. This is something I've talked to Sean about as I don't want him joining up and getting upset cause he can't get home for our mum's birthday or his mates' birthdays. I guess with me being away now he's learnt that and he accepts it. That's why I think he'll do well, he's going in with the right attitude.

Right, just got time to send Jess a quick text, she knows I won't get the chance later but I'm seeing her tomorrow. Actually I'm really looking forward to it, well my cock certainly is, he's never had so much fun as he's had this past week and

I'm sure he's going to get a lot more, well for the next few months anyway.

Me: [Hey, thought I'd drop you a quickie before I head out xx]

Me: [Have a great evening at Fred & Hazel's say hi from me xx]

Me: [Hmm well if you want to, not sure how you'd explain that one lol]

Me: [Oh & if you decide to have a play with your vibe send me pics]

Right then, mum's bag off the bed, got it. Aftershave on, yes, clean clothes, yes. Time to go and get smashed and have some fun with the family.

' 'Ere you go mum. Oooh! Mam you look lovely,' I tell her, she really does. 'Hey Sean, we'd better keep an eye on 'er tonight, she'll pull in that dress, looking like that,' and I wink at Sean as I say it.

'Sod off, you cheeky shit,' she says, putting me in my place.

Our Sean tells her that she needn't bother bringing some bloke back here who thinks he can boss him around! Not that our mum ever has, in fact I don't think our mum has ever even had a date with another man since our dad died. Perhaps when Sean leaves she should start to think about it, I'll speak to Breda - she'll know what to do.

When I think about it, we've been really lucky with our mum, some of the kids in school had a different dad every weekend, I know Ash's mum had six kids, all with different men and not one of their fathers have anything to do with them. We're lucky, I know it.

My phone chirps and I know it will be a message from Jess, it's typical that she replies just as I'm getting in the cab. I'll nip to the loo when we get to the hotel and check it. I don't want my mum seeing a text from a woman, she'll jump to all sorts of conclusions and have me married off by the end of night - I can picture it now! *Nah, Jamie lad keep this one quiet and to yerself.* A smirk comes to my face at the thought.

The hotel is about twenty minutes from our house, apparently it's where the wedding reception is going to be held, so my mum keeps telling me. 28 May 2022, that date is well and truly etched in my brain and our Sean's. Mum keeps telling us "I know you're both gonna be busy but you have to tell the army it's your sister's wedding, you have to be home, besides it's a bank holiday you should be free and you'll not be in Cyprus Jamie, it's a few months before you go. I made sure Rosie knew that, that's why they booked it for then instead of September".

When she first announced the date I told my mum, "it's not written in stone Mam, it's just an option at the moment, the regiment could be deployed somewhere else in a couple of years, you never know what's 'appenin' in the world these days" and as for our Sean, well she's warned him "you make sure you are back here with yer brother in yer best uniform, I want everyone to see how well yer both doin" bless her she will miss him for sure.

I'm starting to worry about her being in that house on her own. Not that anyone round there would do anything, we all grew up together and she's like a mum to most of them. I worry about her financially, it's a big house and she's not earning megabucks. That's one of the reasons I opted to go to college for two years instead of straight into the British Army at sixteen. I decided to do the Public Services course. Plus it really helped me get my fitness up, when I did join there was only one other lad who had done the same course. I wouldn't say it was a breeze but we didn't struggle as much as the others who'd come straight from the streets. Mum was grateful I know, she held onto my benefits for an extra two years, I don't think it was much but it was a help that's for sure.

I've spoken to our Joe about my idea with these new houses being built, surprisingly enough he had been talking to Jacqui about something similar, he said he'd build an extension on the side of the house and she could live in that, that way she still has her own place but it isn't costing her anything. I think he called it a 'granny annex' I did laugh at that word 'granny' our mums only forty-six, "she's not a Granny" I said to him. Although technically she is I know. Anyway, our Joe is going to look into it, he'll even help me with the deposit. That'll be a great help, I'll pay the mortgage, then if we ever come to sell up it'll be fifty-fifty split, a nice little investment for us both.

'I need a slash,' I say to my mum and Sean as we get out of the cab. Giving her twenty quid I ask her to get me a pint, whatever she's drinking and a pop for Sean. He scoffs at that and I hear something about "probably drinking me under the table soon".

I head for the bogs, my adrenaline is rising now, I can't begin to describe how hard it was not to open her message already, so I'll have a quick slash now I'm here and check it after.

Jess: [You too, have fab night & say congratulations to your sister and her fiancé, it works both ways btw]

Jess: [We'll see, I may surprise you. Oh & here's a thought, bring your work stuff with you tomorrow & go to work from mine on Monday. If you want to? Xxx]

Me: [Good idea, saves me getting up early and nipping home, more time for a quickie, set you up for the day]

Me: [Text you later, don't forget my pictures xx]

CHAPTER 14

Family

'This is proper nice Rosie' I say to her, when a hand taps me on my shoulder. Turning around to see who it is, my mum's looking at me with a wide brimming smile and our Sean hands me a pint at the same time. Once I focus on who it was that tapped me I realise it's Jed's little sister, well she's not so little now, compared to how I remember her. She looks about eighteen, all dressed up, heels and make up on. 'Wow, when did you become all grown up, Tara?' I ask, thinking that maybe our Sean should really make a play for her. She tells me she turned seventeen in September and attends college doing a nursery nurse course. I give her a hug and quick peck on her cheek as she is being beckoned by her mum, I wave at Jean and she waves back.

'I'll be over soon to see you Jamie,' she says. They're a lovely family and I'm so pleased for our Rosie.

My mum starts to tell me about Jed's dad, he's not been well and Jed and his brother Finlay have had to start taking on more and more of the work. Brian, Jed's dad, set up an electrical business, so when Jed and Finlay left school they got an apprenticeship with his company. I don't think they had much choice either, it was drummed into them from the off. But they're all doing well out of it.

I say to our Sean about Tara and making a move on her, but he doesn't seem interested. I'm not going to push it, I wasn't that much interested either at sixteen. He's focused on his career choice and that's way more important than any girl.

My mum is as proud as punch, she can't stop smiling as she has all her children in one room, all grown up and all doing well in life. That, I know, was a massive task, looking at where we've all grown up, but hats off to her she's done a cracking job and she loves us all unconditionally, so she tells me. I'm looking around the room as it's starting to fill up with lots of familiar faces and lots of new ones too, I have a feeling this is going to be a good night, and I look over at my mum and give her a wink. There's one thing for sure, no matter where I am in the world I'll always have my mum and my brothers and sisters, because we're family and that's what's important.

CHAPTER 15

Time for Reflection

I woke with that 'morning after the night before' feeling. Shit, my fucking head is banging and I promised our Sean a last run before I head back. A shower, pint of water and I'll be as good as new, fingers crossed.

I get downstairs around 0830hrs and Sean is already waiting for me, 'Come on then Sean, let's get this over with.' Honestly, I don't know how I'm going to get through this run but I'll give it my best shot.

We're about three miles into our run and I can feel my stomach churning, all the alcohol from last night swishing around. It takes all my might to stop myself from spewing. After another half mile I have to stop, and as I retch my guts up, our Sean harps on about too much drink, mixing with shots and then something about Tara. I wave my hand up at him to *shut the fuck up,* I don't need a lecture on drinking - I'm not normally out running the morning after a good sesh.

This is not good, I'm sweating buckets and still have six and a half miles to go, I need to pull myself together. 'Come on,' I say to Sean, 'let's get going. The sooner we get this done the sooner we'll be back home.'

Asking him what he said about Tara, he tells me that he thinks she fancies me by the way her arms were wrapped around my neck last night, like she was flirting. I'm a little taken aback by this because I don't remember it. I know I was wasted but I vaguely remember her coming over again to talk to us. I laugh at him and tell him she's more his age but he's having none of it. I'm hanging out of my arse now and have to listen to him telling me how he doesn't like blondes and that she's only two years younger than me, so when she's a bridesmaid for our Rosie she'll be a woman as she'll be nearly nineteen and I'll still only be twenty-one. I just laugh it off and keep running.

I've known Tara practically all her life and see her more like a little sister, not a potential girlfriend. Apart from all that I have Jess, she's the only woman I need in my life for now. I tell him to stop being silly, that "I don't have time for any kind of commitment" as that's what a girlfriend is. I'm too busy with work and that's my main focus. I know it's not entirely true but I just want him to stop going on so I can focus on this run.

Mum's cooked us a big breakfast when we get back to the house, because I'm heading back to base around lunch time, to make sure I have enough time to get my stuff sorted for work tomorrow. Then I'll head to Jess's for around six-ish. I wonder if she wants to order a take away or cook something to eat? I'll give her a quick call when I'm on the road.

'Right that's me car sorted,' I say to my mum, giving her a big hug and telling her I'll be home for Christmas as we break up on 16 December. I hug Sean too, and tell him to keep up with his exercise and if he can, try and get a run in before school two or three times a week. Also, if he speaks to his PT teacher he'll be able to give him some pointers as well. My mum gives me one more hug, and I sense her sadness because I'm leaving again, I don't think she's ever going to get used to it especially with our Sean joining up, she'll have double the sadness soon. When I think of it like that it cuts me in two.

I say goodbye for what seems like the millionth time and head off on my journey south, back to base but most importantly back to Jess and her wet pussy.

It's on these kind of journeys when you're alone that you often reflect on your life, where it's been, where it's going and what you want out of it.

When I think about my past I always think of home and my mum. Knowing this woman has sacrificed everything in life for us and here we are, all deserting her at the earliest opportunity. I guess that's the natural progression of life. Hell, in the military you move every two or three years!

Perhaps now's not the time for reflection. Just concentrate on the journey ahead Jamie lad.

CHAPTER 16

Driving with a Boner

'Hiya,' now that I'm well on the way, I give Jess a call.

'Hi, how are you?' her soft voice is a welcome sound.

'I am okay now, now I hear your voice,' soppy I know.

'I wasn't expecting your call.'

'I know, that's why I'm doing it,' I reply with a chuckle. 'I was thinking about coming round to yours about six.'

'Yes, that's perfect. I'm just cooking a pasta dish, do you want some putting aside?' she asks.

'If you've enough but don't worry I was thinking of ordering in.'

'It's up to you babe, see how you feel when you get here.'

'Yeah ok, so what happened to my photos you promised me last night?' I tease her.

'I never promised anything, cheeky,' I can hear her grinning, even on the phone.

'Ha, that's not how I remember it, but most importantly did you have a good play?'

'It wasn't a good play but I did have a play.'

'Go on, I'm listening.'

'Go on, what?' she asks with a little nervous laugh.

'I'm waiting for you tell me how wet you were,' I reply.

'I was very wet actually, I was thinking of you and what you'll do to me tonight.'

'Mmm... I have a semi already,' which is totally true, she has this power over me.

'I'm not distracting you whilst you're driving, am I?'

'Nah baby, it's fine. Carry on, let me know what I've been missing all week.'

'As long as you're safe driving, especially with a hard on,' she sounds genuinely concerned, bless her.

'Yeah baby it's cool, go on I want to hear how much you came, tell me.'

'I was so wet and it tasted so good. I could feel your fingers deep inside me and your tongue licking my clitoris.'

'Yes baby. I can taste your juices,' I say, imagining how it would be.

'My nipples are hard waiting for you to suck on them.'

'Mmm, I can't wait to suck on 'em.'

'I'm licking my fingers, one by one tasting my own juices,' I love it when she plays along with the dirty talk.

'Tell me how it tastes baby.'

'It tastes good, so good. Just like it will when I'm kissing you and tasting it on your tongue and your lips.'

'Mmm, I have such a boner, driving with this is gonna be interesting,' I say laughing out loud.

'Mmm, I'm waiting for you so I can slide my mouth over your thick hard cock, will you like that darling?'

'Yes, oh yes. Carry on.'

'I want to run my tongue all the way down your hard cock, down to your balls, tasting my cum all over them.'

'Mmm. Oh fuck! Baby, my Sergeant is calling me. I'll see you at six.' Shit, that certainly brought me back to reality.

'Ok, see you,' she hangs up and I connect the incoming call.

CHAPTER 17

Home Cooked Food

The cheeky sod, as if I'm going to say "Hi" to Fred and Hazel, that's a can of worms I don't want to open. I hear Hazel asking me if I want a top up. Walking towards the kitchen I smile to myself at the thought of Jamie, not only his normal text messages but our sexting, which I find very erotic, so much so, I read our conversations over and over. Usually while I play with my clitoris, my fingers in and out of my wet, warm pussy, licking them, imagining I'm licking his fingers, his erect cock and his perfectly shaped balls. At least I don't have to wait much longer, in less than twenty-four hours I will be seeing him, his beautiful face and his gorgeous blue eyes.

As I walk into the kitchen I hear Hazel say to Fred 'Ooh! Someone's put a smile on her face,' and then she says to me, 'Well whoever he is love, have fun, it's what you deserve.' She's so right, it is what I deserve and having fun is exactly what I intend to do.

I tell her it's not what she might think, there is someone I have become friends with, but that's all it will be. I don't want to get involved in any kind of relationship, not at least for a couple years, I want to enjoy being single.

I pour myself another glass of wine and top Hazel's up. Fred is on his home made brew, he's told me all about it, how he found the local company where he gets everything he needs and how it's done. I didn't even realise people actually brewed their own beer.

Hazel is a wonderful cook, real home cooked food like the way my mum cooks, absolutely no concern about the fats or cholesterol, everything is fried, roasted in butter or cooked in goose fat. But boy does the food taste good.

I ask Hazel what's she cooking for us and she tells me to wait and see. She asked me about my doctor's appointment on Friday and how did it go.

'Urgh! Where do I start?' I say, rolling my eyes in frustration.

'At the beginning,' she says. I laugh, take a big gulp of my drink and begin.

'Well I arrived at 8.50am for my nine o'clock appointment, as I was on ten till six shift. I thought I'd be out by 9.30am latest, plenty of time to get to work and most importantly - find a bloody parking space. I check in and ask the receptionist if the doctor was on time, to which she replies "Sorry Ms Willets, he's running late, he got caught up in the accident on the way in this morning". Well, how would I know there'd been an accident in the next village? So the next thing was, do I stay and get to work late or do I cancel and rearrange for one evening next week? I decided to call work and speak to my team leader and explain the situation, and then depending on what she said I'd make my decision. So, she told me to stay, and if I'm late not to worry, "it's unfortunate but these things happen. Just get in when you can Jess".

'I finally got called in for my so called medical, forty minutes after my original appointment. Honestly, if I turned up forty minutes late the receptionist would scold me and tell me to do one. But hey ho, he finally got around to seeing me. He's a youngish guy around early forties with a warm smile, dark curly hair and dark eyes. I imagine he is a bit of a ladies man with that smile.' I laugh inside at this thought especially as I'm thirty-six and messing around with a nineteen year old, *the irony of it Jessica*. 'He shook my hand and introduced himself along with an apology for running late. I didn't have the heart to stay angry then, so I just smiled and sat down.

'I could see he had my completed application form in front

of him and I started to feel like I was at a job interview and waited for the questions about my past experience and what makes me think I'm right for this role etc, only this time it's a doctor and I want to join his practice. He started talking about my amenorrhea and what treatment I'd received in the past. Then he talked about contraception and asked what I had been using. "Erm, none," I said and I told him my ex-husband had a vasectomy. I thought "Contraception? Why is he talking about this? I can't get pregnant I know I can't, I've been told I need IVF" so I told him this, and he looked at me strangely and then went on to explain that although I'm not menstruating I may still be ovulating. At this point I think the colour drained from my face, because I heard him saying "are you okay Ms Willets? You've gone very pale" so I gathered my thoughts and told him I was fine and if I were to try any contraception what would he suggest? So he had a look through a book, and then on his PC at which point he said "if it's ok with you Ms Willets, can we try the pill? I'm going to prescribe three months for now as a trial and then we can look at how you've got on with it? If you start taking it today you'll be covered from next Friday. So in case you are sexually active it might be worth using condoms until then" and I thanked him and left.'

Hazel asks if I got it, the prescription. I tell her 'Yes, and I've started taking it.' Then I babble something about being ready just in case I find someone. She laughs and tells me not to be daft, that I'm a young beautiful lady, and I should be enjoying what's on my doorstep. I've never blushed so much, I think my whole body is flushed with embarrassment.

'It's okay Jess, he is beautiful and if I was your age I'd do the same,' says Hazel, 'Make the most of it and enjoy it, well at least until his next posting. Like I said earlier you deserve some fun,' and I nodded in agreement with her.

Fred calls from the living room, 'What you girls laughing at?'

'Women's talk. You wouldn't understand,' Hazel tells him. He laughs and tells us to carry on, he'll put the television on whilst he's waiting for dinner.

We sit down to dinner and I'm slightly light headed as a result of drinking on an empty stomach. I'm so hungry. Dinner looks amazing and smells divine. The last time I had Moroccan lamb stew was in Marrakech about four years ago, I tell Hazel. But I've never had it with colcannon potatoes before. It's a lovely combination especially as it's gone so cold these past few days and along with the dark nights it's what you call 'food to warm the cockles'. Definitely better than my tea and toast that I've been living on lately.

It's getting on for nearly eleven and I need to go home, but the thought of walking home in that weather is not at all inviting. Nonetheless, I am horny and want to have a play. I want to feel my wet soft pussy, feel what Jamie feels and taste my juices as Jamie would.

Fred walks me home so he can give Buster, their little Jack Russell, his last walk before bed.

CHAPTER 18

The Air of Silence

My alarm clock says 7.52am. Even on the weekend after a few wines the night before I still don't sleep past 8.00am. I refuse to get up this early, so I snuggle back down into my quilt. It's wrapped around my naked body like a cocoon. The wind is really picking up out there, it's a miserable day already and I can hear the rain again, we're in for a proper nasty winter I think.

It's no good, I need the toilet, I'll pop the heating on to warm the house up, nip and get a cup of tea then climb back into bed and read through my messages from Jamie. My stomach flutters as I think of him, my lust for him is nothing new now I guess or the way he makes me feel. I haven't been in love for a very long time, not since my teenage days and I don't think I'm in love with Jamie. Maybe his looks, who wouldn't be? But I *am* so attracted to him, I just can't seem to get enough - that's definitely lust.

My nipples are erect at the mere thought of him and it's not only because of this cold house. I enter the bathroom and notice how still everything is, this new house of mine is really silent, not even broken by so much as a squeaky floorboard. Perhaps Fred was right when he said I need a dog, it'd be good company and the house wouldn't be so silent. My only problem is I'm at work all day, and I told him it wouldn't be fair on it being cooped up. "You can drop it off to us every morning or I'll come around at lunch time and take it out with Buster, besides it'll be good for him (Buster) to have a play mate" Fred had responded, totally sincere with the offer.

Another thing for me to think about. I'll discuss it with my mum when I call her at lunch time, see what she says. She'll probably have some wise words of advice for me.

Climbing back into bed, I can feel the house has warmed up a bit. My nipples are still erect however and my pussy is warm and tingling ready for something. I feel with my finger to see how wet I am, parting my lips slightly I feel warm wet juices, yes, I'm wet, I suck my finger to get that early morning taste. I swear it tastes different in the morning than at night. Perhaps it is imagination, but I swear it does, well, to me anyway.

Sitting up in bed, drinking my tea, I look down at my breasts, they are perfectly shaped and not at all saggy, I think that's because they aren't big, 34C, and also according to Lizzie in work, because I've not had kids. She says apparently, once you have kids everything goes south. *So perhaps a dog is a better alternative after all*, I laugh out loud at he thought.

My tea is finished, and my tummy rumbles, nothing new these days. I don't think I'm not eating because I'm being lazy, I think it's more the stress of everything I've gone through these last few months. Food is not a priority, not at the moment, but I'm sure that'll change once my divorce is over and my settlement has been paid, after my solicitor takes her cut. Honestly, I'm in the wrong job, she charged me fifty-five pounds for a bloody letter last week telling me she's sent the proposal over. I wasn't happy, I called to tell her not to send me letters like that, just email me, it is quicker, easier and cheaper on my account. I got off the phone and realised that the call had just cost me twenty-two pounds and any email I receive now will cost me thirty-five pounds plus VAT!

I scroll through my messages from Jamie, needing a distraction. Thinking about my divorce and the costs just gets me worked up, so I'll avert my attention on to him, my gorgeous, sexy nineteen year old soldier. I realised last night, I've not watched any porn in the last week.

I start reading through our sexting, imagining that he's here next to me, kissing and caressing my erect nipples. I reach down and part my smooth lips, touching my clit, getting my juices flowing. It's wet down there, moving my fingers down I slide two in and feel how soft and warm my pussy feels. My other hand is gently tugging on my nipple, and I start to caress my whole breast as my fingers go deeper. It feels so warm deep inside, my fingers aren't as deep as Jamie's go but I feel what he feels, it feels good. Taking my fingers out covered in my juices, I rub it all around my nipples then I move back to my clitoris. I need to cum soon, I'm so turned on. I've cum so many times like this, it feels so good. As my fingers move faster I get closer to cumming, faster and with more pressure, I imagine his hair brushing my inner thighs, his tongue licking me as I'm rubbing my clitoris. His tongue deep inside as I cum, it's so powerful this way, I bring my knees in together as I orgasm. 'Oh my God!' I moan with the pleasure. So good.

That'll do for now, I'll have him here tonight and his head will be down there, his hair touching my inner thighs for real, with his tongue deep inside, I won't need to imagine it. It will be happening.

9.03am, time to get up now.

CHAPTER 19

Two Sides to Every Story

Coming downstairs after my shower, I decide to let my hair dry naturally. The warm baggy jumper I'm wearing that would normally rest on my thighs, seems to be hanging loose today. My fleece lined leggings also feel a bit loose, I wonder if I'm washing them wrong? Also I notice my suede, fur-lined slippers that Anthony bought me for Christmas are also a bit sloppy. I love these slippers, they cost him over one hundred pounds but they're the best, especially on these cold winter days. I've decided winter has definitely set in. Time to get my warmer clothes out for sure!

Looking through my food cupboard, I see it's a sorry state. You can hardly even call it a food cupboard in reality. That saying about 'Old Mother Hubbard and her empty cupboards' rings true here. I really do need to get my arse into gear. I need to start looking after myself better. Perhaps I should look at home delivery, I can order groceries online and get them delivered in the evening or on the weekend. Hazel was telling me she has hers delivered every Saturday morning. It helps her plan her meals for the week. She did send Fred shopping once as she forgot to book the delivery, but that'll never happen again, he came back with a boot full of crap, not a decent meal for a week. I couldn't help laughing when she told me, poor Fred, he's provided well for Hazel over the years, just don't let him loose in the supermarket. Thirty-three years in the Army, he joined straight after leaving school and didn't retire until he was fifty. They've lived all over the world, I wonder if this is the reason they never had children? I should think they'd have made great parents. Hazel being the soft one, a fab home cook and the most caring woman you could meet. Fred would have been stern, there'd be no in-between. There's no grey area in Fred's life, you're either right or wrong, good or bad, black or white. It's that simple.

I opt for porridge for breakfast, I have a big bag of oats lurking in the back of the cupboard. It's one of my 'go to' breakfasts in the winter months, definitely warming.

I think I hear my phone vibrating, which is strange because I normally leave it on loud so I can hear it ring. Oh damn, where is it? I leg it upstairs to find it, I can still hear it vibrating somewhere and then it stops. There, on my bedside cabinet. I pick it up, wondering who it could be, 10.18am and I'm not expecting Jamie to be calling as he's still with his family.

It shows a missed video call from my mum. I'll call her straight back now, as I really miss her and Dad even though they're only an hour away, I know, it's not like it's the other side of the world.

'Hi Mum,' she looks worried, 'is everything ok? Is dad ok?' *Why is she looking so worried?*

She starts ranting on about my new profile picture on Facebook , saying 'Oh Jessica, you look so thin, I know you aren't eating properly, even your dad says you look thin.' I reassure her I'm fine, I've just been busy with work, doctor's appointments and doing the house up. I tell her they're not to worry about me, I'm a thirty-six year old woman and I'm learning to stand on my own two feet, in fact, I tell her how much I'm enjoying single life. At this point I hear my dad saying 'hey Barb, (Barbara) perhaps you should try it, you never know you might like it,' I howl with laughter at this, my dad always makes me laugh but I can tell my mum isn't impressed by her response.

'Tony, any more of your nonsense and you'll be the one to find out first,' she says, meaning every word.

'Oh mum, he's so funny, you have to admit that was very quick of him.' Personally I think he was being very brave, a bit too brave if I'm honest. My mum certainly wears the trousers in their marriage.

Then she goes on to grill me about what I'm eating and how much shopping I have in. I can't lie to her so I'm honest and tell her my eating has become a bit lax and I'm not really shopping, only for the essentials. I also tell her I went to dinner at Hazel and Fred's last night.

'Moroccan lamb stew with colcannon potatoes,' I say.

'Colcannon Jessica,' she says as if correcting me.

'Yes mum Colcannon potatoes,' I repeat.

'No Jessica, it's just 'Colcannon' and if someone doesn't know what it is then you tell them, its mashed potatoes and cabbage.'

'Ok Mum,' I say to placate her, then I tell her about my plan to order on line and have my shopping delivered, she agrees it's a great idea. She says she's done some batch cooking and is sending it down with my dad tomorrow, apparently he is close by so he can drop it off and I'm to put it straight in the freezer.

'I'm thirty miles away Barb, how is that even remotely close by?' Dad says from somewhere in the background.

I can tell my mum isn't listening to a word he's saying. I let her know I'm on nine to five shift tomorrow and I'll be home by 5.30pm. If Dad is around earlier, he can leave it in the porch, otherwise he can stay and have a cup of tea with me before he heads back.

I then start to tell her about the doctor's appointment and how it started off, 'Honestly Mum, I felt like walking out and cancelling it, but I stayed and finally got to meet my doctor.' I told her what he said about me not being on contraception and that I could be ovulating.

'That's great news, so you won't need IVA treatment' she interrupts. I chuckle at her remark.

'It's called IVF mum, short for In Vitro Fertilization' I correct her, she doesn't look impressed so I tell her not to scowl at me, anyway, in any case she doesn't look happy.

I know my Mum well and I know her frowns, this frown is not a happy one. It's nothing I've done or Dad has done, no, this frown is something different something more, so I ask her 'What's wrong?' and she lets out an almighty sigh, now I *know* this is something more.

'Mum, tell me what's wrong, I can see you aren't happy,' I ask her again. She takes a deep breath and starts to babble on about my dad going to the clubhouse yesterday, having arranged to play golf with the usual lot but then couldn't because the weather took a turn for the worse. Anyway, while he was there having a drink Anthony walked in. Now, my dad has never got involved, and he often tells my mum that it's "their business and no one else's".

Fair play to my dad, he always stays objective, he never bad mouths anyone and always says that there's two sides to every story. He's a very level headed man, my dad.

' So Anthony joined your dad for a quick chat and bought him a pint and was talking to him about the divorce settlement, how it's not fair that you should walk away with more than him and that you're making all these demands,' she tells me, still frowning while she's talking.

I interrupt my mum and more or less shout, 'I'm not making any demands, the only thing I've asked for is that the offer on the house, regardless of the price, only be accepted from a family, one that will love and cherish it, and turn it into a proper family home as it should have been!' my blood is boiling now, *how fucking dare he talk to my dad about this, who the fuck does he think he is?*

'Don't you worry, your dad put him in his place and rightly so' she continues with a righteous tone, 'He said to him "Now Anthony, you know as well as I do that there's two sides to every marriage, unless you're married to Barbara, then there's only one side, hers!",' she finished with a smirk.

I literally spat my tea out everywhere, 'Mum please tell me Dad actually said that,' and she assured me he did because by the time he got home he was two sheets to the wind and full of courage.

'Oh Dad, you are so funny!' I shout so he can hear from wherever he is in their house. 'Anyway, Mum, carry on.'

'Well your dad tells him that he's kept out of your separation and divorce so far and would appreciate it if he would keep his feelings or any grievances he has about his daughter to himself and that this is not the time or the place, and he doesn't want to hear that he's been dragging your name through the mud, not in there nor anywhere else. He also went onto say "Now if you have any decency left in you, you'll do the right thing and give her what she wants, she's entitled to it after all," honestly Jessica he is so lucky I wasn't there, he'd have felt the wrath of my tongue, I'm still livid. How dare he, deny you of a family, and me and your father of grandchildren. It wasn't right, he's so damn selfish. No Jessica, you did the right thing, you left him and now you can find someone who will give you the family you deserve. It's a woman's right.'

I feel so many mixed emotions right now, I don't know whether to cry with anger, hug my dad for sticking up for me or just... I don't know what I'm feeling. I know my mum can see it on my face, I'm trying so hard to keep back the tears - I don't want her to see me cry anymore. I need to be strong now.

'Mum, it's fine, don't upset yourself over him, I'm happy now and like you say, I've got the chance to look forward to the future and hopefully have a family of my own.'

She asks me if I got my prescription yet. I never usually lie to her, but I had to, I don't want to raise any suspicions that there's someone in the background, especially a soldier and especially one who is only nineteen. I tell her I haven't had a chance yet, but I'll get it at some point in the next week. After all there's no rush.

We've been on FaceTime for over an hour so I tell her that I need to start my online shopping, so I'm going to go but tell dad I look forward to seeing him tomorrow and how much I love them both, and blow her a kiss good bye.

Ending the call, all the emotions I was suppressing with my mum rise back to the surface and I burst into tears.

CHAPTER 20

Sudden Change of Emotions

I'm lying on my bed, curled up in the fetal position. I don't know how long I've been here, I think I must have dropped off to sleep, exhausted from crying and I can feel my pillow damp against my cheek from all my tears.

12.28pm and my phone is ringing. I'm really not in the mood to speak to anyone, but I reach over to my mobile on the bedside cabinet. *I hope this isn't Mum calling me again.*

My heart misses a beat, it's Jamie. I wasn't expecting him to call, do I let it go to voicemail or do I answer it? What if he hears the sadness in my voice, it might put him off? All this shit, it's unnecessary.

No, I need to answer it, so I sit up and accept the call. I can hear he has me on hands free so he's definitely driving. I feel my mood change almost instantly, like a switch. The sadness gets pushed to the back of my mind and all I feel now is happiness, euphoria. Definitely a good change in my emotions.

We were on the phone for nearly an hour, my whole day today seems like it's been spent on the phone or on FaceTime but I'm happy. I played with myself too while he was driving, listening to his gorgeous voice, it's so calming, it's definitely what I needed although I'm gutted his Sergeant just called him interrupting our call, but I guess it's not a bad thing, after all he is driving.

Now, I need to nip to the shop and pick up some things to make the pasta dish that I said I was already cooking, *why didn't I say I was lying down on the bed? That's two white lies I've told today*, I scold myself. *No more* and I jump up to nip to the village store and get the ingredients.

I'll cook a decent meal, perhaps I'll have enough left for tomorrow night as well, then I'm going to get myself ready for six o'clock. I'm all energized again now my mood and my emotions are all back to normal, well, whatever is normal these days.

CHAPTER 21

Good Vibes

Driving down the motorway for another hour with this hard on would have been really uncomfortable, I might have even exploded in me boxers! The Serge calling when he did was probably a saving grace, God knows what mess I might have found myself in.

So, the first day back after my week off is going to be interesting. I always worry about accidentally sleeping in when I've had a break, I don't know why, I've never overslept my alarm in my life, 'a natural riser' my mum always use to say. My Serge wants me in earlier than 0900hrs tomorrow as he wants to discuss my plans and the options for my first promotion to Lance Corporal. That's why he called, we've arranged for a meeting at 0800hrs before everyone else arrives.

I know one thing, I'm really looking forward to seeing Jess tonight but I hope she doesn't mind an early alarm. I'll wake her at 0530hrs, have a good play, a good fuck then I'll get ready and head out for 0745hrs for my meeting. The perfect way to start the day, an early morning fuck.

Well Jamie lad, I don't think you're going to be Private James Michael O'Halloran for too long, I'm guessing another year to eighteen months max then it's Lance Corporal. I reckon another two years and I'll be a full Corporal. I've set my sights on becoming a Sergeant within seven years, by the time I'm twenty-five. I figured if I work hard and keep my head down I'll get there. I know I'll have to make some sacrifices, I've been doing that all my life really.

I need to concentrate on the driving now, at least my boner has gone, thanks to the Serge. I've only got about an hour left till I reach the village but I should really stop off for some bits, like milk and sandwich stuff for work. I'll go food shopping straight after work tomorrow, get stocked up.

CHAPTER 22

The Taste of Chocolate

Jamie: [Hi sexy, just finishing up here, then I'll be round xx]

I pick up my phone and open Jamie's text message with my stomach feeling full of butterflies. My mind is wandering to the chocolate mousse I bought earlier from the market, and all the erotic things that we might do with it later. *Like smearing it all over the tip of his cock and around his nipples*. I would start with licking it all off his nipples, then sliding my tongue down his torso to his patiently waiting, erect cock, teasingly licking it off while slowly wanking him at the same time.

Well that has definitely got my juices flowing!

Jess : [No rush, I'm not going anywhere xx]

Of course he needs to rush, I've been waiting and fantasising over him all week, playing with myself, tasting my juices and feeling deep inside my pussy, feeling what he feels when his fingers are deep inside me.

Jamie: [You are, you're going straight upstairs, my hard cock has missed your warm wet pussy]

Jess : [Ooh, I'll leave the door on the latch, and wait upstairs for you]

'Shit!' I exclaim to nobody in particular and leg it upstairs, pulling my jumper off and pushing my leggings down with my feet. I scrabble around in the drawer for suspenders and a new pair of stockings, black lace thong and matching bra as I planned previously.

Looking in the mirror I have to agree, for once, with my mum, I have lost a lot of weight. *Oh well, I'll worry about that tomorrow*. After very awkwardly taking a photo, I send it to Jamie with a caption.

Jess: [Ready & waiting for you]

Jamie: [Wow, stay right there. I'll be right up]

Jamie: [You look sexy as fuck xx]

I decide not to text back, I don't want to distract him any further, if he has to keep stopping to text back it's going to take him longer to get round.

Running downstairs, making sure not to be seen through any windows, I put the latch on the front door and run back upstairs, fluffing up my hair with my fingers. Then I fix my lipstick and wipe under my eyes to make sure my mascara hasn't run and then I lay back on the bed as provocatively as I can manage, waiting for Jamie.

CHAPTER 23

Euphoria

Parking up, a little way down the street from Jess' house, I can't believe how dark it is already. Probably a good thing really, after all it's a small village and people do like to gossip, and that wouldn't be fair on Jess, I'm sure it's the last she needs just now.

I grab my toiletry bag, boots and uniform, all neatly pressed of course, lock the car and move swiftly toward the house. My phone is on silent, as I don't want anyone disturbing us, not tonight. My cock is already getting hard before I even reach the door, left on the latch as she said it would be and my heart is beating so fast, it feels like I just did another ten miles with my brother. Letting myself in, the house is so quiet, really deathly silent. *She needs a dog or something*. Maybe I'll suggest it. Closing the front door properly I remove the latch so no one can walk in.

I find a space to drop by boots and toiletry bag down in the hall and hang my uniform up on the living room door, then I quickly slip off my trainers, socks, Jeans, boxers and T-shirt, folding them neatly onto a sofa chair before making my way, naked, up the stairs. My cock is fully erect and my balls full, swinging awkwardly as I climb the stairs. I call out her name to make sure she is awake. She calls back, 'Ye-es?' The house is in darkness apart from the hall light and as I reach the top of the stairs I see the bedroom door ajar with a dull light coming from it, so only the bedside lamp must be on.

I walk into the bedroom and there she is, lying on the bed facing me, wearing exactly what she had on in the photo she sent earlier. Black stockings and suspenders with a black lace thong and bra. I realise I've stopped breathing as I look at her, taking in every inch, *fuck she's beautiful*, she seems a bit thinner than last weekend though, hmm, yes, she definitely looks gaunt in her face.

'Wow, you're a sight for sore eyes' I tell her and she flashes me a sexy smile.

My cock is throbbing and my stomach is tight in anticipation, I'm mesmerized at how fucking sexy she looks.

'I think someone has missed you,' I look down at my erect cock.

'Well don't just stand there, come closer and I'll show you how much my pussy has missed your thick hard cock,' she sits up and beckons me with her forefinger.

'Mmm, lie back and spread your legs.' I move forward as she suggested, then I have another idea and go to the foot of the bed.

'Like this?' and she moves her legs apart, her thong is just covering her lips.

'No wider.' As she does what she's told, her thong disappears inside her smooth lips and she takes a sharp intake of breath.

'Mmm , yes, like that.'

I lift her left foot and start to kiss it, running my hands slowly and erotically up and down the same leg, I can already smell her juices faintly. I take hold of her right foot and rub it against my hard cock. She's smiling, but nervously.

'What's wrong?'

'I'm a little ticklish,' she giggles.

I lower her foot and push her legs apart and take a deep breath, deciding there's not going to be any foreplay, I need to fuck her, deep and hard in what she's wearing, minus the bra.

Moving up closer, I kiss her firmly, my tongue looking for hers as my hands fumble behind her. She's arching her back to it make it easier for me, but it's no good. We're both laughing now, and she has to sit up for me, so I can finally remove her bra.

Laying her back down I now have full access to her beautiful perky assets and begin to cup the left breast in my hand as the kissing begins again. She wraps her legs around mine, rubbing against my calves with her feet, my muscles are extra firm and defined, from all the running this week with Sean.

My hard cock is pressing on her pelvic bone with my balls rubbing against the outside of her thong. I move my hand down from her breast, slightly lifting myself up on my knees, and place my cock near her pussy. Pushing her leg out wide to make her thong give way to her lips, she makes a little gasp. I pull the thong completely to one side and put the tip of my cock just inside her pussy so I can feel her juices as I slide once up and down over her clitoris, making her moan with pleasure and anticipation.

I thrust my thick hard cock deep inside her, not holding back this time, fast and deep, pushing harder, the harder I thrust the louder she gets and the louder she gets the harder and faster I thrust.

She's practically screaming with euphoria now, I've not heard her like this before, I'm thrusting my thick cock hard and deep, her juices are pouring out of her, she's cumming with forceful spasms all over my cock, she's moaning with pleasure. I watch her face and listen to her moans, my orgasm is close, I'm ready to explode, deep inside her, I give one last deep, hard thrust, grabbing and pushing down on her shoulders, she screams, and my cock explodes, emptying my balls deep inside her as my whole body shudders, and her cum soaked pussy is filled with my spunk .

CHAPTER 24

That Touchy Subject

Collapsing next to Jess, my chest is heaving as I try to catch my breath, I can hear her ragged shallow breathing too as she tries to recover. She says she feels light headed, and is struggling to catch her breath still.

Turning onto my side I place the palm of my hand on her forehead to see if she's hot. She does feel clammy still, though after the vigorous sex I wouldn't expect her not to be sweating, I am too. I suggest that it could just be hunger if she's not eaten much today.

I cuddle into her as she turns toward me and smiles, that beautiful smile, it lights up her whole face. Planting a kiss on her forehead I ask her if she feels hungry, which fortunately she does. Good because I'm starving. We opt for Chinese and after ordering a takeaway to be delivered, I jump in the shower and Jess gets in when I get out.

Heading downstairs, I just put my boxers and T-shirt on, *I should have brought a pair of shorts with me really* and shout up to Jess, 'do you fancy a drink?'

'Yes please, I'll have a cup of tea, milk no sugar.'

'Not what I had in mind, but that'll do for now,' I answer, laughing.

Walking into the kitchen, wondering where to find everything, I realise this is only the second time in her house and I'm making her a cup of tea, *Damn, she has me whipped already,* I laugh to myself. Anyway a kitchen's a kitchen, I'm sure I can find my way around, I'm only making a cuppa.

I hear her coming down the stairs, so I shout to let her know I'm still in the kitchen. She joins me, with her hair wet and hanging down and her baggy jumper looking very baggy indeed. Not that I've seen it on her before but I can see from the style of it, and her leggings look loose in places I'm sure they're meant to fit.

I know the majority of men take very little notice in the details of a woman's appearance, whether or not she seems to have lost weight for example but I've grown up in a household with three women, so I learned from an early age how important it is to notice the smallest of changes in a woman, especially around period time. They were fucking big, red flags, trust me. Three females in the house all on their period at the same time, I can assure you us boys stayed the hell away for that week.

I'm going to have to tread carefully here I decide, women are touchy about their weight. Perhaps she has a lot of stress with her divorce and she's one of those women who just loses weight through stress? My mum and Rosie are both like that but Breda will hit the goodies cupboard and eat her way through the stress, and then moan she's got spots or her jeans are tight.

One thing's for sure, although I hardly know this woman and we really do have the best sex, here I am, stood in her kitchen making us a cuppa and worrying about her weight loss - I think I care for her more than I realise. I definitely need to be careful, can't afford to fall in love. Care for her yes but fall in love? *Nooooo*.

'Nice of you to join me,' I tease, grinning at her.

'Ha ha! So you found your way around the kitchen then?' she winks at me, obviously thinking the same as I did earlier about me being *whipped* already.

'Don't get too excited, it's just a cuppa Jess,' I wink back.

There's a knock at the door and Jess goes to answer it, must be the Chinese. That didn't take long, I only ordered it about twenty-five minutes ago before showering. I start looking in the cupboards for plates, the good thing about MOD houses is they're all the same 'carbon copy' layout as each other.

'Hmm, that smells good,' the smell reaches my nose before she even walks back in the kitchen.

'Yeah it does, I'm actually really hungry now.'

Aah good, this is my way in, I can now safely bring up how thin she's looking. 'Are you not eating properly Jess?' I tactfully ask.

'Erm, I don't think I am to be honest Jamie.'

'I noticed tonight when I first saw you lying on the bed and even now standing there in that baggy jumper, it looks baggier than it's supposed to be. You've lost a lot of weight, even since I saw you last Sunday.'

'I know, my mum video-called me today, right before you called and she was telling me off, telling me I look gaunt. In fact she's batch cooked loads of meals for the freezer for me. My dad is popping by tomorrow after work to drop them off.'

'Oh okay, so your mam is worried as well. I couldn't help noticing when I looked for plates, you have hardly any food in your cupboards. Why aren't you food shopping?' I said, thinking afterwards that I sounded a bit accusatory, 'You can tell me to shut the fuck up if you like,' I add, laughing at my bluntness.

'Here you go, get that down yer,' I hand her the biggest plate of food she's probably ever seen. I'm going to make sure she eats tonight.

'Bloody hell, I won't eat all that!' she says, her eyes nearly popping out.

'Give it yer best go.'

'I will, promise.'

'So, why do you think you've lost so much weight so quickly?' I query, between mouthfuls.

'I think it's a combination of lots of things, the stress being a big contributor, the lack of food shopping is another for sure and if I'm honest, I've gotten lazy with cooking and eating. But all of you are right, I need to start cooking again, I need to go shopping each week and I need to start taking a packed lunch to work as well.'

'You don't eat in work?'

'No, I don't have breakfast either.'

'So the first meal you have in a day is when you get home, and what would that normally be?'

'Yes, most nights a cup of tea and toast but if I'm really feeling adventurous I might have scrambled egg or beans on toast.'

'For fuck's sake Jess, that's not good. One thing me mam always told us "breakfast is the most important meal of the day," you should have that at least.'

'I know, I use to eat really well, I'd take breakfast to work along with my lunch, get home and either I would cook if I was home before Anthony - erm, he's my ex-husband - or he would cook and quite often, especially on the weekends we would eat out. So in my defence, it's only really been the past couple of months I've not eaten properly.'

'Ok, I get that. Me, if I'm stressed, I go for a run or hit the gym, I know other guys who hit the booze. Me mam and younger sister Rosie are like you, they lose weight with stress but me oldest one Breda, she's terrible, she'll hit the goodies cupboard and eat and eat. But then she gets stressed out 'cause she's got spots and her jeans are too tight from all the shit she's eaten,' I can't help laughing now and Jess joins me too.

'Honestly though Jess, I don't want to sound harsh, but you need food, you need the vitamins for definite. Is money tight, is that why you aren't eating?'

'Good God no! Money isn't an issue, it's me, plain and simple, I've been lazy and just not hungry,' she looks at her plate, 'but this is good, what do you think?'

'Yeah, it's really tasty, I wonder if they have a new chef? I noticed last week it was really tasty.'

'Oh yes, you did make a similar comment last week,' she winks suggestively, but I'm not entirely sure why.

'Ok, I'll just eat and be quiet,' I respond, with a little chuckle, playing along.

'You? Be quiet, really? I don't think you know how to.'

'Have you ever had any pets?' I ask her.

'What? Where's this going? That was a quick subject change. No I haven't, we had a really nice house and busy lives. We didn't have the time for pets.'

'It's just when I came in earlier, the house was deathly silent, I mean it almost felt empty. What about getting a dog? It would be company for you as well. I would have loved one growing up but money was really tight, so we never could.'

'Funny you should mention that. Fred, said the same thing when he walked me home with Buster, he's even offered to walk it at lunch time when I'm working. In fact, I was going to speak to my Mum about it when we were on Facetime earlier but I forgot.'

'Well, if you ask me, I think it will be good for you. Think about it.'

CHAPTER 25

Punishing Oneself

I'm not sure what I just experienced there. Some kind of animalistic sexual behaviour, but one things for sure, I've never in my life experienced that before and if I never experience it again, I can honestly say it was the best, most euphoric thing I've ever had.

I'm sure at one point I was screaming. Oh God! I hope no one heard me. Shit! The neighbours, what will they think of me when they see me in the street? I'll keep a low profile for the next few days, hopefully they'll have forgotten by the time they see me again.

I'm still feeling blown away by what just happened. We're just lying side by side on my bed, breathing heavily, regaining composure. The touch and feel of his naked body on mine as he cuddles into me is something I've longed for and that tender kiss on the forehead, now that's special. It shows the softer side of a man, his compassionate side, it shows he cares, even if he doesn't always show it. I've learned in life that a kiss on your forehead means *she's special*.

I watch him as he gets out of bed and walks towards the door, he's going for a shower before the Chinese arrives. We only just ordered it, so there should be plenty of time for me to shower after him. I feel a little gutted that I went to that much effort earlier to get the pasta dish ready, but actually I can use it for lunches in work, I know I really do need to start eating properly.

Showered and dressed, I tiptoe downstairs with a spring in my step. His uniform is hanging on the door, and I brush over it with my fingertips, getting a tinge of excitement thinking of his beautifully toned body underneath it and that perfect peachy bum in his trousers. Here we go again with the butterflies and yes once again I'm getting warm and wet between the legs, even after the sex we just had. There's no denying it, I just can't get enough of him.

Hmm, he seems to know how to make a good cup of tea too, I could stand here for hours watching him moving around the kitchen in his Boxers and T-shirt, my God he is sexy!

With more tact than most men, he brings up the subject of my weight. Oh no, not him as well, even *he's* noticed I've lost a lot of weight, so how did I not notice until today? Mum's right, I need to start eating properly.

I use to love my food. Is this just a reaction to the hurt, anger and emotional distress of my marriage breakdown? Perhaps, I'm depriving myself of food, like it's a punishment. Maybe I'm subconsciously punishing myself, but why? It's not like I'm the one to blame.

I was every bit the faithful wife, I stayed way longer than I should have, anyone else would have been long gone within a year I'd bet. But no, not me, I stayed. Not because of love, well not for him anyway, no this was deeper, far deeper. This was out of love and respect for my dad.

CHAPTER 26

Fate

My dad is the hardest working man I know, he's fifty-nine now and still works a fifty hour week. He's regional manager for a national building company. He left school at fifteen and went straight into his apprenticeship as a bricklayer, and over the years he's worked hard, even gained a qualification in business management from night school when I was younger. That's when he moved into the offices and from there he has progressed through management.

Forty-four years he's been with the firm. He received his gold watch after twenty-five years, I can't remember what he got for thirty years but I do remember for his fortieth year anniversary he was given an electric golf trolley. Now I'm not much of a golfer but according to Anthony they cost a few grand. Knowing how much my dad loves his golf, this present would have meant the world to him, I for one was really chuffed, probably as chuffed as he was.

It's funny how life plays out, *if it's meant to be it will be.* Take my mum and dad, they both worked for the same firm. Mum started there as a filing clerk at the tender age of sixteen, "always out of the way of the blokes" she said, as the men never needed to go into the offices.

Their business was always conducted in the yard or the works' cabin, where there was a foreman in charge, whether it was work related or picking up the pay packet at the end of the week, it was always the foreman that the men dealt with.

It just so happened that the girls in the office wanted a cabinet moved to make way for some new office furniture. So on this particular Friday my dad and the mate he was working with arrived back slightly earlier than the others and were asked to lend a hand in the office to move this cabinet in preparation for the furniture arriving on the following Monday morning.

So in he went, his usual chirpy self and he saw my mum, a quiet and pretty sixteen, soon to be seventeen year old standing by the much talked about cabinet.

Dad was nineteen at the time and he "knew a good looker" (his words not mine) when he saw one. So on my mum's seventeenth birthday, (which he took the trouble to find out on a sneaky visit to the office) he turned up with a bouquet of flowers and asked her on a date.

So the rest of the story is that Mum started dating Dad at seventeen, got engaged at eighteen, married at nineteen and had me the following year aged twenty. I know I've been lucky, as Mum never went back to work, she stayed home and brought me up, while my dad provided for us and provided well.

They never had more children, my mum suffered two miscarriages after having me, and I know on the second one she was quite far gone, well over twelve weeks. I think it was this miscarriage that scared my dad, so much so he said to her "Barbara, no more, I can't go through this again, the next time I might lose you and I'm not chancing it, it's not worth it. If you want any more we'll look at adopting". They never did adopt though, which is a bit of a shame really as I would have liked a sibling, however, both Mum and Dad were loving parents and gave me the best childhood and memories anyone could wish for.

After Anthony 's proposal my dad told us that no matter what the cost we would have the wedding of our dreams and that money was no object. It turns out that he had set up a 'wedding fund' in a savings account when I was born and had been paying into it ever since. I think the total cost of my wedding came in at over £30,000. It was a huge wedding, just over two hundred people in attendance. I must admit I've never seen my mum and dad so happy, they really were the proudest of parents that day.

This thought makes me really sad as I know now it was all fake on Anthony's part, though not on mine. I wanted a marriage like my mum and dad's. When Anthony and I decided to buy our last house, we weren't sure if we could quite afford it, the mortgage was ok, that wasn't the problem. We were short on our deposit, as the mortgage company wanted a twenty-five percent deposit, due to it being a new build. So with all the fees and the deposit we needed just under £160,000. We were over £40,000 short.

My amazing dad gifted us the difference. We said we could get a loan or we'd just look for something else but he was adamant "No Jessica, your mum and I are more than comfortable, if we can't help our only child out then we will have failed as parents" at which I laughed and told him to stop talking rubbish.

So no, the question of me punishing myself would not be over Anthony. If anything it would be over my parents, especially my amazing dad. When I think of how much he has given us for the wedding and the house, and for what? For it all to go up in smoke. Divorce, chucked back in their faces, or so it feels. This is where all the anger comes from, and a feeling that I've let my dad down!

Anthony is such a bastard.

CHAPTER 27

Sleepover

I swear he's given me his share of the Chinese, my plateful is humongous! It's really nice to have company when you eat though, actually it is nice having someone else in the house. I realise I do miss company but the alone time has been good, definitely what I needed. While we're on that subject, has he been talking to Fred? He too thinks it would be a good idea for me to get a dog. Changing the subject I bring the conversation around to him staying the night.

'What time do you need to be up tomorrow?' I ask him, between mouthfuls of my plentiful Chinese dinner.

'I have a meeting at 0800hrs with my Serge, that's what he called me for earlier. So I was thinking about 0645, leave by 0745. Is that okay with yer?'

Oh that's good, I'll let you get ready first and I'll get up once you're ready. I don't need to leave until 8.30am.'

'Cool, I'll set the alarm for 0530 then,' he says with a wink and a very wide grin.

'Five-thirty?' I'm confused, I swear he said 6.45am.

'Yeah, early morning sex, best way to start the day!'

'Aah, yes, true,' I agree, though I've never actually had early morning sex before. 'So five-thirty it is then,' I giggle.

'I've never stayed over at a woman's house before, then got up to go to work, this will be a first.'

'Really, how come? How do you feel about it?' I hope it's not a problem. I don't want him to be uncomfortable, I just thought it would be nice to spend the night together.

'I just haven't, never really got past the one night stands to be honest. I've been so focused - and still am, on work. A girlfriend or a relationship, whatever you want to call it, I never really, er, I wasn't bothered to be totally straight with yer, I thought it would interfere, distract me, yer know? I am quite looking forward to it, actually, I never did sleepovers, even as a kid neither. So this really is a first. Hey I'm a virgin sleepover-er.' We both laugh at this.

'Well, I promise I will be gentle with you,' I smile and blow him a kiss.

'So your dad is visiting yer tomorrow, are yer excited? I best not leave me boxers hanging on the back of the bathroom door,' he says with a wink.

Nooo, God no, I might be thirty-six but there are some things you don't want your dad to see, a man's pair of boxers hanging in your bathroom, is definitely one of them.' I laugh and cringe inwardly at the thought of it. 'I really am looking forward to seeing him, yes, he's a great man, the best in fact.'

I've missed living close by, where I could just pop in for a drink or would see him down the clubhouse at the weekend. I do miss that part of my life, but that's in the past. This is my life now, I need to think about me and my future.

'See? Yer were hungry. Yer've nearly polished all that off. Yer need to eat more Jess...ica.'

Hey, you're beginning to sound like my mum.'

'Seriously though, we didn't have a lot growing up, but we always had food. It wasn't shit loads but it was enough. I learnt from a very young age that yer start yer day with breakfast and yer finish it with an evening meal.' He gets up and takes his plate to the kitchen.

'Since joining up, I've learned a lot about the vitamins that our bodies need, the calories we burn up in exercise, and what happens to yer if yer don't eat correctly. Our body is like a car and food is the fuel. Yer have to put the fuel in to keep the car going. Does that make sense?' he looks to me for some kind of acknowledgement, like a teacher at the front of the class.

I nod, like a good pupil, to show him I understand.

CHAPTER 28

Cannodling

'Right then missy, let's get yer lunches prepared, then we can cuddle up on the sofa, while I play yer tit.. er breasts and yer can tell me about yer childhood. I'll let yer talk for once!' he laughs.

'Ha ha, that will just lead to more sex, if you start caressing my breasts.'

'Yeah, I know,' he winks and gives her his cheeky boy grin.

'That's fine then,' she says, her stomach awash with butterflies.

'See, the beauty of these containers is they can be used for yer lunches, like so.'

'Oh, you are a clever man. Bravo, bravo,' she says with a mock round of applause.

She can't help but think to herself, last week he was the loud mouth, cocky guy you would avoid at all costs, but behind closed doors, he is the sweetest, most caring man she's met. Next to her dad of course. He doesn't act like a normal nineteen year old, compared to the boys in work, now they really *are* boys. But Jamie is way more mature. One things for sure, his mum has done herself proud.

She looks at him, his beautiful blue eyes and oh so long eyelashes, she can't get over his beauty. Or should that be handsomeness? She wonders. She gives him a warm, caring smile as he turns to look at her.

'What? What yer looking at?' he asks.

'Just you, how different you are to when we met last week, that loud mouth yob in The Bowl.'

'Ha, he's still there, I save him for the lads. Besides yer don't want me shouting in yer house that I'm going to fuck yer, imagine what the neighbours would think, or is that what yer secretly want?'

'No, no. No way, you're fine the way you are. I like this side of you.'

'Where's yer lunch bag? Have yer got any fruit?'

'No, but I'm thinking of getting some fruit for work, perhaps when I'm on my break. Oh and I don't have a lunch bag, that's another thing on my list of things to buy.'

'So, the carrier bag from the chinky it is then, and I'm the one from the council estate?' he asks, laughing at his own joke.

'Hey, cheeky. I've got a lot to learn I know, but I've not lived on my own before, this is all new to me, I thought I was doing well.'

'Yer doin' fine, I'm just jesting with yer.'

They lay on the sofa together, and true to his word he undoes her bra and cups her breasts in his hands , caressing her nipples, squeezing them, softly stroking them, as he's doing this his cock is twitching.

He listens intently as she tells him about her childhood, her parents meeting at work, her mum marrying at nineteen, having her at twenty and about the two miscarriages. He can't imagine growing up without his brothers or sisters, he can only imagine that she must have been lonely. In fact he's never met an only child until now.

His hand moves down to the top of her trousers, teasing her as he moves his hand along the waistband, kissing her neck, telling her to carry on, that he's listening.

Jess was struggling to concentrate and tell him about her life, all she wanted to do was rip her top and bottoms off and lay there completely naked. Naked for him to do whatever he wanted.

'I'm not stripping yer off down here, so yer might as well carry on,' he tells her, laughing as he continues kissing her neck. She lets out a sigh from the tingling pleasure and continues. She tells him about her school, that she didn't go to a private school though it was a very good one. She did her A levels but decided whilst studying them that she wasn't going to university.

She wanted to go to work, she wanted to 'earn her keep' as she puts it. Her mum and dad were supportive of her decision and helped her apply for jobs. Her mum drove her to the interviews and when she landed her first job as a customer service advisor, her parents paid for her driving lessons and bought her first car when she passed her test.

His hands are stroking her, up and down her body, feeling her tits, his cock semi hard, he can't help but enjoy the cuddling on the sofa, something he's not really done before. In fact he's never been very attentive towards a woman before, he just fucked them and left them.

She stops talking, she wants him too much, she doesn't want to talk anymore, in case he asks about her fake marriage, that's how she sees it now and thinks about it as just a 'fake marriage'.

'Go on, keep talking, I'm listening,' he tells her. He's nibbling on her ear lobe and asks her if she wears earrings.

'Yes, I do,' she says, 'but I just didn't put any in today.'

'Mmm, do you fancy going to bed?' he says, feeling excited at spending a whole night with her, sleeping naked and feeling her naked body close to him, kissing and cuddling. Waking up naked and having morning sex, emptying his balls deep inside her before starting the day. Yes, Jamie's very excited about this indeed.

CHAPTER 29

A Nice Neat Pile

Jess gets up off the sofa, snatching up her bra off the floor as she does so. She goes through her usual bedtime routine, checks the backdoor is locked, checks the front door is locked and turns off the lights. Jamie picks up his neatly folded pile from the chair, his toiletry bag and his uniform and heads upstairs. He knows the front door is locked, he was the one who locked it, he tells her, but she has to check herself, for her own piece of mind she says.

She runs up the stairs like a kid on Christmas Eve, giggling to herself as she goes. She's so turned on, in fact she has been the whole time she was lying on the sofa, her juices are flowing and she can feel her thong is damp. She walks into the bedroom and sees how neat and tidy Jamie's little pile is, his uniform hanging from her curtain pole, taking pride of place in her bedroom. *He is very tidy, must be his training*, she thinks to herself.

Throwing her bra on to the chair in the corner of her room, she pulls off her jumper and discards it on top of her bra followed by her bottoms and thong. She can see him looking at her naked body. Suddenly she feels shy and wants to cover up. *Why is he looking at me like that?*

'Stay there,' he says, 'and spread your feet apart, not too wide though.'

She does as he asks, and as she moves her feet she hears the sound as her lips slightly part, because she is so wet, even more than she realised.

'What do you want me to do now?' she asks.

'Close your eyes. With one hand feel your breast, your nipple, caress it, play with it. With the other, I want you to feel yourself as you work yer way down to yer clitoris, feeling yer smooths lips, parting them further, touching yer wet pussy,' he smiles as he says it, feeling turned on by describing it. 'I want yer to tell me what yer feel and what you want to do next. I want to see yer standing there playing with yerself, making yerself cum, tease me. Show me what I'm missing, what my hard cock is missing.' He moves the quilt back to show her his erect cock, and his hand stroking it. 'Tell me how it feels, what you want to do next,' he repeats.

'I'm so turned on, I can feel my juices flowing,' she begins but lets out a nervous laugh, 'I feel a bit stupid.'

'Nah, don't baby, I love it, you look sexy as fuck. Imagine it's my hands touching yer, where would yer want them to go, what would yer want me to do next? Go on.'

She closes her eyes and does what he says.

'My breast is so soft, it feels smooth but my nipple is hard from playing with it, it makes me feel horny. I can feel your warm breath on it, your tongue licking it, warm and wet. I feel your lips lightly touching it. I want to pull your head in tighter, I want to feel your whole mouth on my breast and your hair touching my skin, I can feel my stomach tightening and my pussy releasing more juices. Mmmm,' she lets out a moan.

'Yes baby, I can smell your juices, I feel your heart pounding, I know you're turned on. I make you feel like this, don't I?'

'Yes, yes you do!' she says breathlessly.

'Good, now tell me what you want me to do next?'

His cock is so hard, his balls are aching and all he wants to do is pin her up against the wall and fuck her there, deep inside her wet pussy. But he can't yet, he needs to let her finish, he wants to see what she wants from him, right here right now.

'I feel your fingers parting my lips, they are so wet now. You take your hand away and lick them to show me how much you like it.'

'Mmm, tell me how it tastes.'

'It tastes good, sweet,' she says between slowly licking her fingers.

'Yes it does, it's really good. Carry on.'

She moves her hands back down and opens her lips again. She's using both hands now. 'My clitoris is erect, I'm so horny. I can feel your other hand playing with my lips, parting them, I feel your finger touching, feeling and moving inside my pussy. Ohh!' she groans with pleasure, 'it feels good. I want you to go deeper, to put another finger inside me.' She inserts another finger while Jamie watches.

'How does that feel with two fingers? Spread your lips a bit more, try three fingers now.'

'My arms aren't long enough to position for that, I'll stick with two,' she says with a little laugh.

'Ok then, no problem,' he laughs too.

'I can feel my juices, it's so wet and warm. I want to cum all over my fingers, feel it between them.'

'Don't cum, not just yet. Take yer fingers out and rub your juices all over your nipples.'

As she does as she's told, he gets up off the bed and walks her backwards to the wall. Bending down slightly he sucks and licks her nipples, tasting her juices, they taste sweet, just as she described.

He lifts up her leg and holds it at hip height and with his other hand he places his cock in her pussy and thrusts deep inside her, moving in closer to her, fucking her faster and deeper, she moans in his ear, he knows this is going to be quick.

'Are yer ready to cum?' he asks.

'Yes!' she shouts.

He thrusts his cock deep once more, exploding deep inside her, they cum together, just as he wanted.

He can feel her body going limp, her leg is giving way, but he holds her up, holding her tight, her naked body pressing against his as he lowers her other leg, he can feel her collapsing in his arms, but he's got her.

CHAPTER 30

Alarms

0530hrs. A single beep and his eyes open. Jamie seems to be aware of the alarm, pre-empting it before it even goes off these days. Lying there cuddling into Jess, spooning behind her, she hasn't stirred. He looks at her sleeping peacefully and forgivingly thinks it would be unfair to wake her. He decides to reset the alarm for 0630hrs and dozes back off for another hour of sleep.

0628hrs. He turns the alarm off. Leans over and kisses her neck. He'll easily get ready in forty-five minutes if he has to. His cock is hard, his morning glory. Jess stirs, she can feel his heat against her skin, he's nibbling her ear and his cock is digging in her back. She laughs.

'Good morning,' she says sleepily, 'What time is it?' She turns over on to her back, looking up at him as he smiles down at her.

'Good morning sleepy head, coming up to half six.'

'Oh, I thought you was waking me at half five?'

'Nah, you were fast asleep. I didn't want to disturb you. Anyway, you're awake now.'

As he begins to kiss her, her legs automatically part. But he's decided he's not going to be on top this morning, he wants Jess on top. Lying down he pulls her over him.

She straddles him, legs either side, moving his cock into position, just teasing her pussy lips, she's not surprised anymore how wet it's getting these days, in fact she's loving it, the feelings of horniness, easily turned on at mere thoughts of him.

She sits on his cock, and it feels tight as it slides in, but oh, it feels damn good. She starts to move slowly up and down. He fondles her breasts, cupping them in his hands as they bounce with the motion of her rising and falling, enveloping the length of his morning hard-on.

Leaning forward slightly she holds on to the headboard with both hands, so her breasts are sitting just above his face. He grabs them and sucks on them one at a time, as she continues to rock back and forth.

Her breathing becomes heavier and her moans get louder, her lower muscles get tense, she can feel she's about to cum soon, she wants to make sure he's ready, she hopes he's ready so they can cum at the same time.

'I want to cum, are you ready to cum?'

'Nearly baby.'

She sits back up, supporting her weight in her thighs, she rides his cock hard now, feeling it really deep, he groans, getting closer and closer to his orgasm. She bounces up and down a little longer and then he says,

'I'm ready, I'm going to cum.'

'Me too,' she says as she feels the tension peak, bringing her right to the brink of orgasm.

He thrusts hard up into her and she hears him moan, feels him explode deep inside her, bringing her fully into orgasm with the feeling of his now pulsing cock, her juices mixing with his, her body is flushed with heat, his body is tensed and he's gripping her knees with his hands as he shudders .

They savour the intensity for a few moments, lost in their own pleasure, and then she climbs off and lays back down next to him, both of them still breathing heavily, lying in complete silence, both feeling exhilarated. *It's definitely the way to start the day*, Jamie thinks to himself and a smile crosses his face.

0700hrs, one beep, he jumps out of bed and plants a kiss on her lips before walking off towards the bathroom for a shower and shave, to get ready for his first day back and his meeting at 0800hrs. This meeting will hopefully hold the key to his future.

CHAPTER 31

Shower Time

As Jess is lying on the bed, waiting for Jamie to finish his shower, she's sure she can hear him saying something, but with the noise of the water there is no chance she'll be able to hear him clearly.

'Hold on, can't hear you, I'll come there,' she shouts.

She gets out of bed, walks into the bathroom and stands there for a moment watching him in the shower, he's not the tallest of guys, at five feet seven inches but he is perfect in every way. She looks at his muscular legs, his perfect peachy bum and the muscles in his back. He really has got the perfect physique, even from the back.

'I couldn't hear what you were saying, sorry.'

'Ok, I'm nearly finished, do yer want to jump in? I'll have a shave in the sink.'

'Yes sure, let me grab a couple of towels.'

She gets some extra towels from the airing cupboard, and goes back in to the bathroom, expecting to see him standing at the sink, but he's still in the shower, waiting for her.

'I have a couple of minutes, I'll help yer wash.'

She immediately feels horny again and practically jumps in the shower as he's lathering his hands with soap. He gives her a tender kiss on her lips, the shower water pulsing onto their faces, he starts to wash her neck, rubbing in the soap, moving down to her breasts, paying extra attention to her nipples. He begins to move one hand down towards her bum and the other towards her vagina.

She opens her legs slightly so he can get his hand in. As he lathers her up she feels his fingers teasing her around her clitoris, she chuckles at his directness and he winks at her, guessing the reason for her amusement.

'Turn around, and lean towards the wall.'

He turns the shower off as she turns around, placing her hands up against the wall and leaning slightly forward. He rubs the soap over her buttocks, sliding his hand down the crack of her bum then pushes his thumb into her anus and moves it gently back and forth. She starts to moan, softly, she's liking this. He gets a little faster and her moans get louder.

He reaches forward with his other hand and rubs her clitoris, the pleasure is intense now and she can't control it, her legs shake and she cums hard, in a matter of seconds. He keeps his thumb inside her arse while she cums and puts his fingers inside her pussy so he can feel the full intensity of the spasms. Then he turns the shower back on.

'If I had longer, it would have been my cock instead of my thumb.'

'Next time then?' She laughs as she says this, but she is serious, next time she wants to be on all fours and she wants his cock deep inside her arse.

'Yep. Right I need to get shaved. I'll leave yer to finish off showering.'

He steps out of the shower, wraps a towel around his waist and fills the sink with hot water, splashing it around with his hand to make sure it's the right temperature. It only takes him a few minutes to shave, being blonde he doesn't have a lot of facial hair, he is lucky. He brushes his teeth and heads back toward the bedroom to get dried and dressed.

As she walks into the bedroom, she looks at him, he's beautiful, there really is no other way to describe him. But she can't help feel a tinge of sadness, 'if only he were a few years older. I could quite easily fall in love with him,' she thinks.

There's no getting away from it. He excites her in a way no man ever has and this scares her. What if she never finds that excitement again, how is she to meant find her life partner, someone she can have a family with? Or is it that how it's meant to be, boring? *Perhaps he will always be 'my dirty secret' or 'my guilty pleasure.' Whatever he is, he will always be 'my soldier'* she decides.

7.30am, her alarm clock starts buzzing and she jumps at the noise as it snaps her out of her thoughts. Still set for the usual time she would be getting up. The early morning was certainly worth it today though.

'I'll go and put the kettle on and leave you a cuppa on the side,' he says.

'Ok, thanks,' she smiles as he walks toward her, cups her face in his hands, gives her a tender kiss and heads for the bedroom door.

'Send me a photo before you leave for work, I'll text you later,' he calls back to her and he's out of the bedroom before she can string a word or two together.

This boy, no, this man, he isn't a boy, he's mature way beyond his years, has really got to her, he seems to be showing her what a relationship and even a marriage should be like. She smiles as she sits down to dry her hair.

'Jess I'm leaving!' he calls up the stairs, 'I'll text yer later, yer tea and breakfast are on the side. Don't forget yer lunch!'

'I won't, thanks. Speak later.'

CHAPTER 32

First Day Back

He parks up outside the unit, a single storey building probably built towards the end of World War II. The village became a military village in 1940 when the base was built. It still has some of the old bomb shelters, old storage and housing blocks, though the majority have been replaced with new ones except this unit, but Jamie likes that he's working in one of the original buildings, it's good, it reminds him of home, *the old meets the new*.

His Sergeants office is on the right as you walk in. The equipment room is opposite and a kitchen next to that. There are also a couple of classrooms and a meeting room just before the main hall. That's where they do training, any necessary equipment cleaning/inspections, some PT work and various other miscellaneous activities.

His Sergeant calls him into his office at dead on 0800hrs, telling him to stand at ease, and Jamie puts his hands behind back and spreads his legs slightly. He listens intently to what he is being told, nodding when required or answering a simple yes or no.

The meeting is informal, but important nonetheless, as Jamie has his sights firmly set on promotion to Lance Corporal in the next eighteen months. He leaves the office with a smile and goes to make a drink before everyone else arrives at 0900hrs. He re-runs every word around his head. "There's a good chance you'll be promoted to Lance Corporal with your next posting" were among the Sergeants words.

By then Jamie's initial training will be over and the Serge thinks he'll do well with his own section. A section is a small group of up to four soldiers, which a Lance Corporal is expected to supervise. He said he'll be putting him forward, a recommendation from the Serge himself.

His phone alerts him to a text message with a photo from Jess.

Jess: [Hey, just leaving for work, hope you like the photo? Xx]

Jess: [Sorry forgot to say, Hope the meeting goes well & thank you for everything. <3 xx]

Shit, why the heart? He looks at it intently. *That seems a bit intense, hope she's not getting all serious, though maybe that's not a bad thing. Anyway, no time to think about that now. I'd better reply though, I'll just keep it simple.*

Jamie: [No worries Jess, thanks for the pic, looking gorgeous as ever. Have a good day. Xxx]

Jamie: [Oh, meeting went well, my Serge is putting me forward for promotion on the next posting in June xx]

He suddenly wants to tell his mum about the meeting and the promotion, but forces himself to wait until after work otherwise she'll bombard him with loads of messages. He'll call her later when he has the time to explain it to her. There's a lot of chatter coming from the hallway now, and he pops his head out to see who it is and sees Nobby, Gavin and Stick. (His real name is Andrew, but he's stick thin hence the nick name.)

'Alright lads? Hey Nobby, how did yer shopping trip go?' Jamie laughs, remembering that conversation he overheard when they were all on their three week training exercise.

'Expensive Jamie mate, bloody expensive,' Nobby replies, shaking his head. At this moment the Sergeant comes out of his office.

'Well, well, I hear congratulations are in order Nobby.' Some hand shaking and back slapping then occurs, as it turns out he got engaged whilst away - no wonder it was an expensive trip!

CHAPTER 33

No Respect

The morning was spent like most Monday mornings. In the classroom, for a brief on what is happening, what is expected of them and what they should be doing. The Sergeant began with a talk about fitness, how it was noted that on the last training session it was apparent that some are not as fit as they should be and that he will be talking to them in a one to one.

'At the very least you should all be out running three to four times week and using the gym daily if not every other day,' he says in a slightly raised tone. The meeting is over and they all head out to start the tasks they've been assigned.

Jamie overhears Gavin and Tommo (Thomas) talking about their run yesterday down the lanes in the local area and how they decided on the way back they'd run through the village, as it is good training for road work. His ears prick up at the point where Gavin asks Nobby and Charlie if they've seen the new blonde in the village. By now he's using all his effort not to blurt out that she's off limits, but he knows he can't, not now, possibly not ever.

'Hey Jamie, isn't that the bird that was speaking to you before we went on training?' Nobby asks.

'When was this?' asks Gavin, 'I don't remember no blonde bit chatting you up Jamie lad!'

'You weren't there Gav, I think that's when you was getting a blowie in the bogs from that bit of old skirt,' Nobby replies, with a knowing wink aimed in Gavin's direction.

'Oh yeah, ha, gave her a right seeing to an' all. Good job I *weren't* there, if Blondie had seen me first I'd have had her pants down and bent over a table giving her one!' Gavin is laughing at his own comment and the other two are rolling their eyes but Jamie, well, his blood is boiling. It takes all his self-control to keep his cool.

'Seriously Gav, have yer no respect?' Jamie says, always the one out of them all to show the most respect to women generally, due to his upbringing.

'Erm, nope. None,' he says, still laughing.

'Yer really are disgusting sometimes, honestly,' Jamie shakes his head. 'Well if you must know, she ain't like the old skirts yer go with, she's actually a very nice lady and she's a very good friend of Fred and Hazel's. So bloody show her some respect.'

He has to walk away at this point as he can feel his rage is starting to overshadow his thinking. He can't believe that someone who has been brought up by both their mum and dad together has very little respect for women. Perhaps that's the way his dad is?

He hears Nobby running after him.

'Hey Jamie, come on mate, you know what he's like, don't take it to heart.' Nobby says as he catches up with him.

'Yeah I know Nobbs, it's just his lack of respect for women really gets to me sometimes.'

'I know mate, but he's just a southern twat, he can't help himself, not like us northern soul boys,' Nobby grins, and they both laugh and get on with sorting the equipment cupboard, their currently assigned task. They get it done easily, while Nobby tells him about the shopping trip and how he proposed and the shops expecting four times your monthly salary for a ring.

'I told the guy, "Mate, I'm a soldier in the British army, how much do you think we earn?"'

'What did he say?'

'He offered me finance, so now I gotta pay a hundred quid a month for the next three years for a poxy diamond. Honestly

Jamie if yer get a gal and yer think o' proposing, buy the ring first, yer'll save a fortune.'

'How's that then?' I ask him.

' 'Cause they have some at less than a grand, and they looked alright to me, but no, I gave 'er a choice and she chooses the fucking mother of all rocks.'

'So have you set a date yet?'

'Not quite, we've got a couple in mind but need to put a request in, so I'm gonna speak with the Serge later, you will come won't yer?'

'Yeah, course. I love a good wedding. Our Rosie gets married in two years' time, May 28.'

'Just before we post to Cyprus, if we go?'

Jamie laughs at this, he remembers telling his mum it's not for definite and here's Nobby making similar assumptions as his mum.

'Yeah Nobbs, before Cyprus,' he agrees with a laugh.

CHAPTER 34

Shopping Trip

Mondays are generally the worst day of the week, and that term, the 'Monday Blues' is normally very apt, but not today, not for Jess.

It started off with some early morning sex followed by some foreplay in the shower, it couldn't get any better than this, surely? She hasn't heard from Jamie since this morning, which is a little unusual, but it's his first day back from annual leave, so he's most likely been really busy. She's just finished work now, so decides to message him when she gets in the car, see how he is.

Jess: [Hey, how's your 1st day back been xx]

Jamie: [Yeah good babe, still here, be about 30 mins, have you finished now?]

Jess: [I have, just heading home now xx]

Jamie: [Ok, did you remember your lunch? Xx]

Jess: [lol, yes I did, thank you xx]

Jamie: [Enjoy your evening with your dad, give us a shout when he's gone, if you want? Xx]

Jamie: [Drive carefully babe xx]

Jess: [I will to both]

Pulling into her street she sees her dad's car parked on the roadside, it's a lovely colour this new one, 'Midnight Blue' it's called, navy to everyone else. He gets a new company car every two years because of the amount of mileage he puts on them, although this model is a 4x4 range, where previously he always had estates, mainly for his golf trolley though he denies that. She laughs as she thinks of the times he's tried to convince her mum of that.

Pulling onto the drive she sees her dad, he looks like he's in deep conversation with someone and he's frowning, he looks tired and weary. She smiles at him when he looks her way and he makes a hand gesture which she interprets as *I'll be two minutes*.

Getting out of the car, she opens the front door and stands on the doorstep waiting for him, thinking it would be rude to just walk in and wait for him to knock on the door. She looks around, it's nearly five-thirty which means Jamie will be finishing now, she may even see him drive by on his way home, but then again she's sure he'll be going for some shopping straight after work. *It would be nice to see him passing though* she thinks.

'Finally! I thought you were going to leave me standing on the doorstep!' she says to her dad with a laugh.

'Sorry darling, bloody builders merchants, they can't do a simple thing, they have to over complicate everything. Anyway, less of my woes Jessica, get the kettle on and let's get this food inside for you.'

'Okay dad. Oh! Car's nice by the way.'

She goes inside, closes the living room curtains against the already dark evening, and puts the lights on as she is walking into the kitchen. She fills the kettle and gets two clean cups out.

'Here you go, there's about two weeks' worth here, your mum says keep three in the fridge and put the rest in the freezer, when you're on your last one take another out of freezer and pop it in the fridge, it will defrost in time for the next day.'

'Ok, thanks Dad. But I don't understand why mum is so worried, I'll be fine.'

'It's our job to worry Jessica, now I see you, I can see you've lost a lot of weight. Are you struggling? Is money tight? Is that why you aren't going shopping?' he asks, a grave look of concern across his face as he looks me up and down.

115

'No Dad it's not, honest, I've just got myself into a bad habit, I don't feel hungry so I just don't think about it. I've got lazy but I realised at the weekend I need to snap out of it.'

'Ok, but if you are struggling don't be afraid to say, that's what we're here for.'

As she hands him his tea, she can feel herself welling up but holds it back.

'I know dad, and I really appreciate it. Honest,' she manages to maintain her normal tone and appear calm, when really she was overcome with emotion, at the endless love and support her dad has always given her.

'Are you staying for dinner?' she invites, hoping the answer is yes, though she's not been shopping and has nothing in except the dinners he's just brought with him.

'No not today, I had a late lunch with a business developer. It was nice, three courses, don't tell your mum, I told her it was pie and mash,' he says with his familiar cheeky laugh that she remembers so fondly.

'I tell you what, throw one of those dinners in the microwave and I'll take you shopping, Daddy's treat!'

'Oh Dad, you don't have to do that, I'll go tomorrow straight from work,' she protests, though it really is lovely spending time with him.

'No, Jessica, I insist, besides I can show the new car off to you,' he says, so now she can't refuse or she'll hurt his feelings, especially having already complimented him on it when she got home.

So she does as he suggested, pops a meal in the microwave and eats it while they drink their tea and once she's finished they head off shopping. Her dad asks about her new job and her house, he is genuinely interested and praises her for making the move, but he also makes it clear how much they both miss her and then he asks her if the divorce is going ok.

'I haven't heard from my solicitor since last week, she said she'd only contact me once Anthony has responded to the proposal put forward. So hopefully after you spoke with him on Saturday he might have agreed it with his solicitor now. Fingers crossed hey Dad?' she says with hope in her voice, and he smiles and grabs her hand, giving it a loving squeeze as his sign of agreement.

They pull into the car park of the supermarket and her dad drives around looking for a space, then, even in the dark, she recognises Jamie's car.

Oh no, he's still here, she can't help feeling a little nervous, what if they bump into him, she might give it away, her dad might guess that she's messing around with a soldier and not just any soldier, one that's only nineteen.

'I'll get the trolley. Your mother's bags are behind the passenger seat, grab them, it'll save me some pennies and according to your mum, the planet.'

'Oooh Dad, if I didn't know you any better, I'd say there's a hint of sarcasm in there,' she teases. He tuts and walks off towards the trolley bay.

As they walk inside together, she notices her dad's mood is still quite heavy, she wonders if it is worry about her or something else or is it just what he said, trouble with the builders merchant. She decides to drop it, it's not her place to pry.

'So, what do you need? Shall we just wander around each isle and if you see something you fancy, pop it in the trolley?'

'Good idea,' she agrees with a decisive nod. 'I'm sorry Dad, if I've worried you. I never meant to,' and for all her resolve not to cry earlier, her eyes now fill with tears.

'Oh Jessica, don't be silly, it's my job as your dad to worry, but, I can see you are happy again so that makes me happy.'

'Can you?' she asks, genuinely surprised by this.

'Yes, I was watching you stood on the doorstep and pottering in the kitchen, you look much happier than you ever looked in your old house. And that's all I care about,' he gives her a hug and a tender kiss on the top of her head.

As they're wandering around the store, chit chatting about the village and her friends from work, she suddenly she spots him, Jamie, he is in the same isle, but he has his back to them. She ponders whether to ignore him, pretend she didn't see him and apologise later or should she do the right thing, say hello and introduce her dad.

'Oh! Hello Jamie,' she says.

He turns around startled by the sound of her voice, he could have sworn her dad was visiting tonight.

'Jess, Hi,' he leans in and kisses her on her cheek.

'Jamie, this my dad, Tony.'

The two men exchange pleasantries then Jamie says that's him finished with his shopping and he'll see her around sometime. He gives her a little hug and another kiss on the cheek, says bye to her dad and walks off. Jess and her dad continue with their shopping and once they've finished they head to the check out, pack the bags and walk out to the car.

Whilst in the car Jess brings up the deposit her dad gave them for the house, she tells him that she wants her and Anthony to pay him back as it's only fair. Her dad remains adamant that it was a gift and you don't take back gifts and that she is to drop the subject and never mention it again. So Jess does exactly that.

Back at the house her dad helps her unpack the shopping, says his farewells and then leaves, remembering to take Barbara's shopping bags with him.

CHAPTER 35

Unexpected Gift

Walking back into the house, after waving her dad off, Jess goes about preparing her lunch for Tuesday, she's bought some fruit with her shopping and she chops some up and pops it in a small container, thinking *that's for my break*, *and for breakfast, I'll make a pan of porridge up, that way I can just pop some in a bowl and heat it up and eat it before I leave for work.*

She sends her mum a quick text thanking her for the food and promising to call her tomorrow after work, also asking her to let her know when her dad gets home.

She's pottering about in the kitchen when she hears a knock at the front door. She feels a bit nervous, as she isn't expecting anyone, but goes to answer. Putting the outside light on again she looks through the peep hole but can't see anyone, hesitantly she unlocks the front door and opens it carefully, no one there, she opens the door a little wider and at the same time she says 'Hello, can I help you?' but there is no response so she opens the door fully and notices something on the ground. She bends down to pick it up and laughs out loud. She walks back in, shuts the door, locks it and turns the outside light off.

'Hello,' says Jamie, when she answers her phone which began to ring on her way back into the kitchen.

'I can't believe you bought me a lunchbox!' she says, still laughing.

'Haha! Yer got it, will yer use it?'

'Of course. I can't wait to go into work tomorrow with my unicorn lunch box. I'll be the envy of everyone.'

'Glad you like it. No excuses now for not eating lunch.'

'You're so sweet, thank you, honestly, I mean it.'

'It's fine, I saw it when I was food shopping, picked it up and then you and yer dad walked around the corner, that's why I pushed me trolley forward so yer didn't see it. Well I hoped yer didn't.' They're both laughing as he's telling her.

'Aww, bless you. Well I've got my lunch made, I got some fruit for my break *and* I'm making some porridge for breakfast.'

'Good. It was nice of yer dad to take yer shopping.'

'Yes it was. He insisted, so I didn't have much choice in the matter. But I'm glad I went. Right, I need to get my porridge made. Speak to you later, goodnight Jamie.'

'Yeah okay, speak to yer tomorrow at some point, night.'

CHAPTER 36

Early Morning Run

0530hrs, one beep. *Right let's get this run over with*, Jamie says to himself.

He's arranged to meet Gavin and Tommo at the gates as they're going on a six mile run before work, to help maintain their fitness, and it's more motivating to run in groups.

Shorts on, trainers on, t-shirt and lightweight jacket, even though it's the second week in November, the mornings are dark still but the weather quite mild, no frost on the ground and it hasn't dropped below five degrees yet, so there's definitely no need for a sweater.

Opening the front door, he looks out, no one else in the street is awake and all the houses are in darkness, with only the street lights to keep him company as he starts on his run.

He has arranged to meet them at 0600hrs so he decides he's just got time to run through the village before they get there. Passing Jess' house, he can't help looking up to her bedroom window knowing she's still fast asleep, *just like she was on Monday* he thinks and he wishes he was back there with her now, snuggled in her warm bed next to her naked body. He hasn't seen her for a couple days now and although they text and talk it's not quite the same, he's starting to miss her, *perhaps I should take her out for a drink, preferably before the weekend*, he thinks to himself. *I'll text her later and see what she says.*

Thinking of her makes his cock twinge. *Not now sunshine* he thinks, I need to get this run out the way, no distractions this morning. I'll have plenty of time for that later, this evening.

Approaching the back gate he sees Gav and Tommo waiting for him. You can only exit this gate between the hours of 2000 and 0700hrs, whereas the main gate at the front of the base is manned 24/7. With a bit of luck by the time they get back, this one should be open for them.

Gavin shouts 'What kept ya?' as he approaches. He laughs at him and looks at his watch, 0557hrs.

'What yer chatting about, we said 0600, its 3 minutes to,' he says and Tommo gives Gavin a slap on the arm.

'Told you it was six, you dickhead, he had us here at 0545, the knob, I could've had an extra fifteen minutes in bed.'

'Yeah yeah, whatever, we getting this run in or not? Ya pair o' pussies,' says Gavin impatiently.

Jamie rolls his eyes and Tommo tuts as they start to run, out towards the back lanes, where they expect it to be quiet with no traffic this time of morning, so it'll be safer.

The three of them run the first fifteen minutes in silence. Jamie has his pods in his ears, they were a present from the family for his birthday, which he couldn't get home for. It was his nineteenth birthday this year, on May 19 as it happens.

He was still learning to drive at the time, his test was booked in for the following month, on June 26. He passed first time, much to his delight. The family surprised him for a belated birthday celebration, coming down to see him on the Sunday, a few days later, three cars all in convoy travelling down the motorway, making the two hour journey. He'd only been expecting to see his mum and Sean, she'd told him they'd get the train and then a taxi from the train station to the base and should be at the main gate by noon.

He'd pre-arranged with the gate house to allow his mum and brother in, but he wasn't aware of the others. Fortunately, Anne (his mum) had called earlier in the week and spoken to the gate house who then arranged for the station commander to call her. She explained what was happening and that Jamie didn't know the whole family was coming and asked if it would it be a problem. The station commander was 'very understanding' (his mums words) and left the vehicle details of all three cars plus the passengers who were to be booked in and given a one day pass.

He thinks about this difference between him and Jess. A family get together is a big thing, it takes planning, especially now there are partners involved and kids to add in. There are upwards of ten at any given time and growing. For Jess on the other hand, it's just the three of them.

He mulls over how that must feel, almost boring in his opinion, no chaos, no loud chatter as everyone talks over each other. Just calm, quiet chit chat between three mature people. How would she cope with it all, the volume and the chaos? Then he thinks about himself and more to the point how would he fit in to her life? How very different their worlds are.

'You ok J? You're very quiet,' asks Gavin. Jamie takes a pod out of his right ear.

'Did yer say something?' he asks after seeing Gavin mouth something in his direction.

'Yeah, was asking if ya ok, 'cause ya quiet.'

'Listening to music mate, helps me keep me pace, yer should try it.'

'Nah, I like me wits about me, like to hear what's going on.'

'Gav, we're running down a country lane, what do ya think will happen? Ain't no one jumping out on ya, no ambush to worry 'bout.'

'Yeah, I know that, but still I like to hear everything going on, just in case.'

Tommo and Jamie laugh, Jamie pops his pod back in and they continue running down the lanes just as sunrise is starting.

Twenty five minutes later they reach the next village, their pace is good. Fairly fast, three miles covered already. Running through the village they watch it start coming to life, lights come on in some of the houses, the resident cockerel is awake and crowing and they hear a dog barking in the distance.

On the way through the village centre they pass the local pub, not for the first time, they've run this way many times, but they've never actually been in this village after 0630hrs.

'I wonder what that place is like?' Jamie says to the others after they pass.

'What? The Watering 'Ole?

'Yeah.'

'Probably no different to the SOS, full o' locals who look at ya funny when ya walk in,' Gavin answers. The SOS is their abbreviation for the Sports and Social Club.

'The SOS isn't like that, it's full of ex squaddies and a few locals,' Tommo says, 'so I've heard.'

'Well, till Gav walks in and they 'ear 'is accent, yer know, that southern charm of 'is,' says Jamie, to wind him up.

'Fuck off and put ya music back on, ya bell end,' says Gavin and they all laugh and Jamie does just that.

Jamie thinks about Tommo. Even though he comes from the south, he too is from 'good stock' just like Jess, he'd fit in well with her and her parents, better than he would. He believes this even more now after meeting her dad. Jamie could see he is a proper business man, at six feet tall, standing smartly in his grey pinstripe suit and Gold Watch. Jess is definitely on the 'posher' side of life just like Tommo. His dad works in aviation and his mum is a school teacher. Tommo grew up in a nice big four bedroom detached house and didn't have to share a room with his brother either. Not like any of that really makes a difference when it comes down to it, he knows Tommo's a good lad, always has your back no matter what.

That's the thing with the British Army, you get people from all walks of life coming together. Me growing up in a single parent household, Gavin growing up with both parents but rough as fuck and Tommo, growing up in a four bed detached with plenty of privileges I'm certain. In the end it doesn't matter where you're from because in the army we're all one, 'a band of brothers'.

When they arrive back at camp at 0650hrs the back gates are still locked. Gavin and Tommo decide to jog the half mile round to the front ones and Jamie heads home to collect his kit before going into the gym.

CHAPTER 37

Waiting for the Alarm

Jamie knows her alarm should be going off about now. Jess hits the snooze button, mumbling to herself that it can't be seven-thirty already, she turns over to go back to sleep but the sound of her phone vibrating distracts her.   She knows exactly who it's from and her heart skips a beat, she's getting quite used to these early morning text messages, even if it's only a couple, she thinks of them as 'short but sweet' and starting the day with a smile.

Jamie: [Morning gorgeous xx]

She gets a warm fuzzy feeling inside, thinking how sweet he is. She's smiling at the message, she hasn't felt this good in a very long time, although she hasn't seen him since Monday, so she is starting to miss him.

Jess: [Hey, Good Morning xx]

Jess: [How come you're up so early? Xx]

'He didn't text until 8am the last couple of days, I wonder why he's awake?' she actually says to herself out loud.

Jamie: [Went for an early morning run at 0600, got back and hit the gym for 0700, need to get an hour in before I get ready for work. xx]

'Oh he's at the gym, I swear he don't sleep, or needs very little. Urgggh! I need more sleep,' she's mumbles to herself, eventually conceding, throwing off the covers and getting up for work.

Jess: [Just got to jump in shower, want to join me?]

Jamie reads the message and gets an instant hard on.

Jamie: [Don't tempt me]

Jess: [I wish : ( ]

Oh shit why did I send a sad face, if he questions it I'll say it was an accident, but I really wish he'd join me, I'm not sure what I'm missing most, him or the sex or both? I'll text him when I'm ready, see if he's busy tonight, see if he fancies staying over. Actually tonight will be good for me, I'm off tomorrow as I'm going home to my parents for the weekend.

Jamie: [Babe, why the sad face? Xx]

Jamie: [Anyway, are you free tonight? If so, fancy going out for a drink?]

Jamie: [There's a nice pub in the next village, I pass it on my runs, do you fancy going? Xx]

She walks into her bedroom, a towel wrapped around her, her hair in a bun, she wasn't in the mood for washing it, it's going to be an 'up-do' day today. She looks in the mirror at herself, she looks healthier today, not so pale, even she can see the difference, It must be because she's eating properly again. Picking up her phone she clicks on the message to see what Jamie has sent.

Oh, he wants to see me as well, oh no, that's the pub I went to on Halloween, what will they think if I'm in there again with a different guy, mind you, how would they know or even remember it's me?

Jess: [Yes, that would be lovely, do you want to come here and drop your stuff off and we'll go in my car? I really don't mind driving? Xx]

Jamie: [Ok, sounds good to me, we'll have something to eat in there as well, I'll be round for 7 xx]

Jamie: [Oh, I meant to say, have you got any flatter shoes? xx]

Jess: [Short arse, yes I have some 'flatter' xx]

Jamie: [Hey, I'm all in proportion, besides, I don't hear you complaining about my height when you're flat on your back! xxx]

Jamie: [Get ready, text you later, I need to get finished here. Xxx]

Oooh the cheeky git, but he's right, I don't complain when I'm lying on my back and his head is in between my legs, his height doesn't matter then. Hmm, what I wouldn't give for his tongue to be deep inside my pussy now!

Jess: [xxxx]

Damn, I need to get my arse in gear, I'll be late at this rate, looks like I'm taking my breakfast with me!

She heads down stairs, puts some porridge in a tub, adds some milk and pops it in her unicorn lunch bag that Jamie bought her.

When she walked into work on Tuesday with it, she got a few laughs, it's not every day you see a grown woman walking into work with a lunch bag that is effectively designed for kids. But she loves it and she doesn't care. Besides, no one knows who bought it for her!

CHAPTER 38

Branded

Jamie has decided not to go to the gym after work tonight, he wants to get home and get ready for his first ever date night. It feels weird saying it like that, but that's what it is, he's asked Jess out on a 'date'. It feels good.

A few of the lads were talking to him about this Saturday night, he wasn't listening much, well until someone said about going to the 'lap dancing club' about ten miles away which would mean a taxi there and back. Not that he's bothered normally, but he has decided he needs to start saving money, instead of blowing all his pay on going out, he wants to limit himself.

He told them, "it is Christmas next month lads, one more pay day, I don't want to be blowing one hundred and fifty quid on a night out. Let's just stay local, nip into town and have a good night that way" there were some mumbles and grumbles, but they all agreed in the end that it would probably be for the best.

The last thing he wants or needs is to go to some lap dance club like he used to and not be going into a private booth - how would he explain that? Especially, seeing as the last time he saw that dancer Kirsty, he ended up back at her place after the night had finished. He can't risk seeing her, not that he'd do anything this time, he just doesn't want to raise any suspicions with anyone.

He pulls up outside the house, his two housemates are due back this weekend, no more house to himself, he's quite enjoyed that part but he has missed the banter they all have.

The house is quiet, he notices the cleaner has been in, the curtains are open in the living room and the light is off. The lads club together to pay a cleaner once a week, it's good for when they're away, someone is checking on the house and when they're back, they don't have to worry too much if they're busy with work. They each do their own bedroom though, that was the agreement.

He jumps in the shower and notices that the pubes around his balls are starting to grow back. Even though he's a natural blonde, for some reason he has black pubes, he's never got his head around that. Lathering up his balls, he shaves them and around his cock and just below his belly. He then starts to wash his cock, pulling the foreskin back making sure that's all clean, *can't be getting a blowie if your cock is dirty Jamie lad*, he says to himself, then his arse, *and if she wants to give me a rimming then I'd better make sure me arsehole is clean*. He laughs at himself, he's getting a stiffy just thinking about it all. He lathers the rest of his body and scrubs up. He's been thinking of stopping off on the way back tonight and fucking her either in her car or over it, either way she's getting it outdoors tonight. That thought gives him a hard on, *might as well knock one out now*.

Finishing his shower, wank and shave, he walks into the bedroom, towel wrapped around his waist and looks at what to wear. Jamie is very careful with his money, he doesn't squander it, not like some of the lads. He's always put a quarter or sometimes even a third of his salary away, right from his very first wage packet.

He looks at his T-Shirts, they aren't designer brands but he does buy nice high street brands and the odd label if it's in the sale. His jeans are high street brands, but his trainers are branded. He will pay extra for a decent pair. He looks in the mirror, *yeah, that looks good*, he picks his kit bag up, that's easier to manage, *I'll hang everything up around at Jess' house*.

Picking up his keys and wallet, he looks to see how much cash he has, he counts eighty quid, which should be enough for tonight, but takes his debit card, just to be on the safe side.

CHAPTER 39

Date Night

Nervously, Jess looks in the mirror, *oh God I'm too overdressed, for God's sake Jess, it's a pub.*

She's opted for a navy and blush-pink spotted, knee length, chiffon narrow-pleat skirt, a blush-pink capped-sleeve blouse, tucked in with a navy waist length fitted jacket, a pair of natural colour hold up stockings and a pair of two inch wedge navy leather shoes. She picked these up on her last trip to New York, they were in the sale for one hundred and eighty pounds reduced from three hundred, the last trip she had with her ex-husband, it was her valentine's present.

She hears the doorbell chime, *shit is it seven already?*

Running down stairs, carrying her earrings, she opens the door and he's standing there, that beautiful face, his smile and his faultless physique. *He looks perfect*, she thinks to herself *and smells amazing.*

'Hi, come in I'll be two minutes.'

'Wow, you look amazing!' he says as he looks her up and down. He puts his bag down and starts to take his uniform out, hanging it up on the curtain pole and pops his boots in the hall.

'Here let me help you,' he offers as she's struggling with some earrings.

'Oh thanks, my hair is getting in the way. Am I overdressed? Shall I change?' she asks, a little self-conscious now.

'Nooo! No way, you look amazing, I love your hair with the curls in.' He gives her a kiss on the lips, lingering for a few seconds before he puts her earrings in. 'These are nice Jess.'

She is wearing her pear-drop diamond earrings. One of the many gifts from her ex-husband. She thinks about the fact that everything she wears has either been bought with or by him, she really does need to have a good sort out, sell what she doesn't want, of her jewellery and designer bags. After all, *how can she move forward with her future when she's still living in the past or at least wearing it!*

'Thanks. You smell nice,' she compliments in return.

'You sure you don't mind driving? I feel guilty, we can get a taxi if you'd rather, just don't let me get pissed!' he says with a wink.

'No it's fine, honest. Right. Keys, phone and bag. You ready?'

'Yeah, although I'm beginning to think I'd rather stay in now! Only kidding, come on let's go, sooner we get out sooner we get back.' He makes a growling noise, almost like a dog on heat. There's no mistaking, he's smitten with her, after all she's the older woman he always wanted.

Pulling up outside the pub, Jess tells him she's been here before with work colleagues, but hasn't eaten and hears the food is good and not too expensive either.

'It's really strange, I never had to think about money before, never thought about the prices of anything, if I wanted it I bought it, didn't matter the cost. If I wanted it, I got it,' she muses out loud.

'Really? So how do you feel now, do you miss it?' he asks, not really sure if he should feel something about this, whether it makes him uncomfortable knowing that her ex provided for her in this way.

'No, surprisingly. I feel more like I live in the real world now, I get paid each month and pay my mortgage and my bills and I've started budgeting for the first time in my life.'

'That's really good.' He says with a little laugh at her comment "the real world" and thinks *perhaps money doesn't buy happiness after all*.

The village pub has a restaurant area, serviced by waitresses, and a waiting area to be seated. When the waitress approaches he asks for a table for two and the waitress shows them to a booth. The waitress is smiling at him, like she knows him, so he is polite and smiles back. Once seated she hands them a menu each, takes their drinks order, and looks at Jamie as she says thanks and walks away.

It hasn't gone unnoticed.

'Someone you know?' Jess asks him quizzically.

'Not that I know or can remember,' he says honestly with a frown, as it's beginning to annoy him. Jess gets up to visit the ladies' as the waitress brings their drinks over.

She smiles at him again and asks if he remembers her. He says he's sorry but actually he doesn't. So she tells him they danced and kissed in one of the night clubs a couple of months back. Jamie feels embarrassed, as he has no recollection and can see she is now embarrassed, he smiles again with a slight shrug of the shoulders as he doesn't know what else to say. At this point Jess returns to the table, and the waitress asks if they are ready to order. As Jess has only just come back, she hasn't had the chance to check the menu, so Jamie asks her to give them five more minutes.

'What do yer fancy?' he asks Jess, sensing that she's a bit narked, but not really sure what he can do about the situation, he truly doesn't remember the girl and certainly wouldn't bring Jess to somewhere he knows a previous 'conquest' would be working.

Jess is definitely feeling a little bit pissed off and can't keep the negative thoughts at bay. *He obviously knows her but doesn't want to say. How many girls has he slept with?* This is all new to her, she's wondering *is it something I need to get used to or do I tell him to do one?*

'I fancy a steak,' she answers curtly, 'with a sparkling water please.' He can see she isn't happy, so he tells her about the short conversation and that he really has no idea who she is and feels rather embarrassed by it all. She looks at him and begins to laugh at the hilarity of the situation. She decides that this probably won't be the last time this happens and she'll just have to get used to the female attention he attracts and not let it get to her.

'Yeah, I think I'll have the same,' he says, relieved that the tension is gone. The waitress returns for their order and Jess gives her 'that look' as she approaches, it's a look only a woman will understand, a look that says 'I know what happened, and I know you fancy him but he's my man so keep your distance' and she takes their order and leaves without any smiles this time.

Jamie reaches out across the table, prompting Jess to place her hand in his. He holds it affectionately as she tells him she's planned to go to her parents this weekend and she's booked tomorrow off as she's arranged a massage in the afternoon for her and her mum at a local spa, close to her parent's house.

He watches her expressions while she talks, her eyes as she smiles. He feels some kind of emotions rising, unfamiliar to him because he's never had a girlfriend before. The only women he's really cared about before are his mum and his two sisters. But these emotions are different.

Once their food arrives and they are both more relaxed, they order a pint for Jamie and a glass of red wine for Jess to drink with their dinner, and they continue to talk while eating. It's a really pleasant evening, really nice comfortable chit chat, catching up on events during their week apart. Just after nine-thirty they agree to leave. On the journey back, Jamie casually asks Jess if she's ever had sex outside before.

'Yes, once. Way before I was married and it was fun.'

'Pull in on the left just up here,' he says.

'What?' She laughs, a little surprised but excited.

'Come on, let's just do it, here and now,' he says pulling her skirt up above her thighs to reveal her hold up stockings and thumbs the lace tops feeling his cock spring into action.

Pulling into the lay by, Jess turns the engine off and moves the driver's seat back away from the steering wheel and lowers it, then lies back in the seat, her legs parting for his hand to gain better access.

Jamie also pushes his seat back, lifts her skirt all the way up and sees she has no thong on, just her hold ups. He feels almost ready to explode at the sight of her and quickly undoes his jeans and climbs on top of her. Lifting her legs up as much as possible he inserts his erect cock into her wet pussy. He thrusts it in hard, and she lets out a moan, her noises getting louder as he gets harder and faster, the windows are steaming up and the car is rocking from side to side. She doesn't care if someone drives past, she wants him, deep inside her and she can't get enough of him. She's never felt this way before.

With his face close to hers he can feel her breath on his neck as she moans, he loves the sound of her moans, the louder the better. He tells her he's close to cumming, she is too but he tries to hold out a little longer, wanting to make sure he doesn't leave her behind in his enthusiasm. He asks her if she's ready, she tells him 'yes, yes,' one last thrust and they climax together, his body shuddering, her body temperature rising with her orgasm. Jamie collapses onto her, though he's conscious not to put all his body weight on her and he holds her tight. He kisses her gently and passionately, feeling how perfect she is to him. He knows she's special. He feels it.

Getting up and moving over to his seat, he pulls up his jeans and gets out of the car to sort himself out standing up. Jess pulls her seat back to where it was, adjusts her clothing and laughs as she wipes the windows. They still have another mile and a half to go and when he gets back in the car he gives her a kiss and they both grin like the cat that got the cream as they continue the journey home.

CHAPTER 40

Insatiable

Jess parks her car on the driveway and they walk hand in hand into the house, even though it's no more than two metres away from the car.

She is still smiling, feeling the happiest she's felt since, well, she can't remember the last time she felt this happy. She's not worried anymore what people think, about him being only nineteen, it proved it tonight, she's never experienced such jealousy before as when she saw that waitress smiling at him. She didn't feel threatened, of course not, but she didn't like it.

As she walks into the kitchen, she hears Jamie fiddling around in his toiletry bag, thinking nothing of it she puts the kettle on to make a cup of tea, and then as he stands close behind her, she realises he has other ideas. *He's insatiable! He can't possibly have another hard on already*, she's shocked but really turned on. *He has, wow! How is that possible?*

He kisses her neck, still standing behind her, his hands caressing her boobs on the outside of her blouse, he tells her how much she turns him on, that he's never been this turned on before, the thought of her wearing no thong is driving him insane. He tells her to spread her legs for him. She does as she's told, knowing she's still wet with their cum.

He unfastens her skirt, letting it fall to the floor, then removes her jacket and starts to unbutton her blouse, still kissing her neck or nibbling her ear lobes around her earrings. Once he's removed her blouse and unhooked her bra she's completely naked apart from her hold ups and her shoes.

He strokes his hand over her bum cheek, and then gives it a light slap. She likes the feel of this, and the sound, she can feel his erection pressing against her. He slaps it again, not too hard but enough for them both to enjoy it, she turns to look at his face, he's looking at her intensely, with lust, clearly enjoying it as much as she is.

All of her inhibitions are gone, she doesn't care that she's stood there completely naked, full of cum from the sex on the way home no more than ten minutes ago, she wants him, she knows he wants her, she's turned on and ready for whatever he wants to do to her.

He tells her to lean forward over the sink, and she begins to take her shoes off.

'No leave them on,' he says. She leans forward, her bum is the perfect height for his cock. She listens to the sound of his jeans being unbuttoned and falling to the floor, he moves in closer rubbing his hard cock against her bum.

He kneels down and spreads her cheeks apart and starts to lick around the outside of her anus, leaving his saliva everywhere with his tongue, he can smell her juices, he knows she's still full of his cum from the sex they had in the car, he wants to keep it that way, at least until he's filled her arse with cum.

He stands back up, and she feels his finger slide along her pussy. Wetting it with her juices he then starts to rub it over her anus, *hmm, he needs to lubricate it, damn I have some upstairs* she thinks to herself and wonders if she should tell him, but she doesn't want him to stop and spoil the moment.

'Lower,' he instructs and she bends lower, which is pretty difficult in the position she's in but she goes as low as she can, sticking her bum out, Jamie's hands are holding her outer thighs. He moves in closer and holding his cock in one hand he places it against her anus and very slowly pushes it in. Now she realises what he was up to in his toiletry bag earlier, he must have brought some lube with him, he came prepared.

She feels it going in, Oh boy can she feel it! It's a little tight but he continues, wow, this is something else, something she's never experienced before, she's only ever watched it on porn. This is definitely a new level of pleasure.

He can feel she's a bit tight, but the lube will help, he's loving the feeling so much already, this is what he's wanted, all these years, this feeling of complete freedom to do everything. It's so tight around his cock but it's good, it's better than good, it's fucking amazing.

He begins to move slowly, he can't rush this, but he's so turned on by her, this is all he's thought about all day, in fact for as long as he can remember. Fucking someone in the arse, and he's finally doing it, he can feel what it's really like. Is it all that he hoped it would be? Fuck yeah, and more.

She can feel he's in deep, he's taking it much slower than when he fucks her pussy but it's still so good, she's moaning with the pleasure, his cock is deep in her arse, she wants more, she wants it harder and faster.

'Go faster,' she whispers.

'You sure? I don't want to hurt you.'

'It's fine. You won't.'

He pushes in harder and she moans louder, he loves to hear her, the louder the better.

'Like this?' he asks, still being cautious but increasing the speed and pressure as her volume increases with it.

'Yesss,' the sounds of her enjoyment send him to even greater heights of pleasure. He carries on thrusting, feeling like he's never felt before, it was worth it, worth the wait, he's so glad he waited until now.

'Baby, I'm gonna cum,' he groans.

She can barely hear him over her own noises but she nods fiercely in agreement, she feels him, she knows the signs, his body has gone rigid, his hands squeezing her outer thighs, he's cumming, she can't feel his cum but she can feel him, she knows that shudder.

CHAPTER 41

A Rude Awakening

Jamie wakes up early again, he's hot, a bit too hot. He realises he's cuddled into Jess and holding onto her so tight, it's like he's holding on for dear life.

He can't remember waking up next to someone like this before, probably because he's never stuck around after the sex, he always left, no matter what time of the night or how pissed he was, he would literally fuck them and leave them. The amount of times he'd hear them say "stay till morning, you can't go now surely?" But he wouldn't stay, he couldn't, he had to get out, he didn't want to wake up in their bed, it just didn't feel right.

He's lying there now, thinking of all the girls he's shagged, and there was a fair few of them, well the ones he remembers, the ones he can't quite remember he still knows he did as he always checked his wallet the next morning to see if his condoms were still there, they never were.

He's never felt like this, is this the reason he never stayed over? He didn't want to get close, they weren't what he really wanted, they were just a substitute until the real thing came along.

He looks at the alarm clock 0553hrs, he could actually go for a run, *sleeping beauty there wouldn't know and she'd probably still be asleep when I got back!* He laughs at this thought, knowing he's right. He moves back towards her and snuggles in, kissing the back of her head and goes back to sleep for another hour. At seven o'clock the buzzer goes off.

'That's the worst alarm ever,' he says more to himself than anything, as he's not sure she's even awake yet. He's fumbling to turn it off, it's an awful piercing noise and it's giving him a headache before he's even woken up properly.

'How do yer turn this fucking thing off?' he growls, feeling all wound up and agitated now.

'Here, I'll do it,' she says, so sleepy she turns it off without opening her eyes or moving apart from her hand reaching out from under the quilt. She quickly pulls it back under, wraps the quilt around her and snuggles back in to him. He laughs at her, he's never met anyone who loves their sleep as much as she does. He cuddles into her and gives her another kiss on the back of her head.

'I need a shower,' he says into her neck.

'Why so early?' she mumbles in response.

' 'Cause I'm sweating me bloody bollocks off lying next to yer, wrapped in yer cocoon,' he answers with a laugh.

'Ok, I'll wait here for you, and sleep a bit longer.'

'Okay,' he's laughing now, she's such a sleepy head.

'How did your first date go?' she asks him.

'Shit. How was yours?' he teases.

'Hey, that's not nice,' she elbows him and laughs. Jamie laughs too and holds her tighter to stop her elbowing him again.

'Nah, it was amazing babe, if that was our first date what's the second gonna be like?'

'Who says you're getting a second?' she says with a grin.

'Woah, now who's not being nice?' he tickles her and she tries to wriggle away, laughing.

'Ok stop! You can have a second one.'

They're both laughing now and he bends over to kiss her lovingly on her lips. As she turns over towards him he climbs on top of her. His cock is erect and throbbing for her, he just can't get enough of her, the more he gets the more he wants. He spreads her legs wide enough for his to fit between them and she wraps her legs around his calves, her soft feet rubbing them. His calf muscles feel tight from all the exercise and running he's done this week.

Lifting himself up slightly, he parts her smooth soft lips and positions his hard cock just inside her pussy. She's wet already, he can feel her juices on the tip of his cock. Slowly he pushes in, kissing her the whole time, feeling her tongue with his, his cock in deep, slowly and sensuously he slides it in and out.

He's making love to her this morning, he knows the difference now, last night was sex, this morning is making love, it's soft, sensual and most of all it's meaningful. His hips are rotating, his cock is in deep, it feels so good, soft, warm and wet, she's so wet, he loves this feeling. Moving his hand down, he caresses her breast and her nipple. He's really aroused now, he can feel his balls, they're tight, ready to release his sperm, deep inside her wet pussy.

'I'm gonna cum,' he says, not waiting for her to answer, he releases, deep inside her, he can't control his body any more, he's shuddering, his head feels light, pure pleasure, it's like his brain has just released a thousand hormones all at once. He waits for a moment, until he knows he can move, opens his eyes and he's looking deep into hers. She smiles the most loving, caring smile and lifts her head to give him a kiss .

CHAPTER 42

Property Developers

She's been looking forward to today, spending some quality time with her mum and enjoying a much needed massage and facial treatment.

'What time yer leaving today?' Jamie asks her.

'About eleven, get to mum's around noon and then straight to the hotel for our spa at one o'clock.'

'So, you go pamper yerself, while I work me boots off,' he tuts, 'typical woman,' he winks and blows her a kiss.

'Priorities baby, priorities,' she catches his kiss and plants it on her cheek.

'When yer coming back?'

'I'm not sure yet, either tomorrow late evening or Sunday mid-morning, I can't decide, so I'll see how I feel when I'm there.'

'Ok, well I'm out with the lads tomorrow night, celebrating Nobby's engagement,' he's sure he did already mention it last night, but she may have forgotten. 'Right that's me ready, make sure yer text me, let me know yer ok, yeah?'

'Of course and vice versa. And no kissing strange girls, especially waitresses,' she winks at him, but she's actually entirely serious.

'So as long as they aren't waitress...' he stops when she pretends to slap him. 'Hey, I'm kidding, 'cause I'm not gonna kiss anyone. These lips are for you and your pussy only.'

'Hmm, make sure they are,' she laughs. She can't help wondering if he really is serious, the thought of him looking at or touching another woman fills her with dread, jealousy is an emotion she's never experienced before. *I need to be careful here*, she tells herself.

'Ok, one last kiss, I really gotta go, mmm those nipples,' he says as he pinches one whilst he kisses her goodbye.

'Ouch!! Go on, get gone, you'll see me on Sunday, it's not that long,' she's already counted the hours in her mind, missing him already. She watches him walk out of the bedroom, she has no idea where this feeling has come from, but she doesn't ever want him to leave her, she can't imagine her life without him. *That's a scary thought, I can't afford to feel like this, it's dangerous, it'll end in tears, he's due to leave in seven months. Time to get a grip Jess,* she tells herself.

Climbing out of bed, she jumps in the shower, and when she's all refreshed and powered up, she decides to go and make a cup of tea to enjoy while she finishes getting ready. Walking into the kitchen, she picks up her clothes up and places them in the dry cleaning bag, pops the kettle on and gets some breakfast. Mini shredded wheat today, she's had her fill of porridge this week. When she has finished her cereal she takes her cup of tea upstairs and searches through her wardrobe. She chooses something smart but simple for today and throws a couple of outfits and her toiletries in her weekend bag. All packed, hair dried and dressed, she heads downstairs, grabbing her phone to text Jamie before she leaves.

Jess: [Hey babe, I'm just about to leave, I'll text you when I get to my mums xx]

Jamie: [Ok baby, enjoy your spa, don't do anything I wouldn't do]

Jess: [That doesn't leave much does it?]

Jess: [Really got to go, text you soon xxx]

She heads out, following the back roads, music on, her thoughts full of the past few days. She wonders how she's going to tell her mum and dad about him. Will they like him? He's hard working and yes, he is young but he makes her happy and that means more than anything, doesn't it?

Pulling up outside her mum's house she opens her text message to let Jamie know she's arrived safely. She sees a message from him, it must have come through while she was driving.

Jamie: [Ok babe, drive safe, let me know when yer there? Xxx]

Jess: [Arrived safely, text you later, miss you already xxx]

Jamie: [Miss you too babe, have a fab time xxx]

Jess walks into the house, and calls out to her mum to let her know she's arrived. She hears her answer from upstairs to say she'll be down in a minute. She always feels like a little girl coming home from school again when she walks into her parent's house.

They moved into this house when Jess was thirteen years old, it's a big four-bedroom detached house, with three-quarters of an acre of land. Tony being a typical builder has extended it over the years, making it really impressive. The house prices in this catchment area have increased greatly since they bought it, she knows if her dad wants to retire at sixty (which is only next year she realises) he'll be able to, and they could sell the house, downsize and still have plenty left over, it's probably worth over a million now, not bad considering they paid just over £320,000 twenty-three years ago.

All of the houses in this cul-de-sac occupy plots of at least half an acre. One property developer or another has approached everyone at some point, including my parents, offering silly money, well over the asking price. My dad says that if he sold to a developer, they would knock this house down and build multiple properties on the plot, then they would sell them all at half a million for each house and they'd easily get ten good sized three to four bedroom houses on this plot.

It saddens her to think that's what her dad might be planning, but he is a business man through and through and has lots of business associates in the property industry. He also works for one of the biggest building companies in the country. She knows her dad already has a plan for this house and his retirement, he's probably already offered it to his own employer. She guesses they'll soon find out, when the time is right.

'Oh Jessica, you look so much better, you can tell you've been eating this week. You are glowing!'

'Thanks Mum, the dinners are gorgeous, I forgot how much I miss your cooking,' Jess says and gives her mum a big hug and a kiss.

'We need to get going Mum, shall we go in my car?'

'Yes love. My bag's in the hallway.'

Jess goes out to the car, to check her phone in case of any messages from Jamie but there's none and she '*humph*'s out loud, feeling a little disappointed. She gets in the car and starts the engine, waiting for her mum to set the burglar alarm and lock up.

'Right then, what time is our first massage?' asks Barbara, as she gets into the front seat next to Jess and puts her handbag down at her feet.

'One o'clock mum, so we have about forty-five minutes. Plenty of time to get there, check in and get changed.'

'Oh good. For some reason I had twelve-thirty in my head.'

'No Mum, it's definitely one, I had the confirmation come through on my email.'

'So, how are you Jessica?' Barbara asks, giving her daughter her full attention, looking directly at her while she is driving.

'I'm good Mum but I've really missed you, I wish you'd come down and visit me sometime soon.'

'Jessica, I came down when you moved in and since then I've been very busy with my voluntary work and your dad is working ridiculously long hours.'

'I know he is, he looked really tired on Monday, is he ok?'

'He says he is, but he's had an awful mood about him just lately. I don't know what's wrong with him other than working too hard and too many long hours. Your dad forgets he is sixty next year, I tell him "Tony, you're not a spring chicken any more. Let the youngsters do it" and other similar things to try and get him to take a step back.'

'What does he say to that?'

'He says he just can't, that the youngsters haven't got a clue. That their qualification isn't worth the paper it's written on, and so on.'

'It must be very frustrating for him, especially if he wants to look at retiring next year.'

'Yes, and their *incapabilities* are not his problem, I've told him "Tony, you've given forty-four years, let someone else take over".'

'Poor Dad. Here we are, that didn't take long, did it?'

'Oh, already? That was quick,' Barbara says in surprise.

'You head in Mum and get us booked in, I need to send a quick message, then I'll follow.'

Jess: [Hey, how's your day going? Just arrived at the Spa. Catch up later xxx]

Jamie: Selfie photo with a caption [On treadmill, building up a sweat, wanna come join me in the shower after?]

As much as she'd love to get into the thought of joining Jamie in the shower, she needs to catch up with her mum, so she keeps it simple.

Jess: [Sunday then]

She sends the text and turns off her phone as it's going to be locked away in a locker, so she may as well save the battery life.

CHAPTER 43

Chilled out Evening

'Dad's home, Mum!'

Jess is lounging on the sofa, back at her parents' house, feeling totally relaxed after her facial and massage - it was definitely what she needed. All the recent months of stress with her divorce, moving house and starting a new job had begun to take its toll. Lying on the sofa, watching TV and eating snacks at what she still refers to as 'home' is like her safety net. Even though she's thirty-six, when she's here she feels like a teenager again, back at school without a care in the world.

She wants to talk to her mum about Jamie, she wants to tell her she's found some who makes her happier than she's ever been before. But how can she? Should she lie about his age? *No, that's not a good way to start.* She's going to have to figure this one out for herself.

Her dad pops his head in the door to say 'hello' before heading upstairs for a shower and to change into something comfortable for a relaxing Friday evening while her mum is in the kitchen preparing their 'Greek Salad' a favourite of Jess' from her childhood. It's not a traditional Greek Salad, not like the ones they've had on many holidays to Greece and on the Greek islands, this is the 'Willets Greek Salad' – it's probably fair to say that it's more English than Greek, in fact the only Greek thing about it is the Feta cheese and the olives.

She's picking up her phone to check if Jamie has sent her anything when she spots an email from her solicitor. She looks at it for a few seconds, and considers whether to open it now and potentially ruin her evening or to wait until tomorrow. She decides to wait and just open Jamie's text and then maybe later she'll check her email.

Jamie: [Hey baby, just checking you're having fun?xx]

Jamie: [My cock is missing your wet pussy]

Jamie: [Sorry shouldn't have said that, but I'm missing you and your texts xx]

Jess: [About to eat now, text you later. Missing you too, but I'm relaxing xxx]

'Mum I've had an email from my solicitor, I'm not sure if I should read it now or wait till tomorrow,' she decides her Mum might impart some wisdom and tell her what to do.

'You do what you think best Darling, but remember it's not worth stressing over either way.'

'True. Oh sod it, I'll open it.'

Dear Ms Willetts

Ref: Proposed settlement of £240,000

I am pleased to inform you that I have today received an email response from Taylor, Mead & Croft, acting on behalf of your estranged husband Mr Anthony Blakely.

As you know I put forward a settlement proposal for a total of £240,000 based on the information you provided.

The proposed offer received from them is £220,000

I would suggest you consider this offer very carefully, but feel free to contact me to discuss it further.

I look forward to hearing from you in due course with your instructions on how you wish to proceed.

Kind regards

Jennifer Webster LLP

Ashton, Leigh & Swift

She sits in silence, reading the email over and over, not noticing her mum and dad bringing the food in and laying it out on the table. The sound of her mum's voice snaps her out of her thoughts.

'Sorry Mum, did you say something?' she asks.

'Well? Is it a response on the settlement? Is he prepared to settle sixty-forty?'

'Yes! Yes he is,' she smiles, a feeling of relief washing over her as it slowly sinks in.

Deep down, she's elated. Finally she will be free from him. Time to start planning her future. Time to move forward and leave all that well and truly where it belongs, in the past.

'Oh Darling, that's wonderful news. Tony? Did you hear? He's accepted the settlement offer!'

'Great news, finally. Looks like that chat last week worked.' Her father winks at her, feeling huge relief for his only daughter.

CHAPTER 44

A Clear Road Ahead

Putting his pods in as he heads out for his early morning run, Jamie texts Nobby to make sure he's at the gate. He thinks about how much he enjoys running on Saturday and Sunday mornings, so long as he's not hanging, tomorrow morning he's sure he'll be hanging. He definitely won't be out running tomorrow.

Nobby sees him coming down the road and signals to him to turn right, they're going to run along the footpath of the dual carriageway, they're both carrying some weight today as they need to maintain their stamina for long distances and carrying their Bergan or indeed any other equipment.

'Do yer fancy the junction for town then left there, into the village and through the lanes back to here?' asks Jamie, planning the route.

'Sounds good to me mate, but we might need to be careful this time of the morning. That farmer's normally out walking his cows down the lane back to their field.'

Looking at his watch it's exactly 0700hrs now, by the time they hit the farm it should be around 0750hrs and he doesn't fancy his chances with a load of old heifers.

'Can we cut through the village and come out the back of the farm?' he suggests as a solution to Nobby's concern.

'Yeah, don't see why not,' Nobby agreed. So they had their plan which meant that all in all they'd get a good fifteen mile run in today.

'Jamie mate, I need to talk to yer, but yer promise yer won't say anything to the lads, not yet anyway?' Nobby looks totally serious and a little scared at this point, so Jamie takes his pods out and pops them in his pocket, he and Nobby are good mates, he's a sensible lad with a similar upbringing to his and from the same part of the country.

'Course yer can talk to me, what's up?'

'Shelley's pregnant.'

Jamie tries to hide the shock from showing on his face, he doesn't actually know what to say. Is it congratulations or commiserations, from Nobby's expression, he doesn't look happy. He decides he's going to go down the celebration route, after all they are engaged, and perhaps that's why he popped the question.

'Mate, that's fab news, congratulations,' he says, patting Nobby on the back and watching his expression change from misery to happiness, Nobby starts to smile.

'I've got to be honest, I wasn't sure, I'm still not sure how to handle it. Thank fuck you're with me J, I reckon I'd have carried on up that road and found myself in bonny Scotland or somewhere.' They both laugh, especially as Scotland is a good four hundred miles away.

'Nah mate, its fab news, you'll make a great dad.'

'I hope so J, well I can't do any worse than that old twat. At least I'm going to be here for it, give it as good a life as I can,' says Nobby with determination in his voice.

Nobby's dad was and still is an alcoholic. His mum took him and his two brothers back to live with their grandmother when Nobby was eight. It was the only way she could afford to feed them let alone keep a roof over their heads and it stopped his dad stealing all the money and leaving them without. I do feel sorry for him sometimes, especially when he tells me the stories of waking up on Christmas day with nothing, not even a slice of bread in the house let alone any presents.

Not that Jamie's dad was like that, from what he has heard he was a good man, a caring one, but sometimes when he hears

Nobby talking he's glad it was just them, his mum, his two brothers and his two sisters.

'So are yer gonna get married before the baby is born or wait until after?' Jamie asks.

'December 28th mate, its booked,' says Nobby.

'Fuck! That's quick.' He understands now why Nobby got engaged, he obviously knew that week and he is doing the right thing by Shelley, the decent thing.

'I know, I need to talk to yer about it and ask yer if yer'll be me best man? I know I have me brothers and could've asked them, but me and yer are like brothers. That's if yer can make it?' Nobby looks at Jamie with hope and possibly even a little fear in his eyes. Jamie is flabbergasted, but he feels really honoured that he's been asked.

'Mate, of course I'll be there, honestly it'll be an honour. Have you spoken to the Serge?'

'Yeah, we'll move into married quarters hopefully by the end of January and she can stay with her parents till then.'

Jamie gives him a congratulatory pat on the back and puts his pods back in but doesn't turn his music on. He's thinking of Jess, he wants to talk to Nobby, tell him about her, he'll know what to do. Taking his pods back out, he puts them back in his pocket.

'Actually Nobbs, I need some advice about a woman,' he begins.

'Don't ask me, she'll end up pregnant,' Nobby laughs, 'Yeah course, I'll try me best J, what's up?'

'Well, I've met someone, she was just meant to be a shag,' says Jamie, 'but I've fallen for her, and the thing is, she's older.'

'Mate, as long as she feels the same way, age don't matter. Who is she?'

'Her name's Jessica, erm Jess. Fred and Hazel's friend.'

'Woah! She's in her thirties ain't she mate? But she's a good looking one from what I remember. J mate look, just enjoy yerself, have fun and as long as you two are happy don't worry about anyone else. Ain't she a bit on the posh side?'

Jamie nods, agreeing with Nobby, he really does feel like he's punching above his weight, how can he have fallen in love so quick and with a woman nearly twice his age. What will his mum say? He needs to talk to Jess when she's back, he needs to make sure she feels the same way.

He curses himself, this is exactly why he didn't want a girlfriend, they are a distraction, he should have stuck to fucking and leaving. But he likes this feeling with her, he likes the warmth of her body, her kisses and how her eyes light up when she smiles but most of all he likes how he feels when his cock is deep inside her wet, warm pussy, covered in her juices and how his body shudders when he climaxes.

He hears Nobby speaking again and it snaps him out of his thoughts.

'Say again Nobbs,' he says, apologetically.

'So the invite is Jamie plus one then?' Nobby says, giving him a smile.

They laugh as they're running. Jamie nods in agreement, yes, well why not, he doesn't want to hide her away, he's proud he's pulled an older woman, she's what he needs, he doesn't need any immature silly girl who will just cause him too much drama. He puts his pods back in, turns his music on and looks at the road ahead, it's all clear, and he actually feels content for the first time in a long time.

CHAPTER 45

Floating on Air

Jess: [Hey babe, I'm just leaving my parents now, I should be home by 11]

Jess: [Missing my early morning wake up kisses]

She turns the engine on and waves goodbye to her parents as they're stood in the porch to see her off. She can see her mum is tearful, it breaks her heart to see her mum so upset when she leaves. If only she understood or accepted that she'll never move back, Jessica is resolute that she will never return to live in the town she grew up in. She's happy with her life, living in a small village where no one knows anything about her, unless she tells them. She hears her phone ping, with a reply from Jamie, so pulls in just around the corner out of sight of her parents' house and opens her phone to read it.

Jamie: [Ok, drive carefully, I'll be round to you for 1105, with your early morning kiss and an erect cock, he's missed you too]

Jamie: [Oh & I'm slightly hanging, so if you fancy cooking something together that'll be great. Xx]

Jamie: [Can we have a talk as well, nothing serious, I just need to talk about what's going on with us. I mean I know nothing is going on other than we're having great sex, but, I need to make sure you feel the same way as I do? Xx]

Jamie: [Sorry, hope I haven't scared you or anything, ok I'll shut the fuck up now. See you at 1105]

Jess: [Yes to all the above. X X]

She pulls away again, smiling to herself, feeling content in the knowledge that it's not just one sided. He feels the same way she does.

The drive home is a breeze, she feels like she is floating on air, occasionally talking to herself out loud. 'So this is what it feels like. Being loved, passionately *and* sexually, this is how it feels.' She also feels a little apprehensive, how does she tell her parents? She didn't say anything over the weekend, it was all too much, they were so happy about the divorce settlement she didn't want to risk spoiling it.

She thinks of the bits of chit chat with her mum during the visit to the spa, adding to the discomfort. She hears her mum telling her to be careful, that she is vulnerable right now and the young boys will try take advantage of that, to steer clear of the army lads, they are not good for her etc.

But, her mum hasn't met Jamie and Jess is sure if she did she would change her mind. She needs to think this one through, she needs to get her mum to visit and meet Jamie. That's how she'll do it, an accidental meeting, just like the shopping trip. She pulls onto the drive and sees Jamie is there already waiting for her. She's excited to see him and her stomach is full of butterflies, she loves this feeling.

He walks over to her as she gets out and he holds her face in his hands and kisses her passionately, searching for her tongue, he needs to taste her, he's longing for her, as is she for him.

'Hey, what kept yer?' he says when he finally breaks away from the kiss.

'Well, some gorgeous squaddie kept texting me,' she winks at him.

'Come on, let's get yer bags in before I burst right here on the driveway,' he looks down at his crotch as he speaks and lets out a cheeky laugh.

'I think I should get you a spare key, what will the neighbours think? Leaving you sat outside like that?' she says.

'He's one lucky bastard?' and winks back at her.

She silently nods at him in agreement, as she feels like the luckiest woman in the world.

CHAPTER 46

Heart to Heart

Jamie wakes up just after 0930hrs and looks at his phone, no message from Jess yet but a couple from his mum and his brother Joe. He's feeling rough, self-inflicted of course, and as he sits up to get a drink, he looks for his wallet on his bedside cabinet, it's not there. Smiling to himself he has a drink and lies back down.

A couple of months back, before he met Jess, he would wake up and check his wallet to make sure he'd used a condom. Call it his subconscious or whatever, but no matter how drunk he was he always made sure he placed his wallet next to him, if the condom was still in it, then he'd be taking a trip to the clinic. Fortunately for Jamie it was always empty. All that remains in his wallet recently is the imprint of where the condoms were. This morning he hasn't even left his wallet near the bed, meaning he did not have sex at all.

Checking Facebook as he lies there, he can see from the photos he's tagged in, last night was messy, a bunch of squaddies out on the loose, he can't help but notice how different he looks, he thinks he looks happy or is that just his imagination?

Before he jumps in the shower he calls his mum and she tells him about her increased hours in work, she's started working full time now, with Sean leaving home in a few months he needs to be ready for the loss of his benefits. She also tells him how happy he looked in that photo last night, that even his sisters have text her this morning saying the same thing. She's said to them "there's a girl behind it" she's sure, a mother knows these things and she knows her son.

'When are we going to meet her?' she asks him out of the blue, taking him aback somewhat.

He can't lie to his mum, so he tells her honestly that she's older, though he doesn't say her actual age and he also doesn't tell her she is getting divorced. Then he tells her about being Nobby's best man in December, so they will probably meet her then.

He knows his mum is smiling, he can hear it in her tone, she tells him that he should invite her to stay for New Year, see it in with the whole family.

'Steady on mum we've only just got together, I don't want yer scaring her away already.'

His mum laughs and calls him a cheeky sod.

'Anyway, I need to get in the shower Mum, I'm hanging and I need to sort meself out. Speak to yer later, love you.'

She tells him she loves and misses him very much and to be careful. She always says that. He's about to jump in the shower when he hears his phone receiving a message, he knows that's from Jess, he can tell by the way his stomach does a 'loop the loop'.

He walks back into his bedroom to read it, knowing now he definitely needs to talk to her. Reading her message, he smiles. She's on her way back, he tells her to drive carefully and then he tells her they need to talk, he needs to lay his cards on the table. He needs to know if she feels the same way. Is it just lust, is she just using him for sex or does she feel the same way he does?

When she replies she finishes it with kisses and then he knows she feels the same way. *Well Jamie lad that was the easiest heart to heart ever.*

Now he's laughing and feeling happy, despite the hangover as he heads for a shower.

CHAPTER 47

Chemistry

She barely gets the front door shut and he's pressing her up against it, his tongue searching for hers, his hands under her sweat top caressing her boobs, pressing up against her with his erect cock.

She can't get enough of his animal magnetism, the minute he touches her, her body and soul are his for the taking. Their chemistry is electrifying. How can this be? She doesn't care, she's not questioning it anymore because she wants him as much he wants her.

His jeans are off, he pulls his top off over his head (no neat pile this time) he doesn't care, he strips her off and turns her around walking backwards towards the stairs.

She sits down on the third step and he lifts her legs, he looks at her pussy, her lips are wet from her juices already, bending down he licks them tasting them, making appreciative 'mmm' noises and goes in with his tongue. There's no romance here, it is pure lust, it is sex. He has missed the taste of her juices, he's rough, he's sucking, biting and fingering her, using two and sometimes three fingers, he wants to hear her moan, the louder the better.

She's lying against the stairs cumming time and time again, she can feel her stomach tightening hard as she cums, he's rough, he's never been like this, she loves it, it is such a turn on, she wants to feel the pain, what it's like to be stretched from his fingers, she wants to feel his knuckles as they force their way inside her pussy, opening it up like it's never been opened before. He's not using lube at all, it's all her own lubrication, her juices, her cum, 'Oh God!' she hears herself saying in a deep growling voice as she cums yet again.

Grabbing his head she holds it just above her clitoris, she can feel or think she feels his whole hand inside her pussy, is he fisting her? She needs to know. He tells her, no, it's just four fingers. He takes his fingers out dripping with her cum as he tells her to turn over on all fours. She's leaning up against the stairs, with her arse out towards him, he slides his cock into her pussy, it's soaking wet, he's struggling to keep it in for the moment. He pushes it in deep and holds it there for a few seconds, giving her pussy time to contract back around it.

He's not holding back now, he's going for it, his cock is throbbing, he's not had a wank for two days, saving it for this moment. She's getting it, all of it. He pushes in deeper and deeper, faster and faster, she's begging him for more, 'hurt me,' he hears her saying, 'yes, yes' he hears as he slams his cock so deep his balls are hitting her clitoris, holding her outer thighs as tight as he can, his muscles clenching, his jaw is clenched and he's ready to release. He's not telling her this time he's just going to do it.

He rams his hard cock in one last time, holding on to her thighs as he grunts loudly, releasing two days' worth of cum, filling her already cum soaked pussy. Holding onto her as if for dear life as his cock fills her, his body rigid for a few seconds and then the now familiar shudder.

She stays there motionless on all fours feeling the aftershocks of pleasure as Jamie says, 'welcome home Jess.'

CHAPTER 48

PDA (Public Display of Affection)

Walking into the supermarket, Jamie very proudly holds her hand, he's very affectionate in private and that doesn't stop in public. He doesn't care who sees him with her or what people think of the age gap, after all '*it's just a number*' he thinks to himself.

Jess on the other hand is more reserved in public, she's not used to having her hand held or any show of affection, she is also conscious of what people might think of the age gap, it is going to take her a bit longer to get used to, out in the public eye anyway.

Jamie pushes the trolley with ease and he's happy and comfortable in her company, slapping or pinching her bum, grabbing a quick kiss whenever he can and telling her how beautiful she is.

They head to the till to pay and as always with any local supermarket there is always someone you know or someone you don't want to see, in this case it was definitely the latter. Jess's work friend or maybe just colleague would be more accurate, Lizzie, is right in front of them as they walk towards the tills, so Jess introduces Jamie as her fella, to which Lizzie asks, 'Does he have any single friends?'

They all laugh, and Jess reminds her she's married and what would her hubby say. To which she replies, 'He doesn't need to know Jess,' followed by a wink.

She gives Jess a hug as she's about to walk off to finish her food shopping, and whispers in her ear, 'he's a beauty, enjoy,' Jess hugs her back and nods in agreement.

Pulling up onto the drive, Jamie gets the bags from the boot of the car and they both hear a very familiar voice behind them.

'Hello you two.'

Startled, Jess turns to see Fred walking Buster while Hazel sorts the Sunday dinner out. Jess walks over to him and gives him a hug, while Jamie stands holding the carrier bags. Before he continues his walk he asks Jess if she's thought anymore about getting a dog. She tells him she hasn't really, but will definitely think about it, perhaps it's something she can look at for the New Year.

Finally, they get into the house and Jamie suddenly remembers what his mum said this morning, he must talk to her and tell her about the wedding invitation and if she wants she can spend New Year's Eve with his family.

He starts to prepare the veg as Jess gets the pork joint ready, and he tells her about Nobby and his engagement, their run yesterday, him being asked to be his best man, how honoured he feels and that he spoke to Nobby about her and Nobby said that "age is just a number".

Jess is listening intently, adding the odd "Yes" and "Oh" here and there where appropriate. She can't help thinking how different they both are, he's happy and open about it, happy to tell his mum, yet she can't, not just yet, her parents - well her mum in particular - are way more complicated. They've seen her go through too much over the last twelve months and they have a very different outlook on life. Oh how simple his life is.

'So what do yer think?' he asks at the end of his big long ramble.

'About what?' she replies, having been in her own little world and worried that she might have missed a direct question at the end.

'The wedding invitation and staying at me mams for New Year's Eve?'

'What date is the wedding again?'

'December 28th, it's a registry office wedding and then a good knees up at the social club afterwards. Her dad's a member so they're getting it cheap.'

'Yes, it sounds fab. I'm off until the second. I'm at my parents from twenty-forth but intend on coming home on twenty-seventh anyway.'

He looks a little bemused, he thought she'd be happy, or at least seem happier.

'What's wrong babe, yer look a little down.'

'Nothing darling, absolutely nothing. So you really told your mum about me?' she asks, genuinely surprised that he's so relaxed about this.

'Yeah, I didn't really have much choice, she guessed so I told her. Oh, you'll get to see me in me best clobber as well, we're wearing our number one uniform, so I'll need to take something to change into straight after speeches.'

'Well I'll drive there in the day, so you can keep it in the boot of the car.'

'Yeah ok, I'll book a hotel tomorrow for us.'

He leans in and gives her a kiss, he can't help thinking something's not quite right but he decides whatever it is, if she wants to talk about it she will.

'Oh, my divorce settlement has been agreed,' Jess begins to tell him, 'I received the email on Friday, so all being well, once the house sale has completed and my decree nisi is through, I will get my settlement sooner than I thought.'

'That's fab news Jess. Are you pleased?' he asks, maybe that's what was on her mind.

'Yes, definitely.' She wraps her arms around him and as he turns around to face her she gives him a tender, loving kiss. She has a moment of realisation that he is her future, she never saw it before but now it's clear. She just has to work out how to tell her mum. She decides she will at some point in the next few months, she'll definitely tell her.

CHAPTER 49

Sleeping Beauty

0545hrs. One beep from his alarm and he turns over and gives his sleeping beauty a kiss. He's stayed over three nights this week and risen early for a run every morning at 0545hrs, gone for his run and is back by 0700hrs, yet she hasn't moved, she doesn't even realise he's out of bed. It amazes him and he so wishes he could be more like her.

He meets up with Gavin and Tommo this morning to run together, these two come as a pair, thick as thieves, he thinks to himself and laughs.

'Yer alright lads?'

'Yeah J,' they reply in unison.

They start running out of the gate and down the lanes, Gavin is unusually quiet, so Jamie asks him if he's ok.

'Yeah mate, I'm good, but I owe you an apology.'

'What for?' Jamie asks, shocked that Gavin is offering an apology, although he has no idea what for yet.

'I didn't realise ya was with that blonde girl from the village, I wouldn't have said what I did if I'd have known mate.'

Jamie is more than shocked, it was silly nonsense, it wasn't even an argument, but he is touched that Gavin feels he owes him an apology. 'Mate, it's fine, it was all forgotten about.'

'So things serious between you two then J?'

'It's a bit early to say it's serious, but it's definitely heading that way.'

'Nobbs says she's coming as ya plus one to the wedding, so she must be special, does she know what she's letting herself in for?' They all laugh as they know how messy their nights get.

'Yer think that's bad? She's spending New Year at me mams, seeing it in with the family.'

'Shit! That's some serious stuff mate,' says Gavin with a disbelieving shake of the head.

'Well I'm pleased for ya Jamie, ya deserve it,' Tommo chips in, as they continue their steady pace down the country lanes. He nods in agreement and they carry on for the rest of the run mostly in silence with the odd bit of chit chat here and there.

Back at the house Jamie lets himself in with the key that Jess gave him on Sunday, he pops the kettle on, goes for a shower, has a shave and nips back down to make a cup of tea before waking his sleeping beauty. Lying down next to her, he kisses her neck as he wakes her up. She's on late shift again this week, ten till six, and Jamie is booked into the gym this morning for a session with the PT (Personal Trainer) at 0930hrs.

She stirs and in a groggy voice asks him what the time is. He laughs at her as he tells her it's seven forty-five, her tea is on the side and gives her a kiss.

'Honestly Jess, yer could sleep for England.'

'Hmm, I know,' she replies, snuggling further into the quilt, 'I thought you were going for a run this morning?'

'I was and I did, I got back at seven. Not that you would know, sleeping beauty,' he laughs. He decides to lie down next to her and snuggle in, although he's on top of the bed, the heating is on and he feels warm. Jess turns over to face him, smiling at him, she can't get enough of him, looking at him in just his towel she admires his amazing physique.

'Have you decided when you're going up to your mums for Christmas yet?' Jess asks him.

'Yeah, I'll go on the twenty-forth, same day you go to yer parents, so I'll stay here from sixteenth.'

'Ok, cool, I get you all to myself.'

'I've got a couple of work parties before I break up,' Jamie tells her, 'the one on the tenth is wives and girlfriends, so I've ordered yer a ticket. Is that ok?'

'Yes, of course. I'm going shopping Saturday with Lizzie, I'm going to get some party wear for over Christmas and I'll have a look for an outfit for the wedding too.'

'Babe, you don't have to buy anything special, yer could wear a black bag and still look a million dollars,' he winks at her.

Jess starts to discuss her Facebook account with him, she tells him she's decided to delete it because all her friends on there are basically her ex-husband's friends, that when she got married his mates became her mates. They went on holidays as friends and went out as friends. When they separated it was inevitable they would stop communicating with her, that they'd take sides and in this case they took his side, which is fine as they were his friends to begin with. She lost touch with all her mates from school long ago once she started working. She doesn't want those old friends seeing anything on Facebook, seeing her building a new life, so it's probably safer to delete it. He agrees with her and agrees if that's how she feels it's better to be safe than sorry.

What she doesn't tell him is that her mum is on her friends list and if they are going out to Christmas parties, and the wedding and New Year at his mum's, someone might tag her in a photo and she doesn't want her mum to see it as she still hasn't told her, she's not figured out how to tell her yet. So the best option is to delete it. Like he said, it's better to be safe than sorry.

CHAPTER 50

A Sombre Mood

Finishing work on a Friday in the middle of November, it's dark, cold and raining, but she feels good, why wouldn't she? Jamie is cooking dinner for them tonight and she gets to spend the whole weekend with him, waking up next to him, feeling his naked body next to hers, his hard cock pressed against her, her passion awakening, just like now, thinking of him.

Rushing out of work to get to her car she turns on her phone. By the time she reaches her car she can hear a chorus of tunes as it comes to life. Once she's in the car she'll have a quick check of the messages to make sure there's nothing serious or important. This is her routine every day when she finishes work.

She opens her text messages and there are messages from her mum, Hazel and Jamie. She opens Jamie's first as she puts her seatbelt on, going through the motions of putting her bag safely on the floor and starting the car for the drive home.

Only she hasn't started the car yet, she's caught up in his message. Her stomach wrenches as she reads it, her heart sinks, she can't hide her disappointment or sadness as she leans forward on the steering wheel and cries. This is definitely a new and unwelcome feeling but is it something she's going to have to get used to?

Jamie: [Hey Baby, I'm going away for work, I'll probably be gone by the time yer get this. I'm so sorry, I can't tell you anything else other than we shipped out on four hours notice, we've been training for this kind of scenario and today is the day. I shouldn't be gone for more than a week to ten days, most of which will be out of communication, but I promise as soon as I'm able I'll message or call you. You'll get used to it, I promise. See you soon, I miss you already and love you very much x x]

The drive home is a sombre one, the journey takes no more than fifteen minutes, but it feels like an hour. The rain is heavy just like her heart. Her mood is grey but her mind is running at a million miles an hour with thoughts and questions, the most prominent one 'will she get used to it?' she asks herself over and over.

Pulling onto the drive, she sees that Jamie has made sure the house is lit, the outside light on, the curtains closed and his car parked on the roadside.

She wonders why he left it here, reassurance he's coming back perhaps. These are all new emotions, this is what it's like being with a military man, the wife of a soldier, or his girlfriend. Wow, she is filled with fear and worry but also feels so much love, already.

Opening the front door, she smells something, it's not the plugins, this is something different, it's a sweet fresh smell. Walking into the living room she sees what the smell is, on the table is the biggest bouquet of flowers with the biggest red bow she's ever seen.

She can't control her tears, they're a mix of emotions along with the biggest smile, 'Oh Jamie, they're beautiful,' she says out loud. She notices a little present in front of them too as she's walking over to the table, she leans in and smells them, picks up the card and reads "Love you Ms Willets, from the moment I saw you x x".

She picks up the present, unwraps it and opens the box, she laughs out loud and says, 'Oh my God! A butt plug! Jamie you bloody idiot, you are crazy.' The card inside reads "I definitely want a picture of you wearing this before I come home xx J xx".

She puts the kettle on to make herself a cup of tea and checks the rest of her messages.

Hazel: [So it's official then? Do you and Jamie want to come for dinner on Sunday? Xx]

Barbara: [Just checking if you need any more dinners cooking? Xx]

Jess: [Hi Hazel, it seems he's away, something to do with a four hour notification, you'll understand it more than me! but if the offer still stands, I'd love to come]

Jess: [Hi Mum, it's fine, I'll batch cook a load over the weekend, but thank you. Love you xx]

Hazel: [Aaah, saw the trucks going out down the back roads earlier, wondered what that was all about. Yes definitely, are you ok? You'll get used to it! We'll talk more on Sunday. Xx]

Jess: [Yes I'm good, I'm sure I will. I look forward to seeing you xx]

Barbara: [Ok Darling, just make sure you do. We'll speak over the weekend. Love you too xx]

Pouring herself a glass of wine, sod the tea, she goes and runs a bath, she needs a good long soak, bringing her present upstairs with her, she wants to see how this works.

Taking the butt plug out to have a good look at it, the purple jewel in the top of it looks really nice, and she knows it sounds daft, but she thinks *this will look good in my bum*, she imagines wearing it whilst on all fours and Jamie looking at it as he rides her from behind, this could be a real turn on.

After her soak in the bath and her glass of wine finished she looks in the full length mirror thinking *hmmm, how do I get a photo of this in my bum.*

She piles up some books on the floor and sets the timer on the camera, practicing taking photos of her bum, adjusting the height of her phone, until Bingo! That's it. *Right now let's get this bad boy in.*

Rubbing a bit of lube on to make it easier to slide in, she's anxious as to how this will feel, foreign objects in her anus is still new to Jess, in fact anything in her anus at all is a very recent occurrence.

Getting up from the floor she starts to move around tentatively, she can't believe how comfortable it feels, she could get used to this and can only imagine that date nights will never be the same!

She gets into position with the jewelled butt plug in her bum, facing the camera waiting for the fifteen seconds countdown. Click. Opening up her messages, she clicks on to Jamie's.

Jess: [< photo attached > here you go my darling hope its everything you imagined and more. xx xx]

Jess: [I love you too. Miss you already, xx xx]

CHAPTER 51

Trust

'Aah, Jess, hello love. Come in, I was just about to take Buster for a walk, Hazel's in the kitchen,' says Fred on his way out as she arrives.

She walks into the kitchen and sees Hazel peering into the fridge, so she says, 'Hello,' so as not to make her jump and Hazel closes the door and gives her a big hug. Jess thought she might just turn into a wobbly mess in Hazel's arms, if anyone can empathise with what she's going through, Hazel will.

'It'll get easier, I promise, its early days. You just need to keep yourself busy love,' she says, wisely and with genuine affection.

'I know. I feel kinda stupid, after all people work away all the time, but I just didn't expect it, not like this, I thought you got loads of notice, like weeks or months.'

'Yes ordinarily you would, but sometimes it happens like this, not very often, but it does. He'll be back before you know it.'

'When I got home that day he'd left me a beautiful bouquet of flowers on the table. I haven't had flowers for years Hazel.'

'Aah lovely. Fred was very good at ordering flowers when he was away. Even though like Jamie sometimes it would be a week or two before I'd hear from him, he always made sure I got flowers. A reminder that he was thinking of me, trust and patience. That's so important to them.'

'Trust and patience,' Jess repeats, 'what do you mean by that?'

'These are not normal men Jess, they can't be worrying about life or their girl back home. They choose a girl they know they can trust, one who will wait and have the patience when there's no communication when he's away, that way he can concentrate on the job at hand knowing his woman is waiting for him, not worrying she is off with some nine to five Joey. It takes a special woman to live this life Jess.'

'I can understand that, I see now why Jamie never bothered with anyone before, he never met anyone he trusted, until now, that is. I see it now, he knows I was in a shitty marriage for ten years and still never strayed, stayed faithful, when others might not have.'

'Exactly, he knows you're the one, that's why he's fallen so quickly. He was just waiting. Waiting for the one he could put his trust into.'

'He's taking me to Nobby's wedding next month and then to his mum's, we're spending New Year there.'

'That's lovely, he sees a future with you Jess. How do you feel about it?'

'I feel the same way, I know people will think I'm stupid, it's too soon, but I can't imagine my life without him now.'

'Have you told your parents?'

'Urgh! Hazel, they're complicated, my mum especially. Even though I'm happy, I don't think that would matter to her. I need to wait, I want her to like him not hate him. She's going to take time, and I need to work this one out.'

'Well make sure you tell Jamie this, he needs to understand, don't hide it from him. This is where the trust comes in, something as simple as this.'

'Yes, ok I will.'

CHAPTER 52

The One

It's been a long week, a mixture of early mornings and late nights. If he's had more than two or three hours sleep at any given time he's been lucky. But this is what he thrives on, this is what Jamie loves. The uncertainty of the next minute, hour or day.

He really thought he'd get some down time, time to send Jess a message at least but he hasn't, he's in the thick of it, the middle of nowhere, surrounded by dense forest. Even if he had his mobile he'd not get any signal, so it's pointless. *It'll just have to wait till I get back, I'll surprise her, regardless of the time of day.*

Boy has he missed her, he thinks of her soft lips, the taste of her juices and the feel of her tongue against his. He's thinking of the last time he kissed her, made love to her and fucked her, wondering what he'll do when he sees her after this. *Will it be tender or will it be downright animalistic?* He keeps this question in his mind, playing out both scenarios in his thoughts.

On these kind of training exercises, they test you, test your ability to cope without communicating with the outside world, they test your resolve, your trust and your strengths. This is why they train physically, day in day out.

He has some time out right now, he has no idea what day it is or what time it is, he doesn't care, he just wants to get some sleep, but he can't. He's dog tired but his brain won't switch off, thoughts of home, Jess, his mum, Nobby's wedding, his speech and most importantly taking Jess home to meet his family.

That's a big deal for him, but he knows she's his future, he waited for her and took his time, it was the right thing to do.

'Nobbs, you sleeping mate?' he whispers over to Nobby.

'Yeah,' Nobby laughs, 'I wish mate.'

'Shit ain't it? Yer bringing Shelley to the WAG's one?'

'Yer, but she can't drink. It'll be good for 'er to get to know Jess, at least she'll know someone when she moves down there.'

'Yeah,' Jamie pauses a moment. 'When did yer know Shelley was the one?'

'Dunno exactly mate, just did, just knew I couldn't imagine life without 'er. Why?'

'Was it quick?' asks Jamie.

'Yeah, within a few days. Maybe a week. Yeah it was quick. I trust her man, that's important to me, especially at times like this.'

Jamie lies there, thinking about every word Nobby just said, that's the same as he feels, right here right now.

'Yer think Jess is the one?'

'Yeah, I do. I trust her. It's like yer said, just can't imagine going home now to an empty room, I just want to get back and see 'er. Yeah, can't imagine my life without 'er.'

He lies there a while longer and finally drifts off to sleep, feeling content knowing that he's finally found the one and what it actually feels like to be in love, true love.

CHAPTER 53

The Long Journey Home

He's not sure how long he was asleep for, probably most of it, they all were. The five hour journey sat in the back of the truck takes forever, but they're limited to 56mph, so they'll never get anywhere fast, which is fine on the return journey when you're that exhausted, you don't care, you'll sleep anyway.

Waking up as they come down the back lane, he feels the excitement rising, he's still no idea what day or time it is, it's dark, there's no traffic on the roads, so that means it's probably late at night or early hours.

They drive past the back gates, as they're closed and edge towards the front ones. Once they're on the base they can get the equipment away, have a quick debrief, find out when they're due back in and most importantly find out what day and time it is.

I need to get my phone, and head home. Home to Jess. I don't care how tired she is, or if she's got work tomorrow, I'm waking her up. I'm going to kiss her and take her there and then, well on second thoughts, I may just cuddle into her and go to sleep I'll have loads of time after a good sleep. I feel like her at the moment, like sleeping beauty, I feel like I could sleep for England. Back to reality, they're finally pulling up at the unit. They all jump out of the truck, with a burst of false energy driven by the thoughts of being so close to going home.

Letting himself into the house, he doesn't look in on her because he'll just want to wake her and he desperately needs a shower, he's not had one for seven days, just a 'field wash' with baby wipes. It's 0300hrs and its Saturday. He's not back in the unit now until Wednesday. *I wonder if Jess can book a couple days off with me,* he thinks.

Showered, shaved, teeth brushed he can now go and wake her.

'Baby? Babe, wake up, I'm back,' he whispers. He leans forward and kisses her and she starts to come to. Suddenly her arms are wrapped around his neck hugging him like a vice, he feels her kisses, and some muffled sounds against his neck. He can't make out what she is saying, she's crying, her emotions have got the better of her.

'Hey, hey, it's ok, I'm back now,' he reassures her. He takes his towel off and climbs into bed next to her, he's too tired for anything now, that can wait until they wake up.

She's facing him, kissing him, her tongue looking for his, she wraps her legs around him, she's gentle as she feels him wincing with every touch, her heart aching, wondering what he's been up to for the past week, she can't begin to imagine so she's not going to. She doesn't care now anyway, he's back. Back in her arms.

'Turn over, let me cuddle into you. I need to sleep,' he tells her. She grabs his hands and he winces where they're sore from living in the woods for the past week. She pulls them closer and kisses them while telling him she loves him.

'I love you too,' he says and pulls her in close towards him, he's not letting her go, not tonight, not ever.

CHAPTER 54

Cum Swap

11.05am Jess looks at the clock, she can't move as Jamie's grip is like a vice but she doesn't care, she's just happy he's home. She hears him mumbling, he's coming to, waking from his sleep. He was exhausted she can feel it, hearing it in his breathing. She'll look after him this weekend she decides.

'Mmm, morning baby,' he says in a gruff and groggy voice.

'Hey, good morning Sleeping Beauty,' she laughs.

'Cheeky,' he says with a grin, 'What time is it?'

'Quarter past eleven, you should go back to sleep.'

'No, no, I won't sleep tonight, I need to get back into a normal sleep pattern.'

'Ok, only if you're sure.'

'Yeah, I'll tell yer what I do need to sort out,' he says as he caresses her breast and kisses the back of her neck.

'Oh yes, what's that?' she questions, laughing, sure she knows what's coming next.

'Toilet,' he's laughing as he pulls his arm out from underneath her, getting out of bed to stretch, his bones clicking as a result of sleeping rough for a week. When he walks back into the bedroom, Jess is sitting up in bed, smiling at him with messy morning hair. She melts his heart, he definitely loves her and so many things about her.

'Mmm I've missed that look.'

'What look?' she says, still smiling at him.

'This look, the messy morning hair look,' he laughs as he bends down and kisses her.

'And this, mmm, I've missed your kisses.'

'Just kisses?' she says, raising her eyebrows.

He laughs at her as he climbs back into bed. Jess needs the toilet now, so she gets out of bed and as she's walking to the bathroom she asks him if he got his photo. He tells her he only got his phone when he arrived back on base and didn't have a chance to check any messages before coming straight to her at 0300hrs and that he'll look later.

'Did yer like yer flowers and pressie then?'

'Yes, they were beautiful. Thank you.'

She climbs on top of the bed and kisses him, his hands holding her face, his tongue looking for hers. He's missed this, she's missed it too. They're not going anywhere for the rest of the day, they're staying right there in bed.

She pulls the bed clothes back, finding his cock erect and feels her juices start to flow. She straddles him and he moves his hands down to her breasts moving them around, caressing them.

She places his hard cock just inside her wet pussy, he can feel already how wet she is, he smiles as she sits down onto his cock, feeling it deep inside her warm wet pussy.

'That feels good,' she says after letting a little moan escape her lips.

'Oh yeah, God it does, fucking amazing.'

She starts to move up and down, riding his cock, he's holding her tits, he's moaning, it feels amazing, his cock deep inside her and her wetness all over it.

Leaning forward she holds on to the head board, she's going faster, her tits are bouncing up and down with the motion of her body. She's going to cum. She's cumming all over his cock.

'Tell me when you're going to cum,' she tells him.

'Any second now babe.'

She climbs off and starts to lick his cock, licking off all her cum, she covers it with her mouth, sliding it in and out. He holds her head, he's cumming.

She doesn't swallow, she holds it in her mouth. When he's finished cumming she gets up and starts to kiss him, sharing his cum, swapping it from mouth to mouth.

'Mmm, that was good,' she says.

'Yeah, never done that before, it was different.'

Jess laughs and gets back into bed, the truth is neither has she, so it's a first for them both. She's glad she watched porn this week, she learnt something new.

CHAPTER 55

Breakfast in Bed

Jess gets up to go and make a cup of tea, puts her dressing gown on and realises her butt plug is in the pocket. Laughing, she takes it out and shows him.

'Mmm I cant wait to see it, especially when you're on all fours,' he winks.

She laughs too as she walks out the room, heading down stairs she calls back up to him asking if he wants some breakfast.

'Please babe, whatever yer fancy making.'

He's decided he's not getting out of bed today, he's staying put, relaxing in bed and making love to Jess at some point this afternoon. He's also decided he's not turning his phone on either, that can wait, he'll call his mum tomorrow to let her know he's back home safe. He needs time to recharge.

Arriving back upstairs with a tray of tea and a plate full of pate on toast, Jess is telling him about her shopping trip with Lizzie. She bought two dresses for work parties, an outfit for the wedding and a nice top for Christmas day.

He listens as she's talking, he's really missed hearing her voice, it's so soft and calming. He listens as she describes the dress for his Christmas party, she tells him it's an emerald green, slightly off the shoulder, knee-length fitted dress with a chiffon wrap. He has no idea what a chiffon wrap is, but he's sure it will look amazing on her. He tucks into the plate of pate on toast, it's not something he would eat normally, as he's careful with his diet not to eat too many fatty or high calorie foods, but he's enjoying this, it's a treat, he's not had breakfast in bed for years, if ever.

He asks about her Christmas day plans, he knows what his Christmas day will involve, it will be hectic. They'll get up, exchange presents, have a bit of breakfast, visit Joe and Jacqui's, watch his niece open her presents excitedly as any child on Christmas day does and wait for Breda, Steve, Rosie and Jed to arrive.

After exchanging more presents, all the women will go into the kitchen, chatting and finishing the cooking, while the men drink in the living room and talk about men's stuff, which will have nothing to do with Christmas. Men don't talk about Christmas.

When they sit down to the table the conversation will no doubt turn to Jamie and Jess, there'll be a thousand questions. What's she like? Will we like her? How did you meet her? He smiles as he thinks about it. He knows they'll love her, almost as much as he does.

'Christmas morning is traditional, we exchange presents, have a little breakfast. Then we'll get ready and go to visit my Nana, my mum's mum. She's in a care home,' Jess tells him.

He never knew this, in fact he knows very little about Jess's family, she doesn't talk about them much.

'Then we're booked in for Christmas lunch at the hotel where I went for the spa day, after that we'll head back home, Dad will fall asleep because he's had too much to drink and Mum and I will watch TV and talk about, well, anything really,' she continues.

'Have yer told your parents about me yet?' he asks her.

Jess thinks carefully about how she should answer this, how to tell him about her parents and how complicated her mum is. She remembers what Hazel said, "make sure you tell Jamie this, he needs to understand, don't hide it from him. This is where the trust comes in, something as simple as this".

'No, I haven't yet,' and she looks at him. He looks at her, with disappointment and a frown appearing on his gorgeous face.

'It's not that I don't want to babe, honestly I do. I want to shout it from the roof tops.'

'So what's stopping yer?' he asks.

'They're complicated Jamie, well my mum is. My dad doesn't care as long as I'm happy and you treat me right. But my mum, well, she's complicated. I don't know how else to describe her. I will tell them, honest, I just need to find the right time because I want them to like you from the start.'

'You're not embarrassed by me are you Jess?'

He almost never calls her Jess, always baby or babe. He's hurt by this, she knows it.

'No, no way!' she assures him. 'I'm so in love with you, I don't care what anyone thinks. It's me and you. I promise, when you meet my mum you will understand. You do believe me don't you?'

'Yeah babe, I believe yer.' He leans forward and gives her a kiss, after all, he's met her dad. He can only imagine what her mum is like, seems like a right old snob. He doesn't care for snobbery. He doesn't care if she doesn't tell them or if they dislike him. He probably won't like them anyway.

'Well I hate to say it and I'm warning yer now, me Mam and sisters will love yer, yer'll love them and it's very chaotic in me mam's house, so be prepared.'

She leans forward and gives him a kiss, moving the plate out of the way, leaning in and kissing him passionately. She tells him how much she loves him so she knows she'll love his family. It's something Jess has never really experienced in her life, a big family full of love. She's looking forward to meeting them and being a part of his family.

'So, yer butt plug,' Jamie changes the subject, and they both burst out laughing.

CHAPTER 56

Afternoon Snooze

Waking up he looks at the clock 1645hrs, he obviously fell asleep again, he felt so tired when they were talking earlier, he knows that this is one of the problems with these exercises, they drain you mentally and physically. That's why the first day back he makes no plans and keeps his phone off, he needs a day to recover, to recharge his batteries. Looking over at Jess, who's also asleep, he can't help but laugh to himself, he's never met anyone who can sleep so much.

Taking full advantage of this, he starts to play with her nipples and caress her breast, even before she's awake her legs open as he moves his hand down to feel her smooth lips and parting them slightly, he teasingly strokes her clitoris.

She's stirring, feeling something, waking up horny and wet and realises now why, as she feels his fingers playing around with her clitoris.

He starts to kiss her ear as he moves his fingers down her wet pussy, putting one finger in and then two, 'Mmm' he says in her ear as she starts to moan and move her hips.

Turning her head towards him to kiss him, he lifts up slightly and leans forward to kiss her, his tongue looking for hers as he slides another finger in, she's moaning as he kisses her, his mouth pressed heavily on hers, she's going to cum, he doesn't stop, he knows she's about to cum and moves his hand a little faster. He feels her juices on his three fingers as she's cumming.

He's not wasting time, his cock is throbbing, climbing on top of her she opens her legs wider and he slips in between them. Letting her wrap hers around his, he places his cock inside her wet pussy. His cock is hard, it feels harder than it's ever felt, *two weeks' worth of wanks* he thinks to himself and chuckles at the thought. Jess looks at him.

'What's funny?' she asks, so he tells her his thought and all she can do is roll her eyes, tut and laugh at him.

Her arms wrap around him and she gently scratches his back as he slowly slides his cock in and out, her wetness all over it as he makes love to her, her moans and groans of pure pleasure along with the most overwhelming sense of love, it's so emotional she can't help herself or contain her emotions anymore as she feels the tears seeping out of her closed eyes.

Moving his hips in a circular motion, his cock sliding in and out, it feels amazing, his hard thick cock deep inside her wet pussy, a feeling he'll never get tired of. The more he gets the more he wants.

He's close to cumming, a few more minutes, he moves his hips faster but not too fast, his cock deep inside, his balls are ready to release, one more gentle thrust and he cums, exploding deep inside her pussy, his body, rigid for a few short seconds then the shudder as he climaxes.

CHAPTER 57

Going Home

Jess gets up to go and have a quick shower before she makes some dinner, she's going to make a spaghetti bolognese tonight with focaccia garlic bread, because it's a quick and simple dish to make, perfect for times like this when she would rather not be slaving in the kitchen.

Jamie is saying something in the bedroom as she walks back in, but she couldn't quite make it out, so she asks him again. Seeing as he's not back in work until Wednesday, he wanted to know if she could book the two days off with him.

'I don't have enough annual leave left, plus it's too short notice, we have to give fourteen days to book any time off.'

She's considers whether to call in sick, but quickly decides against it, as it goes against her morals, she wasn't brought up like that. No she has to go to work but she tells him if he wants to he can drop her off and collect her. He laughs and tells her he'll pass on that but will have dinner ready for when she gets home. Jess likes the sound of that, coming home to a nice warm house, a cooked dinner and most importantly, Jamie.

She heads downstairs to start preparing dinner and Jamie gets up for a shower, he tells her he can't stay in bed any longer, they'll eat downstairs, she's definitely happy with that, she can imagine the mess eating bolognese in bed would make. Laughing to herself she shakes her head at the thought.

Jamie comes downstairs around half hour later. Walking into the kitchen he's tells her he needs to go to his house on

Monday, he needs some bits and bobs, he'll drop his share of the cleaners money off and let the lads know he'll be back Wednesday, he'll stay here for a couple more days.

Her heart sinks at this thought, she really doesn't want him to leave her, not that he is, he's only three streets away, and what will she do when he posts out of here next year? That thought terrifies her at the moment, she's not ready for it, not now, not ever.

'You're more than welcome to stay here, don't feel you have to go if you don't want to.'

He looks at her, surprised. Has she just asked him to move in?

'I mean, I know you have to go back at some point but there's no rush, ok?' she clarifies, having seen the shocked expression on his face with her previous statement.

He laughs at her, she's blushing, he loves this innocent woman and the fact that he can make her blush is an added bonus. Winking at her, he tells her he'll go home Wednesday after he's finished work, a couple nights there then he'll come back on Friday so they get to spend the weekend together.

She nods in agreement but deep down inside she's dreading it already, coming home on Wednesday and Thursday to a dark, empty house.

CHAPTER 58

The Purple Gem

Sunday morning and it's cold, dark and raining, a typical winter's day. Jess snuggles back down into the quilt, wrapping her naked body around his, after all he's permanently like a hot water bottle.

'Do you not feel the cold?' she says.

'Sometimes, but not like you, obviously,' he grins.

'Urgh! I hate this weather, I never feel warm, no matter how many layers I'm wearing.'

'That's 'cause yer cooped up in an office with heating on full and when yer come home yer heating's on here. Don't forget babe, ninety percent of my job is outside and its physical, yer don't get the chance to get cold.'

'I prefer my office job to yours then. No way would you get me outside in the wet and cold. I'm a sunshine girl.'

'Yer my ray of sunshine that's for sure!' he winks at her. Anyway, I guess I need to turn my phone on at some point this morning, I need to call me mam and check out this pic yer sent me.'

'Shall I go and have a quick shower and put it in, show you it for real?'

His cock rises instantly at the thought of her wearing the butt plug and more so at the thought of her on all fours and him looking at it as he rides her from behind.

'What do yer think?' he pulls back the quilt to show her his hard cock.

She gets out of bed laughing, goes to her top drawer and gets out the butt plug along with the tube of lube.

'Leave it there, when yer come back I'll put it in,' he suggests.

She feels a bit embarrassed about this, she doesn't know why. But nods in agreement with him. Getting out of the shower she looks at her petite body frame, at five feet six inches tall, fitting into a size ten in clothes she wonders what she would look like pregnant, there's no denying it - Jess is broody. She is more so since meeting Jamie, she can only imagine what their babies would look like. Blonde haired, blue eyed and very beautiful, they would look like him, she knows they would.

She walks back into the bedroom, and sees him standing there, his cock as hard as ever. Walking toward her he puts his arms around her and kisses her, lovingly and passionately.

He motions for her to go to the bed and she gets on all fours, he loves this sight, her bum cheeks slightly open, her pussy facing him, he could have her on all fours all day long if she'd let him.

'Mmm babe, you're wet already.' He runs his fingers down her bum to her pussy and back up.

'I'm tempted to just go in with me cock.'

'Put the plug in first then if you still want to do that, you can take it out.'

'Yeah, I'll do that,' he puts some lube on the plug, not loads, but enough to make it easier to push in.

'Wow, that's fucking amazing,' he says, seeing it in place.

'I know, it looks good doesn't it?'

'Yer you have to wear this to the Christmas ball and no thong, definitely no thong,' he tells her.

'Ok,' she'd already thought that but she'll let him think it was his idea, after all he bought it.

Pushing his cock in, he can't believe how amazing it feels and looks, he's going to try not to cum so quick today, he needs to go longer than he was capable of yesterday, well, longer for him anyway.

'I swear I can feel it rubbing against me cock,' he says, enjoying the sensation as he slides in and out.

'Really?' she's trying to answer him, in between moans of pleasure. She wants to tell him how amazing it feels, but just gives up, she can't talk, the feeling is too intense and she cums hard, groaning loudly.

His cock is deep inside her, holding onto her outer thighs he can't take his eyes off her arse, the purple gem glitters as he slams back and forth in her wet pussy. He's never seen a sight so fucking amazing in his life, he's only ever imagined. This? This is off the chart.

'Where do you want me to cum?' he asks, nearing his climax already.

'Anywhere you want,' she says breathlessly.

He pulls his cock out, covered in her cum, he feels her pussy with his fingers, its wet, soaking. He puts three straight in, he wants her cumming all over them before he cums in her arse.

Taking the plug out he drops it on the floor and lifts his cock into position, it's still wet and so are his fingers, she can feel how wet they are on her bum cheek. He pushes the tip in slightly, making sure not to hurt her, then slowly he pushes it in, it's ever so tight, he knows he will cum soon.

He pushes his cock deep into her arse, gently, not wanting to hurt her. He loves this feeling, she likes it, he can tell by the sounds she makes, now a bit faster, he's ready, he needs to know if she is.

'I'm going to cum babe, are you ready?'

She nods, she can't speak, he gives it a few more thrusts, holding her thighs tighter as he does, he feels his cock releasing, his body rigid then the shudder - he's climaxed.

CHAPTER 59

Flowers

Deciding he has to get up, he turns on his phone and then sorts his gear out for washing. Jess has already said he can use the washing machine, not to worry about the mud and any other crap he has on his kit.

Walking into the living room, he sees the flowers still sat in the middle of the table, taking pride of place, Jess moved them back after dinner last night.

'Babe, when was the last time you had some flowers?' he asks her, curious as to why she was giving them so much importance.

'Oh crikey! Years ago, probably for my thirtieth, from my work colleagues. Why?'

'Just curious, but didn't your ex ever buy you them?'

'Nooo, he wasn't romantic in any shape or form. I mean he always bought me nice gifts for birthday or Christmas, but he didn't do romance. We didn't even celebrate our wedding anniversary.'

'Wow, really? But you like romance, well you do with me, don't you?'

'Yes. Yes I do, I struggle with the kissing in public, but I love the fact that you hold my hand.'

He just smiles at her, he wonders how she stayed with someone so cold and unfeeling all those years, what was it that made her stay? He knows it wasn't the money, he can't help but think it goes deeper than that, he wonders if it had something to do with her parents, her mum perhaps. After all she did tell him that her mum was more upset about it ending than Jess was and that her mum was and still is, upset over the house.

It would be interesting to know what the house was like, how much it sold for. Her ex-husband definitely had a lot of money, you can see that from her jewellery.

Well, he decides, he's not about to start a competition, he can and will give her all the love in the world, he'll buy her gifts that are meaningful, special to her. Like when he goes away, he'll make sure she has flowers, he knows from his mum how important flowers are for a woman, especially one who is with a military man.

They tell you this in training, how important it is to send flowers or leave flowers depending on the length of the tour. It gives comfort to your loved one back home, let's her know you're thinking about her, after all it can't be easy for the women on their own, that's why it's so important for them to bond with other military wives and girlfriends, often referred to as WAGs.

Having turned his phone on, he heard all sorts of sounds of messages coming through, Facebook notifications, WhatsApp notifications and other social media accounts, all coming back to life. He doesn't know why he bothers with Instagram, he hasn't used it for ages, the same with Facebook, he never uses it, just gets tagged in loads of stuff. He opens the messages from Jess first.

'Mmm babe, I'm saving that one for me bank.'

'Your bank? What's that?

'Me wank bank. You never heard that saying before?' he grins.

'No, never,' she laughs.

Then he opens his messages off his mum, too many to read them all at the moment, so he decides just to text her to say he's back, and he'll call her later or tomorrow, that he's missed her and loves her.

He then looks on Facebook notifications, he's been tagged in Annabelle's christening, the date, time and place. He shakes his head, 'why can't they just text me and tell me?' he says aloud, Jess looks at him, so he shows her. She thinks it's sweet, but understands what he means.

Nothing much happening in the world of Facebook, so he then checks out his Instagram. He has a follow request from T4R4_2002. He looks at her profile and sees that it's Tara, Jed's sister. He accepts and follows back.

All in all, thirty minutes later he's answered his messages, set the updates to kick in during the early hours of the morning and now time to get that washing sorted.

He empties his Bergan on the kitchen floor, damp, dirty and stinking. He puts the first load in the washing machine on a hot wash and as there's too much for one wash, he'll sort the next lot afterwards.

He goes about cleaning his boots - these he takes great pride in. He sits on the floor with a bowl of warm water, a tub of Kiwi parade Gloss polish and a yellow cloth and slowly works his way around the boot, painstakingly, bit by bit, in tiny anti-clockwise circles. Once he's finished cleaning them, the first load is already finished so he pops this in the tumble dryer and puts the second load in. He was feeling recharged already.

Jess walks into the living room and comments on how shiny his boots are, that you can see your own face in them. He tells her that's how they're meant to be. He won't be wearing them now for a while, he'll revert back to his brown combat boots tomorrow.

'So why have you just sat there for two hours cleaning them?' she asks, with a look of confusion on her face.

'Because yer have to, yer can't put your kit away dirty. If yer do then yer have no respect for it or yerself. If I had an inspection tomorrow and my boots were dirty, I'd be cleaning toilets for a month with a toothbrush.'

'Oh, ok,' she nods with a new understanding.

He knows she doesn't really understand, that fine ninety-nine per cent of civilians don't either but give her time - she'll learn.

CHAPTER 60

In a Relationship

The day went by quite quickly with Jess preparing and cooking dinner, while Jamie finished his laundry, ironed and hung up his uniform, as well as changing the bed and helping with Jess's washing.

She likes this domesticated man, it's so refreshing to have someone to help at the weekend, getting the house ready for the long week ahead, although she did have a cleaner when she was married, there was no way she was working full time and cleaning that big house every weekend, no, she paid for someone to come in every Wednesday and give it a 'spruce up'.

Jamie decided to call his mum in the end as she didn't respond to his text message, which had him slightly worried. It turned out she was out with Breda, Christmas shopping, to his relief.

They've had their dinner and settled on the sofa and Jamie is trying desperately not to fall asleep. *What is it with Sunday dinner and a snooze afterwards?* He gets to talking about his Christmas shopping, he's thinking of buying his mum a piece of jewellery, but like most guys he wouldn't know where to start. He needs Jess' advice.

'Why don't you look at a keepsake type bracelet or a Pandora. That way you can buy her a charm each year, either Christmas or Mother's Day.'

'Pandora?' he's not heard of it, has no idea what she's talking about.

'Yes, give me your phone and I'll show you.'

He gives her his phone, but he hadn't heard his Facebook messenger notification. She sees a message on the screen from someone and it looks like a young girl. Her stomach wrenches and she feels all shaky. She hates the thought that he might be talking to someone else, someone his own age. She thought she could trust him, he said she could and she believed him.

'You have a message on Messenger,' she says, handing him his phone with still slightly shaky hands.

'Have I? Ok, let me see,' he says, clicking on the message, 'Oh, it's Tara, Jed's little sister, she's just asking if I'm going home for Christmas and New Year.'

'Oh, how old is she?'

'Erm sixteen, no seventeen. She told me at the engagement, the last time I saw her she was a spotty teenage school kid,' he laughed.

Jess knows what she's doing here, she has to be careful not to show she's jealous.

'What are you going to tell her?'

'I've replied, look,' Jamie shows her the screen.

She reads it, he tell her he is coming home and that his girlfriend Jess will be coming up for New Year with him. Jess is pleased about that part.

'I don't think she realises you have a girlfriend,' she says.

'No. Well I didn't have until recently, did I?'

'Why don't you change your relationship status on Facebook from single to in a relationship?' she suggests, wanting him to do it, to show others he's not available anymore.

'What? I don't bother with Facebook babe, you know that,' he answers, but he can see she's worried, she has a frown on her face. He's never seen this look before. *Is she feeling threatened by a seventeen year old?* He's known the girl most of his life, she's more like a little sister and he's never really looked at her in that sort of way.

'I know you don't, but girls, erm, I mean people…erm you know what I mean.'

'Hey, come here, don't be like this, I'm not interested in anyone else,' he assures her, giving her a passionate kiss and squeezing her tightly. He wants to reassure her he isn't the cheating kind.

'Look, if it makes you feel better I'll do it.' He changes his status to 'in a relationship' and she smiles and feels a sense of relief, for now anyway.

Jess decides she really needs to get a grip on her emotions, she's never experienced this before, she never realised she had such a jealous streak in her, but then she's never loved anyone so deeply and she certainly hasn't felt it before. Jamie definitely makes her feel so loved, it's very special - he's very special.

She shows him different bracelets he could buy for his mum, she tells him which ones she likes and which are the best for quality. His Facebook notifications have been going crazy with people congratulating him on his relationship, most people asking *who is the lucky girl?* and a few of the lads asking *who's the lucky fella?* – the usual squaddie banter. He can't be bothered to answer all the messages, so he just puts a thumbs up on most and on the squaddie ones a laughing face.

One thing he's learned during his time so far in the army is personal protection, he doesn't like to say anything on social media, he knows it's not safe, the less people know about you, the better.

CHAPTER 61

Divorce Settlement

Jess leaves for work at 7.30am feeling really tired, not through any difficulty sleeping, in fact the chance would be a fine thing. It's definitely through all the sex. She's not complaining about it though, she just needs some more sleep, being woken at five in the morning by a horny soldier is okay at the weekend but Monday morning is another matter, plus they didn't even get to sleep until gone midnight last night.

She can't help thinking that Jamie going home on Wednesday is probably a good idea. In fact, not probably, definitely! She knows she'll be able to get a good, early, undisturbed night's sleep.

She pulls up at work by seven forty-five and gets out of the car. Across the car park she sees Lizzie, and another colleague Vicky. She's shocked at how awful Vicky looks, she looks like death warmed up. Walking over to them she asks Vicky what's wrong and is she not feeling well? It turns out she found out she was pregnant on Friday and this morning she's suffering with really bad morning sickness.

Jess gives her a hug, and as she walks ahead of them Vicky comments on how happy Jess is today compared to last week. So Lizzie follows up with, 'He must be home then.'

Jess laughs out loud, nodding her head in agreement and says, 'Is it that obvious?'

All three women laugh as Jess walks into the building. As happy as she is, she still finds it uncomfortable to be around someone who is pregnant or who has just had a baby, when she so wants one of her own.

She's been thinking about her divorce settlement, she'll have around a hundred thousand left after clearing her mortgage. She wants to do some modifications to the house, like a loft conversion or a nice kitchen extension on the back and she figures that will eat up around sixty thousand of it.

She's going to put thirty thousand into an ISA or some equivalent savings plan and the money she has left over she's decided she wants to undergo IVF treatment. It's around five thousand per treatment, so with the money she's saving on her mortgage and the ten thousand remaining she can afford three treatments over the course of twelve months.

Obviously, she hasn't spoken to Jamie yet about this. *How can she?* She actually doesn't know how to broach the subject, but one thing she is sure of, he's definitely the one for her, the one she wants babies with.

For the meantime she'll carry on taking the pill, for what good it's doing her but she was given three month's supply and told to re-order when she runs out, which she doesn't intend to do. Her last pill is the end of January, then she's not going to bother with them anymore. Who knows, if she's lucky it might have kick-started her ovaries and she could get pregnant naturally. *Ha! One can only hope*, she thinks to herself, and then turning off her phone, she starts work.

CHAPTER 62

Jewellery Box

Once Jess left for work at 0730hrs, Jamie decided he'd go for a run and do a couple of hours in the gym before sorting his stuff out. He'll need to take a lot of it back home today and get some clothes for the next couple of days.

Jess has cleared a couple of drawers for him to keep boxers and socks in, plus some T-shirts and anything else he wants to leave, so it's going to be easier when he stays over Friday until Monday to have some stuff here. Ideally he shouldn't need to bring anything with him, it should all be here.

He sends a message to the lads in the WhatsApp group seeing if any of them fancy ten miles plus gym afterwards, or at least to try ten miles as he hasn't been running in ten days. It will definitely have an impact on him, he's sure he'll struggle, he's going to have to really push himself today.

The replies come in quickly, a couple of them have already been out, hitting the road at 0600hrs and the rest are going to the gym. There's a new PT instructor who they think is on secondment from the Royal Marines, apparently he's *brutal but good*, really puts you through your paces.

He opts for the gym, he likes a challenge, plus he'll see what this PT guy is all about, if he is as 'brutal' as they say. He nips back upstairs for a quick shower before he goes, he doesn't want to turn up smelling of early morning sex and Jess' cum all over his face and fingers, not that he'd mind but he doesn't think anyone else will appreciate it.

Now he's not a nosey person, not by nature anyway, but when he saw Jess' jewellery box this morning he couldn't help wondering what's in there and should he take a look? *After all, if he asked her she'd show him, wouldn't she?* Actually, maybe she wouldn't. She's very secretive about her past and her marriage. He can't fathom out why, but for whatever reason, it will come out one day, it always does. With his towel wrapped around his waist and his body still wet from the shower, he opens it, ever so slowly, careful not to dislodge anything, he doesn't want to arouse any suspicion that he's been snooping.

The jewellery box is navy blue velvet, rectangle in shape with a door at the top and a pull out drawer on the bottom. Not that he's an expert in jewellery boxes but this one looks quite big, he reckons it's about twelve inches long by eight inches high and six inches deep.

Opening it up he can see it has another compartment in the top. He wasn't expecting to see anything other than a few pairs of earrings. But he's shocked when he sees how many pairs there are, he recognises the pear drops, and glancing at the others he sees some single diamond ones, a deep-red stone pair, and a couple of black-stone earrings. *Looking in this box is like looking at the crown jewels*, he thinks to himself.

He carefully lifts out the compartment and places it on the chest of drawers. There isn't a great deal in it, a few little boxes, like trinket boxes, he picks a couple out and opens them, there's a nice chain in each of these, one of them has a diamond pendant on it, *hmm she likes her diamonds*, he thinks. The next one he picks up nearly knocks him off his feet, he really wasn't expecting to see anything like this. Straight away he can see it is her engagement ring and her wedding ring. The most sparkling diamonds he's ever seen, even her wedding ring is just a mass of sparkling diamonds.

'Shit! Fuck me! Yer could buy a house with these,' he says aloud. He puts them back, he's seen enough, he knows now Jess' ex-husband replaced love with possessions, showering her with fancy expensive jewellery rather than actually showering her with love itself.

197

He carefully puts the compartment back and closes the lid. He pulls the drawer out, it's full of bracelets, mostly chunky things and a few diamond ones but nothing he'd expect to see on Jess, they are awful in his opinion. Not at all what Jess usually likes, she's petite in stature and her wrists are so tiny they'd be lost in those bracelets, if she ever wore them!

He closes the drawer and walks away from it, as if he'd never opened it. He knows what Jess likes - simple but elegant jewellery. He might have only been with her a short while but he decides he knows her better than the man she was married to for ten years did.

He realises now, he doesn't need to compete with her ex-husband, it's not material things she needs, it's love and a family of her own. He remembers her reaction when he told her that Shelley is pregnant. He can and he will give her everything she needs, that he is sure off.

Right, let's hit the gym, see what all the fuss is about. Pffft, brutal my arse, we'll see how brutal he is, I bet he's no marine either!!

CHAPTER 63

Dressed for Summer

Jess pulls up on the drive just before five o'clock when Jamie comes to the front door to greet her. All he's wearing is a pair of training shorts and a T-shirt with the regiment logo on and a pair of flip flops.

'Have you missed the memo?' she laughs.

'What?' he says, looking confused.

'We're in the depths of winter and you're dressed like its thirty degrees out.' She walks towards the door laughing at him and gives him a kiss. He puts his arms around her shoulders and embraces her lovingly.

'I went for a run this afternoon, after the gym, had a shower and put these on for comfort, then couldn't be bothered to get dressed again.'

'Have you been out like that?' she asks.

'Yeah, I went food shopping, I did get some weird looks,' he laughs.

'Really? I can't imagine why.'

As they walk into the house, she can smell food, he's made chicken stir fry and noodles for dinner. He's not the best cook in the world but he tries his best, he tells her. She goes upstairs, takes a shower and gets into her warm PJ's and dressing gown and heads back down.

He's made her a cup of tea and she leans against the sink holding the cup to warm her hands. She tells him about the conversation in the car park and he laughs with her.

He starts to tell her about the gym session this morning, that there's a new PT instructor on secondment from the marines. He tells her about his reputation for being brutal, 'and I don't mean a little,' he says 'I mean fucking brutal, two hours he had us doing stuff *even we've* never done before.' He continues his explanation, that it's the way they train the marines, and how he always considered himself fit, but no way, even the instructor called them "Couch potatoes, unfit pricks the lot of ya!".

'You'd never get away with talking like that in my workplaces,' she says, shocked.

'That's the military babe, it's how we are, it's not personal, they're just words,' he laughs. She shrugs her shoulders, she doesn't understand it and doesn't intend to try, to be honest.

They have dinner and then cuddle up on the sofa with a nice film, after all, there's not much more you can do on a cold winter night.

CHAPTER 64

Party Preparations

The last couple of weeks have flown by, Jamie is spending more and more time at Jess' house, they have been out and about in the village and the local town for nights out. People know they're a couple now, there's no hiding it.

It's the night of *the* Christmas party and Jess is busy getting ready. She managed to find a hairdresser to do her hair, a bridal hair specialist which is perfect for these type of events. As she was leaving for her appointment, Jamie was polishing his boots (again) his number one uniform hanging up in the bedroom, the brass buttons so shiny *you could see your reflection in them*, she thought to herself.

Now three hours later she returns, her hair looking amazing, long flowing curls with diamante grips pinning bits up here and there. Jamie is lost for words, all he can think about is showing her off tonight. She sets about sorting out her make-up, careful not to ruin her hair and she has a strip wash before she gets dressed, luckily she had the foresight to have a shower earlier, before going to the hairdresser.

Jamie gets in the shower, as Jess is practically ready, all she needs to do now is put her butt plug in and get dressed, she had a dummy run with it last weekend and it was really comfortable so there shouldn't be any problems. If she needs to take it out, she's taking the black pouch that came with it, it'll fit in her purse till she gets home.

She goes and sits on the toilet to talk to him whilst he is showering, something she does quite often. Mindful of her hair, she leaves the door open wide to let the steam out. She's asks him what Shelley is like and has he been to these kind of events before. He tells her he only met Shelley once and she seemed really nice, that he's sure they'll get along and not to worry. He hasn't been to this kind of thing before so it's all new to him, but they're good fun from what the lads tell him.

Tommo's girlfriend is coming too, he tells her she's a seventeen year old, A level student, that they have something in common and they're both going to the wedding at the end of the month. She reminds him it's only eighteen days away.

'Shit! I need to get me fucking speech sorted,' he says, feeling a bit panicked.

'We'll work on it in the week, besides you break up next Friday, so you'll have the week to yourself, maybe do it then?' she suggests.

'Yeah, I need to do me Christmas shopping too, but that'll take me about an hour,' he winks.

'That doesn't include my present as well does it?' she asks, pretending to look scared, he's laughing and nods his head, so she chucks a cold wet flannel at him and it makes a slapping sound as it hits him.

'Hey, that's not nice,' he laughs, shrugging it off.

They're both laughing as Jess gets up and leans over to kiss him before she leaves the bathroom. Walking back into the bedroom, she shouts to him that he needs to put her butt plug in, so he walks in with an instant hard on at the thought of her on all fours while he inserts it. There's no way he's doing this without sticking his cock in her pussy.

She's done that on purpose, he's sure of it. *Oh well, who is he to complain*, besides he'll probably have a hard on all night anyway at the thought of her wearing it.

She's already on the bed waiting and the sight of her sends him wild. He decides to insert his cock first and give it a few good thrusts then he inserts the butt plug. She tells him to be careful of her hair, but don't stop. The feel of his hard cock in her wet pussy, deep inside makes her cum in no time.

He doesn't last long, he never does when she's wearing her plug, that's something he's noticed, he tells her he's going to cum and she nods in agreement. He gives it one more thrust and she feels him explode inside her, she feels his body go rigid and the grip on her thighs tighten as he does.

He pulls out, his cock dripping with their cum and tells her she should go out with her pussy filled with his cum.

'Eeuww' she says, 'no way, it'll leak all over my dress.'

He goes in the bathroom to jump in the shower for a quick wash and Jess has a wash at the bathroom sink. Now she needs to get dressed.

She opts for a simple pair of diamond earrings, a half carat in total, probably her favourite ones, elegant and classic at the same time. She sprays her perfume and gets her dress on but Jamie needs to do the zip up, so she'll wait, he is in the spare room getting ready.

Finding her little silver clutch purse, she puts on some new silver sandals that she bought for tonight. They're a criss-cross diamante strap with a two inch heel, so she'll only be an inch taller than Jamie. No one will notice, she thinks to herself and chuckles.

She hears him walking towards the bedroom, she doesn't want to see him straight away, she wants her dress doing up. She stands with her back to the door as he walks in, he can see how amazing she looks from the back and immediately feels a sense of immense pride.

With the zip now up she turns around slowly, catching her breath at him standing there in his uniform. This man in front of her, whom she loves with every ounce of her being, is breath taking. She begins to feel emotional, tears welling up in her eyes. *No Jessica, not tonight*, she tells herself and she smiles from ear to ear, the biggest proudest smile possible.

He is wearing his number two uniform known as the 'Mess Dress' which consists of black trousers with a red stripe down the outside leg, a red tuxedo with black lapels, tails and the tux cutting off at the waist, a withering shirt with a black bow tie, and of course some extremely shiny black boots.

She's totally in awe, she can't believe how amazing he looks and he's taller too. *Mmm,* she thinks *perhaps I won't be taller than him tonight after all.*

'Wow, fucking hell babe, you look a million dollars,' he says, struggling to find the words to tell her how amazing she looks in her tight fitting, emerald green, off the shoulder dress. Her body looks divine, there's not a lump or bump anywhere it shouldn't be and her perfect shaped tits are like they have just been placed there on her chest. He notices her earrings, she's opted for the delicate diamond ones and they're perfect, just like she is.

'What time is Shelly picking us up?' she asks.

'1830hrs, so yer got fifteen minutes left. Fancy giving me a blow job?' he asks, laughing out loud.

'What? No! No way, later,' and she winks at him.

They head downstairs to wait for Nobby and Shelly, glad they're being picked up as it's a long walk to the hall where the party is on camp. One things for sure, he's got a semi on already and will have all night, with thoughts of her wearing that butt plug and no thong. It's enough to drive him wild.

'Yer know on the way home, I think I'm gonna lean yer up against one of them trees, and give yer a good fucking outside in the woods, back to nature and all that!' he says, unable to stop thinking about her butt plug.

'Ha, no! Those trees are on the edge of a park and anyone could see us!' she says.

'Yeah, I know,' he winks, and squeezes her slender hand.

CHAPTER 65

Christmas Party

They hear the horn of Nobby's car outside, as he very kindly comes to pick them up, even though it isn't very far, they want to arrive freshly dressed and scrubbed up. Jess gets in the car as Jamie locks the front door.

Nobby immediately introduces her to Shelley, his fiancé. She's exactly as Jess pictured her, the type of woman she would expect him to be with - shoulder length blonde hair, curvy, probably a size 16 and very bubbly personality.

Jamie gets in the car and immediately gives his key to Jess to pop away in her bag. He sees the black pouch and asks what it is, Jess has no idea what to say, so she makes up some sort of excuse saying it's for any loose change she has.

'Babe, you're the same as me Boss. "Sorry Ma'am",' Jamie says, making reference to Her Majesty Queen Elizabeth, 'neither of you carry any money.'

They all laugh, as Jess blushes, but in the back of the car in the dark, thankfully it can't be seen. Driving onto the base itself, Nobby drops them all off at the entrance to the mess where the party is, he needs to go and park his car. It's less than a five minute walk back from the car park, so the three of them wait just inside the foyer.

Jess makes conversation with Shelley, asking her if she's excited for the wedding and what colour are the bridesmaid dresses. She needs to make sure that the dress she bought isn't the same colour, it has happened before so she doesn't want to make the same mistake twice.

Shelley tells her that due to it being a Christmas wedding her two bridesmaids will be wearing red and gold. Jess can tell by the mixture of chuckles followed by a huge smile, that she is extremely excited. She's excited to be marrying Nobby, starting a new life, making new friends and having a family.

It's evident that they are a young couple very much in love, Jess can't help wishing that's how she had felt when she was getting married, instead of full of fear.

In the still of the night air they hear Nobby's boots crunching, as he approaches.

'The pouch is for my plug,' Jess whispers in Jamie's ear.

'Shit! Sorry,' he puts his head down and sniggers quietly.

They stand in a queue and wait their turn for having a photo taken, the two men swapping their usual friendly banter and the women chit chatting, getting to know each other. When Shelley tells Jess how stunning she looks, Jamie hears and looks at her also, giving her a wink as he says 'You really do, my gorgeous girl,' and leans forward and gives her a kiss.

Jess thanks Shelley for the compliment and asks her how she's feeling with her pregnancy, telling her about her work colleague Vicky who is suffering with terrible morning sickness.

Shelley tells her that the first few weeks she felt awful, a permanent headache and nausea, though no actual vomiting, but she says she is sure the constant nausea is worse than actual being sick. Other than that she feels fine and has her twelve week scan on 20th December.

'Blimey, so you're due when they post out?' says Jess, having worked out the dates in her mind.

'Yeah, I'm going to move back to my mum's two weeks before, I'm not changing my doctors or hospital, so I'll just go back for my appointments,' says Shelley, seemingly unfazed by the way the timing has fallen.

'What about work?' Jess asks.

'I've still got four weeks holiday due, which I'm going to take before my maternity leave starts at thirty-four weeks, so I'll actually finish work mid-April.'

'That's good, I take it you're staying at your mum's until April, coming down at the weekends?

Shelley nods and she and Nobby go for their photo.

'See? I told you she'd love you,' Jamie says, kissing her again and pulling her in closer by her waist, he doesn't want her leaving his side, she looks at him and gives him a broad smile, leans in and whispers, *love you*, and he mouths back, *love you too.*

Photo done, they go and find their seat, it's on the same table as Nobby, Shelley, Tommo and his girlfriend Clementine, as well as Gavin and another guy and a couple she doesn't know.

She can't help but stare at Clementine, she's tiny, probably a size six, very beautiful with long flowing black hair and beautiful green eyes with long, jet-black eyelashes.

Jess introduces herself as Clementine is looking very shy, Tommo tells her he's going to the bar and that seems like the cue for all the men to follow suit, leaving the women at the table. They all start chatting about the party, it turns out it's a first time experience for all of them.

'What A Levels are you taking Clementine?' Jess asks, to break the ice.

'Biology, chemistry and physics,' she replies.

The other two women both look stunned and ask her what she wants to do when she's finished sixth form. She tells them she wants to be a doctor and has had some offers already for university, pending her results.

'Wow, Clementine, you're brave. I studied English Literature and Geography and I thought I wanted to be an English teacher but by the time I'd finished my A Levels, the stress of the exam pressure put me off going to Uni.'

Clementine agreed that this year, her final year, is very stressful indeed. With the amount of course work she has that needs to be handed in by January 9, she can't see herself having any time off from her studies over Christmas.

The men all come back to the table with what seems like an endless number of drinks, and Jess can't help but feel sorry for

Shelley not drinking. The night is fantastic, all the women are bonding really well, the three course meal is amazing and the drinks are flowing, music is playing and everyone is up and dancing.

Jamie's never felt more proud, he looks at Jess talking and mixing with everyone, he can't believe how lucky he is, he feels like the luckiest man in the world.

'Babe, you're amazing and I've had a semi-on all fucking night thinking of you wearing that plug,' he whispers in her ear.

Jess laughs and thanks him for the compliment, the truth is she feels the same way. She can't stop looking at him in his mess uniform, even though they've all removed their jacket and bow tie and some have even undone the top buttons of their shirts by now, he still takes her breath away.

The night is drawing to a close and it's just gone midnight, so Jess gives Shelley a big drunken hug and tells her how excited she is for the wedding, then she hugs Clementine and wishes her a lovely Christmas and not to stress over her course work plus she'll see her at the hotel on the twenty-seventh.

They all say their good byes, Jess and Jamie are the only ones not staying on the camp so they start to make their way through the base, to the back gates, exiting through the turnstile as the gates are closed.

Walking down past the social club, Jamie motions over towards the park area, telling Jess that his cock is so hard, he's never going to make it home. She laughs at him, she knows he wants to fuck her up against the tree. They get closer, he stops, pulling her towards him to kiss her, he can feel her body heat as she moves into his arms.

Moving her backwards a short distance he leans her against the tree, his hand is undoing his zip and pulling out his cock, it's hard and throbbing, he really doesn't want to have to wait until home. He pulls her dress up to her waist, she's naked from the waist down. She's struggling a little to relax in the location, so while still kissing her he tells her that it's fine, no one is around. Opening his eyes extra wide, he can see it's definitely pitch black, no street lights and he doesn't hear anyone padding by.

He tells her to turn around and face the tree, as she does so she looks to make sure no one really can see them, but he's right, its pitch black and no one is around. Facing the tree, she moves her legs apart, Jamie helps her get into position, he wishes he could see this, in daylight, Jess bent forward, arms outstretched touching the tree, her dress around her waist, her half naked body on show for his eyes only. The gem of her butt plug glistening in the light and her wet pussy ready to take his erect cock.

He places his cock against her pussy lips and wets the tip of it before he pushes it in deeper. She lets out a moan of pleasure. It feels amazing, his cock feels so thick, he thrusts harder in and out, Jess is trying her best not to scream, but she can't help moaning and groaning with each of his movements. She wonders what they look like, what she looks like being fucked from behind up against a tree. The thought is really horny, it's making her cum quickly, all over his cock, he can feel it, he's ready to cum too, he gives another thrust and releases deep inside her, holding her tight as he climaxes.

He leans against her as both of them catch their breath, then moves slightly and his cock falls out just as Jess is straightening up, he pulls her dress down and lovingly kisses her right shoulder, telling her how fucking amazing that was. Once he's finished sorting Jess' dress out he tucks his cock away, does his zip back up and pulls her towards him. He's holding her tight and kissing her one last time before heading home, feeling the intensity of his emotions, standing there under the trees in the pitch black of the night with nothing more than moonlight to illuminate their faces.

CHAPTER 66

Morning After
the Night Before

Both of them sleep until gone ten the next morning. Jamie being the first awake as always, looks at the clock, 1004hrs. His head is pounding, he has the mother of all hangovers, he needs a shower, some paracetamol and a cup of tea. That will sort him out. First he needs to find the energy to get up and get in the shower, but he can't, so decides to lie there a bit longer.

Jess is coming to, she's saying something he can't quite make out, something about head and a sledge hammer.

'What yer saying babe?' he mumbles back to her.

'I feel like someone's hit me over the head with a sledgehammer,' she manages to say clearly enough.

He's never heard that saying before, he tells her, so she explains that it's what her dad always used to say when he woke with a hangover. It must be a builder's saying, maybe, and then she decides to try not to think too much, it really does hurt her brain.

They're both feeling delicate, both hanging from their first military Christmas party, what a night, they talk about the different conversations that were going on around the table, the wedding and how exciting it will be and how excited she is to be spending New Year with him and his family.

An hour passes very quickly, and Jamie manages to get up to go and get some headache tablets, a large glass of water and also makes them both a cup of tea.

He decides he needs to ask her this morning, something that has been bothering him for a while now and he saw it again last night. Her sad eyes when she was talking to Shelley about the pregnancy and that friend from work who just found out she's pregnant. He needs to know why she never had any of her own. He's very observant, he knows every expression on her face, her frowns, her smiles, he knows already the difference, whether it's happy or sad. Jess' expressions are like a conversation of their own.

He wanders back upstairs and she hasn't moved from her 'cocoon'. He gives her a couple tablets, a pint of water and a cup of tea and jumps back into bed next to her. He's not bothering with a shower just yet, he needs more energy for that. Jess moves a little, just enough to take the headache tablets, sip the water and lie back down, moaning about her head.

'Babe I need to ask yer something, something personal and I want yer to be as honest as yer can be.'

Jess freezes, she knows it's going to be something to do with her marriage, but she'll be as honest as she possibly can. She turns over to face him, he looks worried, he has that frown, she's nervous now, perhaps it's not something to do with the marriage after all. Perhaps it's to do with them. *Is he having second thoughts?* Her heart sinks at the thought of losing him, she needs to know now.

'Ok, what do you want to know?' she says, dreading what might come next.

'Why did yer never have kids, did yer not want any?'

She feels only relief when she hears his question, she'll happily tell him the reason why.

'Anthony never wanted any, he said they'd be a burden, all he wanted was to make money, more money for the finer things in life and if you have kids then you can't have that lifestyle. He made sure of it as well, he had a vasectomy for his thirtieth.'

'Wow, selfish bastard, did he ask yer about it?' Jamie says, shocked at the callousness of an action like that.

'No not really. But the other reason I think, is he didn't want to spend the money on IVF, even though my mum offered to pay for a course. She wants grandchildren, I guess like any parents would, it's a natural process.'

'Why IVF?' he looks confused.

Jess explains to him about not having periods, and being diagnosed at eighteen with amenorrhea and being told that if and when she wanted to start a family then she'd need IVF treatment. Because of her medical condition (it's classed as medical) she'll get help from the NHS but it's a long waiting list, so she wanted to go private, after all it's not like they didn't have the money.

Jamie is shocked by this, he's doesn't know what to say, he lies there for a bit in silence, wondering whether to ask his next question or not.

'So for us to start a family, I'm not saying now but at some point in the future, we'll need to pay how much for IVF?' he asks her.

'It's five grand for each round of treatment.'

'Shit! That's a lot. But, yer could get it cheaper through the doctor, so how much is it then?'

As she listens to his questions, she thinks very carefully. *Should she tell him what her plans are with the settlement or should she keep it close to her chest still? No, she needs to be open and honest, it's about trust after all.*

'Well, I've been thinking about my divorce settlement. Once I've paid my current mortgage off I want to look into getting either a loft conversion done or a kitchen/diner extension on the back of the house, I want to put some away for a rainy day, as they say, and I was going to keep some back for IVF. I figured with the money I'm saving on my mortgage each month I could afford three treatments.'

As Jamie is listening to her he's roughly working the sums out in his head and can't help thinking *that's some fucking settlement.*

'Ok, but say yer start the ball rolling now with your doctor, it's cheaper and if it works yer've saved yerself a lot of money,' he suggests.

'Yes, I guess so, but I have to wait now until I finish this lot of the Pill he gave me.'

'What? The pill? Why are yer on the Pill if yer can't get pregnant?' he says, his face a picture of complete confusion now.

'Remember when I had to register with my new doctor?' she says patiently, trying to explain it all as best she can.

'Yeah, I was away at me mams.'

'Yes, that's right, well I went for my medical and the doctor was talking about my condition and asked me what I used for contraception,' she says, seeing the confusion deepen on his face.

'I told him Anthony had a vasectomy so there was never any need for any other form of contraception. But he went on to tell me that even though I'm not menstruating I could still be ovulating so until I start trying for a baby they'll never know, in the meantime he prescribed a three month trial of the Pill.'

'So hang on, what he's saying is, yer could actually get pregnant naturally without the IVF?'

'It seems so, yes,' she smiles at his new expression of surprise.

'Your ex must have known this, that's why he got the snip.'

'No, he wasn't that clever,' she laughs.

Jamie thinks *it's because he was being unfaithful, he didn't want to get caught out. He was being careful, being a sly cunt.*

'So, I have to get this straight, me 'eads all over the place here, so are yer taking the Pill now?

'Yes, I started that very same day, we'd already had sex and I was petrified in case I fell pregnant, not that I don't want to but I didn't know where we were going. Does that make sense?'

'Yeah, of course. Perfect sense.'

'So when does it run out?' he asks, his mind working on its own little agenda now.

'Mid-January.'

'Then what?'

'I have to re-order another three month supply.'

Both their heads are spinning, neither of them sure if it's the effect of the hangover or the conversation and the fact that they are discussing starting a family.

'Don't,' he says, 'don't order any more, see how it goes and if yer've not caught by the time I post out, then let's look into

IVF.' He is serious about this, he hasn't been this serious about anything since he made the decision to join the British Army.

She doesn't know what to say, she's grinning from ear to ear, the thought that she could have her own baby soon is something that she's only dreamed about in the past. All she can do is nod in agreement.

'But, yer know what that means don't yer?'

'No, what?'

'Yer gonna have to tell yer parents about me.'

They both laugh, and she agrees that at some point in the next few months she has to tell her parents. Then again, she could wait until she's pregnant, by which time her mum will be so ecstatic at the thoughts of her first grandchild, she probably won't care about his age.

CHAPTER 67

Better get Practising

'What time are we getting up today?' says Jess, thinking they've probably been in bed long enough, though she's very cosy still under the duvet.

'Soon, I need some food,' Jamie says, feeling much less hungover than earlier, but in need of nourishment nevertheless.

'Mmm, me too.'

'Yeah, yer need to keep yer strength up, we've got a lot of practising to do.'

They both laugh as Jamie starts to move.

'So may as well make a start now,' he says and climbs on top of her, both of them chuckling like teenagers, he leans forward and kisses her, deeply and passionately, the love he has for this woman is like nothing he ever imagined.

Jess moves her legs to allow for Jamie to slide in-between them, she can feel how hard his cock is and she can't help but wonder if there is ever a time he isn't hard. Not that she is complaining, in fact right now she wants to feel his hard cock inside her, filing her with his cum, imagining that at some point it's going to be fertilising her egg.

She knows in the next few months she might have their baby growing inside her, the most precious gift a man could ever give her. She doesn't care if she never gets a piece of jewellery or an extravagant holiday ever again, none of that would compare to having a baby.

His hand travels down to caress her tits, her erect nipples, he moves to suck them, caressing one and sucking on the other,

her legs open wider, her juices are flowing, she gets so turned on by her nipples and he knows this. He wants to taste her before he fucks her, he wants to hear her begging him for more, he wants to hear her cumming over and over again, her juices pouring out of her.

As he climbs off her, she's a bit shocked and asks him what he's doing. He tells her to wait a minute as he nips over to the chest of draws, she can hear him rummaging around for something. He climbs back on the bed and produces a pair of handcuffs, she laughs as she moves into the middle of the bed. She's never been handcuffed before, this is something new - it's a definite turn on.

Holding her arms up he feeds one of the cuffs through the headboard, he laughs as he tells her it was a good choice buying this bed because the head board is solid pine but with an iron scroll pattern in the middle. He puts the cuffs on her so she's completely helpless now and he knows he has full control. This thought is arousing him more, even though he's not a dominant person, not by nature, he does like to feel in control in the bedroom. He stares at her for a while, his finger running along her body, her perfect shaped body, not a mark on it, he can see her chest rise and fall with her deep breathing, she's really turned on and he hasn't even started yet.

Bending down he licks her nipple, his tongue flicking it, his teeth grazing it. He can hear her breathe harder as his fingers part her lips, he feels for her clit, it's erect and longing for his touch, he gently runs his finger around it knowing this will drive her insane. Running his finger down her pussy, he feels how wet she is already. Oh God, he wants to take her and fuck her now, fuck her stupid, but he won't, he wants to enjoy this, he wants to take his time.

She's telling him to put his fingers in, 'please,' she says, 'as many as you want, hurt me, make me cum all over them.'

He lifts up his head to look in her eyes, smiling he leans in and kisses her and she kisses him back. In that moment he inserts three fingers inside her pussy, forcing them in, she catches her breath with the shock. She opens her eyes to see him, smiling at her, his beautiful face, so intense and so young.

He pushes his fingers in deeper and she lets out a deep throated groan, his fingers getting faster, her juices soaking his hand, she's getting louder and louder, he wants her screaming, he forces a fourth one in, its tight, too tight but it'll give.

He's fucking her pussy with his fingers, she's losing control, she can feel it. He's watching her, he wants to see her face as she climaxes, he knows she's close, another thrust of his fingers, he sees it, he hears her, he feels the spasms tightening around his fingers, she's climaxed, her cum all over his fingers, her chest is heaving as she catches her breath.

'Do you want more?' he whispers closely to her ear.

She doesn't open her eyes but nods and says 'Yes, yes I want more.'

'Tell me. Tell me what you want,' he whispers again, softly next to her ear. She tells him, she wants him, his fingers deep inside, stretching her, that feeling of hurting but not hurting. It's pure pleasure, a feeling of euphoria as she climaxes time and time again.

His hand is soaked in cum, she's dripping, she can't control herself, her climaxes are so strong, she's begging him to stop, she feels she can't take anymore, but she doesn't want him to stop because it's the most amazing feeling she's ever felt.

He stops, but leaves his fingers inside for a moment, giving her the chance to catch her breath. She opens her eyes and smiles at him as he slowly takes his fingers out. He undoes the cuffs, and leans in to give her a kiss, asking her if she's okay. She tells him she's fine. He smiles at her and tells her to get on all fours. He's way to too aroused to mess around with love making, he wants to fuck her and fuck her hard.

She turns over on to all fours and finds that her wrists are hurting her from pulling against the handcuffs but she's not going to complain in case he never cuffs her again and she really enjoyed it, the pleasure, the pain, the euphoria, she definitely wants to feel all that again.

He gets behind her and places his cock just inside her pussy, he's not going to last long, he can feel it, he starts to push it in deep, he loves that feeling, that warm wet feeling wrapping around his hard cock. He starts to thrust it in deeper.

'Oh baby, yes, that's fucking amazing,' he says.

'Yeeess,' she's struggling to talk, her moans and groans getting the better of her ability to say anything at all.

He's grunting as he thrusts his cock in deep, he's trying his hardest not to cum but he can't hold on any longer, he needs to cum now.

'Baby, I'm gonna cum, yer ready?' he says. She nods her head in answer, unable to speak.

He holds her thighs tight, she loves the feel of his powerful grip, his strength, his forceful thrusts. He pushes his cock in deep one more time and she feels it, his cock pulsating as he fills her with his sperm, deep inside her pussy, she feels him go rigid for a few short seconds before his body shudders as he climaxes.

CHAPTER 68

Inadequate

It's been a busy week at work for Jamie, they're getting the base ready for lockdown over Christmas. Ninety percent of the lads living in the blocks will go home, they'll be on skeleton staff to man the gates and the ones that live in the married quarters will probably, at some point, go and visit their families somewhere else in the UK.

Jamie finishes work on Friday 16, he's arranged with Jess to go Christmas shopping on the Saturday daytime and out in the night with a few of the lads, a bit of a stag night for Nobby.

He needs to get his family's presents but most of all he needs an idea of what to get for Jess. His plan is that if they go together, she can help to pick out a nice bracelet for his mum but in doing so, she'll show him the sort she likes without realising. Then he can nip into town during the week when she's in work and she'll be none the wiser.

He wakes early on Saturday, around 0530hrs and he's excited about going away for Christmas, seeing his mum and family but most of all about introducing them to Jess.

He gets up and goes through his wedding speech again, making sure it's perfect, it's funny in parts and serious in others. *Yeah, that'll do,* he thinks to himself.

He's not going to wake his sleeping beauty just yet, so he gets dressed and goes for a run. He wants to get about ten miles in this morning, he estimates that it'll take him one hour and forty-five minutes. He sets his watch at 0600hrs, puts his pods in, turns the music on and off he goes.

It's quiet, dark, and deserted, just as he likes it so he can think while he's running, sorting his life out in his head and clearing his mind.

This morning he needs to think through something that has been bothering him, something he's not sure how to deal with. It's definitely too early in the relationship for him to be put to the test, he's never had a relationship before so he doesn't actually know if he's the faithful loyal kind, although he'd like to think he is.

A few miles into his run, he checks his watch, 0643hrs so his timing is good, he's nearly halfway. He feels really good, that PT instructor was right, he's given them some new breathing techniques, saying it'll help with the long runs, increasing your speed without tiring you out.

Jamie has really enjoyed the training sessions with him this week, he's brutal alright, he puts their bodies through hell, but the outcome is that they're fitter and they have more stamina. He's going to show Sean when he gets home, it'll help him with his training, give him a good start.

Turning off the dual carriageway back into the village, he can see some lights on in the houses, people starting to come to life. 0738hrs, that's really good going. He opens the door and decides he'll message the lads and let them know he managed ten miles in ninety-eight minutes, a personal record. Something they'll all try and beat now, no harm in a little bit of healthy competition amongst them.

Taking Jess a cup of tea up, he intends to wake her up before he gets in the shower as it'll take her twenty minutes or so to get herself up and subsequently *actually* wake up. He smiles to himself, *a bomb could go off around her and she'd sleep through it.*

'Babe?' nothing, not even a twitch, 'Baby, wake up darling, it's nearly eight, I've made yer a cup of tea. I'm now going in the shower.' He bends down, his face and hair are all sweaty but he doesn't care, he gives her a kiss and strokes her face and she begins to stir.

'Good morning gorgeous,' he smiles and tells her again that he's going for a shower but not a shave, he'll leave that for later.

She sits up slightly, still half asleep, she can see he's been out for a run. She asks him the time and he tells her its 0757hrs and then continues to tell her about his time that he managed the ten miles in. She smiles, trying to show as much interest as she can but at this time of day it proves to be very difficult. She'll tell him later how well he's done, once she's awake properly and in the talking mood.

She sits up in bed, cradling her cup, thinking to herself, *this time next year I could be a mum or pregnant.* This thought has been playing through her mind all week, she's even contemplated stopping the pill, *there's no point in carrying on is there?*

She thinks about Christmas and the wedding and New Year. The celebrations mean she'll be having a lot to drink, a lot of alcohol and one thing she definitely intends to do is stop drinking when she finishes her pill. She wants to give her baby the best start and she won't know in the beginning she's pregnant because she won't miss a period, which would normally be the sure sign of pregnancy.

No, Jess needs to make sure that if she conceives naturally, then her baby hasn't had any alcohol from the start, it has the chance to be the healthiest baby possible and most definitely the most loved and cared for baby ever. She's smiling at this thought and touching her belly, she can almost feel already what's it's going to feel like having a new life developing and growing inside her.

Jamie walks back into the room with his towel wrapped around his waist and sees her smiling and asks her what she's smiling at. She chuckles and tells him what she's thinking about.

He agrees with her, entirely. He thinks it's the best thing for their baby that when she gets pregnant, there'll be no drinking of any kind. He can't abide seeing a pregnant woman smashed out of her face, smoking and taking drugs like he saw back home, some of the women on the estate, popping kids out yearly, always drunk or high on some sort of drugs. No, his baby will have the best start in life and definitely be the most loved baby to be born on this planet.

Jess jumps up out of bed, she has a new spring in her step this week, she can see her future as a mother coming to reality, it's no longer just a dream.

While Jamie starts getting ready, he asks her how she would feel about moving. That when they start a family he wants her closer to him, he doesn't want to be away all week and only home for the weekend. No, if Jamie is going to be a father, he wants to be there for every occasion possible and he will be the best father a child could have. His kid will never know what it's like to grow up without one.

'We definitely need to talk this through, but let's leave it for now, can we discuss it after New Year?' Jess asks him, not really wanting to think about moving right now, she's only just moved here. Not that she would go against Jamie's very sensible observation about being together to bring up their child of course. Definitely best left until a little later, they have a lot to take care of today and she wants to get into the Christmas spirit.

'Yeah, good idea, I need me thinking head on for this shopping trip.'

'Just make sure you have your wallet, you're going to need it!' she laughs, meaning every word.

There wasn't a lot of traffic on the journey into town. They took Jess' car, but Jamie drove as she added him to her insurance policy earlier in the week, deciding it would make life easier when they visit his family or go anywhere long distance if he drives. She realised in doing this, just how expensive her car insurance is, she never dealt with it in the past as Anthony would always sort it. She'd get her new car every two years and he would sort out all the finance, the tax and the insurance, but now she's standing on her own two feet financially so she is dealing with it all.

'I'm thinking of changing my car,' she shares with him as they enter the town centre and head for the car park.

'Why babe?'

'I don't really need a car like this, it's a luxury car, I don't need anything like this anymore.'

'I know what yer mean babe, have yer thought about what you'd like instead?'

'No, don't be silly, I haven't a clue. I need to talk to my dad, he took over the finance agreement after the separation. I need to see if I can trade it in yet and how much equity I have in it, if any.'

Jamie thinks about how much her dad helps her out financially, he worries that he'll never be able to live up to his mark. After all he's only a private in the British Army, the lowest ranking soldier, *could she really adjust to his way of life?* He does know, however, that with his future promotions his salary will increase. He wants to feel proud to be the provider of his family, he doesn't want Jess running back to Daddy every time they need something like a new car or something for their house.

'Jess, I need to talk to yer about the kind of life I'll provide for yer, I'm worried that it's not going to be the kind that yer' used to.'

He never calls her Jess, he's serious, she can see it. She can sense that he's genuinely worried about this.

'Hey, stop. Stop it now. I'm serious Jamie. If I've learned anything over the years, I've learned that money doesn't buy you happiness. As long as we have a roof over our heads and food on the table, anything else is a bonus,' she says, feeling quite upset at the fact he might feel inadequate as a provider, that he's worried she won't be happy with the life they will live. She squeezes his leg lovingly, in reassurance that everything will be fine. She really doesn't care if they live in married quarters, as long as she's with him, that's all that matters to her.

'I love you Jamie, I love you with all my heart, as long as I'm with you I really don't care where we live in the future.'

Jess has had a very privileged life, she can't deny it, growing up she never wanted for anything. Married life was pretty much the same, however, she never had the love. Although her parents loved her, her mum always seemed disappointed with something, be it her choice of friends or her exam results - it didn't matter, she never seemed happy with Jess's achievements, until she met Anthony. Her mum knew he had a thirst for money and that he could provide a lifestyle her mother wanted for her only daughter. But then look how that all turned out. Perfect example of money not buying happiness.

They pull into the car park, it's pretty empty. Once he's found a space and parked, Jamie can't help noticing that other drivers are looking at him getting out of the driver's seat of the car, it's definitely a luxurious vehicle, the type you'd expect to see an older guy driving not a nineteen year old. He can't help feeling just a little bit smug - he does like this car.

CHAPTER 69

Christmas Shopping

'First things first, let's get a nice breakfast,' Jamie says decisively as they're leaving the car park.

'Ok, what do you fancy?'

'You. Open yer legs,' he laughs as he pulls her towards him and kisses her, she's getting used to him kissing her in public now.

'You're terrible,' she laughs at him.

Finding a nice coffee shop they each order an English breakfast with an Americano. Jamie gets his list out and discusses it with Jess. They decide to start with his nieces as he wants to leave his mum until last, he needs to concentrate and make sure he watches and takes note of what Jess likes.

After breakfast they head to the toy shop to get his nieces' presents, buying Sofia a ride on scooter and Annabel a talking teddy. Next they head to the perfume store as he's decided on gift sets for his sisters, his sister-in-law, his brother Joe and his brothers-in-law, Steve and Jed. Sean is already taken care of, Jamie's bought him a Fitbit to help him with his training, he bought it half price with his mobile phone upgrade.

They decide to take the presents back to the car. It's nearly twelve-thirty already and the town is ridiculously busy. Getting through the crowds without bumping into everyone is becoming very stressful, he feels like he definitely needs a pint. Walking back into the town centre they head for a jewellery shop and as they're looking in the windows he can't help noticing her face light up as she spots something. It's a ring, a half carat princess-cut diamond solitaire. Elegant and classy, exactly the sort of ring he could imagine her wearing, not that big monstrosity of a thing that she has in her jewellery box.

'That's nice,' he says, pointing to the ring, 'it's very similar to the earrings you wore on Saturday.'

'Yes it is, it's beautiful, it's exactly what I wanted the first time around, if *we* ever get engaged, that's exactly what I would choose.'

'Woah, steady on there babe, one step at a time, baby first,' he laughs and gives her a kiss.

'Is there anything in here you think me mam would like?'

'Yes look, that bracelet there,' she says pointing to a lovely silver infinity style bracelet, he really likes it but feels he needs to get some more ideas for Jess, so he tells her he's not sure and they walk off but before he does he takes a photo of the ring she looked at without her seeing. He knows he'll be back for that.

They find a Pandora shop in the precinct and Jess tells him that the bracelets in here are unique and that he'll be able to buy her charms for it every birthday or Christmas.

After an hour and a half of queueing and then deciding what he was buying they eventually walk out with a bracelet that his mum will love, and he bought her a charm to start it off. He's pleased they went in there, he definitely got plenty of ideas for Jess' presents.

They head back to the car, hand in hand and feeling very loved up. Jamie can't help congratulating himself on an enjoyable day and a very productive shopping trip.

He has a lot to think about!

CHAPTER 70

Temptation

They're finally back home, car unloaded and kettle on. Although Jamie is going out tonight for Nobby's stag do, he wants to try and have something to eat that will help soak up the alcohol and hopefully minimize the guaranteed hangover tomorrow. Jess offers to cook beef stroganoff with rice or mash potatoes and broccoli. He thanks her gratefully and opts for the rice option.

He takes all the presents upstairs and puts them in the spare room, it's more like Jamie's storage room than Jess' spare bedroom. He laughs at this thought as he walks out and shuts the door.

'Babe, guess what we didn't get?' he says as he comes back downstairs.

'What?' she says, frowning as she's sure he bought for everyone on his list during their shopping trip.

'Wrapping paper.'

'Oh not to worry, it's okay, I'll pick some up on my way home one evening this week.'

What he doesn't know is she has booked Wednesday afternoon off work, to go Christmas shopping for his presents. Her parents presents are being delivered in the week, she bought them online already.

'Ooh, while I think about it, my parents pressies are arriving on Wednesday, any chance you can stay in for me and sign for them please?

'Yeah sure,' he says, thinking he needs to go into town on Monday or Tuesday latest in that case.

'I'll drop you to work Monday and Tuesday if you want,' Jamie offers, thinking he will use her car to go to town.

'That'll be nice, you'll need to collect me as well though.'

'Nah, you can hitch a lift back,' he teases her with a wink.

'Oooh, cheeky.'

'I'm going out at seven tonight, what time will dinner be ready babe?'

'Around five, once I've prepared it all,' she says, quite enjoying being able to cook for him, making sure he's eaten properly before he goes.

'Great, I'm horny, in fact I've been horny all day,' he tells her, laughing and wrapping his arms around her as he kisses her neck. He felt it as soon as he got out of the car and told her he wanted to eat her. She tells him she's horny too, but she is looking forward to having some alone time tonight.

She prepares the stroganoff and pops it in the oven to cook, soaks the rice in cold water, intending to cook the rice and broccoli afterwards. Jamie chases her upstairs, his cock is hard, it's throbbing for her, he needs to taste her juices, he needs to fuck her before he goes out, he can't go out horny especially to the lap dancing club, he wouldn't trust himself, not yet, it's too soon into their relationship.

He's never really thought about committing to one person before, having sex with the same person forever and a day, well not until he met Jess. But… he still doesn't trust himself, he doesn't know how he'll react in the club, *will it be too much temptation?* Is he strong enough to walk away?

He has his top off and jeans undone by the time they reach the bedroom, daylight is fading, even though its only 3.30pm and the winter night is drawing in. They leave the lights off and curtains open so all they have is the light from the street lamp outside the bedroom window. Jess can't help but notice how different he looks this week, his biceps are more refined, his abs are definitely tighter, she tells him as he's kissing her neck while he undresses her.

'It's that trainer from the marines, he's got us doing different stuff, teaching us breathing techniques and pushing us further. I felt it this morning on the run, there's no way I'd be able to do ten before without struggling the last couple but today I didn't, I swear I could have done another ten if I'd had the time.'

'I like it, I love how fit you're looking,' she says, really turned on by his body, she can feel the strength and power in his arms even if it's a hug or he pulls her towards him, she loves his masculinity, he's strong - mentally, physically and personality wise. He's definitely coming into his own, 'evolving' as the hunter, the provider, the leader. Yes, she can see it now, Jamie is evolving into his role as *the man of the house.*

'So long as it keeps you turned on, I'll keep on going,' he laughs, but he's serious, he needs her to keep her libido high, he has a high sex drive, he knows this, he wouldn't want to give way to temptation because he's not getting enough at home.

CHAPTER 71

Vulgar

He tells her to get on all fours, he wants to fuck her from behind, he can smell her juices before he puts his cock in, he tells her and she agrees, she's always turned on these days. Just the thought of him gets her juices flowing.

She climbs on the bed, in the doggy position. He tells her he's fucking her arse first, he wants to see her cumming before he licks her out and then he'll fuck her pussy, before he climaxes.

He's being vulgar, he's feeling dirty, he's so hard, she can feel it as he goes in, slowly to begin with but once he's in he's fast, it's tight, he loves the feeling of her tight arse around his hard thick cock.

She's moaning loudly, she can't help herself, he wants her to be loud, the louder the better, he gets faster, fucking her arse hard and deep.

'Scream baby, I want to hear you scream, tell me you want me, tell me you want it deeper.'

She can't talk, she mutters a few words like 'deep' and 'hard' but can't say anymore while she's climaxing, the pleasure of being fucked hard in her arse is making her climax over and over. He can feel he's close to cumming, he needs to stop. He slows down and slowly pulls out but tells her to stay there in the same position she's in.

He bends down and starts to lick her pussy, it's full of her cum, it's dripping out all over his tongue, he loves it, he wants more. He pushes his face into her, his tongue deep in her pussy, holding her legs he sucks and licks, over and over, the whole time she is cumming again.

This man has opened her up in every sense, to reveal her innermost feelings, her ability to climax time and time again, she has no boundaries with him, he pushes them, pushes past them. She loves it, she wants him more than she's ever wanted anyone before.

He stands up and pulls her back towards him, he tells her he's going to fuck her, he wants to cum deep inside her. He pushes his cock hard into her pussy, hurting her, she's not sure why he's being the way he is, he's being extra rough, but not in a nice way, its vulgar, it's as if he's treating her like he doesn't care, that's not Jamie.

He starts to fuck her, he's fast, he doesn't stop, she's loud, louder than normal, he's telling her how he wants to fuck her, he wants to hear her scream,

'Scream baby, scream for me again, show me how good it feels,' then he goes quiet, his body rigid and he shudders as he empties himself into her, boy has he climaxed!

Jess collapses on to the bed as he lies next to her. She's looking at him, he looks different, she can't put her finger on it but she's not seen this look before. He leans forward and kisses her, he tells her loves her, he loves her very much.

He's going out tonight with the lads, to the lap dancing club, only tonight he won't be getting a lap dance or going back with the dancer. No, tonight he'll be coming home to Jess, he's made sure of it.

CHAPTER 72

Stag Night Out

Jess drops him off at The Bowl and he leans over and kisses her, lovingly and passionately, telling her he loves her and he won't be home late.

Walking into The Bowl, he sees most of the group are there already, only two more to join them. There's ten of them out tonight, so they'll definitely need two taxis.

'Who's for shots?' Jamie shouts out above everyone as Charlie and Owen walk in. A loud cheer goes up from them all, so he leans over the bar and orders ten Jaeger bombs.

They down the shots and Gavin orders the same again, the night is going to get messy. Ten squaddies out on a stag night and with Christmas celebrations in the air everyone is in high spirits.

After a couple of pints, the taxis arrive and they head into town. One of the guys in the other taxi moons at a group of girls standing outside a pub in the centre of town as they drive past. It causes a rapture of shouts and cheering from the other four lads in the taxi.

They're all pretty well known in the town by the doormen, many of whom are ex-military themselves. The banter on the door with them is always good, there's never any trouble getting in and the guys on the door look out for them, making sure they don't get into any trouble or cause too much of it either.

They make their way around the town, rowdy, drunk and full of excitement, it's nearly eleven when they head for a couple of taxis to go to the club. It's just over a twenty minute drive from the city centre. Pulling up outside, Jamie can see it's busy, it's bound to be, the last Saturday before Christmas so everyone is out.

Getting out of the taxis the doormen greet them, they're fond of the lads, Nigel the head bouncer is ex forces, he still has the stature and demeanour of a soldier and can relate to them all, he often used to sit and chat with them at the end of the night, he's a man with many stories to tell. The lads shake his hand one by one as they walk in, they don't need to pay for entry as he lets them all in free of charge.

The club is split over two levels, the ground floor is the night club and the upstairs is the lap dancing club as well as having the private booths, where you go for a private dance. The stage is in the centre of the room with three poles. One at the front of the stage and one on either side, there are lots of tables and chairs dotted around the room as well as plenty of stools at the bar.

They all head to the bar on the ground floor, they're rowdy and loud and are all known by the bar staff, it's not long before they've ordered drinks followed by more shots.

They stand near the edge of the dance floor, Nobby's talking to Jamie, telling him how chuffed he is that he's his best man and how much Shelley loved Jess. Jamie agrees with him and tells him Jess loved Shelley and how pleased he was they all got on. He looks over his shoulder toward the end of the bar, he can see a few of the girls have come down from upstairs to mix with the crowd and encourage them to go upstairs for a private dance or just to buy some drinks upstairs. He looks again toward the end of the bar and sees Cassie, whenever he's been here in the past she's always made a play for him, always given him a free dance and the last time he was here she took him home. He thinks about the sex they had, it was good for a one night stand, but Jamie being Jamie, left as soon as he'd finished. She took offence to this and turned nasty towards him when he left, he can't help wondering if she's going to make a show of him in here tonight.

He looks at her as she's looking straight at him leaning into a fellow dancer and whispering into her ear, not taking her eyes off Jamie the whole time. Her mate looks at him and they both laugh, like silly school girls, Jamie last saw this kind of behaviour in the school playground, he can't stop himself from laughing out loud and shakes his head in disgust and turns his back on them.

He's drunk, he's had a good night and he's ready to leave. He takes thirty quid out of his pocket, shoves it in Nobby's top pocket and tells him to go and have one last dance on him, he's getting out of here. Nobby knows exactly what's going on, he knows Jamie's probably fucked most of the girls in here and he can see how much Jamie's changed already in the short time he's been with Jess, he's pleased about that, Jamie used to be a bit too wild.

Jamie tells the rest of the lads he's out of here, he's had enough for one night and they'd better make sure Nobby gets back in one piece or Shelley will have their balls on a plate.

As he walks outside to get a taxi, there's plenty coming and going this time of night, he can see Nigel is saying something but can't hear him over the music pouring out from the open doors of the club.

'What did yer say Nige mate?'

'You're not leaving us already are you Jamie?' Nigel asks in surprise.

'Yeah mate, I am.'

'Cassie will be upset, I told her you were here, you got a better offer somewhere else tonight eh lad?'

'Ha, yeah, something like that.'

'Well I don't believe it, Private O'Halloran, you're telling me you're not fucking this one and leaving?'

'Nah, not this one Nige.'

'Ok lad, well wish her Merry Christmas from me.' Nigel laughs and salutes.

Jamie salutes back, gets in the taxi and heads home thinking to himself, *once a soldier always a soldier* and can only imagine what a soldier Nigel would've been.

CHAPTER 73

Some Alone Time

Jess offers to drop Jamie off at The Bowl for his night out with the lads, it's cold out and quite a walk from the house, not that any of that would bother Jamie.

Driving onto camp through the back gates she can't help but feel a sense of pride, pride for Jamie for what he does, she's never felt proud of any one before, other than her dad. She's noticed a difference in him tonight, he's been strange, it's his first proper night out with the lads since they got together, she wonders if it's because he's excited.

He leans over and gives her a loving and passionate kiss, telling her how much he loves her and that he won't be late home. She tells him to have a great night with the lads, it's Christmas and he deserves it, 'Let your hair down babe,' she says.

Walking back into the house, she notices how alive the atmosphere feels, even though it is currently empty. It's changed, it's definitely more homely since Jamie has been staying there.

Jess decides to have a nice glass of wine with a hot bubble bath, so she lights her candles, and puts some music on, not loud, just a little background noise. While her bath is running she starts to write a list of things for her suitcase.

The plan is that she drives to her parents' house on Christmas Eve and Jamie leaves for his mum's, then on the twenty-seventh she's going straight to the hotel, it's pointless her coming back here, over an hour in the wrong direction. She's told her mum that she needs to leave around eleven in the morning, she has a friend's wedding to attend on the twenty-eighth, so wants to head back early to get herself sorted out. *It's kind of true*, she says to herself, *I do have a wedding, but I'm not coming home I'm staying in a hotel two hours away,* that's a little white lie, but the less her mum knows, the better.

Jamie's taking her suitcase with him, so she needs all her wedding clothes, New Year's Eve outfit and enough clothes for the three days at his mum's. That's a lot of to pack, she'll need her big suitcase for this one. Walking into the spare room, it looks like Jamie's own personal wardrobe, all his uniform hanging up, laundered and pressed, shiny brass buttons and polished boots, she touches his number one uniform, the one he's wearing for the wedding, lightly running her fingers down it, the biggest smile on her face, she can see him in it already, her beautiful amazing boyfriend. She feels so proud.

She gets in the bath, and lies down, her hair in a bun so as not to get wet, fully relaxing, she melts into the hot water. What an amazing feeling, at this moment in time she's not got a care in the world.

The water starts going cold and her glass of wine is empty, she looks like a 'dried prune' but she's relaxed, it feels good. She dries off in the warm bathroom and puts her dressing gown on, she actually feels like she could just get into bed now, so she goes down and locks up, turning all the lights off except the porch, she leaves that on for Jamie, God knows what time he'll get in and what state he's going to be in, she can only imagine.

Her clock says 8.30pm she can't believe she's getting into bed at this time of night on a Saturday, but the truth is she's exhausted, she needs a good night sleep. Jamie's insatiable, his sexual appetite is tiring, not that she wants to complain, she loves it, she can't get enough of him herself, but she is tired, the late nights and early mornings, have worn her out, so she's going to sleep.

It feels like she's only just gone to sleep when she wakes up to the sound of a car door, and listening carefully she hears his key in the front door and his footsteps up the stairs, he's home already. She checks the clock, 1.32am, wow, she definitely wasn't expecting him home this early.

He walks into the bedroom and bends down to give her a kiss, he holds her face, his forehead touching her, he holds it there for a moment or two.

'Are you ok?' she asks, wondering why the forehead touching thing, maybe to steady himself, but he doesn't seem as drunk as she expected him to be.

'Yeah, I am.'

'You're home early,' she says with genuine surprise.

'Yeah, I was bored and I missed yer.'

She kisses him again and tells him to get into bed, he's drunk, but not steaming drunk, she's still shocked, she actually didn't think he'd be home until a good few hours later. He gets into bed and completely envelopes her with his body, kissing the back of her neck while saying something she can't make out, his voice is muffled against her.

'What did you say?' she asks him, turning her head to position her ears closer to his mouth.

'I love yer baby, I love yer with all my heart, I'll never be unfaithful, I promise yer.'

Jess opens her eyes as if a light bulb has just gone on, she realises in that moment that the look she saw on him earlier was fear. He was frightened, not because of her but of himself, his own actions, he didn't trust himself and it scared him.

She moves in closer, if that's possible and says, 'I know you won't, I love you too and I'm glad you're home early, let's go to sleep.' She kisses his hands and closes her eyes, she can feel his whole body weight on her, holding her tight with a vice like grip as he engulfs her, his whole body wrapped around her, but she doesn't care, not tonight, not ever.

CHAPTER 74

Princess Cut Diamond

Jamie drops Jess off in work at 0900hrs, giving her a loving kiss before she gets out of the car. She blushes when she sees various co-workers walking past, Jess is a very private person and ordinarily not one for public displays of affection. Jamie is the opposite, he doesn't care what people think, he loves her and shows it, no matter where they are.

He heads straight for town to do her Christmas shopping, he has lots of ideas but wants to check something out first, something that caught her eye on Saturday. He parks up and when he's getting out of the car he hears someone, not sure who it is or what they said, he looks round, it's Nigel, the head bouncer from the club.

'Alright Nige, mate?'

'Nice wheels there Jamie.'

'Yeah, thanks, it's the missus' car, just dropped her off at work and need to do Christmas shopping for her.'

'Fuckin hell, never thought I'd hear them words out of yer mouth Jamie lad!' the surprise shows clearly in his voice.

'Me neither mate, me neither.'

'Joking apart mate, yer seem like yer got yerself a good'un, don't fuck it up, yer'll do well in the army if yer got a good woman behind yer,' he says in an almost fatherly concern for Jamie.

'I won't, I'll make sure of it. Catch yer soon Nige, look after yerself.'

'Back at yer Jamie, stay safe mate.'

Jamie walks off into the city centre, he needs to find the jewellery shop he took a photo of at the weekend. Looking at his phone, he realises it's on a side street. He finally finds the shop and looking in the window he's comparing the rings to the one on his camera, but he can't find it, so he nips inside.

He chats to the very friendly sales woman and she asks him what ring size he needs. He hasn't got a clue, how will he find that out? She tells him to try a ring on his little finger and make a mark where it sits. She gives him all the details of the ring on headed note paper.

Description:

Half carat, princess cut diamond solitaire. £1,150.00, ref: YR201089

A classic princess cut diamond mounted in a stunning tiffany style setting allowing the maximum amount of light to pass through the diamond. Mounted on an elegant D-shape tapered band.

He asks if it will still be available to buy in the New Year, maybe around April or May. She tells him that it's a new season product, so will definitely be available but if it's not in the shop it can be bought online or ordered in. He thanks the lady and leaves, thinking how to find a way of getting her ring size. He knows what he needs to do, he's going to have to try her old wedding ring on for the size, he'll sort that out in the New Year, for now he needs to think about her presents, as that's the main reason he's in town.

He heads to the Pandora shop, it's really empty this morning compared to Saturday. He finds the bracelet, a lovely heart-clasp snake-slider chain and he buys a charm to go with it, Disney's 'Lady and the Tramp' dangle charm. He sees the irony in it and hope's that Jess will too, that she doesn't take offense to it, squaddies have a strange sense of humour.

On his way to the perfume store, he passes Ann Summers. Walking in he wonders what on earth he could buy her from here, but he's soon deep in thought looking at the underwear, in fact he's getting a hard on thinking of her wearing it. *For fuck's sake* he thinks, *I can't be walking around town with hard on*, and he laughs at himself as he walks out with a boxed black lace 'Baby Doll and Brazilian' set.

He goes to the perfume shop and can't decide whether to buy a gift set or just a bottle of perfume, of course the helpful assistant talks him into a gift set, costing him an extra twenty pounds, but what the hell, she's definitely worth it.

Finally he reaches her favourite high street clothes shop, and thinks *fuck me, where do I start?* He has a plan, he calls Nobby and asks to speak to Shelley, he explains to her where he is and what he is doing, so she talks him around the shop and he gets to the tills with a Tote bag, a pair of jeans, a nice cowl neck jumper and a belted knee length, camel coat with a fur collar.

He thanks Shelley and hangs up as the cashier rings up the items, he's not looking forward to this bill, he's definitely using his credit card on this lot. Four hundred and seventy pounds Shelley's just cost him! He should have just asked a sales assistant, he remembers now how much Nobby spent on her engagement ring because he gave her a choice. Mental note to self for future present buying - don't phone Shelley!

The final shop is the card shop, with card and wrapping paper now bought, it's time to head home, he needs to wrap and hide it all somewhere, until Christmas Eve, when they exchange presents before heading off in different directions, something he's not looking forward to. Next year will be different, he's convinced she'll be preggers by then, so they won't be going anywhere, people can come to them.

On his way home he decides to visit a local dealer and get some brochures on new cars, something that will be suitable for when they have a family, he chats to the salesman about finance, he doesn't want her dad involved in this, he's going to sort it, after all he's the man of the house or at least he will be by then. The salesman tells him that he qualifies for their military discount, but might struggle with the finance company due to him not living in the same place for three years, but he's happy to look into it for him when Jamie's ready.

He leaves there feeling slightly deflated, that's really not what he wanted to hear, but decides he's not thinking about it for now, he'll wait till the time comes and weigh up his options. He'll also have a chat with Joe nearer the time and see what he thinks is the best option.

He pulls onto the driveway, unloads the car and immediately starts wrapping everything as soon as he gets it inside. He signs her card and hides it in the wardrobe to wait until Christmas Eve morning. Feeling happy with himself, he starts to prepare dinner, he's making a chili con carne as it can simmer away while he goes to collect Jess from work.

In the meantime, he's so turned on at the thought of her in her baby doll outfit, he goes upstairs for a wank. Perhaps he should give her that present the night before Christmas Eve. Either that or he'll be heading back to his mum's with a hard on, he laughs, it wouldn't be the first time and he doubts it'll be the last.

CHAPTER 75

Half Day

Driving into work this morning, Jess couldn't help feeling a bit lonely, she's quickly become used to Jamie dropping her off and picking her up these past couple of days, in fact she's got used to him being there 24/7.

If they're going to start trying for a baby in January then perhaps they should consider him moving in properly. After all, when he posts out in June, he'll be coming back every weekend so they may as well start the New Year as they mean to go on, as *common law husband and wife*. She smiles at this thought.

It doesn't take long to reach town and she eventually finds a parking space. It's surprisingly busy today, very similar to Saturday, she knows she needs to be finished by four-thirty otherwise she'll be late home and she definitely doesn't want to arouse any suspicion on what she's been up to today, it's meant to be a surprise.

First stop is the coffee shop which they went into on Saturday, she needs some lunch and a coffee, all to go, as she doesn't want to waste time. She chooses a warm croissant, with ham, tomato and emmental cheese and a skinny latte, changing her mind about having it to go as it'll be easier to eat it in - after all you can't shop with hands full of food and drink.

Sitting alone at the table she opens her phone to check her list, she's been getting ideas from their conversations, plus what she likes and thinks would look nice on him. When Jess was married, Anthony was all about labels, which made buying for him really awful - everything had a huge price tag and what he didn't have he didn't need or wouldn't wear, so it just sat in the wardrobe forever and a day, a complete waste of money in her mind. Jamie's list was nice and simple.

Jamie gift ideas:
• Running trainers – size 8 £120.00
• Every day trainers – size 8 £75.00
• Running shorts – 30" waist £25.00
• Running jacket- Medium £65.00
• Jean's - size 30" short £55.00
• Jumper – medium £60.00
• Aftershave - £60.00
• Toiletries- £20.00
• Card -£5.00
• Total £ 485.00

Wow, he's cheap, she says to herself, I could get used to this, not having to spend on credit cards and then take all year clearing them. She realises she hasn't used her credit card since leaving Anthony, her dad cleared the debt on it, it wasn't much, around two grand but he told her he didn't want her worrying about credit card debt, she has enough to deal with. Her dad is her rock, he's always been there, never judged, just listened, perhaps that's how she tells her parents, tell her dad about Jamie, he can then tell her mum. He's met Jamie, he said himself "he seems a nice boy" because to him, anyone under forty is referred to as "a boy" or "a girl". *Yes, that could be the way to do it.*

`She reaches the sports shop, feeling full from her lunch. The shop is busy, and the queue for the till is at least twenty people deep. She needs to find an assistant to pick both sets of trainers, whilst she picks the rest of the sportswear.

She can't help picking up a couple of packets of trainer socks and some branded boxers shorts, adding an extra sixty pounds onto her spend, but she doesn't mind, *he's worth it*, she smiles to herself.

As she goes around the shop, she thinks about something she needs to talk to him about - his car. If he's going to keep commuting from June onwards then he'll need a new car, plus if she falls pregnant naturally she'll soon need a car suitable for a baby, so they need to look into their options. She's sure her car will be a good deposit for two cars, there's got to be at least ten to twelve grand in equity in it. She takes her phone out, fumbling around with the clothes on one arm, not wanting to wait now that it's on her mind.

Jess: [Dad, how much finance is left on my car & how much equity is in it? Xx]

She joins the queue with all his sportswear, his trainers are already behind the counter waiting for her and she hears her phone go already, she knows that's her dad replying to her message.

Tony: [Why darling? xx]

Jess: [I'm thinking of trading it in, something less expensive or luxurious, I don't need a car of this calibre xx]

Tony: [The finance is clear, I paid it off, last month, what you thinking of buying? Xx]

Jess: [Oh, really, wow thank you, you didn't have to, but I'm really grateful, truly, I am xx]

Tony: [It's ok, you've been through enough, we'll talk about a trade in over the weekend xx]

The weekend - she will be travelling up on Saturday to spend Christmas Day and Boxing Day with them, she feels really guilty not being completely honest with them now, but this weekend is not the time for her to tell them about Jamie, it'll have to wait until the New Year at least.

Another thought crosses her mind, that she can't tell Jamie her dad paid the finance off, because he'll never understand that. *He's from a single parent household, I on the other hand, well the last I knew my dad was earning eighty grand a year and that was twenty years ago, he must be on well over one-fifty grand a year now plus they have no mortgage, our lives are poles apart, no, I can't tell him, I don't want him to feel inadequate, because he's not, far from it in fact.*

She concludes these thoughts about money in her mind, that it doesn't make you a better person. It's kindness, empathy and a kind soul, that's what makes a person and Jamie is every bit of that person and some.

Finally, forty minutes after entering the sports shop she was served and is now heading to the perfume store for his aftershave, *now that should be a quick one*, she hopes.

The sales assistant tries her hardest to talk her into buying a gift set, but Jess is having none of it, he only wears the aftershave, as she told her, and eventually Jess gets quite cross with the sales girl's persistence and tells her that if she asks once more she'll walk out and go somewhere else to buy it. Needless to say, the sales girl finally takes the hint and rings up the items.

Walking out of the perfume store, she looks at her watch, ten past two, she's doing well with the time, now for the men's clothing shop, she knows exactly what she wants so that shouldn't take long, that just leaves his card, with a bit of luck she'll be finished by three o'clock and she'll get home early. She'll think of an excuse on route.

CHAPTER 76

Finance

Jamie drops Jess into work again, just as he has done all week except for Wednesday. She's not finishing until five today, her normal time, and he's a bit pissed off with this, he wanted to give her an early present before they go out.

He's heard a lot about this restaurant, apparently it's the best fish restaurant around here, the Serge knows the manager really well, due to the fact he takes his wife there regularly. It seems the manager is a big fan of the military, always gives the Serge loads of discounts, let's hope he does the same for Jamie. Their table is booked for 1900hrs and he's looking forward to it, he just wishes Jess could have finished earlier.

Jess is listening to him go on about it, he has a right moaning-minnie head on him this morning. He tells her how ridiculous it is that she couldn't leave early on the last working day. He's really worked up about this, she needs to know what's wrong, this is not like Jamie.

'What's wrong?' she asks him directly, 'you're like a bear with a sore head today.'

'I'm just pissed off,' he says, 'not with yer babe, just everything else.'

'What's "everything else"?'

'I just wanted it to be perfect, our first Christmas, but yer working till five, we gotta rush getting ready, then tomorrow I'm going home to me mams and yer going to yer parents. I just know I'm gonna miss yer like fuck and I can't even Facetime yer, it's all a fucking joke really, ain't it?'

Jess is quiet, listening as he vents. So that's what this is all about, them going their separate ways, made worse by her parents not knowing about him.

'Babe, don't be like this, it's not like you to be angry, it's our first Christmas, but it's not our last and besides I'll be with you on the twenty-seventh, it's no different from you being away with work.'

She was going to say it's no different for her, because she has to wait for you to text or just turn up back at home. She's only experienced it once and it was hell, she's got years of it to come, but she decided to keep that to herself, she didn't want to piss him off any further by saying the wrong thing, it's not worth it. She's sure he'll go straight to the gym after dropping her to work and release the frustration, that's what he usually does.

'I know, I just ... well, next Christmas we ain't going anywhere, yer'll be preggers and I'm not dragging yer around the country to see everyone, they can come to us. Well, that's unless yer parents still don't fucking know about me,' he's still angry, none of their conversation seems to be calming him. In fact he feels even more wound up than before.

'I'm going to tell my dad about you, he's met you, he liked you, he can then tell my mum but I can't tell them this weekend it's not the right time. I don't know why you're being like this, is there something else you aren't telling me?' Jess says, feeling that all this has really come up suddenly, he wasn't so bothered about her parents before.

He puts his head on his hands on the steering wheel, Jess can see something is eating away at him, and this argument is just an excuse, a front for something else.

'I took the car into a local dealers yesterday to see how much it's worth for yer to trade in, he had a look on his system and told me yer'd get thirty to thirty-two grand.'

'Ok, but why didn't you tell me?'

'I know I should have, but he also told me there's no finance on it. I just don't feel good enough for yer Jess,' he says, shaking his head.

'I only found out on Wednesday myself babe, honestly I didn't know before. Please don't feel like that, money doesn't make you any better than the next person.'

'Would yer have told me?' he asks, wondering why she didn't say on Wednesday.

'Yes, yes I would have. In the New Year, look let's not discuss this now, I want to talk to you about everything later, you, me, trying for a baby, commuting to and from your new base. Let's discuss it all tonight.'

'Ok, yeah let's talk about it tonight, I'm sorry baby, I just worry I'm not going to be enough for you.'

'Oh Jamie, you are more than enough for me.' She leans towards him and gives him a loving passionate kiss, she doesn't care if anyone's watching, a definite first for Jess.

'Now, get that sexy ass of yours to the gym and I'll see you back here at five.'

'Yes Serge,' he laughs and salutes her, but that's exactly what he's doing, he's going straight to the gym, he needs to work it all out of him.

CHAPTER 77

The Eve of Christmas' Eve

Jess is just finishing her hair then all she needs to do is get dressed. She's wearing a little black number tonight, black hold ups and two and a half inch patent black heels, so she'll be slightly taller than Jamie but he doesn't mind an inch.

She sees him standing in the door way with a big smile on his face, he seems smug, but one things for sure he's in a much better mood than this morning, the three hour gym session did him the world of good, just as she knew it would.

'What are you looking so pleased with yourself for?' says Jess, puzzled by his smug look.

'I have something for yer,' he says, smiling from ear to ear as he hands her a present.

'You're not getting any of yours until tomorrow,' she replies, laughing and taking the present from him. She opens it slowly, trying to work it out before she's even seen it, she finally unwraps it fully and reads 'Black Lace Baby Doll & Brazilian set' on the front of the box.

'You're not expecting me to wear this out are you?' she laughs and opens the box. She looks at it closely, she can see it's beautiful, she doesn't want to go out now, she'd be quite happy to put it on and let Jamie's hands and cock fuck her, caress her and make her cum wearing her new present.

'Not out no, but when we get back, yeah, absolutely. I've had a hard-on for four days thinking of you in it.' He leans in and kisses her, placing her hand on his crotch area, he's hard and she's not going to waste it, they have a spare ten minutes.

She slides off the dressing table stool onto her knees, undoing his zip she pulls his hard cock out and places it in her mouth, he loves this feeling, his cock sliding in and out with her lips around it. Her hands pulling him closer so his cock goes deeper in her mouth, she gags a couple of times so shuffles back a bit. He's moaning as she gives him a blow job, pulling her head back she licks the tip of his cock, her fingers are wanking him at the same, he likes this, he loves the gentle touch of her hands, the feel of her tongue as she licks his cock. He holds her head still as he thrusts his cock faster in and out of her mouth, he can feel he's going to come soon, another thrust, he can feel his cock throbbing, ready to release his cum into her mouth.

'I'm going to cum baby.'

He's holding her head, his cock pulsating as he fills her mouth with his cum and lets out a grunt as he's cumming. He holds her head for few moments longer after he's finished, she manages to move it slightly so as to swallow his cum but still keep his cock in her mouth.

She gets up off her knees and gives him a kiss, telling him she needs to finish getting ready or they'll be late, he doesn't care now, he'd quite happily stay in, but he can't, his Sergeant booked the table on his behalf.

They pull up in the car park at five minutes to seven, and it's packed already. Walking into the restaurant Jess realises she's been to one of these back home, it's a small chain of fish restaurants and she's never had a bad meal yet. She doesn't tell him that she's used this chain before, she doesn't want to ruin the night, he's excited to try it out for the first time.

The manager introduces himself when they walk in, Jamie tells him they have a table for two booked under the name of O'Halloran and he escorts them to their table. Once they're seated he returns a few minutes later with a bottle of white wine courtesy of his Sergeant.

Holding Jess's hand across the table, he tells her he's sorry for the way he behaved this morning, he should have discussed it with Jess first, after all it's her car, but he just wanted to help her.

She tells him it's fine, she understands why he did it but more importantly he needs to stop thinking he's not good enough for her, if she didn't think he was good enough she wouldn't be with him, she then tells him how she found out, well not exactly all the story, that she text her dad whilst on her lunch break and the reason she didn't tell him was because she knew he'd react the way he did, and she didn't want that.

'I'm sorry babe, I'm such a twat sometimes. I really put meself through me paces today at the gym to help clear me head. I thought about what yer said, I think, I just... I mean, we grew up so differently.'

Jess interrupts him, she tells him that she can't help it if her dad feels the need to help her out, whether he tells her or not, he shouldn't feel angry or resentful that even during her marriage he would help them out if they needed it, she tells him about the deposit he gave them to help buy the house, the one they've just sold.

He sits there in silence, just listening and thinking, the truth is, he's not jealous, he doesn't do jealousy but he can't help wishing his mum had been so lucky and able to live that life. The waiter comes to take their order and pours Jamie another glass of wine and as Jess is driving home he orders her a soft drink.

'I've been doing some thinking and I want you to hear me out,' says Jess, all serious and businesslike, while Jamie looks a little uncomfortable on the other side of the table.

'Go on, I'm listening,' he frowns.

'Well, we're going to start trying for a baby next month and you have practically moved in already, so why don't you move in properly when we come back from your mums?'

'Yeah, funnily enough, I was sorting me stuff out today for the wedding and the time I'm at me mums and I thought, practically everything I own is at yours, it's almost like I live there already anyway,' he laughs.

'The reason I asked my dad about my car was because I was thinking of trading it in, using it as deposit on two cars, one for you for commuting and the other for me, a family type car, you're going to need a decent one when you post out in June.'

'I'll only be an hour away, I'll be home on Friday and head back Monday morning, but that's something I've been thinking about as well, yer know. I actually think I've had too much time on me hands this week,' he laughs and takes a drink of his wine.

Jess laughs and agrees with him, then their food arrives and Jamie asks for a pint of lager.

'The thing is babe, I wasn't lucky enough to grow up with a dad, and have always said that when I have a family of me own I want to be there, I want me kids to know what it's like to grow up with both parents. What I do for a job isn't easy for anyone let alone a family but living in different parts of the country, well that's a whole new ball game.'

'I know what you're saying but let's cross that bridge when we come to it, take it step by step, but I still think you need a new car.'

He scoffs at her, raising his eyebrows, not in a nasty way but in a *that's because you're posh* way and says, 'We'll cross that bridge when we come to it.'

CHAPTER 78

Trying on her Pressie

Jess runs up the stairs like an excited child. She wants to try her present on so she kicks off her shoes and steps out of her dress, undoing her bra. Opening the box and lifting it out admiringly, she stands there in just her hold ups, puts it on over her head and pulls the pants up but then realises she needs to put these on first.

'For fuck's sake,' she says, as she slips back out of it.

She can hear Jamie shouting up to her 'How much longer yer gonna be?'

She finally gets the pants on and slips the baby doll on again. Standing in front of the full length mirror for a moment she can't help smiling, it looks amazing.

Jamie's stripped off, his cock hard in his hand as he strokes it, thinking of Jess in her pressie, it has driven him nuts this week, every time he thought about it his cock was hard. Finally he gets to see it.

'Are you ready?' she calls down the stairs.

'Yeah babe, my cock's rock hard and waiting,' he laughs. His cock is always hard whenever Jess is around or he thinks of her. *I'm going to explode before she gets in here if she don't hurry up*, he thinks to himself.

Jess walks in to the living room, he's never seen anything like it in his life, he can't contain his excitement, he's leaking pre-cum already, he needs to get control of himself, he's too excited.

Walking over to her and kissing her, he pulls on her hair, pulling her head backwards slightly but on an angle, his other hand rubbing and caressing her tits through the lace, he tells her how amazing she looks, how much he wants to fuck her, that he's going to fuck her, he's going to make her cum and cum, over and over again.

He stops kissing her and looks at her, telling her to open her eyes and look at him, he looks her in the eyes as he talks.

'Tell me baby, tell me what you want me to do.'

She can't think, her mind is blank, she's too excited, she has to think of something.

'Anything you want to do, I don't care.'

'Anything? Anything at all?'

'Yes! Yes, just do it,' she just wants him to get on with it, fuck this talking, her pussy is wet, she's turned on, she wants him to fuck her, make her cum.

He leans in towards her and whispers as he kisses her neck, he tells her he's going to lick her pussy juices, then he's going to stick his fingers in, as many as he wants, he wants to hear her moaning louder and louder, he wants to feel her cumming all over his hand.

She's so horny as he's talking, she can't control herself, he has her all to himself, he can do whatever he wants.

He carries on kissing her neck, his hand going down towards her pussy, spreading her legs apart with his feet, one at a time, he knows she's wet, he can smell her already.

He puts his hand around her throat, gently squeezing it, he looks her in the eyes and asks her 'Do yer trust me?'

She nods, she does trust him, she can feel his hand tightening, the strength in his hand is scary but fuck it's amazing. He squeezes a bit tighter, her eyes open wider, he's watching her, he wants to see her reaction as his other hand finds her wet pussy.

Moving her panties out the way with his fingers and finding her pussy he pushes two fingers inside, she lets out a moan, the fear of what he's doing with one hand and pleasure from the other in her wet pussy is sending her wild, she's no idea what this feeling is, he's in complete control, she knows it and he knows it.

He releases his grip slightly, he doesn't want to mark her but more than anything he doesn't want to hurt her. He starts to kiss her passionately, with his fingers deep inside her wet pussy. She grabs the back of his head, she tries to moan in pleasure but he's stopping her with his mouth pressed hard on hers, his tongue looking for hers. He feels his own strength, his dominance - in that moment he is in complete control of her.

He stops kissing her and takes his hand from around her throat, she moans as she drops her head on to his chest, he hears her, she's cumming already, he can feel it on his fingers, he leaves them in there for a few more seconds before taking them out.

Jamie can't help thinking how dominant he's become in the bedroom over the past few weeks, he's not a dominant person ordinarily but he likes this feeling, he knows it's because Jess trusts him, she's allowing him to be this person to push her boundaries and his, to be adventurous and by doing this they are discovering more and more about each other, their kinky side - it's fun, it's exciting.

'Are yer okay?' he asks, to make sure he hasn't hurt her.

'I'm fine babe,' she answers breathlessly, and leans in and kisses him.

He takes her hand and leads her upstairs, he wants her in the bedroom, on the bed on all fours. He wants to fuck her from behind in what she's wearing, he's going to move her panties to one side, his cock deep inside with the lace rubbing against his hard cock, he needs to feel this, feel what it's like.

They walk into the bedroom and he tells her to get on all fours. She does as she's told, she knows he's going to fuck her, there's not going to be more foreplay tonight, he's too turned on, he needs to cum, she can sense it.

He rubs the outside of her lace panties, over her wet pussy. They are soaking wet from her juices, he loves this feeling, he moves them to one side, holding them with one hand and positioning his cock in her pussy with the other.

Her pussy feels warm on his hard cock, he holds the outside of her thighs, slowly he moves back and forth, his cock moving in and out. He can feel the lace on his cock, the feeling is amazing, he tells her this, he tells her how much he loves to feel her warm wet pussy with his hard cock, as he's telling her this he's starting to thrust a little harder as Jess is starting to moan a little louder.

'Yes baby, let me hear you moan, louder baby, louder, show me how much you want me.'

She can't talk, his cock is thick and hard, it's deep inside, fucking her faster and faster, his grip on her thighs is getting tighter. This turns her on, his strength, his masculinity, him being in control, he has control of her, he tells her what to do, she wants more.

He's thrusting faster and faster as he hears her telling him 'Fuck me, fuck me hard, yes, yes, like that.'

He gets faster, his thrusts reaching deeper in her wet pussy, her juices all over his hard cock. He can't tell her he's cumming, he doesn't have time, he lets out a loud grunt as he thrusts one last time, his balls releasing his cum, deep inside her as he holds her tight, his body rigid followed by the shudder as he climaxes.

CHAPTER 79

Thoughts of Tomorrow

He's not going for a run tomorrow, no need for an alarm, he's decided to have a rest for the next two days. He'll take Sean out on Boxing Day, for a ten miler, so he can use the Fitbit he got him for Christmas. Jamie will also teach him the new breathing techniques to help him in his training.

Pulling Jess in closer towards him, he wraps his body around hers, he wants her as close as possible, after all he won't see her for three days. It's probably the most important time of year and they're going in opposite directions, this saddens him, he wants her with him, he can't bear to be away from her. After all he has to leave her for weeks on end with work, that's bad enough.

He's thinking of the journey home to his mum's, it's a two hour journey, he needs to be on the road by 1000hrs, but he can push it to 1100hrs if it gives them an extra hour together.

Before he goes he needs to pack the car up, his number one uniform is in its bag ready, his boots are on top of his bag, and all the presents that he and Jess wrapped are ready with her suitcase. He has no idea how long she thinks they're going away for, but judging by the size of it, she could last a month away from home, *this woman certainly doesn't travel light*, he smiles to himself.

He needs to go to sleep now, he kisses the back of her head and tells her he loves her, she doesn't answer as she's asleep already.

CHAPTER 80

Christmas Eve

Jess wakes unusually early for her, probably because she can't move, his grip is like a vice around her body. They've slept like this all night, he hasn't let her go, but doesn't care, she's missing him already and has no idea how she's going to cope at her parents' house, especially not being able to call him and talk to him, only a few texts but even that will be difficult in their company.

She feels herself welling up at the thought of not seeing or speaking to him until the twenty-seventh, it's bad enough when he's away with work, she can deal with it, it's what he does, but this, this is something different, this is because her mum is a snob and thinks no one is good enough, *oh Mum, why can't you be more like Dad?* She thinks to herself.

She moves slightly, she's got pins and needles in her arms from Jamie holding her so tight, she actually can't believe he's still asleep, *it's ten to seven, he never sleeps this long usually*, she's thinking to herself, just as she feels him kissing her on the back of her head and hears him say, 'Morning beautiful.'

Her heart melts, she loves this man more than anything, she's even thought about cancelling going to her parents for Christmas and going with him, but she can't, she has to keep up the pretence of being single for a few more weeks or a couple more months at the most.

She wishes him Happy Christmas, it's Christmas Eve, they're going to exchange presents before they go and she can't wait to see his face when he opens his new running trainers, he definitely isn't expecting them, she asks him if he wants to open his presents now or a bit later.

'We can open them in a bit babe,' he says, he just wants to cuddle a bit longer.

She doesn't care, they can stay in bed all day if he wants. She laughs and says 'We should just stay here, tell everyone we've changed our mind and we'll be up after the wedding and I'll tell my parents I'll see them in the New Year.'

'Really?' he asks her, 'do yer really want to do that? I wouldn't mind.'

In fact he thinks it's a great idea. She tells him they can't really, it wouldn't be fair on all their families, besides, they agreed that next Christmas they'll stay here together, just the two of them.

'Right you, I'm getting your Christmas presents, I'm too excited to lie here any longer,' she says grinning like an excited child.

Jamie laughs, he's excited too, to see her face when she sees what he's bought her, but first he needs the loo, then he'll get them from the spare room, where they're hidden.

Jamie's goes to the bathroom as Jess dives out of bed, his presents are all hidden in her wardrobe. How he's not seen them is a miracle. She lays them on his side of the bed, just as he walks in with her presents. Her face lights up when she sees them.

He's watching her as she opens them slowly, her eyes widening with excitement as she sees what's inside each one. She opens her bracelet last, she can't believe it, it's the one she looked at last week.

'It's beautiful, Oh Jamie! How did you know? I love it,' she tells him.

He passes her the last present to open, and she opens it quickly. It's a charm to go on the bracelet, she looks at him and rolls her eyes and says, 'It's a good job I know your sense of humour.'

He laughs, as he takes it off her to put on to the bracelet, her first charm, *Lady and the Tramp*.

It's time for Jamie to open his presents now. She sits and watches as he tears the paper off his running trainers, he's in shock, they cost a fortune. He can't believe she got him these, he's thrilled to bits with them.

He can't believe he has so many presents, he's not used to this many, but he's not complaining, he opens every one of them, thanking her and kissing her after each one. He's never been so spoiled at Christmas. He loves it.

'Baby, I'm blown away with me presents, I can't wait to wear these out running, I'm gonna keep me Jeans and jumper to wear on New Year's Eve.'

'Okay darling, I'm glad you like it all,' she says, with a beaming smile.

'Yeah, it's amazing.'

He moves all the presents off the bed and gets back in, he needs a shower, but not before he's made love to Jess, he'll get a shower afterwards.

CHAPTER 81

All Packed up

Jamie's been busy loading both cars, he looks in his, it is literally packed to the roof. 'I think I've got the wrong car!' he tells Jess.

He laughs at himself, he really has got the wrong car, he loves hers, he loves the smooth drive, the automatic gearbox, everything about its luxury, but his will have to do for a few days.

He checks his watch. 1036hrs, he needs to get going soon, this prolonged wait is killing him, he shouts up to her to see if she's ready yet.

'Nearly but not quite,' she replies.

Tutting, he sits back on the sofa and texts his mum.

Jamie: [Hi mam, I'll be leaving here at 1100hrs, so aim to be with you by 1300hrs. Xx]

'Baby, I've just text me mam and told her I'm leaving here at eleven, can yer hurry up?'

She shouts down, 'I'm just getting dressed now.' *It's his own fault*, she thinks to herself.

He made love to her after they opened their presents. It was sensual and passionate, she thinks it lasted for nearly an hour, his cock was hard and deep inside her, his hands caressing her breasts as he kissed her lovingly. She came so many times, it was soft and rhythmic, his hips gyrating with every movement, his beautiful strong body on top of hers, her legs wrapped around his. She can feel her juices starting to flow again, thinking of him, she's going to miss him, sleeping next to his naked body.

She shouts down that's she's ready and coming, *not quite literally this time though,* she thinks and laughs at her own childishness, but then reprimands herself at not being more grown up in other ways too. *Oh Jess, you're a 36 year old woman, why can't you just be brave and tell your mum, it's your life after all, what can she say?*

She walks into the living room and sees Jamie sitting on the sofa, clean shaven, his arms and chest looking hench in that T-shirt. She looks at the wet, cold weather outside and asks him if he's travelling in just a T-shirt. He tells her that he has his sweater in the car, the heating will be on, he'll be warm enough.

He laughs at her as she bends down and gives him a kiss, he holds her head, their foreheads touching and tells her how much he loves her and that he's going to miss her terribly, but he's looking forward to seeing her on the twenty-seventh and this is the last time they will be sleeping apart, other than when he's away with work.

'Right then, let's get this show on the road,' he says, needing to move on from the awful gut wrenching feeling of leaving her.

He tells her to go and get in the car and that he'll lock up. All the curtains are closed, the bathroom and hall lights are on. She dropped her key to Fred and Hazel's on Wednesday as Fred is going to check up on the house every day when he walks Buster. It was much easier to go round on Wednesday rather than today, she was home early and it was a good opportunity to take their gifts round.

He bends down inside her car, gives her a kiss and tells her to call him once she's arrived and he'll text her when he reaches his mum's. He shuts the door and walks to his car, he can see her eyes are full of tears as she reverses off the drive, he can't help but think that if she'd had the guts to tell her bloody mother, they'd be going to his mum's together today.

Jess drives out on the back road, it's the best way to her parents', she's not looking forward to this, not one bit, for the first time in her life she doesn't want to go home, it's not home anymore, this village, her house, Jamie, all this is home and this is where she belongs. She tells herself, this is the last time, next year will be different, whether they like it or not.

Next year will be so different, for both of them, Jamie moves into hers officially in January, he's going give his notice on the house he shared with his two mates to the MOD, empty his room completely and hand back his key.

When they come back after the New Year, they're going to start trying for a baby, for real this time. He's had lots of practice, he thinks to himself, laughing. He quite enjoys, no actually he loves this part, this is the best part. The sex, the dominance, the love making, tasting her juices, his fingers deep inside her warm wet pussy. 'Shit' he says to himself out loud, as he looks down, he's got a hard-on. The journey home is going to be interesting.

CHAPTER 82

The Long Journey Ahead

Jamie's journey back to his mum's is going well, there isn't much traffic on the road, but then again it's a Saturday and it's Christmas Eve, so he didn't really expect to see much .

He had to stop off at a service station, needing a quick wank. There was no way he could drive any more, his thoughts had gotten him too hard, it literally took him five minutes to cum in a cubicle in the men's toilet, not the best places but it had to be done.

Business finished, he picks up a white coffee from the coffee shop. The young girl behind the counter is really chatty, asking him where's he spending Christmas and New Year, smiling away as he tells her, then he tells her his girlfriend is joining him for New Year and she stops smiling. He can't help but laugh as he walks out, the young girls always make a play for him. He doesn't mind, he quite likes that he's attractive to the opposite sex, but he's not going to do anything, he'd never cheat on Jess, well not intentionally.

Getting back in the car, he thinks about some of the stories he's heard, from the older lads, the long service guys, about the tours they've been on and the places they've been. Some have stories of the women they've fucked while their wives are waiting back home, but then he's also heard about the wives, the ones who mess around with the single lads when their men are gone.

He's never really thought about it in the past, he never had a relationship, but now he has, there's no way Jess is messing around with another man, he will make sure she knows it's not acceptable, they aren't having an 'open relationship' or whatever you call it. No way, she's not allowed to fuck anyone else, ever.

He feels very possessive now, he's never felt this way before in his life. Is this the sort of man he's becoming? He's strong, both mentally and physically, that goes without saying, but he's noticed that he's become very 'dominant' recently. At first he thought it was just in the bedroom, he knows he's assertive and strong minded, that he's finding his feet, and becoming the man of the house, but he doesn't want to be a possessive man. A caring man and a good provider, yes, but not a possessive one.

His phone rings, interrupting his thoughts, it's Jess. She tells him she's at her parents, she is literally outside on the drive, he laughs at her and tells her he doesn't believe her, that she'll be parked up around the corner, like she was the last time.

She assures him she's not as she tells him her mum has just come out of the house and can see she's on the phone, Jess holds up an outstretched hand to her mum, meaning she'll be five minutes, her stomach is wrenching, this is the last time she'll hear his voice now until she meets him at the hotel.

He listens as she tells him she loves him and is missing him already, and to text her as soon as he reaches his mums and to have a safe journey.

He tells her he will, he loves and misses her too and if the opportunity arises, that she should tell her parents, after all they're going to be living together in January, he's not hiding anymore.

The car goes silent again, he looks ahead, and sees from the clock that he's still got an hour or so to go. He puts some music on, settles back in to his driving and thinks about his future, their future, he smiles - it's going to be a long journey but a good one.

CHAPTER 83

Seizing the Moment

Jess takes her bracelet off and puts it in her handbag before she gets out of the car, she doesn't want her mum to see it, not yet, she'll wear it on Boxing Day, they're out for a golf event at the local club which her dad is a member of.

She hears her mum's voice as she gets out of the car, 'Jessica, you're early, I wasn't expecting you until teatime, this is a nice surprise.' Her mum gives her a big hug and tells her how beautiful she looks, and that she's filled out since the last time she saw her, and it suits her.

'Jessica, you look so happy darling,' her mum is still chatting as Jess gets her weekend bag out of the boot along with the bag of presents. She asks her mum to carry her shoes in while she locks the car and they both walk in to the house making chit chat about her journey.

Jess puts the presents under the tree, takes her shoes and bag upstairs and hangs her clothes up in her wardrobe. Her mum and dad have had the house painted and redecorated, including Jess' room. It really doesn't matter that she left home in her twenties and is now a thirty-six year old woman this will always be her bedroom, for as long as they live here.

Sitting on her bed, she can hear her mum pottering around in the kitchen downstairs. This big house, the family home, is starting to feel less like the home she remembers, she looks around and sees it's all depersonalised. To a stranger it would look every bit a family home still but to Jess, she can see they are preparing to sell it.

Her dad will retire this year, they don't need a house this size, so it was inevitable that they would sell up one day, but she was hoping that her children would see this house, that they would come and stay with their nanny and grandad here, sleep in her room maybe, but sadly this won't be the case. She knows it won't happen now, her baby will visit them in their retirement home, the house they downsize to. Neither of these plans are that far in the future, in fact within the next twelve months, she's sure of it.

She goes downstairs into the kitchen where her mum has made tea and lunch for them both, Jess asks where her dad is and her mum tells her he's at the pub, that they didn't think she was going to arrive until around five-ish, so he nipped out for a few pints.

Jess goes quiet, she knows this is the opportunity to tell her mum. She thinks to herself *it's now or never.*

'Mum, I have something to tell you.'

Her mum looks at her with a loving, kind and caring expression, she's thinking how much she's missed her daughter.

'I have something to tell you too, well actually your father and I have something to tell you, but he's not here so I'll be the one to say it. But you first darling.'

Jess wonders what on earth could be so important that both of them wanted to tell her, but she brushes it aside, she has to be brave now, stand up for herself.

'I've met someone, he's a lovely guy, really hard working and…' she braces herself and continues, '… he's in the army, but you and dad will like him, I'm sure.'

Her mum scowls, the last thing she wants to hear is that Jessica has met a man in the army, she doesn't care for people like that, it's not a good life or future for anyone, let alone her only daughter.

'Now listen Jessica, I'm happy you're having fun, really I am, but I've told you before, those kind of men don't have a good future, you won't be able to settle anywhere, you know how much they move around.'

'Mum, this is different, I own my own house, I can stay where I am, besides you don't know anything about him and you're already judging him. Mum, listen, I married Anthony because he made you and Dad happy, it didn't matter to you that I wasn't happy.'

Her mum cuts in, telling her "that's not true, they only wanted the best for her and could see Anthony would do that, that he'd provide for her".

'It doesn't matter Mum, I'm happy and I love this man, whether you and Dad accept it or not.'

'Now Jessica, there's no need to involve your father with this nonsense, you have your fun with him and we'll not mention it again,' her mum purses her lips together, concluding her speech.

Jess has seen this look so many times, it's her 'disappointed' look, her mum has made her feel like a naughty little girl, she feels like she's eight years old again. How on earth is she going to tell Jamie that she tried? No she can't, she's going to have to lie to him, she needs to protect him from her mum.

The two women sit there eating in silence, she wants to go upstairs pack her bag and leave, this is exactly why she moved away, she had to, she could never live her life the way she wanted to around her mum.

CHAPTER 84

Christmas Decorations

Jamie pulls up outside his mum's house, it's all decked in lights and window decorations, something he's missed if he's honest. Jess didn't want to put anything up this year, "they weren't going to be there so it was pointless," she said.

He paps the horn, he's definitely going to need help today, he can't manage all this lot on his own. He hears her before he sees her, his mum is shouting at Sean to come down and help his brother carry everything into the house. She hugs him, her fourth child, the one she misses the most, the one she worries about the most, he was always a mummy's boy and still is, in her eyes.

Jamie hugs his mum and kisses her on the cheek, he tells her he's missed her and has lots to talk about, although he knows she wants to hear about Jess mostly. He's already told her loads over the phone or by text, but he hasn't told her he's moving in with her after Christmas and that they're going to start trying for a family. There's one more thing he hasn't told her, probably the most important one, and that is her age.

The car is unloaded and he and Sean take his stuff and Jess' suitcase upstairs. He can't leave it in the car, not around here, it's not like the village he lives in - it's not safe.

The boys come back downstairs and join their mum in the kitchen. The house is full of Christmas decorations, it looks so festive, with Christmas music playing, loads of goodies on the side, cakes, crisps, chocolates, pop and the obligatory Christmas nuts. A big bowl full, walnuts, monkey nuts, peanuts and some other things that you can't even begin to open for the love of God, and if you *are* lucky enough to crack one open the chances are you'll end up eating half the shell with it, because it's smashed into smithereens and you can't decipher between the nut or the shell. *Nah, them little fuckers can stay where they are*, he thinks to himself.

Jamie sits himself down and in response to a million questions from the both of them already, he starts to tell them about work, what he's been up to and the new breathing techniques he learned which will help Sean (promising to show him later and give him some new exercises to help him). He tells them about Nobby's stag night too, well most of it, he left out the part about the lap dance club, his mum doesn't need to know he goes to lap dancing clubs.

Sean leaves them to it, he's off back upstairs to carry on with his game, he's sixteen, he's seen his brother that's enough, Jamie tells him he'll come up in a bit and have a game.

It's just him and his mum, he really misses times like this, sat here with his mum chatting, telling her about the army, she's heard it a thousand times before but listens again and again, she loves to hear Jamie telling her about how great life is away from here.

'Mum, there's something I need to tell you, before you meet Jess.'

'I'm listening, what is it?'

'She's older than me, and not just a couple of years, a lot older.'

His mum sits in silence, she knows Jess is older, she can see in the photos he's sent her, and if the truth be known she always knew, in her heart of hearts Jamie would settle for an older woman as it's what he needs, she's always said "he's an old head on young shoulders".

Jamie tells her how old she is and watches for his mum's reaction, but she doesn't react, she simply smiles and grabs his hand and tells him,

'As long as you're happy and you love each other, which I can see you do, then I'm happy, and that's all I want, for you to be happy in life,' and she can see from his face, he is.

Anne will never judge her children for the decisions they make in life, she raised them to be strong independent people but to also know that she'll always be there for them no matter what.

CHAPTER 85

Early Morning Text

He wakes and checks his phone, its 0530hrs. Jess sent him a text when she went to bed last night and he got the impression she was upset, though she wouldn't say there was anything wrong. He worries about her, she's not the strongest woman, not like his mum. No, Jess is delicate, he knows it's his place to look after her, he will protect her from everything and everyone.

Jamie: [Happy Christmas baby, I love you & missing you xxx]

Jess: [Happy Christmas my gorgeous soldier, you've no idea how much I'm missing you xxx]

He doesn't like to think of her upset, come to think about it he doesn't like to see any woman upset. He can't handle crying, he sees it as a weakness, but he does know that women are generally emotional, that they'll cry at the strangest thing. Even if it's a happy event, women cry. He shakes his head as he thinks about it.

Jamie: [Hey, are you ok? I'm worried about you xxx]

Jess: [Yeah I'm good, I'll be fine xxx]

Jamie: [Why are you awake so early? Xxx]

Jess: [I wanted to text you before we got up, I set my alarm xxx]

He laughs to himself, but he knows there's more to this. He's only been with Jess a short while but he knows when something isn't right, and one thing he knows for sure is when his alarm goes off at 0530hrs, she doesn't stir, there's no way she set an alarm, she'd sleep through it, she does every day at home. No, there's something she's hiding. But he can't question her now, not like this, he'll wait till he sees her. For now he needs to make sure she's definitely ok.

Jamie: [I can't wait to see you in a couple days, I swear I'm gonna explode when you walk in that hotel room xxx]

Jess: [I'm not letting you out, I've decided, Nobby can choose a different Best man]

Jamie: [Yeah, I'll text him and tell him]

Jess; [I need to go, my dad is up, I'll text you later, Happy Christmas darling, I love you with all my heart xx]

He doesn't reply, it's pointless, she probably won't read it for hours, he decides it's time for a shower, he needs a wank, and can only have one in the shower here. He gets up, his morning glory in full swing, decides to put his pods in and turn a porn site on, this will get him closer to cumming quicker, then he'll finish off in the shower, or at least try.

CHAPTER 86

Festive Celebrations

So the last two days have gone exactly how Jamie predicted, his mum loved her bracelet, she showed the girls and Joe before she even wished them Happy Christmas, his siblings took the piss out of him, telling him he was after brownie points buying their mum such a lovely gift but it was all just banter amongst family.

They spent the day at Joe's, eating and drinking, Jamie told them all about Jess, including her age, and to his surprise no one seemed bothered, no one was shocked. *Is this what they expected of him?*

His sisters were asking what he bought her for Christmas, he told them about the perfume shop, the clothes shop and that it cost him over four hundred quid thanks to Shelley, he did however leave out the Ann Summers part, his family don't need to know that much.

They're all really excited to meet her and that she's coming to stay for New Year, Breda even asked what hat she should buy for the wedding. They all laughed, Jamie told them it will be a while yet and not to get too excited, besides Rosie's wedding will happen before his.

They had a lovely day yesterday and are doing it all again today, only it's at Rosie and Jed's with his mum, dad and little sister Tara, the rest of the family are going to their in-laws.

Jamie and Sean get up and head out running at 0600hrs, Sean is wearing his new Fitbit and Jamie his new running trainers, they're really comfortable, he can really feel the difference and he's not even out of the street yet.

He shows Sean some new stretches and teaches him the breathing exercises while telling him all about the PT instructor on secondment from the Royal Marines. He tells him that he's brutal but amazing, "no wonder they're fit," he says, Sean agrees with him, tells him he considered the marines but didn't think he'd make it, but it's something he wants to look into in a few years' time.

Jamie nods, he's impressed, Sean's thinking about his future in the forces. He thinks of Nigel the head bouncer, he can see Sean being like him, smiling to himself he puts his pods in, Sean has earphones as he doesn't like pods, and off they go, their bellies still feeling full from yesterday but they'll run it off. They're going to try and cover ten miles today and if Sean is up to it push it some more, so maybe even perhaps fifteen.

Jamie sent Jess a text just before he left, he hopes she has a nice day today, she didn't say much last night about how her day was, just that it was 'okay' and the dinner at the hotel was 'nice'. *Oh well,* he thinks, *time to concentrate on me running*, he picks up his pace and gets going into the cold, crisp morning.

Jess finally wakes around 8am, she checks her phone and sees a message from Jamie. Checking the time he sent it, she wonders if he's still out running. She messages back but it's not delivered, he's out of range which means he's still out. He said he'd be pushing himself today, he hasn't been for a run for two days and he probably has a lot of food and drink to run off from yesterday.

She can only imagine what sort of fun filled day he had, his niece all excited to see him, opening her and her baby sister's presents, she's looking forward to meeting them all and to celebrating New Year with Jamie and his family.

Jess wonders what today has in store, yesterday was nice, they exchanged presents before going to see her Nanna, she's not in good health and Jess can't help but think this is her last Christmas. They left after about an hour and headed to the hotel for Christmas Day dinner, she wasn't in the mood for drinking so offered to drive, she was happy to chauffeur yesterday.

Her dad's up, he knocks gently on the door to see if she wants a cup of tea and says that he'll bring it up to her, so she lays back down and waits for her cup of tea. Once she's had that she'll get in the shower before going for breakfast, they don't have to be there until 12.30pm so she'll have a lazy morning, she decides.

CHAPTER 87

Check in

Jess is up, showered and dressed by 8.30am and she's got a spring in her step. She's definitely in a better mood than she's been for the last two days with the hum drum of all the pretentiousness around her. Yesterday felt like her wedding day, it was awful, she couldn't wait for the day to end. She's hardly spoken to Jamie, so as soon as she gets in her car she's going to call him, she needs to hear his voice.

Her mum and dad are up when she walks into the living room, her dad gives her a hug and thanks her for driving over the last two days - it meant a lot to him. He tells her that he's sad to see her going so soon but understands as it's her friend's wedding.

Her mum is making breakfast for everyone, scrambled eggs with smoked salmon in a brioche bun, definitely a favourite of Jess'. It will be good for her to have a proper breakfast this morning, as she has a three and a half hour drive ahead of her.

She checks the hotel reservation to find out the earliest time they can check in, it says any time after two o'clock in the afternoon, so that means she can leave at ten, perfect. By the time she's had breakfast, packed her bag and said her goodbyes she can get on the road. She'll stop off for a toilet break and perhaps get a drink in the second half of the journey and all things going according to plan, she'll arrive at the hotel around two.

She hugs her parents and thanks them for a lovely time and the presents they bought her. Reversing off the driveway she takes a good look at the house, this is the last Christmas in this house, as she expected, they are selling up. They've had it valued, and have found a few bungalows they like within thirty miles of Jess' house. She's not sure how she feels about this, but she's going to put it out of her mind, for now.

Pulling over a couple of streets away as she wants to make sure no one sees her, she definitely can't arouse any suspicion now, she lifts her bag up to the passenger seat and gets her bracelet out. She hasn't dared to wear it since she arrived at her parents, for fear of questions she would have to lie to answer. 'It's beautiful' she says to herself, admiring it.

She sets the satnav, and it informs her of an estimated time of arrival 13.25pm. She clicks on contacts, looks for Jamie and presses call.

'Well hello, stranger,' he answers, sarcastically. He gets up from the sofa and goes up to his room for a bit of privacy.

'Hey, I'm sorry,' she starts to cry at the sound of his voice. She's genuinely upset, she's missed him more than she realised.

'Hey baby, shush, don't cry, what yer getting upset for?'

'I'm sorry. I'm so sorry. I've missed you so much.'

'I've missed yer too but we'll be together in a few hours.'

'I know, but…' she's interrupted by Jamie.

'Stop, it doesn't matter, it's only been a couple of days, it's fine,' he says.

She starts the car up again so she can get moving, and tells him she'll be there around 1.45 -2pm, and that they can check in after 2pm.

He knows this, he's already checked. He lives less than forty minutes away from the hotel but he's arranged for Joe to pick him up at 1300hrs, there's no point in taking his car, he'll drive back in Jess's car.

The truth is, he has been pissed off, not with her but with this ridiculous situation regarding her parents. He spoke to his mum about it last night after they got back from Rosie's house and his mum just sat and listened to him vent about it all.

She told him that some people can't help themselves, they think they're better than others but "you shouldn't hold that against Jess, she's knows her mum," she said, "if she doesn't want her to know then there's a reason for it, don't question it son. Just enjoy your life with Jess and be supportive of her decisions, it'll all work itself out in the wash".'

He told his mum that he's moving in with her in January (officially) and that they want to start trying for a baby. He explained the reason she never had children and that she doesn't know if she can get pregnant naturally or not, so they're going to try and find out.

He was definitely drunk, he told her too much for sure, but that's how his relationship with his mum is, he can tell her anything. He does kind of wish he hadn't told her about trying for a baby just yet though, *oh well, what's done is done.*

He has some lunch and gets everything ready to be packed straight into the car - uniform, boots, toiletry bag, clean clothes for travelling back and his clothes to change into for the evening. Oh and Jess' suitcase also, Joe pulls up just as he brings hers down. He loads it straight into Joe's car, gives his mum a hug and a kiss telling her he'll be back in a couple of days, gets in the car and off they go, butterflies fluttering in his stomach as he thinks about seeing Jess for the first time after a few days.

CHAPTER 88

Honour

He gets to the hotel just after 1330hrs and tells Joe he'll unload the car and wait for Jess to arrive to check in for 1400hrs. Joe wishes him good luck in his duties as Best Man and says they'll catch up when he's back for New Year and then leaves him to it.

He finds a seat in the hotel reception area and gets his phone out to send a WhatsApp message to the lads to see who's here and who isn't. Nobby is staying here the night with them all too, he decided he wanted to be here with everyone and go to the wedding venue tomorrow from the hotel with Jamie. This is the hotel where he and Shelley will spend their first night tomorrow as man and wife. The hotel manager approaches Jamie and asks if he can have a quick chat with him.

'Yeah mate, what's up?' Jamie asks.

The manager tells him it is nothing to worry about, it's just that he's heard there's a few squaddies staying in the hotel for a couple of nights, Jamie tells him he's the Best Man, Nobby and Shelley get married nearby tomorrow and that there's a few coming up for the wedding.

The manager tells him he feels honoured that they're staying in his hotel and he's putting a bottle of champagne behind the bar for them. He's also arranged with the restaurant to provide a free meal tonight for them all, he has booked them a table for 7.30pm for ten guests, and the bride and groom will be upgraded to the honeymoon suite tomorrow, compliments of the hotel.

Jamie is blown away, he's truly gobsmacked. He thanks the manager, almost lost for words but he assures him he will make sure everyone is on their best behaviour while in the hotel. As he finishes talking he sees Jess and waves to let her know he sees her. As she's walking towards him she's wondering who the sharp dressed man is that he's talking to.

He holds out his hand to Jess, and she catches the end of the conversation, she's still none the wiser other than hearing Jamie tell him he's "blown away", she'll wait and find out after, he'll tell her soon enough.

The manager walks away and Jamie turns around and picks Jess up, he's so happy to see her, he hugs her so tight she thinks she might break and then he kisses her. He tells her to wait here with the cases and he'll go and get them checked in.

Jamie stands waiting to check in and sends the WhatsApp message to everyone, adding the news that they've a free meal booked in the restaurant for 1930hrs, and they'll all meet then.

He checks in and the receptionist welcomes him to the hotel and she also tells him that they are honoured to have members of the military staying with them. He thanks her on everyone's behalf, picks up the room key and walks back to Jess.

Giving her a quick peck on her lips, he tells her he's so pleased to see her, and can't wait to get her into the room. She laughs, she can't wait either.

As they head to their room he tells her about the conversation with the manager, the bottle of champagne behind the bar along with a free meal tonight and the upgrade for Nobby and Shelley to the honeymoon suite. Jess is smiling at him, feeling yet another reason to feel proud of him, he's humble.

CHAPTER 89

Catching up

Walking into the room, Jamie straight away hangs his uniform up and tells Jess to get her dress out of the suitcase, it's going to be creased for tomorrow if she's not careful.

Clothes sorted, he can now concentrate on Jess. He tells her they've got some serious catching up to do, she laughs as he wraps his arms around her and kisses her, passionately, his hands caressing her tits through her clothes and he starts to undress her.

Kissing her neck as he undoes her bra, he slides it off, his hands feeling and playing with her nipples, 'Mmm,' he says and he bends down and starts sucking on them. Jess exhales loudly, she's missed this, she's missed his touch and his kisses, amongst other things.

He undoes her jeans and pushes them down, tells her to sit on the edge of the bed and pulls her boots off, followed by her jeans and thong. He tells her to lie back as he lifts up her legs, kneels down and starts to lick her lips, they're dry but he knows they will soon be wet. He parts her lips and licks her clitoris, he can hear immediately that she likes this. He pushes a finger inside her pussy, takes it out and sucks on it, 'Mmm' he says again.

He pushes in two fingers, fingering her pussy as he sucks and licks her clitoris, Jess is moaning, she wants more fingers, she wants them deeper, she tells him, he laughs and tells her soon, be patient.

He sticks his tongue inside, she's wet, its warm, it tastes amazing, he pushes his tongue in deeper, holding on to her legs with his hair brushing the inside of her thighs. She reaches down and touches his head, she can't help moaning louder as his tongue goes deeper, he sucks and licks, licks and sucks, her juices flow and he laps them up.

He moves his head and pushes two fingers back in, pushing them in deep he lets her legs down and moves up to kiss her, letting her taste her own juices, his fingers working her pussy, she's trying to moan but he's kissing her, she can feel she's going to cum soon. He moves back down her body as he pushes three fingers in, she lifts her knees towards her but he pushes them down telling her it's what she wants, she's asked for it.

He wants to hear her moan, he wants her to cum all over his fingers. He pushes his fingers in deeper, its tight, but she's wet, she's moaning more and more, louder and louder, she's groaning deeply, she's cumming, all over his hand.

He slows down and lets her catch her breath, he takes his fingers out slowly, they're sticky with her cum. He stands up to strip off and tells Jess to move up to the top of the bed. Climbing onto the bed, he lifts her legs and pulls her towards him, his cock is hard, he's throbbing for her, he lifts her legs right up onto his shoulders and pushes his cock into her pussy, he starts to thrust back and forth, Jess is moaning, she's loud, he loves to hear her, he wants to hear her louder.

His hard cock is deep inside her pussy, its warm and wet, his cock is throbbing, his balls are aching, he can hear the squelching as his cock thrusts in and out, her juices soaking his cock and balls.

He's thrusting faster and faster, she tells him she's cumming, he's close, he can feel it, another thrust and he tells her he's going to cum too, holding her legs tight he pushes his cock in one last time, and grunts as he shoots his cum deep inside her wet pussy, his body rigid, he shudders, he's climaxed.

CHAPTER 90

Complimentary Dinner

Jamie and Jess decide to shower together before getting ready to go down for dinner and meet everyone. Jamie lathers the shower gel in his hands and begins to wash Jess, starting with her neck then down on to her tits, paying extra attention to her nipples, caressing them as he's washing them, moving one hand down between her legs, he runs his fingers around her clitoris then lets his finger play inside her pussy, as he kisses her, his tongue looking for hers

The hot water is running powerfully over them both, his cock is hard, Jess has one hand stroking his cock and the other caressing his balls as she kisses him, responding to his tongue in her mouth, she continues wanking him with one hand as she caresses his balls with the other, while feeling his fingers deep in her pussy.

Kissing her passionately, he can't concentrate on fingering her while she's wanking him, his cock is hard and his balls are aching, she turns him on, he can't get enough of her. He takes his fingers out and places his hands either side of her head, hands flat on the shower wall, he can feel he's going to cum. He can't kiss her any more, he tells her he's about to cum so she kneels down in front of his cock as he explodes, his cum squirting all over her face, her open mouth and onto her tongue.

She stands up, under the centre of the shower, he kisses her and tells her how amazing it is to watch his cum squirting all over her face, but that they need to get ready otherwise they'll not be going out tonight at all. So they shower each other properly this time, he washes her hair as she washes her body and once she's done she gets out to leave Jamie to get washed.

They're finally ready and head downstairs to meet up with everyone, it's now 1830hrs, so they have an hour until the time of the table reservation in the restaurant. Walking into the bar they can see Gavin there already, he greets Jamie with a slap on the back and leans forward to give Jess a kiss on the cheek. She's not seen this more respectable version of Gavin, she's only seen the rough side of him, his common mouth and coarse behaviour but she sees now he has a gentle side, it's just a shame he doesn't show it more often, she thinks.

The others start turning up and by 1845hrs they're all at the bar, Jamie and Jess, Gavin, Charlie, Owen, Daniel, David, Nobby, Tommy and Clementine, everyone is in good spirits. Clementine tells Jess how she's getting on with her assignments and that she took on board what she said at the party, working harder on them over Christmas so that she can take a break and enjoy herself these next two days.

Jess is really pleased to hear this, she tells her that anytime she needs a bit of a break, even if she's just venting, to give her a call. She knows what it's like, even though it was a long time since she studied her A levels, she remembers it well.

The group is buzzing with excitement and they order a round of drinks, they're not doing shots tonight however as they need to be on their best behaviour and wake up with a fresh head tomorrow. After a little more chit chat and drinking, they make their way to the restaurant. Jamie is holding Jess' hand, but pulls her in towards him by her waist when they reach the entrance, he wants to make sure she is seated next to him, he tells her he needs her as close as possible, he's missed her. She nods in agreement.

The waiter escorts them to their table and Jess sits on the end so Jamie can sit next to her, he says to Tommy for him and Clementine to sit opposite him and Jess, so they can continue chatting. They order another round of drinks and a couple bottles of white wine for the table and when all the drinks arrive, the waitress brings out the complimentary champagne. She opens the bottle and pours each of them a glass and they raise a toast to Nobby.

'To the Groom, on his last night as a single man. May he be happy ever after!' they all cheer loudly and the atmosphere hikes up another notch.

Nobby decides to get the official discussion done now, while it is all fresh in his mind, and then he can relax for the rest of the evening, as much as a Groom about to be married can relax that is. He tells Jamie that they need to be at the registry office half an hour before everyone else arrives. The wedding is booked for 1230hrs at the registry office, followed by a reception in the local social club, Shelley's dad is a member there, so they got it nice and cheap. While she's listening to the arrangements, Jess realises she's never been to a registry office wedding before and doesn't recall ever going into a social club either.

She's excited for tomorrow, especially to see Jamie in his uniform, she's a little frightened she'll cry, which will smudge her makeup. She leans forward and shares her worry with Clementine who says she's feeling the same and that she's bringing some makeup with her for that very reason.

At 1030hrs the evening is winding down, Nobby tells them he needs to get an early night, so he's calling it a day. They ask for the drinks bill, so they can split it eight ways, the two girls aren't expected to pay of course. The waitress brings it out and tells them she's applied her student discount of fifteen percent as a thank you for everything they do, so the whole evening ends up costing them less than fifteen quid each.

Clementine leans over to Jess and tells her how proud she feels of Tommo and what he does, and seeing the way they've been treated by the hotel makes her feel so lucky to be with him, Jess agrees with her, as she thinks to herself, she can't wait to become Jamie's wife, that's her future too, the wife of a soldier in the British Army.

CHAPTER 91

Pre Wedding Nerves

Jamie wakes up at his usual time 0530hrs, he didn't bother setting his alarm last night, there's no point really, he thought. He's arranged with Nobbs and couple of others to go for a run because the gym doesn't open until 0730hrs, that's too late for him, he needs to back by 0800hrs.

He's actually quite nervous, he's never been a Best Man before and he's most nervous about his speech. He doesn't want to embarrass his mate in front of his family or Shelley's so he is opting for a 'clean' speech. He's decided to tell them how they first met, that Jamie arrived on base in the February after completing his training and Nobby was the first guy to introduce himself as he'd been in the Army for four years by then and always made a point of making any new recruits coming into the reg (Regiment) feel at ease, he's the most genuine caring bloke you could meet.

He continues to read to himself, this must be the fiftieth time he's read it, and he's played it out in his head a hundred times, this time he feels a little choked up as he gets to the end "Finally, I would like to thank Nobby for asking me to be his Best Man, I'm honoured mate, truly I am and I couldn't think of a better person I'd want to break my 'Best Man Virginity' with than with you". Jess has told him to turn and look at him when he says this, she thinks it will have a better impact, then he is to finish by asking everyone to raise a toast to the Bride and Groom, as he raises his glass in the air.

He smiles, he's got this, he knows he has, *right, Jamie lad let's get this run done, get rid of these nerves, if this is how I feel and I'm only the Best Man, how the fuck is Nobby feeling?* He can't help wondering.

He walks into the lobby area where Nobby is waiting. He looks nervous to Jamie, as he suspected. Charlie and Owen are going with them, the rest are apparently using the gym when it opens. Nobby knows this area well, he grew up not far from here. When the lads arrive he asks them if they want to head in towards the centre of town which is three miles away or out towards the motorway, five miles away.

There's no country lanes around here, it's a small town, but good for building up stamina with road running. They all opt for the motorway, they'll be back by 0800hrs, perfect for Jamie, as it means he can wake Jess up, go for a quick shower after his run and then head down for breakfast.

CHAPTER 92

Preparation Time

So it's finally here, the big day, Jess has butterflies, she's so excited about it. It's not even her own wedding but still she's excited, perhaps for a different reason, she gets to share a special occasion with Jamie, the love of her life, this man who has taught her so much in the short while they've been together, this man whom she loves with every ounce of her being.

She's seen his number one uniform hanging up for so long now, she's touched it ever so lightly, imagined him in it countless times, but today, it's going to be a reality. Her heart is bursting with every emotion you can imagine, love, pride, joy the whole lot, just complete and utter happiness.

He's left her to get ready on her own, he's gone to Nobby's room, she can't help but wonder what people must have thought when he left their room earlier in nothing but a towel wrapped around his waist, carrying his gear, although in his defence he did have boxers on underneath it.

She sent a text to Clementine to see if she's ok, and asked if she needs a hand with her hair or anything - she could do with a bit of company herself. She opens the door to let Clementine in and it turns out she wasn't the only one deserted, Tommo did the same thing and went off to Gavin's room to get ready. They really do work in unison with each other, they train together, they work together and they get ready together, almost like brotherly love.

The girls get chatting over a glass of wine, Clementine brought the rest of the wine from last night with her, as they were the only two drinking it there was half a bottle left. Jess is glad, she feels like she needs a drink to calm her nerves.

She's not sure how to have her hair, she tries her fascinator on, it is burgundy, the same colour as her dress, simple, with a few small feathers intertwined with some small bows on an Alice band. Clementine offers to curl her hair with the straighteners and shows her if she picks pieces up and clips them it gives her an 'up-do look' without it actually being up.

Jamie sent her a text to tell her he's coming to collect her at 1100hrs, then they'll have a drink or two at the bar before they leave. She tells him Clementine is here with her and for Tommo to come to their room as well. She tells Clementine not to worry about her clothes and make up being here, she can take it back to her room when they bring the boys back later to get changed or she can collect it in the morning, either way they'll deal with it later.

Jamie knocks on the door, Jess' stomach is in knots, she honestly doesn't know what to expect. She opens it slowly to see him standing in front of her, her legs wobble, her stomach flips, she's about to burst into tears from her emotions, but he's already warned her "no tears today" even though they're happy tears "I don't want to see yer cry babe, I'm nervous as it is, I can't be having yer crying on me" he said this morning before he went to get changed.

He stands there, like he's on parade, well he is on parade, kind of. He looks so tall, his cap and boots give him extra height. He looks breathtakingly handsome, his blond hair and blue eyes really stand out in his green uniform, it suits him, the black cap with the thick red band pulled down to his eyes accentuates them even more. She continues to look him up and down, she can't help herself, admiring his jacket with the shiny brass buttons on and white belt around his waist, even the brass clasp on it is shining.

She looks down to his boots, his 'ever so shiny' boots, she swears she can see her image in them, they're like mirrors. She's told him that time and time again as he's been sat on her living room floor polishing them, "that's how they're meant to be babe" he always says, she sees it now, she understands why he takes so much pride in what he does. It is all clear to her now, watching him stand to attention outside their hotel room.

CHAPTER 93

The Big Day

Jess is beaming as they walk down to the lobby area to reach the bar, just off to the side. She's looking at Tommo and Clementine and thinking, *even in her four inch heels she barely reaches his arm pits, she's so tiny, but beautiful.*

Her dress shows off her tiny figure - a navy blue, one shoulder, tuck-detail midi dress, her long black straight hair just passes her waist, her strappy diamante sandals no bigger than a size three match her bag and her fascinator matches her dress but she's cleverly added little diamantes to it.

They walk in to the bar where the rest of the guys are waiting. Nobby is nervous, you can see it, so Jess goes up to him and gives him a peck on the cheek and tells him that "this is the worst part, it'll get easier once the ceremony is out of the way".

Jamie orders drinks, getting himself a Jaegerbomb with a pint to calm his nerves and Jess is driving so he orders her a soft drink. He can't help looking at her every two minutes in admiration, she looks stunning, her blonde hair is all curly and he loves it like this, with her hat thing on. He's no idea what it's called, she said "it's not a hat" and told him its name, "if it's on yer head, it's a hat" he replied.

She's so tall and slim, the colour of her dress really suits her too, she told him it's burgundy, and that it's an embroidered-waist Bardot dip-hem dress. Of course he had no idea what she meant, "it's a dress babe," he said. "As long as you like it and I know you'll look a million dollars in it, then I'm happy".

She looks more than a million dollars, she looks amazing, beautiful, he's so proud of her, he knows one day this will be them. He knows he's going to marry Jess, after all he's picked out the ring, he just needs to find the right time to propose - when he's figured that out he'll go and buy it.

People are looking, staring and shaking hands with the lads, eight soldiers standing near the bar in their best uniform, looking very proud and rightly so.

'Its times like this I am proud to be British,' one guy has just said to Gavin.

'I have to admit it, I'm proud and feel very honoured to be a part of the British Army,' she hears him telling the fellow hotel guest.

The manager approaches and asks if he can take a photo, he'd like to put it on the hotel website next week, the boys agree, but will need to check first if he can put it on the website, Jamie told him he'll let him know once he's back on base, he took the managers number so he can contact him direct.

She hears Jamie say, 'It's time to go, drink up you lot, I have to get this twat to the registry office on time,' and they all laugh. Jess would never dream of talking like that to her friends, that special banter is something only a squaddie will really understand.

Jess pulls into the carpark adjacent to the Registry Office and Clementine parks next to her. Jamie and Nobby get out, put their caps on and march off to meet with the Registrar. The rest of the lads get out of the cars, put their hats on and escort the two women.

It's cold standing around outside, and guests are starting to arrive, so Jess motions to Clementine to go and wait in the foyer, 'it's a bit warmer in there,' she says. The two of them watch from there as people arrive, and much shaking of hands and patting the lads on the back begins. Both ladies are continuously smiling ear to ear, each very proud of their respective partners.

The Bride arrives, she looks beautiful, an ivory A-line, embellished, strapless dress with a matching short veil. She looks so happy, you can see that these two are marrying for love.

Jamie comes closer and holds Jess around the waist, he leans in and tells her how stunning she is and thanks her for being with him today, but he can't promise he's going to be in any fit state later for sex, he smiles and winks at her, she tuts and rolls her eyes in mockery of him.

They all walk inside, the Bride and Groom sit in front of the table and the bridesmaids sit in the front row with Shelley's parents, who on this special day are the proudest looking parents in the world.

Jamie is sitting next to Nobby's family on the front row, he keeps looking back at Jess and winking or smiling from time to time, he can't help wondering why she is sitting on Shelley's side. He hasn't worked out that she sat herself there so she can see him and watch him perform his duties as Best Man.

A quick twenty-five minutes, and the ceremony is over. Nobby and Shelley are now man and wife and lead everyone outside for photos.

CHAPTER 93

The Speech

Walking into the room of the social club and looking around, it wasn't at all what Jess was expecting. She had the image in her head that it was going to be a seedy, dingy, smoke filled room, but it's not what she imagined at all, in fact it's the complete opposite.

The room is big and light with a massive stage at the other end and a couple of balcony areas off to the side, these are beautifully decorated, with the buffet food on one balcony and the other with the cake and memory boards of Nobby and Shelley as children, teenagers and right up to this week as an engaged couple. In the middle of the last board is their scan photo of 'Baby Peters'.

Jess is looking around at the decorated room, she can feel the love and happiness that everyone holds for these lovely people, there's no pretentiousness in here, just everyday people celebrating the happy couple's big day. She can't help wondering how she made it through her day when she got married, she knows her own dress cost more than this whole wedding, yet Shelley's off the peg dress is every bit as stunning as hers was.

Gavin interrupts her thoughts, he's asking her something, 'Sorry Gavin, what did you say?' she asks him. He tells her he's going to the bar and asks if she would like a drink. Jamie is on the top table so Jess is sat next to Gavin and Charlie, she can't wait for this bit to be over, it's only been a couple of hours but she needs to be with Jamie.

She hears the pinging of glasses, meaning it is time for the speeches. Shelley's dad gives a lovely one, it brought a tear to the eye, he spoke about Shelley growing up, what a lovely caring woman she's turned into and about the night she brought Nobby home.

'So, let me tell you how Shelley introduced Jake to us. Well, I don't know where to start, as it was simply by waking me up at three in the morning to ask if Jake could stay the night, as he was passed out on the sofa down stairs.'

Everyone in the room is laughing, her dad is funny and a natural entertainer, he continues to tell everyone how proud he is of Jake and that he couldn't imagine anyone else marrying his daughter. He finishes his speech with a toast.

Next Nobby stands, up, he thanks Shelley's parents for allowing him to marry their daughter, he's full of praise for Shelley, telling everyone he knew she was the one for him after their first date, he was home on leave and they met through a mutual friend. He starts to talk about his job and trusting your buddy, your wing man, and that Shelley is quite simply his wing man, he couldn't imagine living life without her. A round of applause breaks out as he bends down to kiss her and all the women wipe their eyes and the men are clapping and cheering.

Now it's now Jamie's turn. Jess can see he's nervous, in fact he tells everyone, this has got to be the most frightening moment of his life, even when Nobby shot him, when they were on exercise and he forgot to lock his rifle. 'He accidentally dropped it and it's going off, you wanna see half a dozen squaddie's diving for cover as their mate's shouting "shit, fucking hell, sorry lads," needless to say we got our own back in the form of gaffer-taping him to his bunk.'

Everyone is laughing, Nobby is nodding his head as he laughs, he can remember it well, he says. Finally he comes to the end of his speech, he's had everyone in hysterics - this is Jamie, the life and soul of the party. As he finishes he asks everyone to stand and raise a toast to the Bride and Groom, Lance Corporal Jake and Mrs Shelley Peters.

CHAPTER 94

Hangover

'If I feel like this, fuck knows how everyone else is feeling,' Jamie says out loud.

She can hear him but she can't open her eyes or move her head, in fact she's still drunk, she can feel the room spinning. 'Oh God,' she says, as she dives out of bed and into the bathroom.

He leaves her for a bit before asking, 'Are yer ok babe?' and gets out of bed to see what's going on. Opening the bathroom door he sees her hugging the toilet and laughs, although he really doesn't feel much better himself.

'Yer didn't start drinking until we got back, what yer like? Yer light weight,' he laughs as he pulls her hair back, her head stuck down the toilet, he knows what she means now when she tells him "she can't do hangovers".

They got pretty drunk last night, the evening party was in full swing by the time they got back from changing out of uniform into civvy clothes, the drinks were cheap, the rounds plentiful and a bottle of wine with every round. He hates to think of the state Clementine ended up in, he last saw her being carried by Tommo.

He puts Jess back to bed, it's only just after 0700hrs, she can sleep a bit longer as they don't need to check out until midday and he sets about packing everything away ready to check out.

He opens WhatsApp and sends a message to Tommo asking if Clementine is ok and that Jess is really sick, Tommo replies straight away telling him she's asleep but was really sick in the night, so he's going to leave her as long as possible. Jamie sends him a thumbs up.

He's not going for a run today or the gym, he'll end up spewing at some point like the last time. No, he doesn't want to embarrass himself today, once he's finished packing, leaving their clothes out for today, he climbs back into bed for a while as he could do with a bit more sleep himself.

They both wake at just after ten, Jess is still hanging badly, but she knows she has to get herself together as she's meeting his mum today. *Whatever will she think of me turning up in that state?*

'How yer feeling now?' Jamie asks her.

'Ill. I hope Clementine is ok.'

Jamie tells her what Tommo said, and that probably means she feels a bit better now, having got it out of her stomach during the night. He tells her he's packed everything away except their clothes as she snuggles into him, kissing his chin. She's much too delicate for sex, so she's not going to encourage him, not this morning, it can wait until later on this evening.

She asks him if they are sleeping in a single bed together at his mum's and he nods and laughs at the thought, but he doesn't mind really, they'll be closer together, not that they are not any other night.

'We'll have to be quiet, I mean really quiet, and on the floor as well, I don't want no bed creaking when me mam's next door,' he says.

Jess cringes at the thought of it, she's never had sex with anyone in her parents' house or under the same roof even. Jamie gets up for a shower, he needs to get moving to shake this hangover off, once he's finished he's going to start loading the car. He tells Jess she'll need to be up by 1100hrs as they have to check out for 1200hrs.

'Yer got another forty minutes baby,' he gives her a kiss and leaves her be.

Checked out and climbing into the car, Jess feels a mess, she just managed to shower and wash, she still has no idea how, but she did. Thank God Jamie is driving, if it were her she'd have to book another night's stay, she's convinced of it.

They pull out of the car park and wave to a few of the lads loading their cars, Jamie paps the horn and gives a thumbs up as they pull away. It's only a forty minute drive, so Jess settles into her seat, with her arm stretched out holding his inside leg. He looks over and tells her she looks a bit better now, *thank God*, she thinks, *I wish I felt it!*

CHAPTER 95

Protecting his Assets

He pulls into the street, the usual lads are hanging around, hands tucked in their new track pants they got for Christmas, 'the chav brigade' he calls them.

Ash sees him driving Jess' car as he walks down the street towards Jamie's house, he calls after him and Jamie gets out as he's tells Jess to stay put. He walks away from the car in Ash's direction.

'You alright Ash?' he asks, Ash is beaming with excitement, asking him if he'd take him for a "spin in 'them wheels' and whose are they anyway?". Jamie tells him he can't, it belongs to his missus and that he's brought her back to meet the family.

Jess listens as she hears Ash replying, 'Woah, Jamie lad, got yersel' a right one there, yer punching mate, yer punching.' She has no idea what he means by any of that statement, he may as well be talking a foreign language.

Jamie crosses over to him and they shake hands as Jamie tells him to let whoever he needs to know that this car is out of bounds, 'Yer do that for me Ash and I'll sort yer out with a Bullseye,' meaning he'll give him fifty pounds. She continues to watch in her side mirror as Ash walks away saying 'Yeah mate, yeah, sweet, catch yer soon Jamie lad.'

He walks back to the car and pops the boot as Sean walks out, he doesn't need to ask, Sean and his mum watched it all go down, they knew what he was doing, after all the only people driving those kind of cars around here are drug dealers and loan sharks.

His mum comes to the door as he's walking in, she gives him a hug and asks if he's leaving Jess sat in the car, he laughs and tells her he'll get her out once he's unpacked it, she gives him a kiss and tells him he's a proper gent. He smiles and says, 'I'm learning mum, I'm learning.'

CHAPTER 96

Meeting the Family

They've had a lovely few days together, Jess has bonded really well with his mum sitting around the kitchen table, drinking cups of tea. His mum has told Jess about him as a child, the mischief he got into and the proudest day of her life watching Jamie's Passing Out as a soldier in the British Army, something he worked and continues to work very hard at.

Jess has met his two sisters, Sean of course, his other brother Joe and his partner Jacqueline and their two daughters, Sofia and Annabel, and just as he thought they would, his sisters love her, it's like she's been a part of the family forever, he particularly enjoyed watching her as she cuddled his baby niece Annabel and played tea-sets with Sofia.

They've managed to have sex, albeit very quiet, not something Jamie likes, he likes her to be loud, he likes to hear her moaning and groaning, telling him she's cumming, asking him to fuck her harder, hearing her gut wrenching moans as he inserts three fingers into her tight wet pussy, finger fucking her until she can't take any more, until her juices are flooding out of her and his hand dripping in her cum.

The chosen sex position has been mainly 'doggy' although they learned a new position the 'Fifth Element' which he found by Googling, as they have very little space on the floor in the box room. Jess quite liked this position, although Jamie is not sure if he can get used to Jess being in control all the time, he's too much of a strong personality for that, his dominant side wouldn't allow it all the time.

They're getting ready to go out as a family to celebrate New Year's Eve, even Joe and Jacqueline have got a baby sitter, off to the local social club, it's cheap and within a twenty minute walking distance of his mum's house.

Jess has opted for something a bit more casual than usual, she's wearing indigo coloured tight fitting jeans, a black, see-through blouse with a black balconette bra underneath, and black open-toe, two inch heels, when Jamie saw what she was wearing, he got an instant hard on.

They have around ten minutes before they have to leave and his mum and Sean are talking to a neighbour outside while they wait for Jess and Jamie to be ready. Jess grabs Jamie by the shoulders and kisses him hard on the mouth. Instantly his cock begins to rise with the feel of her probing tongue and soft lips. Closing the bedroom door she gets down on her knees to give Jamie a blow job. He leans against the back of the door and she unzips his jeans and slides his already hard cock out. He's holds her head and puts his cock in her mouth and she slides her lips back and forth, up and down the length of it. He begins to thrust it in faster and faster trying not to make any noise.

This is so unexpected and horny for her to take the initiative like that, he's hard, his cock is throbbing as she looks up at him, he pushes it further in to her mouth, right to the back of her throat, he's going to cum, he whispers to her as he holds her head still, he shudders as his cum fills her mouth and she pushes him away a little so she can swallow it. Now they're ready to go out. Jess quickly fixes her lipstick in the mirror, while Jamie tucks himself back into his jeans. Trying hard not to grin like a pair of teenagers, they make their way downstairs.

Walking into the social club is a bit like stepping back in time to the 70's, it is all reds and golds, big flower carpets, big gaudy red velvet curtains, lots of dark wood and huge Christmas ceiling decorations with a massive Christmas tree in the corner of the concert room. This social club is in complete contrast to the one that Nobby and Shelley held their wedding reception in just a few days ago.

During the evening Jamie introduces Jess to a lot of people, Jed's mum, dad and little sister Tara are also out with them tonight. Jess watches Tara around Jamie, she's not sure if she can be trusted, she quickly noticed earlier on in the evening that Tara has a crush on Jamie, she might only be seventeen but she's not letting that stop her from flirting, or trying to flirt at any given moment, Jess has taken an instant dislike to her and the feeling is mutual for Tara.

Everyone is merry, Jamie is drunk, it's getting close to midnight and he wraps his arms around Jess and tells her how much he loves her, that he's never been so happy and he knows he will marry her. Jess responds by kissing him and telling him she can't wait until the day she becomes his wife, the future Mrs O'Halloran.

The countdown to midnight starts, with someone's voice calling out 'ten, nine, eight, seven, six, five…' Jess looks around her at all the relaxed and happy people… 'four, three, two, one.'

'Happy New Year!' everyone shouts together as Big Ben strikes midnight, then she feels everyone grabbing her to hug her and wish her a happy New Year. Anne squeezes her tight and thanks her for being with them all tonight, telling her she couldn't have wished for a better person for her son and can't wait for them to give her a grandchild. Jess is shocked, he's told his mum about trying for a baby, Anne sees the look of surprise and maybe a little discomfort fleet across her face and tells her not to be embarrassed, she brought her children up to be open with her. Jess can only wish she had a relationship like that with her mum.

CHAPTER 97

Home Time

Jess is due back in work on January 3, so they decide to head home on Monday, January 2 , it's a Bank Holiday, as New Year's day fell on a Sunday, which they spent the best part of just lounging around, nursing sore heads and sore feet (in the women's case).

Anne is sad to see them go, she's enjoyed having Jamie home and meeting Jess, she's told Jess that she's not to be a stranger, to come up with Jamie in a month or so and Jess assured her she will, she's had an amazing time and can't wait to visit again, soon.

Jamie gets the cars loaded, he's not happy that they're travelling back in separate cars but Jess protested at him driving back in hers, then catching the train back in the week to get his car, even his mum told him he was being daft and that it's pointless making unnecessary journeys.

He needs to run an errand quickly before he leaves and tells Jess he'll be back in five minutes. He nips out in the car, picking Ash up at the end of the road and they drive to the local shops. Ash stays put while Jamie goes to the cashpoint, he gets back in the car and hands Ash some money, he doesn't need to count it, he knows Jamie's good on his word. For Jamie it was a job well done and well worth it. He drops Ash off, and goes back to say his final goodbyes before they hit the road.

Walking into the house for the first time in nine days felt very strange but welcome, Jess has missed her home, she's missed her bed and most of all she's missed their intimacy. Fred's been in and closed the curtains and put some lights on, it's not late but it is dark for three o'clock in the afternoon, a typical winter's day.

Jamie starts to unload the cars, telling Jess to put the kettle on and that he's putting it all in the hallway and he'll sort it out tomorrow when Jess is at work. She asks him if he wants to drop her off this week and pick her up. He agrees, and mentions that that he can go shopping tomorrow when he picks her up, so for tonight they can just get a take away.

Jamie opens his new calendar and puts it up in the kitchen, starting to mark some dates for work that he knows of, like training days and he pencils in a possible short tour (17 Feb - 20 April) a weekend up to his mum's, birthdays, and the two most important dates, 2 January 2020, (officially) moved in together and 20 January, the date to start trying for a baby.

With full bellies from a Chinese takeaway, they cuddle on the sofa, talking about decorating the spare room, making it more like a spare room rather than a dumping ground for Jamie's belongings. They agree that it's important to sort out a joint account for bills and savings for the baby and Jess mentions his car again, that she thinks it would be a good idea if he uses her car and they buy a family car, something like an MPV or SUV.

He laughs at her, 'Yer ain't giving up are yer?' he says, she shakes her head as he starts to tickle her, she screams at him to 'Stop!' as she hates being tickled.

He climbs on top of her and holds her hands above her head, leaning down he kisses her, she's completely helpless, he's so strong, she gives in to him, not that she was going to put up much of a fight anyway. He kisses her, just long passionate kisses, French kissing, pecking, long lingering kisses, he's missed this, the intimacy of kissing.

His cock is hard but he doesn't want just sex tonight, they've had quick sex all week, he wants to make love, he wants to feel that rush of emotions as his cock is deep inside her, kissing her as his hips gyrate, slowly and meaningfully. He holds her hands in one hand as his other holds the back of her neck, her back is arched upwards and her breasts exposed through her dressing gown.

She's turned on by his touch, he's strong but sensitive, caring but dominant. Although his hard cock is rubbing against her, he's not in a rush, he wants to take his time. He moves his hand from the back of her neck, stroking her breast slowly, cupping it in his hand, he moves his head to suck her nipples in turn, they are erect, as his tongue licks and sucks them.

He lets her hands go, but she keeps them raised as he pulls her dressing gown open, exposing her naked body, his cock is throbbing as he gazes at her perfect body, but he can't rush this, he won't rush. Climbing off her, he pulls her up from the sofa and leads her upstairs to bed, he doesn't want to make love on the sofa.

She lies down and he climbs on top, his legs sliding in between hers, he places his cock in her pussy and pushes in slowly, she's wet, he's hard, his thick cock filling her tight pussy, a sigh of pleasure escapes her lips as he pushes in deeper.

Moving his hips side to side slowly kissing her lovingly and passionately he feels her juices all over his cock, she moans quietly, he holds her shoulders as he pushes in deeper, as she moans again he thrusts it in deeper, his hips gyrating faster, making her moans loader, this is what he's missed, he tells her, 'Louder, let me hear you.' Her moans of pleasure excite him, the louder she moans the more excited he gets.

She feels his cock deep inside her, his body moving all over hers, his muscles flexing every time he moves, she wants him, she wants him deeper, harder, she's ready to cum.

She climaxes and he feels it, he hears her groan, he knows he's close too, he wants to let go but doesn't, he tries to stop himself, he slows down but it's no good, he tells her he's going to cum, he pushes his cock in deep and releases his cum, grunting loudly, his body rigid as he climaxes and that overwhelming feeling of love, as his whole body shudders.

CHAPTER 98

Log Cabin

It's been a busy time since returning home, Jamie has been training hard, he's going away on a short tour in a few days for ten weeks, they've decorated the spare room, bought a new single bed, bedding and curtains and they managed to finish it just in time for his mum to stay when she came at the end of January.

Jess has bought an ovulation home test kit as she needs to know if she's ovulating. As much as she's loves their sex and love making she needs to know when she's ovulating, otherwise she has no way to know if she's pregnant when she doesn't have periods.

She's not spoken to her mum much since Christmas, it's not that she doesn't want to, it's just more difficult now Jamie is living with her so she's decided she'll go and visit when Jamie goes on tour, it will help break up the loneliness of him being away.

It's their first Valentine's Day this year and Jamie wants to surprise her with a weekend away, he's booked a log cabin with a Jacuzzi and although it's to celebrate Valentine's Day they're going away on the weekend immediately before, as he has too much to get ready before he goes on tour to be away on the day itself.

Jess booked a half day on the Friday so they can leave around two o'clock. It's a three hour drive south, but Jamie doesn't mind the drive, in fact he'd been looking forward to it, though not quite as much as he's looking forward to the Jacuzzi, he's never had sex in a Jacuzzi before.

They arrive a little later than planned due to traffic, so it's nearly seven o'clock after stopping for some snacks and a bit of shopping and some beers for Jamie to drink over the weekend, Jess isn't drinking now in case she falls pregnant but doesn't realise.

The cabin is big, with a nice big double bed, a kitchenette and a living area, with patio type doors onto a veranda where the Jacuzzi is. He unpacks the car, opens a beer and Jess gets a cup of tea. He can't help feeling guilty, but it's for the best that she's not drinking, it won't be forever he tells her, easing his own guilt.

He switches the outdoor heaters and the Jacuzzi on, 'After all, there's no point waiting,' he says, as Jess unpacks her weekend bag.

She laughs at him, 'You're so impatient Mister,' but she's secretly excited and she strips off ready, walking outside in just her towel, ready for a bit of 'skinny dipping' as she calls it.

The water is hot, it's a bit noisy, more so than she expected, but she likes the idea of this, she tells Jamie they should look into one for back home, but he dismisses it, he has other plans and they don't involve them living at that house in January next year.

He has a six month tour out in the Middle East next year and he wants Jess close to his mum so he can deploy knowing she'll be looked after and won't be lonely while he's away, especially if they have a baby by then. He hasn't told her about this tour, not yet, he doesn't want to worry her as it's not set in stone, it should be confirmed by September this year, for deployment next May.

He climbs in and joins her, kissing her as he does, there's something sexy about a naked body in water, 'It feels so different,' he tells her as he pulls her towards him. She straddles him and starts to kiss him, feeling the bubbles stroking all over her body and the steam of the water rising, she sits down on his cock, it definitely feels different in water, the Jacuzzi is loud, so she's sure that no-one in the next cabin will be able to hear her.

He wraps his arms around her and begins to kiss and suck her nipples, she moves up and down on his hard cock, quietly moaning, she gets faster, her tits bouncing close to his face, his arms around her with his hands holding onto her shoulders encouraging her movements. He tells her he loves her, he loves how much she turns him on, how he can't get enough of her. She nods, she can't speak, she's starting to cum, it's happening quickly in here, more than she thought it would be.

She tells him, 'I'm cumming,' as she lets out a loud moan.

'Yes baby, let me hear yer, louder,' he tells her as she gets louder and faster, 'come on baby, I'm close, let me hear yer,' her loud moans are turning him on, the bubbles of the Jacuzzi with her naked wet body against his is exciting him to the max.

She's moaning - a real deep intense pleasure moan – and he's starting to grunt, his cock thrusting hard and deep inside her pussy, he holds her tight as he starts to cum, letting out a loud grunt, his arms wrapped around her body as he climaxes.

CHAPTER 99

Tour of Duty

Well the day is here, the day Jess dreaded, Jamie leaves for his ten week tour of duty, the only consolation she has is that it is nowhere near a war zone, or so he tells her, she's just pleased that the Afghan war has all but finished, that any regiments out there today are there on a peacekeeping mission, however, she can't help but worry as there's a three hour time difference, and communication will be minimal.

He's marked the calendar on the day he is due to arrive back into the UK - Monday 20 April. Jess has booked the week off from work and she's also going to collect him from the airport upon his arrival. She doesn't want to have to wait for him to come back on the coach provided by the MOD.

Jess goes about her usual daily routine for the first couple of weeks, she's kept herself busy, visiting her parents, going out for dinner with work friends, seeing Hazel and Fred and she's even going up to stay with Anne in March for the Easter weekend, she's getting on really well with Anne, they text or call each other every other day.

She's still yet to hear from Jamie, he messaged her when he first arrived but she hasn't heard from him since, although she's trying not to worry, she's spoken to Clementine and Shelley but neither of them have heard from Tommo or Nobby, she understands now why the wives and girlfriends are so close, they support each other when their men are away.

She's used her vibrator more these past few days than it's been used in a while as well as watching porn, she's horny, hornier than she expected to feel whilst he's away.

She's noticed recently that she's been getting a lot of stomach cramps, something that Lizzie suspects are period pains but without the period. She hopes so, this would mean her ovaries might be kicking into action, she's going to do an ovulation test in two weeks on 20 March, it's marked on the calendar. She loves this calendar, she understands now why he bought it, it's vital for his job and their home life.

Jess woke up feeling down today, tearful and missing Jamie even more than usual. Clementine called her last night as she was feeling emotional, worrying what effect this could have on her at Uni. Jess told her not to worry about it like that, it's not always like this, and she hopes that they will get used to it to some extent. She can't deny it, this is the part she hates but this is what they do.

Typical, she can hear her phone ringing and she's in the shower, her shifts are 10-6pm this week, it stops but then goes again, she has to get it, it must be important. Running into the bedroom she picks it up and sees three missed calls from Jamie,

'No! No! Why didn't I get out and answer it?' she wails and tries to call him back but gets the overseas engaged tone, then realises he's calling her again, she disconnects her call and answers his.

'Hey Baby, are you ok?' his voice is thin at the other end, but it's still her Jamie.

She's crying, she can't help it, the sound is crackling in waves, it is a really bad line.

'Hey, don't cry please, I don't have long, I needed to hear yer voice, love yer and missing yer so much.'

'Sorry baby, I'm so sorry, I just miss you, I miss you so much. I got your flowers they're beautiful, thank you.'

'Aah good, miss you too. It's long days here, we're on patrols, nothing serious to worry about but no mobile coverage. This is the first time.'

'Ok, as long as you're safe. I'm going to your mum's for Easter, spending the weekend there.

'Are you? That's great baby, when is Easter?'

'In a couple of weeks darling, I'll be going up on the Friday, coming back on the Monday.'

'That's great baby, hang on, someone's talking to me.'

She hears him saying something but can't make out what it is, something to do with "ARV's… and see Scottie".

'Darling I gotta go, I love and miss yer, see yer soon,' he says, his voice tailing off as the crackling line takes over.

She tries to answer but his phone has already cut off, she can't help herself now, she cries big hearty sobs, it's upset her more hearing his voice than not speaking to him. She needs to get a grip, this is how life will be, the Tours, the training exercises, surely it must get easier?

Jamie's call was cut short, but he needs to text his mum while he has signal he needs to make sure Jess will be ok.

Jamie: [Mum, speak to Ash for me, tell him Jess' car is out of bounds, I'll see him right when I'm back from this shithole, love yer and miss yer xx]

CHAPTER 100

Home Coming

Jess had a lovely time at Easter with Jamie's mum and Sean, she's spoken to Jamie a couple more times, she writes to him regularly and sent him some photos that she had printed. She also had some printed for herself, there's one on her bedside cabinet and a big one of the two of them at the wedding is framed and on display in the living room.

She counts down on the calendar, another eighteen days, it's coming around more quickly now, but she misses him terribly, that doesn't ease, she can't imagine it ever getting any easier, the terrible emptiness she feels when he's away.

She's decided to go and stay with her parents this weekend, it's the last week of Jamie's Tour, next weekend she wants to clean the house from top to bottom. She's booked into the hairdresser on Saturday along with the beauty therapist for all her waxing, she wants to be fully prepared for his home coming.

The last week of his tour dragged for Jess, every day at work felt like a week. She woke early Saturday morning excited but also a little emotional, she knows she is going to cry on Monday when he walks through the arrivals gate at Brize Norton, she doesn't care what he says or thinks about her crying, not this time, she's going to tell him to "suck it up, buttercup", she's allowed to cry on this occasion.

She didn't sleep much Sunday night, she was too excited, the most excited she's ever felt in her life. She got up at six in the morning, the online shopping delivery was booked for seven and by the time she had put that away, had her shower, dried her hair, and got dressed it was nearly half nine.

'No point hanging around girl, may as well get on the road,' she says aloud.

It's roughly a two hour journey to Brize Norton, but Jess likes Oxford, she used to shop there a lot when she was married. The drive down was a breeze and she has stopped off for a light lunch at a cafe she knows well near the retail outlet, she only has twenty-three miles left of her journey, she's due to arrive at Brize Norton for half-past one so she gets back on the road around twelve forty-five and it'll take her around thirty-five minutes to finish the journey.

Shelley is already there when Jess arrives, she can't believe how much her baby bump has grown, the two women hug each other really tight, both have tears in their eyes as they chat about the baby, Shelley had her twenty week scan while Nobby was away and she sent him lots of scan photos and a couple of wedding ones, she tells Jess.

The time spent in the arrivals area went quickly and the flight has landed. Jess' stomach is a tangle of knots and butterflies but most of all she's elated, she's never felt this kind of emotion before, but she knows this is how it's going to be, forever and a day, her life as the wife of a serving military man, and a very proud one.

CHAPTER 101

A Time for Thought

The last ten weeks have been pretty much as he expected, the mid-day heat regularly reaching over fifty degrees, carrying one hundred and thirty pounds of gear (body armour, weapons and back pack) not knowing what day, week or even month it is, he arrived on location, completed his tour and now he's going home that's all he knows. One thing's for sure, he's no idea how he's going to do six months of this next year, there's no getting used to it, you just deal with it and get on with it.

There's not much down time, there's no phone coverage and the place is a shithole, there's no other way to describe it. It's hot, it's dry and it fucking stinks, the only consolation is that the locals are nice, very welcoming, they love the 'English' which is ironic, *probably the only foreign country to like us,* Jamie thinks to himself, *but I can tell you now, it's not on my list of holiday destinations, I'll give this place a miss!*

He's been thinking a lot about the situation with Jess and her parents, he doesn't care if he never meets them or if they don't like him, she just needs to tell them, they're living together for fuck's sake and she's going to have his baby at some point in the next twelve months and that's another thing he's been thinking about.

He doesn't want Jess working when they have a baby, he's going to work hard and get his promotions under his belt which in turn will give him more money to provide for his family, that way Jess doesn't have to worry about working and she can concentrate on looking after the family and their home.

His reason for this way of thinking is that his mum didn't have a choice, she *had* to work, they all helped raise each other, during school holidays they'd be on their own while his mum was at work. He doesn't want that kind of life for his children, he'll be away from them a lot as it is, they'll need their mum at home, she'll be the only bit of stability in their life and his for that matter, she'll be their rock.

Even though Jess owns her own home, that's hers and it always will be her house, any money she has now, belongs to Jess. Any money they earn or property they buy in the future will be jointly theirs, he's not one for handouts and he's certainly not going to take anything in the way of a hand out from her marriage, even if it is her share of everything - that belongs to Jess.

Jess has been a diamond sending him cards, letters, photos and a few boxes of goodies, it's been a welcome treat, something to keep a man going out there, and if he is honest, it is a proper morale booster knowing he's got his woman to go back to, which is something that can't come quick enough for Jamie right now.

The long flight home will be difficult, he hates the return journeys as he is impatient. In his mind, he's been away, done what he needs to do and just wants to get home to Jess. He's missed her so much, more than he thought he would, he's told her she's not to cry when she sees him, it's not that he can't handle her crying, he's actually frightened he's going to cry too, he feels himself welling up just thinking about her now, that first kiss, their love making, the cuddles and just being home.

CHAPTER 102

An Emotional Reunion

She can't see him, she's on her tip toes looking over everyone, she hears Shelley screaming, "Nobby!" and waving frantically and Jess knows Jamie is never far from Nobby, they're like Tweedle-dum and Tweedle-dee those two.

She sees him, his sun bleached blond hair and the most beautiful blue eyes accentuated by his tanned face. She tries to move forward through the crowd but it's no good, she goes around them and stands in a clear space, waving at him, calling him, her tears streaming down her beaming face, he's grinning like a Cheshire cat, as he makes his way through the crowd .

Finally, dropping his bag at his feet, both throwing their arms around each other, his face buried into her neck as his emotions take over, his tears flooding out as he squeezes her, this is the moment he's been waiting for from the moment he left all those ten weeks ago.

Cupping her face in his hands he kisses her, lovingly, her arms wrap around him holding him tight as she kisses him back, she doesn't care if anyone is looking, not this time. They walk out to the car, anxious to get it packed, get on the road and get home. He feels grubby and in need of a proper decent shower, shave and some clean clothes, ones that aren't covered in sand for a change.

The car is loaded and Jamie tells her he wants to drive, he's really missed driving. Before he gets in the car he has to give her one more kiss, this time his hands are caressing her breasts through her clothes, he doesn't care if they're in the car park of the airport at Brize Norton, if he felt clean he'd be giving her one by now up against the car, he's sure of it.

They get in the car and set the satnav for home, Jess can't let go of him, she's holding his leg tight. It feels like he's lost weight, in fact he looks like he's lost weight in his face. She tells him this and he agrees with her, he thinks he's lost about a stone in weight, he's not done any running, not proper running in the time he's been there, it was too hot in the day and too dark by the time they got back in the evening. He's managed to use the gym out there on his days off but it wasn't like the gym back here.

He asks her about Easter at his mum's, and says that they'll go up for the weekend before his birthday next month, even though he's got two weeks off now, he wants to stay home with Jess and when she goes back to work next week he'll be able to start his training again - early morning runs and the gym every day to get him back into shape, he also needs to look at gaining this weight back but in a healthy way.

The two hour journey home goes quickly, chatting non-stop, as they pull up at the house he tells her he's been thinking about his car, he thinks he'll be better suited with a diesel if he's going to be commuting to and from work in June. He was chatting to a couple of guys during his tour who commute now as their family live in the village and they didn't want to keep moving them around, they told him it's ok if you're an hour or so away but it can get a bit difficult when it's more than two hours.

He unloads his gear into the house, intending to sort it all out tomorrow, including his washing. Tonight is all about relaxing and being with Jess.

CHAPTER 103

First Night Home

He strips off and puts his shorts and T-shirt on, he's going to have a shower in a bit but first of all he needs a drink and a cuddle from Jess. Walking into the kitchen and looking at him, Jess can't help welling up, he looks so thin, you can really see the weight loss. He hugs her, not saying anything, his emotions are too strong to speak.

He kisses her, lovingly and passionately, his tongue looking for hers, oh how he's missed this, his hands caressing her boobs, his cock is hard, he knew it wouldn't take long, he's had a wank from time to time but it's been difficult and apart from anything else he's been too exhausted most days.

Her arms are wrapped around him and she holds him tight, she can feel his hard-on, she's missed all these feelings, she smirks as she kisses him, 'that didn't take long,' she says.

Both laughing he tells her 'Babe, he's not had any action for ten weeks, what do you expect, hardly even a wank, you're gonna have to take it easy on him for tonight,' and he laughs, what he means is he's going to cum quick but he'll be fine tomorrow.

She asks him what he wants to do about dinner, he tells her he wants to go out, he needs a beer and some decent food, so he'll have a shower, get dressed and they'll go out. She follows him upstairs, she's going to sit on the toilet and talk to him while he showers, she wants to be with him, she doesn't want to let him out of her sight.

Getting him a towel from the airing cupboard, she walks in to the bathroom where he is standing under the shower, his hands against the wall, the water running over him, and he looks lost. She asks him if he's ok, and he tells her he's never felt better and how amazing this shower feels, something he won't take for granted again.

He washes his hair, then starts on his body, his pubes have grown a lot as he couldn't shave them while he was away, but he's going to today. Jess passes him a razor and watches as he shaves around his balls and his cock, then washes it all off.

He must have had four body washes in the shower, he was in there for more than half an hour, almost as if he was trying to wash the tour off his skin. She's not seen him like this before, she wonders, *how long will it take him to adjust to being back?*

They head out to the pub in the next village, he wants a decent steak and a couple of pints, he drives there and Jess drives back, not in complete silence but with minimal chat. He is tired from the journey, she guesses. When they get home they cuddle up on the sofa and he kisses her neck.

'Babe, can we just cuddle tonight? I'm exhausted and I just need to hold you, you don't mind do you?'

She turns over towards him wrapping her legs around him, stroking his face she tells him 'Of course not, just having you home is all I care about.'

She feels slightly deflated, she honestly thought that they would be fucking all night long, she's horny and she thought he'd be rampant but he's not, quite the opposite in fact. She never realised how much this short tour would take its toll, she has no idea what he'd be like if it were any longer, she dreads to think. It's something she'll discover in time no doubt.

CHAPTER 104

Second Time Around

For the first time in a very long time Jamie slept in until 0930hrs, he's had nearly twelve hours solid sleep, he's not sure if it's the lack of sleep for the last ten weeks or just that he's home, perhaps both and waking up with a hard on is exactly what he needs this morning.

Jess is stirring, Jamie's body has been wrapped around hers all night, she lets out a little giggle as she feels his hard cock digging in her back, 'Someone's awake,' she says.

'Mmmm, good morning, yes and pleased to see you,' he says as he moves her hair away so he can kiss the back of her neck, he starts to caress her tits at the same time, 'Oh! How I've missed these.'

She lifts her leg over his and feels herself, she can feel how wet she is. She rubs her juices from her finger onto her nipples as he moves to let her lie flat so he can suck it off. Climbing on top of her as she opens her legs, he slides in between them, he's not bothering with foreplay, he wants to lick her out and taste her juices, he wants his fingers deep inside her wet pussy, feeling her cum all over his hand, but that can wait until later, he has absolutely no intention of getting up today, it's going to be a day of love making and sex, lots of sex.

He positions his cock into her wet pussy as he starts to kiss her, pushing it in deeper he tells her he might cum quick this time, but it's just a warm up, followed by a big smile and a wink.

Moving his hips slowly, he starts to kiss her, pressing his body lightly onto hers, he needs to feel her naked body against his, his cock deep inside her wet pussy, he can feel her juices all over it, it's throbbing as he thrusts slowly, gyrating his hips and listening to her moaning softly.

His hip movements are faster as he kisses her, he can't help himself, he needs to cum, he starts to thrust his cock in deeper, her moans are louder, the louder her moans the more turned on he gets, he thrusts harder and deeper, he can't hold on any longer he's going to cum, his cock is deep inside, her pussy is so wet, another deep thrust and he feels the release of his cum deep inside her, his body rigid then the shudder as he climaxes.

'Sorry baby,' he says as climbs off her, 'I didn't realise I'd cum so quick,' he leans over and kisses her, 'I'll make it up to yer later,' he says.

Jess smiles and touches his face lightly with her hand telling him, 'It's fine, it's your first day back, it's going to be like this.'

She gets up to go to the toilet, she really wasn't expecting this, she's feeling dissatisfied, disappointed even, their sex life was amazing and exciting, she really hopes it'll get better, back to how it was before his tour. Jess jumps in the shower, she's sweaty and feels dirty, putting her hair in a bun she steps into the shower, she can't hide her frustration, she feels her emotions building as her tears start to flow .

Jamie, hears the shower, he's exhausted but wants to join her, 'Fuck it,' he says as he gets out of bed, he walks into the shower as Jess is facing it, the water running over her, she sees him and she's shocked, she wasn't expecting him to walk in.

'Babe, what's wrong?' he could see the look on her face as he walked in, before the look of surprise, and it wasn't a happy expression she was wearing.

He climbs in to the shower and puts his arms around her, kissing her shoulders. He knows what's wrong, he never thought it'd be like this, he thought it'd be like before he went away, exciting and amazing.

'Babe, I can't explain it, it was a shithole, hot, actually really fucking hot and really long fucking days,' he tried to explain to her what it was like and maybe why it seems to be hard for him to adjust.

Jess feels guilty, she tells him she's just being selfish and she doesn't know why she's so upset. He cuddles her and lifts his hand up to her face. Kissing his palm and each finger one at a time she tells him how much she loves him and how much she's missed him.

He continues to kiss her shoulders and up her neck, nibbling on her ear as he starts to caress her breasts and around her nipples. With her back to him he moves one hand down, parting her legs and begins to rub her clitoris with his thumb, pressing on it as he does.

Jess starts to moan, she loves this movement he makes, it makes her cum so easily and Jamie knows this, he moves his other hand down and places his cock in between her bum cheeks, he's hard already, but before he cums again he wants to make sure Jess has climaxed.

Playing with her pussy, he pushes a finger in, the shower still is running over them so Jess turns it off and places her hand against the shower wall.

With two fingers in her wet pussy, Jamie's thumb continues rubbing her clitoris, making Jess moan, just as he likes her to, the louder she is the harder his cock gets. As his fingers go deeper he can feel her juices squelching between them. He rubs her clitoris faster, increasing the pressure, her legs are shaking, she's cumming, making deep stomach wrenching moans.

Jamie steps out of the bath and helps Jess out, he tells her to lean over the sink in the doggy position and parts her legs with his feet pushing hers, placing his hard cock in her wet pussy, he holds her outer thighs as he pushes it in. He moves his cock in and out slowly and Jess resumes moaning in continued pleasure, as her moans get louder his thrusts get faster, deeper, he can feel her juices all over his cock as he pushes in harder and harder.

He tells her, 'Louder baby,' and she tries to answer him but she can't, his cock is so deep and fast, 'I'm going to cum again,' she manages to tell him weakly.

Jess is cumming, her legs are shaking, she's moaning loudly, he's going to cum, one more deep hard thrust and he explodes, his body shuddering as he fills her pussy with his cum once again.

CHAPTER 105

Watching Porn

A day in bed is exactly what's needed, for Jamie it was about recharging his batteries but for Jess it was the reconnection, the sex and love making.

Although their relationship isn't based solely on sex, it goes deeper than that, she can't help but wonder how she'd cope if it became a 'sexless' relationship, she wouldn't cope, not this time, she couldn't imagine a life of celibacy with Jamie, never feeling his hard cock deep inside her wet pussy, the touch of his hands as he caresses her breasts and most of all his kisses, tender, loving and passionate.

He's young, fit and virile, he gets her juices running just thinking about him. She realises that the tours are going to have an effect on him so when he first gets home she'll need to learn to be patient as he adjusts back into normal life.

She turns around to kiss him, touching his beautiful tanned face as she does so, he asks her what she did whilst he was away. As she's talking, telling him about work, doing this and doing that he laughs at her, 'No, I mean, did you use yer vibrator and watch any porn?' he asks. She must have blushed as he responded with, 'Good, I want to see what yer did, show me babe, show me what I was missing.'

'What now?' she asks in a slightly high pitched voice.

He nods, as he says, 'Yeah, now.'

He opens his phone and clicks on a porn site asking her what she watched, she tells him it was a threesome video, he looks at her shocked and tells her under no circumstances would he ever want to watch her being touched let alone fucked by another man and to get that idea out of her head.

Jess tells him she doesn't want one, she just likes to watch it, 'It's just porn babe, fantasy, I'm sure there's stuff you like to watch but wouldn't do, right?'

He looks at her, he can't tell her he likes to watch the girls at the lap dancing club and yes he's fucked most of them, he'll never be able to tell her that or that he wants a lap dance, where he can look but he can't touch, that turns him on, so he just shrugs his shoulders and tells her he'll put a normal one on.

As she's lying on the bed listening to the porn and the fake moans and groans of the woman being fucked she starts to play with her nipples, then moves one hand down to rub her clitoris, after a few minutes she turns her vibrator on and licks it like she would Jamie's erect cock.

He kneels up to watch her, his cock semi hard as he strokes it, he likes watching her play with herself, it's a turn on, in effect she is telling him what she wants him to do but without speaking.

His cock is hard, she's inserted her vibrator in to her pussy and her juices are all over it, taking it out she licks it and rubs it on her nipples, he wants to bend and lick it off but he won't, he wants to see her cum first.

She inserts her vibe back into her wet pussy, pushing it in deep, she starts to moan, not loud but enough for him to hear, she slides it in and out with one hand and plays with her nipples with the other, Jamie is hard, he masturbates at the same time, watching her and listening to her.

Her vibrator is really deep inside, and she moans softly, then takes her vibrator out and rubs it over her clitoris, this always makes her cum quick, so she inserts it back into her wet pussy, pushing it in deep, soaking it in her juices.

He asks her to tell him when she's cumming, he wants to cum all over her tits, she's close he can see it, he's close to cumming, he wants to cum at the same time. He hears her, she's cumming, her vibrator still deep inside her as she cums, he moves up the bed on his knees next to her, cumming all over her tits.

CHAPTER 105

Back to Normality

Jamie gets up early and leaves his 'Sleeping Beauty' to sleep longer, she's back to work tomorrow and he still has another week off, so he'll drop her off and collect her. He's going to start back with his running tomorrow and will use the gym each day, he needs to start getting his fitness levels back to where they were.

He checks his messages, he can see he has some Facebook notifications, a message on Messenger and a couple of WhatsApp messages, he'll sort these out later, his head is slightly sore from last night, he thinks to himself, *I really can't be arsed with talking this morning.*

He collects their clothes from the living room, smiling as he recalls Jess doing a strip tease, his cock is twitching as he thinks about it, he loves it when she teases him, stripping off, fingering herself and licking her juices off her fingers while he watches, it gets him hard and she knows it.

He picks the chair up and pushes it back under the table, he knocked it over in his rush to get Jess on the table, facedown, he fucked her doggy style, she was literally sprawled out over the table, his cock deep in her arse, it was so tight on his cock, it felt amazing - it was amazing.

His cock is hard again now, remembering last night's action, he laughs as he looks down at it, 'Haven't you had enough this week, meat?' he says aloud.

Life is definitely back to normal, his uniform is washed, ironed and hanging up in the spare room, they've had plenty of sex, he's definitely made up for the last ten weeks, he also drove Jess to her appointment with her solicitor on Friday, her house will be completing in a week's time, her decree will be through around May 10, then all she has to do is wait for her settlement, the solicitor will transfer it into her account.

Jamie had a night out last night with some of the lads, he needed a blow out, a good drink, generally just let his hair down. He only went out to The Bowl on camp and Jess went out with Angela and Jodie, a couple of new friends she met at one of the 'WAG's' wine tasting evenings, whilst Jamie was away.

Jess had told Jamie earlier in the week about Angela - that she is also going through a divorce - and Jodie is fairly new to the village, her husband's regiment posted here four months ago. She also told him about Angela messing around with a couple of the young lads from the barracks, "she's definitely making up for lost time" she said, laughing.

Jamie knows Angela, she's come on to him a few times, whenever he's seen her out down town but he always blew her off, he also knows Gavin is one of the 'lads' she's messing around with, he actually doesn't want her hanging around with Jess, so he told Jess to be careful, Angela has a bad reputation among the squaddies and he doesn't want Jess being tarred with the same brush.

CHAPTER 106

Birthday Month

It's been a busy first week back to work for Jamie, it's his birthday in a fortnight so he's arranged to go home to his mums the weekend before, he's looking forward to seeing her as he's not seen her since the end of January and he has missed his mum a lot. He knows Jess is organising a surprise the following weekend with his friends, he's told her not to make too much of a fuss, he's happy with a night out with her, he loves their date nights and nights out together.

Marking the calendar with his birthday weekend at his mums, his birthday (May 19) and the following weekend surprise, he looks back over it and sees Jess has marked it with her negative ovulation test for March but nothing for April, 'The silly bugger,' he says aloud, she forgot to do it in April. He marks May 20 for her next ovulation test and June 20 also, the week before his posting.

He's finishing work early this Friday, he's asked Nobby to go with him to town, he wants to buy Jess' engagement ring as he's finally figured out the day he's going to propose. Saturday June 26, the night before his posting, he wants a Christmas wedding, that way they can move into married quarters in January at the start of 2021. Jamie smiles as he closes the calendar, he has it all worked out in his head, all planned and ready. Lost in thought and distracted into his own little world, he hears Jess talking to him as she walks into the kitchen.

She's telling him she's getting a lot of pain in her lower back, she's never suffered with a bad back before, she also noticed for the first time in her life there was a bit of blood in the toilet, if this is what periods feel like she's glad she never had them.

He can't help but smile, he shows her the calendar, her ovulation test in March and that he's marked it for May, if she's starting to bleed, then she must be ovulating, he feels excited as he says this, perhaps they should get some pregnancy tests in and use one each month, he opens the calendar again and marks it on the tenth, starting from June.

CHAPTER 107

Jamie's Birthday

Jess has been trying to organise Jamie's birthday, she's no idea what she's buying him yet but she's booked a table for fourteen people at the fish restaurant that he's taken her to on a couple of their 'date nights', something she's never going to tire of, it's a chance for them both to actually have some quality time together even if it's only an evening, its special.

She's looking forward to seeing Clementine, she hasn't seen her since the wedding, although they chat regularly and Shelley is living in the village now, having moved down to live with Nobby in married quarters as she's now on maternity leave.

They're off to his mum's the weekend before and she's looking forward to seeing Anne, she has grown really fond of her, they chat regularly, more so than with her own parents of late and this saddens her, her mother's snobbery is pushing her away - that's something she's going to have to sort out in time.

But now's not the time to deal with her mum, she has to try and figure out how to tell Jamie that her dads sixtieth birthday and retirement party is booked for Saturday, June 5, she needs to go to it obviously, but she knows it will cause uproar with one of them, and if she's perfectly honest, she actually doesn't want to go without him, she feels like a 'pawn' between her mum and Jamie, trying to keep both sides happy yet neither of them know or realise how she feels.

The month of May seems to be flying by, she can't believe that today is already the day they'll be travelling up to his mum's, they both finish at half-four and aim to be on the road by six o'clock which means they'll be there by eight to eight-thirty latest. She's feeling a little apprehensive but she's not sure why, perhaps it's because they'll be sleeping in a single bed and trying to have sex with his mum next door, which is way too difficult, but they managed it over the New Year, so there's no reason why they can't this weekend, but she's definitely not felt right all week and now to add to her many discomforts, her boobs are hurting too.

Jamie's packed the car up, she took his car to work today, it meant he could get her car all packed ready for when she got home, then all she has to do is have a quick shower and get changed in to something a bit more comfortable for the journey.

She stands and looks at herself in the mirror, forgetting that she doesn't really have the time. She can't help thinking her boobs look different, she's not sure how, but they do.

'Babe, do my boobs look different to you?' she asks, walking into the bathroom while he is showering.

'What?' he says, not sure if he heard her clearly over the running water.

'My boobs, do they look different to you? I think they look fuller, they're bloody hurting I know that.'

'Baby, they look amazing, come here, let me have a suck and I'll tell yer,' he laughs.

'We haven't got time, we need to get to your mum's.'

'There's always time for sucking on yer tits,' he grins, 'I'll just tell her we got stuck in traffic.'

She climbs in the shower to join him, sees his cock is erect already and starts to stroke it as he caresses her boobs, she winces a couple of times, they really are tender. His fingers are rubbing her clitoris, making her gasp with pleasure, he pushes a couple of fingers inside her wet pussy, she's going to cum fast, she can feel it, he's sucking on her nipples as his fingers are fucking her, she tells him she's cumming, his fingers deep inside her, fucking her faster, moaning loudly as she cums.

She climbs out of the bath and leans over the sink, doggy style, his cock is so hard now, he pushes it into her soaked pussy, she's really wet, he slips out a couple of times, but quickly pushes it back in, he's thrusting really deep and hard, fucking her fast and making her moan, she can hear him telling her, 'Louder baby louder, let me hear yer scream,' this excites him, she can feel it, his cock is deep, thrusting fast, she's cumming again all over his cock, she's losing control, her legs are shaking as he thrusts hard and deep, she doesn't even hear him tell her that he's ready to cum but she feels him, his body going rigid, followed by the tell-tale shudder.

CHAPTER 108

Birthday Weekend (Part 1)

He hugs his mum tight and apologises for being late as the traffic was really bad and slowed them down. He tells her how much he's missed her, and she tells him she doesn't mind, they've arrived in one piece, that's all that matters.

Sean helps Jamie unload the car as Jess walks in with Anne, nattering like old school friends, Jamie can't help smiling at them, he can see they've got a bond, like a couple of best mates, they're the two most important women in his life and they get on like a house on fire. He nudges Sean and says 'That's charming ain't it, I do all the driving and she just walks off like the queen bee.'

Sean laughs and nods as their mum hears what he said and calls out 'That's why I raised two strong men like you two,' followed by, 'the cheeky sod,' to Jess as they both laugh and step inside the house.

They have a quick chat over a cup of tea and then they all head to bed, as it's nearly 2300hrs and Jamie and Sean are going running at 0600hrs, so he needs a good night's sleep, well, as best he can while snuggled with Jess in a single bed.

Saturday is a lovely sunny day, with temperatures in the early twenties all around the country, so they all head out to the countryside where there's a lovely country manor about forty minutes from his mums, it's open to the public and has lots of picnic areas and a coffee shop that serves afternoon tea.

Jess is totally up for this, this is her kind of thing. It's not something Jamie or his family are used to but he's happy to go along, after all he wants his two favourite women to enjoy themselves - if they're happy he's happy.

Jess is right about one thing, her boobs are looking and feeling fuller, he noticed this morning when he was cuddling her and holding them in his hands, they felt hot and heavy. He's got absolutely no idea why as he knows very little about the workings of the female body, except how to please her, make love to her and fuck her until she cums.

The family are going out for a big family meal, Jess is driving as she's still not drinking, Jamie is so proud of her and her resilience, they've been out a few times since he's been back and she's still resisted.

His family give him his presents at the restaurant even though his birthday isn't till Tuesday, it's an extra day later than last year as it was a leap year, it took Jamie a while to work that out as he was away in February, he also didn't realise until tonight that he missed Annabel's Christening in February, though his family know and accept that he will miss lots of family events, it's inevitable.

Joe, Jacqueline and his two nieces have bought him a nice designer T-shirt, it's not something he'd buy for himself as they're at least eighty quid, but he loves it, Rosie and Jed give him his favourite aftershave, Breda and Steve give him a fifty-pound gift voucher and his mum buys him some jeans and a couple of tops from his favourite shop on the high street.

He tells them all about the tour, about how hot it was, the midday heat reaching over fifty degrees, but that the saving grace was that the locals love them, they're very friendly and welcoming but it's a right shithole and it stinks. He warns Sean, that no amount of preparation can prepare you for it, you just got to deal with it when it happens. Joe asks if he will have to do another tour any time soon. He can't tell them yes as he's not told Jess yet, so he skirts around it by saying, 'Cyprus is on the horizon for September 2023 after your wedding Rosie, but otherwise I'm not sure.'

Mentioning the wedding works, diverting the attention away from him and on to Rosie, he takes a drink of his lager, feeling relieved, that's a can of worms he doesn't want to open just yet, he'll deal with it after Christmas, once they're married.

The night is drawing to a close and everyone but Jess, Jacqueline and Sean are drunk or merry, he listens in as Jacqueline tells Jess it doesn't get any easier after the babies, you still can't drink, especially if you're breastfeeding, and that she's saved all of Annabel's newborn babygrows and vests, as they're all neutral colours and if she has a sickie baby, she'll need as many as she can get. He realises that it's now common knowledge amongst the family that they're trying for a baby. He looks at his mum and smiles, there's no secrets in this family, that's how they were raised and that's how it will always be, even now they are adults.

CHAPTER 109

Jamie's Birthday

Jess has booked the day off work, she told Jamie on Sunday. She's not had the time to go and buy his birthday present, but the truth is she wanted to wait until she saw what his family bought him so she would know not to buy him the same.

He wakes her up when he gets back from his run, she's feeling exhausted like she could sleep all day, when they left his mum's on Sunday she fell asleep in the car, definitely not something she's ever done before, she's no idea what's going on, Jamie thinks she sickening for something, that she should go to the doctors.

She's sat on the toilet talking to him whilst he's in the shower, she's feeling really light headed, almost like she has a hangover, she doesn't tell him this, he's worried as it is, she doesn't want to give him anything else to worry about, but even she's starting to think there's something wrong, perhaps he's right, perhaps she should go to the doctors.

He leaves for work at 8.45am. She'll never tire of seeing him in his uniform, his peachy bum, his muscular arms and beautiful face, he just takes her breath away. Jess jumps in the shower, gets ready and heads into town, she has an idea of what she's buying him but wants to check some other ideas out first. She heads to the jewellery shop and looks at the watches, trying to find the one he liked and then as someone walks past her, emitting a really bad smell of body odour and she can't even begin to identify what else, her stomach turns and she's dry retching in front of the shop window.

'What the fuck was that?' she says out loud, looking around, no one is anywhere near her now thankfully. Something isn't right, she thinks to her herself.

She decides to go and get his card first and wrapping paper, then she nips and gets him some bits from the sports shop, he can never have enough training gear, besides she loves seeing him in T-shirt and shorts, his physique is mesmerising.

Finally, she heads back to the jewellers, she has an idea of the watch and tells the salesman, he knows which one it is and walks over to the display window, he points it out to her, 'Yes that's the one,' she confirms. He tries to sell her an insurance policy for it, but she tells him it'll be covered under her home policy as long as she has a receipt, she also pays on her credit card, as she knows this is extra insurance and she'll pay it off over the next few months, a couple of hundred pounds each month, Jamie won't notice, though now they have a joint account it's not that easy to spend money willy nilly, as they're both answerable to each other.

Wrapping his presents ready for him to come in from work, she looks at the receipt of his watch. *Tag Heuer, Formula 1, Men's Stainless Steel Bracelet Watch. £1,295.00.* She needs to call the insurance company and add it to the policy, she'll do it tomorrow from work. She feels a little better this afternoon as she waits for Jamie to come home, it was probably helped by her two hour nap on the sofa when she first got home from shopping, she won't tell him about that, she smirks as she thinks about it.

He walks in from work by 4.45pm, Jess has butterflies, she's excited to see his face when he opens his watch, she really enjoys spoiling him, as he never has any expectation and is so appreciative of the simple things, even a card - that's enough for him he says.

Handing him his birthday bag, she giggles in excitement, he couldn't even get changed before he opens them, he starts with his big presents, a couple of training T-shirts, some running shorts, and a pair of track bottoms (not chavvy ones) and then he picks up the wrapped watch.

As he unwraps it he tells her she didn't need to buy anything else, and hadn't even finished his sentence when she sees his jaw drop and his whole face light up, it is like Christmas all over again. He keeps repeating himself all night, telling her how amazing his new watch is and she is and how much he loves her.

She can't wait until he sees everyone Saturday night, now that will be a surprise, one she's also looking forward to, how she's kept it a secret she's no idea but it's one worth waiting for.

CHAPTER 110

Sworn to Secrecy

Jamie can't believe what an amazing birthday he's had, 'It's been the best week I've ever had,' he tells Nobby, but he has no idea what she has planned for tonight, all he knows is they're going out for a slap up meal. Nobby plays dumb, he's been sworn to secrecy, Shelley warned him and he's not about to cross a pregnant woman, *no way, that's a fate worse than death*, he thinks to himself.

Nobby tells Jamie to enjoy it, he deserves it and that he and Jess make a lovely couple.

'Have yer thought about when yer going to propose? And where've yer managed to hide the ring anyway?' Nobby asks Jamie.

'Saturday June 26, the night before we post out, mate it's hidden in me Bergan,' he says, laughing.

'Fucking 'ell mate, well I guess that's as safe a place as any, have you thought about when you want to tie the knot?'

'I want a Christmas wedding, then we can move into married quarters straight after New Year.'

'Have you said anything about the tour next year?'

'Nah, I'm gonna wait till end January, what about yer? Yer told Shelley?'

'Nah, same as, gonna wait, don't want to worry her.'

Jamie puts his pods back in and they run the rest of the distance in silence, arriving back in the village at nearly 0800hrs. Nobby decided he needed to run in silence as it was safer, as he heads home he tells Jamie to have a great time tonight and that he'll see him Monday, Jamie gives him a thumbs up and turns towards home.

In the kitchen he looks at the calendar, concentrating on the twentieth, the ovary test – 'negative'. He feels saddened by this result, perhaps they're going to need IVF after all. *How can someone so beautiful not have a baby, when the trollops back home pop 'em out annually,* it doesn't make sense to Jamie.

He takes a cup of tea up to Jess and wakes her, giving her a big sloppy kiss and then jumps in the shower telling her to come and join him in the shower if she wants. They have an appointment this morning with the dealership at 1000hrs to test drive a new car, with Jess paying her mortgage off that's a saving of five hundred quid a month. He also spoke with Joe about finance and he's agreed to be guarantor for him, it makes sense to get a car now, plus with his promotion to Lance Corporal, that's a massive pay rise, an extra six grand a year.

Jess walks in to the bathroom looking ill, he's worried, he's never known anyone have a bug for this long. He tells her she needs to go and see the doctor, he'll take her next week if she's no better by Monday and she agrees with him and climbs in the shower to join him.

CHAPTER 111

Birthday Weekend (Part 2)

Jess is driving, she's really perked up since this morning as she had a good sleep this afternoon and woke up feeling better. She tells Jamie she thinks she's finally getting over whatever she picked up, but she's definitely lost weight, her little black dress she wore over Christmas is hanging like a 'sack of spuds' even Jamie commented tonight, he likes her slim figure but he thinks she looks too skinny at the moment, apart from her boobs, they're lovely and full.

They pull into the car park, they're the first to arrive, *phew,* she thinks, *no one's let the cat out of the bag.* As they're walking towards the restaurant Jamie pulls her into him giving her a loving kiss and thanking her, he tells her he's had the best birthday ever. The manager greets them and Jess introduces herself and tells him, 'Party for O'Halloran.'

'Party? What party? Babe what yer done?' he says with a shocked tone.

She smiles and tells him, 'Shush, be patient,' as they're led into a private room, it's all decorated, in 'Happy Birthday' banners and balloons. Jamie is gobsmacked, he has no idea who's invited, but he knows there's obviously going to be more people arriving. He's never had a birthday like this.

'Baby, I'm blown away, how have yer managed to keep it a secret?'

'With great difficulty,' she grins.

The door to the room opens and in walks Nobby and Shelley, Jamie laughs and calls him 'a sly bastard,' Nobby tells him he has no idea how hard it was keeping his mouth shut, they hug and laugh, he then hugs Shelley telling her how beautiful she looks.

By the time they've all arrived, Jamie is feeling emotional, he's not one for emotions generally but this has touched him in a way he never thought possible.

Looking around the table at everyone, Tommo and Clementine, Gavin, Charlie, Fred and Hazel, Nobby and Shelley, Jodie (Jess's new friend) and Martin and of course Jess, his beautiful wife to be, not that she knows it yet, he's wishing he'd have known about this surprise, tonight would have been perfect to propose, *Oh well it can wait until next month*, he thinks to himself.

He's chatting to Martin, asking him about his length of service and what bases he's been on, Martin tells him he's just passed his tenth year, he started off in Germany, his first posting, then moved back to the UK four years ago, this is his second posting here and he's hoping to stay three years, give the kids a chance in school, they were both born in Germany and he and Jodie got married a month before he signed up, when they were both twenty.

The room is alive with different conversations, the food is amazing and the alcohol plentiful. Jess couldn't have wished for anything better, the night is perfect, *just like him*, she thinks as she watches him talking, smiling, laughing and most of all enjoying his surprise birthday party.

CHAPTER 112

A New Car

'Babe, I need the details of the car, I'm gonna register it at the front gate when I'm at work today.'

'Hold on,' she replies from the bathroom.

He hears her, she's being sick again, she's not been able to go to work this week, the stand in doctor said she has a 'gastric virus' and it should pass in about a week or two and he's signed her off work for two weeks.

Jess shouts down that she'll text him the details, she's going back to bed, hopefully she'll feel better by this afternoon, she has to take him to pick his car up. He got a really good deal on it, with his twenty-five percent military discount and twenty percent deposit, the payments work out at just short of three hundred pounds per month for four years.

Jess needs to text her mum that she's off work sick and that she might not be able to make it to the party, not that she's using it as an excuse but it is a great one and she truly is ill, she's not lying.

Jamie comes upstairs, sits on the edge of the bed and bends down to give her a kiss, he moves her over and lays next to her, he has plenty of time to get into work.

'Yer feeling rough babe, do yer want me to get one of the lads to take me and pick the car up?'

'I am, but I know I'll be ok later, I'll take you.'

'What card we putting the deposit on?'

'Put it on my credit card then we'll clear it next month,' she says.

'I need to pay my credit card by the weekend, can yer leave a few hundred in the account?'

He has to pay her engagement ring off, he bought it on his credit card intending to clear it each month, that way she won't know any difference, as they have a joint account now so he can't just spend without her seeing it, but he likes having a joint account, they both earn good money, and it makes life easier when he's away, he knows Jess won't go without.

'Yes I've left two hundred and fifty pounds in, use that, have you swapped the insurance over?'

'No, I need the reg, but we'll have a cover note for seven days from the dealer. So I'll sort it tomorrow.'

'What are you doing with your car?'

'Gonna sell it, I reckon I'll get a grand at least, I should have asked about part exchange.'

He gives her a loving kiss and cuddles her, telling her he needs to get going to work, he asks if she wants him to come home at lunch time but she tells him she'll be fine and she'll see him around four-thirty, the dealer closes at six, so he mustn't be late. She listens for the door to close, turns over and goes back to sleep.

Jess wakes up just after noon, knowing that she needs to get up, her energy levels are at an all-time low, this gastric bug has really knocked her off her feet. The nausea is as bad as the sickness and she's lost over a stone in weight. The last time she weighed herself she was nine stone thirteen pounds and when the doctor weighed her on Monday she had dropped to eight stone eleven. The doctor told her not to worry, once she starts eating properly again she'll gain it back.

'Shit,' she says aloud, 'I haven't text the reg over,' and she looks through the paperwork for it.

Jess: [Here you go darling, WV20 PTE xx]

Jess: [Sorry it's late, I just woke up xx]

She thought it was ironic that the end of the registration plate represents his current title, she's sure the salesman has done it on purpose, and thought it was a nice gesture if he has.

Jamie: [Thanks baby, how are you feeling? Xx]

Jess: [So so, I'm just going for a shower, care to join?]

Jamie: [Tease. See you at 1600hrs, love you xx]

Jess: [Love you too xxx]

She checks the rest of her messages, Lizzie and Jodie have text her and she has missed calls from Shelley and her mum. She gets in the shower, deciding she'll deal with them later.

Jess is up and eating some toast a bit later when she hears the front door, Jamie's home, he's excited to be picking his car up, he's never had a new car before, he tells her he's just going to get changed then they can head out. He looks at her with a very concerned look, he text his mum earlier to say how much weight Jess has lost and that he's worried.

'Baby, I'm ready to go,' he says as he walks in to the living room.

She looks at him, he looks a million dollars, wearing his T-shirt from his brother, his new jeans and his watch, you'd never believe by looking at him now that he didn't like designer brands. Jess wonders if that was a ruse, a way of hiding the fact he couldn't afford them or didn't want to spend that sort of money, as he preferred to save.

When they opened their joint account, they also opened a joint savings account and transferred their savings over, Jamie contributed more than five grand as he saves a third of his salary each month and has done since he joined up. Jess has no worries about Jamie and money, she knows he's sensible, not one to squander it.

They arrive at the dealership to collect his car, he signs some papers, pays the deposit of £3,100 on Jess' credit card, gets his seven day cover note and finally the keys. He opted for a manual gearbox for this car, as much as he loves the automatic he doesn't want to lose the ability to drive a manual, it's better to drive both, unlike Jess who hasn't driven a manual for about ten years, she's told him she'll never be able to drive anything other than an automatic now.

He gets in his car and drives home with Jess following behind in hers, he's spoilt for choice with two new cars to drive now and to think that less than two years ago, he didn't have a pot to piss in and never wore anything with a label. Fast forward two years and he's wearing a watch that cost more than his mum has ever earned in a month, driving a new car that costs more than he earns in a year and is proposing to his girlfriend next month with a ring that he never thought he'd ever be able to afford. How life has changed, life is good, it's what dreams are made of, and if this is a dream, he never wants to wake from it.

CHAPTER 113

Coming Clean

'Babe, I have something to tell you, but I don't want you to go off your head.'

'What? Tell me what?' he asks, frowning and now with a worried look on his face.

'Well it's my dad's birthday next week, Sunday 6th June and my mum has organised a big party because he's retiring as well.'

Jamie looks at her, he doesn't say anything as he moves her head off his lap, then he gets up and stands by the window with his arms folded tight across his chest.

'I didn't know how to tell you, I need to go, because it's his birthday.'

'Of course, and lets not fuckin' forget that I don't fuckin' exist. Carry on Jess, keeping up this pretend bullshit.'

He's livid, she can see it, she needs to be careful what she says and how she says it, she really doesn't want to upset him any further, and besides all that, she's too ill to argue.

'And let's not forget, you're on the sick, but it's fuckin' funny how you miraculously recover to go to a party.'

'Babe, I'm sorry, I've tried to tell her, honestly I have, but…' Jess struggles for words to try to explain… 'but she's not like your mum, God knows I wish she was.'

'Jessica I fuckin' mean it, you ain't goin'. Yer tell yer mother, either we go together or yer don't go,' he finishes, his face red and his hands clenched, feeling all the frustration coming out at once.

He has never called her Jessica, Jess on the odd occasion when they've had a fall out but never Jessica, this is a whole new level, he's never told her she can't do something either. This is worse than Jess thought it was going to be.

'Babe!' she says, desperately wanting this awful argument to be over.

'Don't fucking "babe" me Jess,' cutting her dead as soon as she began.

'Jamie, seriously, are you blaming me for this situation?'

'Yeah I am, yer should have fucking told 'em months ago,' he raises his voice even further, feeling as close to rage as he ever has and shouts, 'How long have yer known about this party?'

He's never shouted at her before, not in this manner, this is fury. Jess starts to cry, he's scared her, not in the physical manner but she's scared now of what this party will do to them.

'Well? And what are yer crying for?' he's still shouting, red in the face now, 'I'm the one being made to look a cunt here, not you Jess.'

Jess opens her mouth to answer but she's about to be sick, her stomach retching, she covers her mouth with her hand and runs up to the toilet. She doesn't hear the front door open as Jamie storms out.

He left for his own safety, he was frightened of what he might say or do, he's furious, beyond furious, he walks around the block, but is still too angry to go home, so he heads towards the base, he's no idea where he's going or what he's going to do.

Jess finally makes it back downstairs, and when she realises he is gone, she cries even more, a lovely Sunday afternoon ruined, she's not getting any better and for the first time in their relationship she's seen a side to Jamie she didn't know existed.

She calls Hazel, she doesn't know who else to talk to, Hazel listens, not saying much, but in her heart she agrees with Jamie. She tells Jess that she has to do what's best for her and her future, to follow her heart. Hazel has met Jess' mum once and that was enough for her, as far as she is concerned, Jamie is better off not knowing her.

Jess tries to call him but he declines her call, she sends him a text telling him she's sorry, she's torn between the man she loves with all her heart and wants to spend the rest of her life with and her mum who is impossible to please. No matter what she chooses to do, she can't do right for doing wrong, she's fed up of feeling like a pawn between two sides.

He blanks her text, he's never done that, whatever or where ever he is he's got to come home tonight, he has nowhere else to go. She calls her mum and tells her she's been signed off again, she has a gastric bug and that she's not sure she'll be able to make it next week. Her mum told her it's a week away, you'll be better by then and in any case she has to go as it's her dads birthday, he's only going to be sixty once.

Jess is beside herself, she tells her mum she's bringing someone with her to the party, but her mum tells her that under no circumstances is she to 'pull that stunt' "Jessica, you make sure you're here next weekend and on your own" Jess hangs up, asking herself, *what the fuck am I going to do?*

She goes up to bed, it's gone eight o'clock and she's worn herself out crying, she can't deal with this situation anymore, she needs to try and sleep. She'll deal with it tomorrow, once Jamie is home and she's had a chance to talk to him, she needs to tell him what her mum said Christmas Eve and that she tried to tell her, she can't keep it from him anymore, she needs to come clean.

CHAPTER 114

Bank Holiday Drinks

I swear If Jess goes to her dad's party Saturday night, that's us done for. He's talking to Angela at the bar of The Bowl. She tells him, 'Blood's thicker than water Jamie, course she's gonna go.'

For the first time in his life he's sat in a bar after having an argument, normally he'd go for a run or the gym, but not this time, this is different, he simply doesn't know how to handle this situation.

There's loads of people in The Bowl, it's been a nice sunny Sunday, the last Sunday in May and tomorrow's a Bank Holiday, he's just going to have a few pints and then head home, he needs to sort this out, she's going to have to choose between him or her parents.

He can't bear the thought of not having Jess in his life, the more he drinks the more upset he gets. Now it's nearly midnight and he's been in The Bowl since early evening, a good six hours so he decides now is a good time to head home, he's not going out late and besides he left Jess throwing her guts up, he shouldn't have stormed out when he did.

He called his mum earlier in the evening, he needed to talk to her, he feels like his heart is breaking in two. His mum is always his rock, his 'go to' when he doesn't know what to do in a situation and this situation definitely fits that description.

His mum told him to go home and to listen to Jess, there's a reason she hasn't told her parents, he needs to ask her if she's even tried. 'But most of all son,' she said in a very calm manner, 'it's one weekend out of your lifetime together, don't ruin everything Jamie with your stubborn pig-headedness'.

He's walking home chatting to Angela about how much he loves her and his plans for the future, she tells him he's young, too young to be settling down, 'Have some fun, live life,' she says, 'it'll only end in divorce,' like hers did.

He's not sure why he's even talking to her, if he remembers rightly, he actually doesn't like her when he's sober, he needs to get away from her before he does something silly, he tells her he's turning left here and if she is out next week he'll have a drink with her in The Bowl.

Walking towards the house he can see Jess has left the outside light on, that means she's in bed. He has no idea why, but he suddenly turns around and catches up with Angela asking her if she fancies some company, he's not in the mood to go straight home.

CHAPTER 115

Too Late for Regrets

He hears Jess walking towards the bathroom, he's washed himself half a dozen times but no amount of scrubbing is going to wash away what he's done. He needs to figure out how to deal with the guilt and more than anything, to get Jess away from the village in case she ever finds out.

'What time did you get in last night?' she asks him.

'About midnight, yer was asleep, I didn't want to disturb yer so I slept in the spare room.'

'Oh, I wondered why the bed was a mess.'

'Babe, this situation with yer parents, it's coming between us and I don't want it to, go to the party next week, but this is the last time, from now on we do things as a couple.'

She nods her head and climbs in the shower with him, telling him how sorry she is, that she thought it was the end of them, and she promises that no matter what after next weekend if he's not invited then she doesn't go.

He starts to kiss her, his guilt is killing him. Why did he do it? All the times Angela came on to him when he was single and he blew her out, why now? The only consolation is that he wore a condom, luckily she has a drawer full, as he hasn't bought or used a condom since he's been with Jess.

No matter what happens I'll deny it, deny it to the hilt, he decides. He'll have to, it will destroy them for sure.

He starts caressing her tits, and playing with her nipples. They kiss, his tongue looking for hers, he stops, 'Baby, I can't do it in here, let's go back into the bedroom.' He can't have sex he needs to make love, Jess deserves to be made love to.

She lies on the bed and he climbs on top of her, kissing her lovingly and passionately, his love for this woman is beyond words, he caresses her tits, plays with her nipples, his cock is hard, he places it inside her wet pussy just enough so he can push it in slowly.

Still kissing her he enters her, his cock sliding gently into her soft wet pussy, her juices all over it. He starts to gyrate his hips in a slow motion, moving them slightly faster he can feel her hands all over his back, she starts to moan as his hips get faster.

He's guilt ridden, he's struggling to make love but he can't stop as he daren't arouse any suspicion, he needs to put it all behind him. He made a mistake, something that he's got to live with but he hopes in time will ease. It was a one night stand. That's all she was.

His hips are gyrating and Jess is moaning, his cock is deep, he starts to thrust faster. The faster he gets the louder Jess gets, 'Yes baby, louder,' he tells her, his hips gyrating faster, his thrusts harder.

He hears her say, 'I'm cumming,' and he thrusts again and again, her deep intense moans excite him, he hears her, he feels her juices all over his cock, he's ready to cum but he doesn't tell her, he cums, he feels his cock explode deep inside her, filling her wet pussy with his cum, his body goes rigid then he shudders as he climaxes.

CHAPTER 116

A Difficult Situation

Jamie's been running on his own this week and going to the gym on his own, in fact he's been distant in work all week. Nobby's concerned, he takes him aside on Friday, books some time out for them both, says its training, but he needs to talk to him and find out what's wrong.

'Mate, what's going on with yer? Is everything ok with Jess?' he asks him, genuinely concerned for his friend.

Jamie's head is in his hands, he's running his fingers through his hair, sighing very loudly.

'I can't say Nobs, I need to try and deal with it myself, Jess is fine, she just can't shift this gastric bug.'

'Mate, I'm worried about yer, yer been snappy all week, distant, I can't help yer if I don't know what's going on.'

'No one can help me with this, it's something I need to sort myself.'

'Look mate, there's a rumour going round amongst the lads, but I've told 'em to shut the fuck up, that's its bullshit.'

Jamie's heart misses a beat as he thinks, *fucking rumours,* but it's not a rumour, not this time. How can he hide this from Jess? He's sure the only reason she's not found out yet is because she's poorly but he knows it's only a matter of time.

'What's the rumour?' he asks, bracing himself for it.

'You fucked Angela Sunday night, the lads have said you were sat with her in The Bowl, and you left with her. She's told Gavin yer fucked her and left, telling her she was a big fucking mistake. But I told Gav "don't believe it mate she's bitter, he's blown her out loads in the past", I told him yer proposing to Jess this month so it's all bullshit.'

Jamie's shaking his head, he can't believe what he's hearing, or how stupid he could be.

'It's not bullshit mate,' he says with his head in his hands.

'Woah, nooo! Why J, why? What the fuck was yer thinking?'

Jamie tells him about the argument, the party and the parents, that they still don't know about him, that he stormed out, walked around for a while then went to The Bowl to see who was out. Angela was sat there with a couple of the lads, he was venting to her, decided around midnight to go home, he left Angela, went home saw the outside light was on, turned on his heels and caught back up with her asking her if she fancied some company. 'I don't know why I did it Nobs, I'm questioning myself every day but I can't find the answer.'

'Jess is gonna find out mate, everyone knows, yer need to tell her before someone else does.'

'I can't, Nobs, it'll destroy us, its destroying me already.'

His head in his hands, his eyes are full of tears, he's frightened of what this will do to them. He knows what it will do to them, he doesn't want to face the truth - life without Jess.

'We've not had any sex this week, I've tried but I can't, I've just cuddled into her, used her sickness as an excuse, I'm scared Nobby, really scared.'

'Shelley knows mate, Angela was at a coffee morning on Wednesday and told her, in fact she told everyone, was boasting that she conquered yer, she said "now let's see how miss prim and fucking proper feels when she finds out her toyboy is fucking around" she's a nasty fucker Jamie, of all the women to choose, why her mate? Honestly.'

He can't help himself, he can't hold it in anymore, he's crying, silently, but he's crying into his hands.

'Jess has gone to her parents today, she's back on Sunday. I'll tell her then. What do I do Nobs? She's gonna end it, I know she is.'

'Yer need to deal with it, give her time, she loves yer mate.'

He nods his head, there's nothing else he can do until Sunday, only then will he know the full extent of what he's done.

CHAPTER 117

Time for the Truth

Jess has left her dad's party before 9pm, she's too ill to stay, she tells her dad she's left his present in her room, that she's sorry but needs to go home, she's going back to the doctor on Monday, she can't cope with this any longer.

Her dad gives her a hug, but understands, her mum is worried and tells her that if the doctor doesn't do anything on Monday to go to the hospital, it's not right to be this ill for near on three weeks.

Jess texts Jamie to tell him she's coming home and she needs to go to the doctors on Monday, he texts her back letting her know he's at home waiting for her and he loves her. She tells him she loves him back, she's glad to be going home, she's missed him, she hates sleeping without him.

She pulls onto the drive, the house is practically in darkness except for the living room lamp. He walks out to help her, getting her weekend bag out of the boot, he gives her a big hug and tells her he's missed her and puts his arm around her shoulders as they walk in.

'Why's the house so dark?' she asks.

'I was just chilling on the sofa, didn't realise it'd gone so dark babe.'

He laughs, but it's a nervous laugh, he's not slept all weekend, he knows his future lies in the balance with what he's got to tell her. He doesn't know how to tell her though, he doesn't want to see her world destroyed because he was a twat, a drunken twat.

'Babe, I need to tell yer something, but I also need to tell yer how much I love yer and don't want to lose yer.'

These words put the fear of God into Jess and she's shaking before he's even told her what he wants to tell her. *Does he want to finish? What could be so important or bad that he's sat in darkness, that's what this is about*, she's thinking.

'What's wrong? Whatever it is we'll sort it.'

He sits forward on the sofa, his head in his hands. He lets out a sigh and begins.

'When I stormed out last week, I walked around and around for ages, then I went to The Bowl, sat with the lads and Angela was with them.'

Jess's heart stops, she knows what is coming, she's known something has been up with him all week, she thought it was because she was sick.

'I came home and saw the outside light on, knew yer was in bed and then because I was drunk I turned and went back after her. But yer got to believe me it meant nothing, she means nothing, I told her it meant nothing. Baby I'm sorry, I'm so fucking sorry, yer gotta believe me.'

Jess can't talk, her heart has just broken into a million pieces, the one person she trusted in the world, has just destroyed her, destroyed them, how can she ever trust him again? She can't. She'll never trust him, ever again.

His tears are streaming down his face, he's telling her he's sorry, please forgive him, it's never going to happen again.

Jess can't breathe, she's going to be sick, she runs upstairs into the bathroom and he follows her, he tries to pull her hair back off her face but she shrugs him off, yelling at him 'Don't touch me, ever!'

'Babe, please, don't do this, we'll sort it, I promise, I can't lose you, please, I'm begging yer, please babe, I love yer.'

'Get out, get the fuck out, you came home and made love to me after you fucked her, how do I know you haven't given me anything?'

'I haven't, I swear.'

'Oh, you swear, you wore a condom?' She looks at him as she's asking him this question, he doesn't look back at her, just nods his head.

'You bastard, you fucking bastard, get the fuck out of my house,' she screams at him, she knows he hasn't bought condoms since they've been together, she doesn't want to know any more, she's heard enough. Her world has just caved in around her.

She hears the front door slamming, his car starting, then his tyres wheel spin as he drives off, she collapses on the landing floor, unable to move, she lays there, crying like she's never cried before, wondering how she's going to get through the night.

CHAPTER 118

The Arms of a Mother

Jamie pulls up outside his mum's, it's just gone 0100hrs, he's no idea how he's reached home, the two hour journey is just a blur.

He gets out of the car, the house is in darkness, she's obviously in bed fast asleep, he needs her, he needs to tell her it's all over between him and Jess. He needs to hear her tell him that he's going to be okay, that he'll get through this. His heart is broken and it's his own fault he knows, but he needs to know it will mend.

Anne wakes to the sound of banging on her front door, she always puts the latch on when she goes to bed, that way no one can pick the lock, she listens, she can't make out what they're saying at first then she realises it's Jamie, he's banging on the door, she can hear him crying 'Mum, Mum, let me in, Mum I've fucked up, Mum wake up.'

She dives out of bed and runs past Sean's room shouting to him to get downstairs quick. She opens the front door to see her grown son fall through it, crying uncontrollably as he collapses on the floor in the hallway, he's trying to tell her what he's done but he can't get the words out.

Anne sits on the floor with him cuddling him like she used to when he was a child, when he would cry for his daddy, asking why he never came home from work. Her grown son lying on the floor of the hallway is like that little boy all over again.

She doesn't know what he's done, she can't understand what he's telling her, but her instinct as a mother knows she doesn't need to hear the words. All she can do is sit with him, cuddling him, her heart breaking in two for him. She reassures him it will be okay, that he will be ok, her silent tears run down her cheeks, just like they used to. Only she knows this time it won't be okay.

CHAPTER 119

The Sound of Knocking

Jess wakes up with a start, her heart pounding, it's got to be the early hours of the morning, she can hear sounds from downstairs, knocking, someone's at the front door.

She looks at the clock, 4.18pm, she has no idea how long she's been asleep for, or how or when she got into bed even. Lying there she hears a man's voice, he's talking to someone, she can't make out who it is but it's a woman's voice, a familiar one.

She walks to the top of the stairs, and calls out, 'Who is it?' She hears her reply, it's Shelley, so she goes down and opens the door to find her and Nobby, they've been trying to get in to check on her, no one's seen or heard from her in three days and her phone is off.

Three days, it can't be, I haven't been asleep for three days, and she hasn't, it's true. The last three days have been spent crying for hours on end, her heart aching so much she thought it was going to burst and she's slept in between for a couple of hours here and there.

Shelley asks when was the last time she ate, she shrugs her shoulders, she has absolutely no idea, they take her into the living room, the curtains are still closed so Nobby opens them and the afternoon sun shines through, lighting up the room.

Nobby goes into the kitchen to put the kettle on, Shelley's talking to her but she's not listening, everything is like a haze around her, her senses sluggish and cloudy.

'What? I didn't catch what you said,' Jess says to Shelley, the haze beginning to lift a little.

'Jamie needs his stuff, he's coming back this evening, he's moving into the block for the next two weeks.'

'No, he's not stepping foot in this house, I don't care what he needs.'

'Don't worry, Nobby will sort it, he doesn't need to come round.'

Jess stares ahead, her eyes red and puffy. Shelley looks at her, seeing her pain. Her face is drawn, much too thin. Jess feels Shelley's caring hands holding hers, she's trying to talk but her words are not coming out, only the tears, finally she hears herself saying, 'I loved him Shell, I trusted him, the one person I trusted with my life.'

Shelley hugs her, she can't do anything else, no matter what she says it's not going to make anything better right now, only time can do that.

The sun is starting to set as Nobby finishes packing the car up with Jamie's things, he's made sure his Bergan is intact and everything is in place. Jess has eaten something and had a couple of cups of tea so Nobby leaves the two women alone while he takes Jamie's stuff up to him.

Shelley tells Jess she's going back home to her parents on Sunday but she's going to call and see her tomorrow, and that she needs to go to the doctors. She'll make her an appointment and take her before she leaves. Nobby gets back quickly to collect Shelley and they say their goodbyes, making Jess promise to eat some breakfast in the morning, even if it's just some dry toast.

She closes Jess' front door behind her and gets in the car, she looks at Nobby, his face is sad, he's never seen his best mate cry, in fact he's never seen a grown man cry before, he holds Shelley's hand for a few moments before he drives off, both of them sitting there in silence, thankful for each other but saddened by what they've seen, seeing how one person's actions can destroy everything.

CHAPTER 120

Jess is replaying the conversation with her doctor over and over in her head. She took the urine sample, went for the blood test, rebooked an appointment for the Friday, June 25 and was signed off for another two weeks. Her sickness bug was not getting any better and she had no idea how or when she would start feeling normal again.

She hears the door, more precisely the letter box and a letter dropping to the floor. It is Sunday morning, there's no post on a Sunday so she gets up and walks downstairs. She picks up the letter and recognises his handwriting, it's from Jamie. She wants to tear it into tiny pieces but she can't, she needs to read it.

My Dearest Jess,

Nothing I can say or do is going to change what I did, but I hope one day you can forgive me.

I'm truly sorry for what I've done, you have to believe me when I say this, I never ever wanted to hurt you, I've only ever loved you, from the moment I saw you, I knew you were and still are the one..

Jess, these past two weeks without you have been a living hell, I miss you more than I can tell you, I love you Jess, I love you with all my heart and always will.

If there's a chance, no matter how small, please, I'm begging you please give it to me, I promise you, no matter what it takes, I will be that man you loved and trusted once again.

Today is my last day in the village, and the chances are I'll never return to this base, but you have to know this before I go, no matter how long it takes, weeks, months or years, I'll be waiting, I promise you.

I love you Jess, my Sleeping Beauty.

Jamie x

She lays the letter on the table with her eyes full of tears. She looks at it then looks at the note beside it, from the doctor, showing her blood tests and urine tests result.

'Pregnant – Positive'

She reads it again. She knows that the only person she can trust is herself and that the only person she needs to think about from now on is the 'little person' she's carrying inside, her baby.

For now she will keep it to herself, for a few more weeks at least, letting the dust settle on her past before she moves on with her future.

Epilogue

Jamie

I left this base on Sunday, June 27, 2020. Since then I've had three further postings, another promotion to Corporal and now this, a twelve week secondment with a possible extension to twelve months.

It was a long drive coming here, it felt like I was driving from one end of the country to the other. Picking up my pass from the gate house, I ask if The Bowl is still open. Some of them have closed down on other bases, but it was good to hear this one hasn't, I'll pop by later once I've unpacked and prepared my kit for tomorrow.

It doesn't matter what military base you stay on, the blocks are all the same even in Cyprus it was no different. I guess they're not meant for comfort, they're just blocks. Designed for young lads to live in until they either move on or get married and then it is married quarters, something I'll find out about soon, no doubt.

I guess I'm just like any other guy, it's not that I'm not interested, It's a woman's thing planning a wedding. Just tell me where and what time and I'll be there. Oh and 'how much', the all-important question. Only this is different, I don't have to worry about the funds. When Tara's dad, Brian passed away, not long after Rosie and Jed's wedding we found out he'd arranged a 'wedding fund' for Tara. He figured if he wasn't going to be around to give her away the least he could do is pay for it. God love him, he was a good man, a hard working one at that.

I've settled in really well on the new base since returning from Cyprus, it's within an hour of my mum's which makes it easier to nip back home each weekend, especially since she now lives right by the motorway. A fairly new house which I purchased from new for her after first seeing the development on one of my visits back home in 2019.

The good thing about nipping home every weekend is I get to spend time with Tara. It's definitely been easier since the regiment posted back to the UK. Although I enjoyed living in the sunshine I missed my mum, Tara and the rest of the family, although Tara would come out to visit. In fact it was on her last visit that I proposed to her.

I decide to take a wander down to The Bowl, the beauty of these places is they're cheap, they do good food and if you've been on the base before, like me, you're bound to bump into an old friendly face. Well, hopefully.

'Well if it isn't Jamie O'Halloran,' I hear as I walk in. It's a familiar voice and as I look around, I see my old friend Fred sitting in one of the booths, beckoning me over. *At least I'll have a bit of company for the next hour or so,* I think, happy to join him.

I order a pint and take a seat opposite Fred, he's asking me how I am and what I've been up to and what in God's name brings me back. I tell him I need to order food before anything else and ask if he has eaten, or does he want to join me. To which he replies 'No, not yet, Hazel is away for the week so I've been left to fend for myself.'

'You're doing a good job of it so far Fred, you're in the best place,' I laugh.

Food and another pint ordered, I start to tell Fred what I've been up to these past five years and the reason I'm back here for the next twelve weeks. He listens intently, and when our food arrives I think to ask Fred where Hazel has gone and who with. Fred tells me that she's gone abroad for the school half term, with Jess.

My heart misses a beat as my stomach practically hits the deck. *She's still here, still in the village, shit, she stayed.* I was sure she'd have moved back to her mum and dads by now. *Oh Jess, why couldn't you have told them about me? I wonder if she slept with any other squaddies after me…* I feel a pang of jealousy at the mere thought of her with another man, let alone a squaddie.

I really need to snap out of it, but I can't. She was and still is my first love, I can't deny it I loved her and still do. When I think of her, it's painful, that love is still there. There really are some things in life that never die and this is an example, my love for Jess, the amazing sex we had and what an amazingly beautiful woman she is.

Perhaps coming back here was wrong, perhaps my mum was right, after all she saw me, she saw the mess I was in, 'a broken man' she called me. It was my own fault, I caused it. I was the unfaithful one, no matter how I look at it, I went against everything we stood for 'honesty, trust and loyalty' shot to pieces.

Those two years on my own were the worst, I threw myself into every exercise going, if it hurt I did it more, the physical pain was better than the emotional pain I was feeling. By the time our Rosie got married I was finally feeling like a person again, I was in good shape physically and getting better mentally. That's when things developed between me and Tara.

Oh, sweet Tara, she loves me, she is in love with me and always has been, so she says. I love her, I'm sure I do, after all, I asked her to marry me so that must mean something.

The sex is different, very different but it's good, she's not adventurous like Jess was, I don't shudder when I climax like I used to with Jess but it's good, I enjoy it.

'Did she ever re-marry?' I ask Fred, secretly dreading the answer.

'No, she never re-married, in fact she's been on her own since.'

I'm relieved to hear this but sad to think she's still alone, that's not fair, she deserves to be loved and cared for.

'You know Jamie lad, I always thought you were good together. It's a shame you did what you did, I'm sure in time she would have told her parents.'

'I was immature Fred, thought I knew best, thought I was getting me own back, yer know? I was feeling hurt so I wanted to hurt her, but the truth is Fred, it destroyed us, me included.'

I feel a rush of emotions and that pain again, five years later I still feel it, it's feels as raw today as it was back then. I can hear Fred is still talking, so I pull myself back to the present and start to listen again. He tells me that 'little Mikey' started school in September so now they have to take holidays during half term breaks. So that's what they've done - they're on holiday. Hazel has gone with her to help Jess look after him.

I actually can't think or speak at this moment but I have to, I open my mouth but nothing is coming out. I take a drink of my lager.

'So, she has a child? A little boy is it?' That's all I can muster up, over the shock.

'Yeah, little Mikey. And to think she was told she couldn't have kids, that she'd need IVF,' says Fred casually, then stops, 'Hang on, you didn't know?' he asks with genuine surprise.

All I can do at this point is shake my head.

'Look I'm not saying he's yours, but I told Hazel if he is, you have a right to know.'

My mind is racing at a million miles an hour. *Little Mikey, is that short for Michael, my middle name?* I need to know more, I need to concentrate on what he's saying, but right now I actually feel like I'm going to be sick.

'But she was adamant it was a direct result of a fling with a work colleague, to get over you apparently, only she falls pregnant, and told us that he didn't want to know. Anyway, Hazel and I have been on hand to help out, because even though her mum and dad moved closer after her dad retired, they're still half hour or so away. But it's great for us, not having any children of our own we've been there to help them 'cause he's the cutest little guy, with the biggest blues eyes you ever saw and the blondest hair.'

I think by this point all the colour has drained from my face and I can hardly breathe.

'You okay Jamie? You look like you're in shock,' he asks and I just nod, what else can I do?

'What date was he born?' I ask, barely able to string two words together

'January 12, 2021', she called him Michael, but I call him "Mikey" or "little Mikey".'

Fred carries on talking about how amazing Jess is with him, that she now only work three days a week and that it can't be easy being a single mum.

I can hear him talking about this and that but all I can think is *I need to get out of here, I need to get back to my room.*

I barely finish my dinner and make an excuse that I have to be up early tomorrow for my first day. I say goodbye and Fred tells me he'll be back here tomorrow if I fancy some company.

I get back to my room and think about everything I've just been told, January 12, 2021, I pop that date in my calendar and rewind forty weeks - to April 21, 2020.

Fuck!

9 781913 568757